OUT WITH THE TIDE

A Novel by

Lola Faye Arnold
2015

Lola Faye Arnold

This book is a work of fiction. The characters, names, places, organizations, incidents, and dialogue are a product of the author's imagination or are used ficti- tiously. Any resemblance to real people, living or dead, is entirely coincidence and is not to be considered as real. The author has intended to create an authentic, yet fictional work.

Dedication

In loving memory of

My Mother
Caroline Marie Price Tripp
&
My Father
John Thomas Tripp (J.T.)

ACKNOWLEDGMENTS

As an author, how do I begin to say thanks to the many people who have influenced and assisted me through the process of writing and publishing a book? Without a doubt, it's a daunting task.

When I think of my Southern American heritage and the zany things we do and say in the South, I have to smile and say a warm thank you to my many acquaintances and good friends that got my giggle box turned upside down over the years, especially during those times when I felt like crying my guts out. This love of life, in the South, and the ongoing use of humor to help lighten one's burdens became the impetus to include fictional humor in my novel. I would have to say that my sister, Susan Tripp, has to be included, along with that group of friends, because I thought of her so many times as I wrote, wondering how I could make her crack up when she finally gets the chance to read what I wrote. I'm confident that my fictional character, Uncle Doyle Earl Pritchett, will make Susan roar when she reads about his "prayer of all prayers" because she and I were forever laughing when we were supposed to have been quiet, as kids.

MaKayla Davis, you're another one who knows how to keep me laughing like a hyena, especially when times are rough, and your funny personality makes me want to pass on that joy of laughter to my readers. Graeme Robertson, I would have to say the same for you, with your fabulous sense of humor, Kiwi style; you're almost as hilarious as a Southerner. To my late brother, Les Tripp, I hope you're laughing in paradise, because you motivated me to write with humor, too. Les was the type of guy, who would've always kept a straight face while he was being funny as heck. Please note, I didn't quote any of you'uns, promise, and all of my nutty characters are figments of my own vivid imagination.

When it comes to a portion of the medically technical wording in *Out With the Tide*, I have to shout out a special thanks to Dr. Otto AhChing, M.D., who shared his knowledge as a physician. Additionally, I would like to acknowledge my former physical therapist, Chris Cobb, for his input as a PT. Gentlemen, I certainly could not have written those sections of the novel without your help.

For editing and support, I would like to thank Ross Arnold and Nancy Weiss. Ross, there is no way that I could ever have done this without you giving me the constant encouragement that you gave me and the benefit of your excellent editing skills; you're a gem of a man. Nancy, I don't know whether you were a glutton for punishment to read the entire novel and to offer another set of eyes over the manuscript or just a super supportive friend. At any rate, if there are still errors or typos, I'll take the responsibility as it is probably due to the fact that I had to add a few thoughts, here and there, just could not keep my big mouth shut. By the way, the capitalization chosen for the title of *Out With the Tide*, was intentional; so, to my perfectionist "English major" type readers, I would say, "Don't get your panties in a wad," but read to the end and you'll figure it out.

I would also like to acknowledge Will Mulholland, a very talented Kiwi, for his excellent graphic design work leading to the beautiful finished product of my book cover. I love it.

I cannot close without taking the opportunity to acknowledge my three wonderful children: John Christian, Tara Caroline, and Joseph Clayton for the beauty that y'all bring into my life. Without the three of you, and my beautiful grandchildren, I wouldn't have a reason to want to write successfully. You always have been and always will be, my life. I want you three children to know that your mother never lets adversity take her down; when life gives you lemons, you remember mama said with a chuckle, "Make lemonade, or better yet, make SWEET tea, so sweet it'll sting yer teeth."

CONTENTS

INTRODUCTION

I reckon, true Southerners are a rare and dying breed. I would say a dying breed because too many Yankees have infiltrated the Southern states and purchased much of the farm land to build "snow bird" condos and nursing homes, have owned the textile mills and baseball teams, to boot, and have had the gall to "clean and polish" the school systems, almost to the point of obliterating our charming accents by derogatory comments about our use of non-standard English. Heck they even observe new teachers to be sure they use good grammar, and the poor rookies fail if they let a "she don't" or a "he ain't" slip occasionally. That's a bunch of hogwash, because there's nothing more delightful than going to the movies and hearing a good ol' Southern accent in full swing, and the more authentic, the better. People pay good money for that, and Y'ALL know it, too, NOT you guys.

So it's high time for the belles of the South to fill up on shrimp and grits, fried okra, buttered biscuits, and two jars of sweet tea and head off to war, a war to keep the culture alive. But if there's one thing that Southerners do best, it is to take their own sweet time;

and a good story teller knows how to keep the long tale alive and pique the interests of the listeners. We don't need the cunning visual effects guys ready to create yet more sex symbols with low cut peasant blouses or tight fitting t-shirts and cut-off jeans tickling their buttocks. What we need are dynamic, strong and intelligent heroines, like Caroline Bethany Carter, and here's her story. Hang on to yer ropes sugah, and start uh swangin', but don't forget yer hanky.

CHAPTER 1
FINDIN' 1981

After suffering through an unpalatable cafeteria lunch on Friday of the Labor Day weekend, Caroline and Emily left the campus, with a superfluous supply of clothing and shoes, as most girls their ages would have, and began the grueling four hour trek to Summerville. Emily, in her short, rough looking blue jean cut offs and hot pink halter top, with all her yellow, bleached hair pulled up into a makeshift updo secured by a large barrette and a multi-colored ribbon, looked like she was ready to play a game of coed volleyball on the beach. Conservative Caroline, looking more like she was attending some sacrosanct church picnic, was wearing white shorts and a modest, indigo colored tank top, with her hair in a ponytail and strays around her face secured snuggly by a paisley triangular bandana, and dazzling white sandals as she knew this should be her last weekend to wear them until spring, according to Momma.

The air, still sticky warm, muggy and uncomfortable, in most of South Carolina, blew through the open windows of Emily's vintage VW Beetle, painted purple by her daddy's friend for her twentieth birthday. The cracked black leather seats were covered with black and white checkerboard seat covers, custom ordered by her persnickety mother so as not to be embarrassed by the hideous condition of the interior of her daughter's car, not only covering the unsightly upholstery but making the seats less apt to make one sweat terribly in the torrid weather of the South.

In the years she'd known Emily, Caroline had never gone home with her for the weekend. In fact, Caroline had spent most of her humdrum weekends, in the confines of a boring dormitory, in Rock Hill, working and studying, the schoolmarm type always prim and proper. This year, the senior year for both of them, racy little Emily had put her foot down and insisted that her best friend have a life and visit one of the most beautiful parts of the southeast, her beloved Lowcountry. She all but dragged Caroline by the hair of her head and stuffed her into the VW.

"I feel like I'm being abducted and carted off in an oversized, mechanical purple insect," Caroline bellyached with the description of the vehicle that might be spoken by a nerdish seventh grader.

"Good...ness, Caroline, it's a holiday weekend. I swear on a stack of rotten old textbooks, I'll get you back in plenty of time to study properly and get your beauty rest," assured Emily.

"Somehow, your tarnished track record indicates that you have every intention of rushin' back at the last minute, dumpin' me off just before the dorm closes, and then sleepin' the next day until noon, while I rise at the crack of dawn to get to my early mornin' classes on time."

"You've got a smidgen of your own past tarnished track record, if I understood you correctly and your chronicles were accurate." Caroline felt a flood of shame devour her at Emily's statement, but, from her days of growing up in church, she remembered the hideous crimes of passion of King David.

"Besides, you know I usually make it back way before they lock the dorm, and I don't sleep all mornin'. I always manage to get to class, somehow, on Monday mornings. Not always in the best of shape, but I do get there."

"Emily, what you've managed to do for the past three years was to get classes that didn't start until ten o'clock in the mornin', some of which you didn't make it to, according to reliable sources. Guess that's par for the course for an art major."

"Well, go ahead and chirp all you want to, Miss Early Bird. You need to stop mournin' and tryin' to make up for things that can't be undone; I'm surprised you're not dressed in solid black today, or black for the next year, for that matter. You need to have some fun, girl! All you do is work, work, and work some more. You know this world would be no different from a sepia image if it were left up to you."

"That's a little harsh, and I'm not trying to rectify any mistakes that I've made in the past," said Caroline. "What's been done has been done, but it has made me more cautious to prepare for the future."

Oh Lord, preparation for the future, you're so cautious, you're afraid to put one step in front of the other. Good gosh, Caroline, you're paranoid 'bout what people are gonna think of you." Emily continued, "I don't care what you, your brother, your preacher, or anyone else thinks about me, to heck with all y'all. I intend to live life with a bang and help things come alive with a streak of fuchsia here and a spatter of chartreuse there and swirls of gold, and crimson." Emily swirled her right arm in a funnel shaped movement. "Furthermore, you shouldn't gossip with your so called reliable sources and act so prejudiced, like some "holy roller", belittling art majors. Now, I'm wonderin' which little rat snitched on me, probably that silly William R. Stone who can't keep his long pointed nose outta other people's business."

"Heavens, you're wound up like a top, Emily," Caroline said, interspersing her words with her good natured chuckle, "and you sound like some Bohemian fashion designer describing the colors

of new fall fabric collection. To set the record straight, I was statin'
my own opinion about art majors. I suppose most of art is illogical,
to some degree. That's why artists starve and engineers buy vacation homes in Costa Rica."

Emily held her left arm out the window, rotated her wrist, for
another spurt of body language, and said, "C'est la vie!"

Caroline tried to conceal her grin as she bit into a soft-baked
chocolate chip cookie stuffed with pecans, allowing the cookie to
melt in her mouth and savoring each morsel, a real treat for her as
she deprived herself of sweats most of the time, fearing that she'd
look bottom heavy with her pear shaped figure.

Emily and Caroline were the best of friends even though they
were quirky and different. They'd argue until the cows came home,
but they loved every minute of it, snipping and snapping at one another and bursting into laughter in the end, opposites attract.

Screaming and teasing one another, it didn't seem to take long
speeding down the highway for the deciduous trees on the hills,
strangled by kudzu, to be dominated by scrubby pines. The sides of
the embankments were filled with ruts in the red clay, washed out
during infrequent but heavy rain, with exposed rock interspersed
with decomposing pine needles and cones. Residual wild blackber-
ry canes arched over the invasive old die-hard dandelion greens on
the dirty red hills. The remaining spent blooms of orange daylilies
were swaying in the moist warm breeze. On and on as they drove
where the forests next to the interstate were dense with pine, oaks,
poplars, and maples, all choking one another out to catch the rays
of sunshine shining on the foliage needed to photosynthesize the
trees. The further they drove to lower part of the state, the more
humidity increased and the landscape looked as if it had morphed
into oblate terrain blanketed with sandy soil with miles and miles of
views of various conifers and low flat fields nearly barren of vegeta-
tion. They were now in the Lowcountry.

They sped along down the highway, trying to hear one another above the droning hum of the wheels needing new bearings. Conversation for a while, on an older stretch of highway, was nearly impossible, so they listened to the radio, cranked up loud to the highest volume, singing familiar lyrics as young girls often do. Caroline grabbed a lavender hand towel from the back seat to wipe the perspiration off her face as a wave of heat and humidity enveloped the car. She made a comment about sweating bullets and retrieved two bottles of chilled lemonade from the small cooler on the back floorboard. They drank the cold liquid so rapidly they felt like their abdomens were distended. Later, in search of a restroom on a side road taken from the exit ramp, the low riding car with poor shocks made the drive feel like a carnival ride when they hit pot holes sending the girls bouncing into the air, nearly touching the stained gray headliner. Emily screamed, "Woo hoot," as she purposely swerved the car left and right up the exit ramp, with Caroline holding onto the hand strap to keep steady while admonishing Emily to take it easy.

Back on the highway for a while, they noticed ill kept ranch style homes in the midst of arid fields and shanties with dilapidated out buildings, Caroline asked, "Seems like we're out in the middle of nowhere; what on earth do people do for a living down here?"

"Farm, plant pine trees, work in pulp and paper, and heaven forbid, some may even teach school."

"Sto...p" she said stretching the word! That's a depressin' thought." Then she asked, "Am I lookin' at cotton fields over there?"

Even though they turned down the volume on the radio, they were practically yelling to each other as they spoke to hear one another over the drone of the bad bearings and the whizzing sound of the wind.

"I bl'eve so. There was a bad problem with boll weevil attacks sometime back."

"I've heard tell of boll weevils before, wipin' out an entire cotton crop. You'd think that livin' in the state of South Carolina, these people would have been contactin' somebody from the Clemson extension service. I guess I was mistaken to think that the pesky insects had been eradicated."

"That's exactly what Daddy said, although he didn't use the word eradicated. He says some of the people down here are just plain "backasserds". Lord, they may not even have a telephone and live miles from one. It's not like pickin' up the phone in Greenville and callin' the extension service.

Daddy might have a thick accent, bein' from Anderson County, but he's no dummy when it comes to agriculture. He'd call his buddies at the university in a heartbeat if he were aware of a boll weevil problem. You nevah seen a cotton field before?"

"No, I haven't seen vast cotton fields like these. Grandpaw has a small patch of cotton in his garden, just to have his grand younguns do a little pickin'. She mumbled on for a few minutes before Emily spoke up.

Emily responded, "Law me, you had a mouthful to tell, didn't you? Sorry, honey, but I didn't understand most of what you said. You'll have to tell it all again over a big fat bowl of ice cream." She wiped the beads of perspiration from her forehead, looked to her left for a moment, and then quickly refocused on her driving. "It's distressin' to look at some of these tumble-down farms," Emily said loudly, like the radio volume had been turned up.

"Is Summerville like this," Caroline yelled, leaning over toward Emily trying to make sure that she heard her question?

"No, Holly Hill is like this, but not Summerville. It's another world from this. It used to be a place for the rich and famous to get away from the hustle and bustle of busy city life. You'll see, it's a beautiful little place, different from the beauty of Charleston, uniquely its own."

"Are you thinkin' of comin' back here when you graduate," Caroline asked?

"What," she questioned, straining to hear everything Caroline asked as a truck passed them on the highway?

"Are you comin' back here in May?"

"I might, or I'll go on to art school in Savannah, if Momma and Daddy will keep on supportin' me. Once you have Lowcountry blood flowin' through your veins, it's hard to stay away from here; I think I'd be afraid to move away for good, unless I was warned to. There are voices, you know, whisperin' in the pines?"

"What do you mean by voices and bein' warned," queried Caroline?

"Don't you know people believe Charleston is haunted? Ghostly voices from the dead can be heard clear up to Summerville. Sometimes, they beg you to stay, and sometimes they tell you to leave," she said with a mystical tone of voice.

"Now, you're gettin' weirder than you usually are, Emily."

"No, I'm serious, people hear voices. I've heard people tell me for a fact that they'd heard voices."

"I didn't think you believed in haints and spooks. And these people you say have heard voices, they've not had too much jigga boo?"

"Good Lord, I nevah heard haunts called haints before. You're a hoot! But you nevah know what people believe in, 'till you ask 'em. What's jigga boo?"

"Booze. You're as naïve as I am, girl. And you don't know the word haint, cus your momma is so proper. I bet most of the people in Charleston call 'em haints."

Caroline was nearly sitting on the hand break trying to get close enough to Emily to be heard and to hear what Emily said back to her.

"How do you know my momma's so proper?"

"'Cause you've been a complainin' 'bout her for several years," said Caroline, smirking.

"Oh, I guess I have. I love her, but I don't want to be like her. And I don't want to live at home anymore. If Daddy won't send me on to art school, I'll just have to get an apartment, maybe in Mount Pleasant."

Getting off on one of her little tangents again, Caroline said, "You know, everywhere in the South, they have different words for different things. Don't you just love it when Hollywood tries to dump us all in the same stewpot? I can sure tell the difference between a Virginian, a Texan, and somebody from South Georgia. Why, our accent is different from the Upstate to the Lowcounty."

Emily wasn't really listening, but she nodded to Caroline as she mouthed away.

They arrived in Summerville in the early afternoon, enjoying Emily's parents' comfortable air conditioned home on the hot, muggy day, the kind of day that made you feel like you'd been in a sauna with your clothes on. Emily's mother offered them fresh squeezed lemonade, which they were grateful for. However, it didn't take long for Caroline to see how annoying Emily's mother could be, as she spoke as if everyone were beneath her. They waited until Emily's daddy got home from work. He was an executive for a big forestry company and had the luxury of leaving early on Fridays. After spending a short time with Emily's parents, Emily nervously stated that they had other plans. She was afraid to get on her mother's bad side. Her daddy was much more down to earth and made some statement about the girls being young and full of energy, and that they might want to go out. Emily's mother cocked her head back and then turned her head in the other direction, giving Emily a clear indication that she thought the young girls were being rude to arrive and leave after such a brief visit with them.

Caroline welcomed the minute when they exited the family room and walked back toward Emily's bedroom. Mrs. Price had already gotten on her nerves, running her mouth constantly, trying to impress Caroline, but being unsuccessful in doing so. She found it hard to believe that someone as earthy as Emily could've been birthed by someone so prissy, so uppity. Emily didn't care one iota about her mother's social calendar, but she'd suffered through her announcements.

As they got out of earshot, Emily made a motion like she was gagging herself and whispered,

"That's why I wanna move to Savannah after I graduate from Winthrop. I won't have to hear so much of her prattle."

"Shame, shame, but I'll not blame," responded Caroline singsong, in a hush and rolling her eyes to indicate her own boredom.

Emily tried to talk Caroline into going to a male striptease performance, but she definitely declined. She had no intention of joining a crowd of crazed drunken women watching attractive muscular guys dance around in skin tight attire, or not much at all, to be stuffed with money at the end of each act. So they decided to go to a beach music club. They soon became bored with clubbin' with kids probably from the College of Charleston, strangers, and a few older guys wearing kakis and golf shirts trying to hit on young, unescorted female coeds, including the two of them.

Emily said, "Let's split from here and go back to Summerville."

The trip back on Highway 61 was eerie where the headlights of the Emily's VW were the only lights around. Ancient oaks shrouded the road, reaching out and arching across it, with their branches, curtained with moss, blowing in the breeze, making the trees look as if the trunks were moving, too.

Once back in Summerville, they drove down Main Street and took a left, near the square, onto West Richardson Street. Passing ten to fifteen houses, Emily finally brought the VW to a screeching halt in front of an old gray house, nestled behind a row of scraggly, unpruned shrubs near the street. A single light bulb, the globe missing, was lighting the front of the house, with insects tapping the bulb and bouncing off, repeatedly.

They parked the VW Bug in a sandy area behind a Toyota, a Mustang, a Volvo, and a restored 1957 Ford truck, the grass not growing beneath the ancient oak, which arched over the vehicles, but the branches on the other side had been amputated to keep the power lines intact. The side of the house, where the back door was located, was dimly lighted giving some visibility of the run-down house and parking area. The house was situated on a corner lot with a narrow, poorly paved road to the right of the property. A glimpse of the old house, with a partially rusted tin roof and a wraparound porch with sagging railings and broken spindles, told Caroline that the house was in dire need of preservation work. It probably had not been restored because the location was terrible. The surrounding old houses were also in a ramshackle state, and needed more than a tender touch to bring them back to life. Emily mentioned that in this section of town, it sounded like thunder every morning at the crack of dawn, as well as every couple of hours, as the train rumbled on the tracks right behind the houses, making the properties even less desirable. In this old house rented by three of Emily's friends, the whole house shook when the train passed, especially in the kitchen, where the drinking glasses on open shelves would clank if stacked too close together.

As Caroline approached the house, noticing the warped condition of the front steps with nail heads sticking up to the right and left, she saw three rocking chairs, that looked like they'd been used at a house on Folly Beach for a couple of decades, weathered grey with uneven grains, splinters and cracks, were placed on the porch in close proximity to encourage conversation. As Emily and Caroline walked up on the rackety steps and knocked on the door covered with chunks of peeling gray paint, they could hear the sound of an Alabama rock band in the background, and lots of raucous laughter. In fact, it was so loud, with the windows open in a futile effort to catch some semblance of a breeze, Emily literally banged on the door on the second attempt to get someone's attention. After she knocked, she had paint chips sticking to the side of her fist that was moist with the humidity still hanging in the air. The noise agitated Sebastian, a medium-size, shaggy mutt with way too much energy, who came bounding around the corner running into empty beer bottles as he tried to zigzag through the collision course of the rocking chairs in his path. In his excitement he tipped over a small round table with an ashtray full of nasty cigarette butts and made a huge mess on the neglected sandy porch. He stopped for nothing until he reached Emily, tucked in his hind legs to sit, and thumped the porch with his thick black tail.

"Hey, Sebastian," Emily said as she knelt down to give him a pat on the head; "Have they been lettin' you party a little too much?"

It looked like someone had been partying too much and forgot to wash and brush the matted, stinky, but friendly, black mongrel.

As Butch, a tall lanky guy with a full beard and round glasses slowly opened the door, Emily could see J.P. and his brother sitting on a burgundy sectional couch. The guys were drinking, and laughing uproariously, having a good old time. The three fellows were college friends of Emily's brother, Drew, so she'd known them for years. Emily thought they were a little on the wild side, with the exception of Butch who was the shy type in comparison to the Yanks.

"Hey! Y'all come on in," Butch said to Emily, and he glanced at Caroline with a welcoming smile. Shy Butch appeared to be embarrassed, standing there shirtless and wearing light summer cotton pajama pants, and turned to the guys and said, in his most pronounced drawl, "Hey y'all, looks like we've got some pleasant comp'ny for a change."

The girls, undeterred, entered the room, and Emily was ready to make a proper introduction to Butch. Caroline, raising her head from a lowered position she'd timidly assumed as she'd entered the room, looked up at Butch and shook his extended hand. He noticed her bashfulness, reminding him so much of his own timidity. She managed to make eye contact, and then her vision drifted toward the left, and she was quite captivated by a unique painting mounted on the cracked plaster wall. The huge painting had an ethereal quality, a surreal depiction of a middle aged woman with a look of weariness, which drew your eyes in to fixate upon her; surrounding the woman's head were the gnarled branches of a tree, and flashes of lightning above the old Live Oak. Caroline's concentration on the anomalous painting was broken when Butch unintentionally bumped into her as he was trying to grab Sebastian as he bolted, like a wild animal lunging toward prey, into the doorway after the girls. Butch felt awkward and flustered. He fled momentarily to put on a wrinkled, blue linen shirt hanging over the back of a chair in the corner of the adjacent room.

"So you like our masterpiece," asked J.P. as he noticed Caroline beginning to study the painting again but having a bizarre look on her face? "One of our friends painted that for us as a house warming gift; she's called Mother Wofford. He's our Woodstock hippie friend who's usually smokin' and drinkin' a whole lot." He was laughing as he glanced over at his brother.

"That would be Rufus," said J.P.'s brother, Chris. "The man is messed up, that's all there is to it, smoked one too many joints to be sane."

"Did he ever think like a normal person," asked J.P. with a chuckle? Then he looked back at the girls, stood, and said, "Have a seat and grab a beer."

"If you got a couple of cold cans of cola, that would be good," said Emily, knowing that they might have to face her momma when they got home, with her barrage of nosy questions. "I wanted y'all to meet my friend from school."

Caroline, having gotten over her bout of shyness, spoke up to introduce herself. "I'm Caroline Carter; nice to meet y'all."

Butch furthered the introduction of J.P. and Chris to Caroline. "Compared to you two young'uns," said Butch with his slow drawl, "we're three old dudes sittin' around and reminiscin' about our days at Clemson, eons ago. We did far too much celebratin' back then. Now, Monday morning hangovers are beyond rough, if you got a job to do. Y'all caught us on one of our weak moments, but we'd rather have the comp'ny of two nice looking women than sit around and act like a bunch of hellions all night. Y'all have saved us," he said placing his hand over his heart and leaning back.

"Thank you, darlin'," said Emily as she looked at Butch. She and Caroline had a seat on the huge burgundy sectional couch. To the left of the peculiar painting on the wall, there were a couple of posters and some Clemson paraphernalia attached with thumb tacks. A piece of fluorescent orange ribbon hung from the short pull-chain on the dust laden ceiling fan. Caroline noticed Sebastian's disgusting dog hair clinging to the nap on the velour sofa, and there were sandy paw prints all over the worn hardwood floor. A makeshift coffee table, nothing more than a thick sheet of unpainted plywood on top of stacks of cinder blocks, was covered in empty beer bottles and soda cans. A clear view of the kitchen, dirty dishes, pots, and pans on every horizontal surface could be seen from the living room through an entryway flanked by a few strands of wooden beads hanging from the overhead molding and tucked back on the sides with tiebacks of three inch long nails.

"Sorry 'bout the place; it's disgusting right now. I suppose most bachelors don't keep things too neat, unless you're the effeminate type. We're animal lovers, and don't mind if Sebastian naps on the couch with us." He began to laugh and added, "He sheds and usually smells like fish - he can sniff out a trash bag full of fish heads in a New York minute - but he's loyal and high spirited." He had to stop describing Sebastian momentarily because he was laughing so hard, but he joked with a feigned drawl so familiar to Caroline, "That dawg lapped up so much beer spilt on the porch he's done gone crazy, got perm'nent brain damage."

Butch interjected, fearing that Caroline would think J.P. was making fun of Southern folk, "We just made a big ol'batch of shrimp scampi; are y'all hungry?"

The aroma of garlic wafted into the room from the kitchen.

"Thanks for the offer, but we just ate down in Charleston. If I'd known I'd be offered somethin' as good as the shrimp scampi smells, I'd have waited to eat here. We ended up eating greasy hamburgers and fries because we were chugged full of beer, and to tell you the truth the combination didn't set well with me." She suddenly felt self-conscious because she'd opened her mouth and a tsunami of explanations had flooded the conversation.

"So you're Caroline Carter. Don't you have a middle name or a first name? Carolina girls use their first and middle names, like Mary Lou or Sallie Anne, don't y'all?"

She was about to get tickled at him but she answered him saying, "My full name is Caroline Bethany Carter, but that's just too many syllables for most people to handle, so I just say Caroline Carter. Southern guys use their initials, like J.T. or T.J., but girls usually don't, but you don't sound like a native to me." She took a deep breath, having opened the flood gate of words again to make some sort of conversation. "Tell me where you're from."

"New Jersey, I was born and reared right outside of Manhattan."

"What's a Jersey boy doin' bein' called by his initials," she asked?

J.P. said, "My full name is John Paul Andersen. When I got down south, I realized a lot of guys here use their initials. I wanted to fit in, so I told everyone to call me J.P. When I go back up north or speak to my mom, I have to answer to Paul; they'd laugh me out of Jersey for calling myself J.P."

Caroline found herself checking J.P. out, even though she wasn't in the habit of doing that, especially lately, trying to finish school and keep guys out of the equation. Guys acting like bloodhounds on a hunt really got on her last nerve, so she usually never gave them a reason to go after her.

J.P. had been working in construction all summer, spending most of his days outside. His tousled dirty blond hair had a sun bleached look which set off his ocean blue eyes. He was stocky in stature, strong, and healthy looking with a nice tan. His eyes were the intoxicating type that made you want to stare into them, but she resisted and tried to seem simply interested in what he had to say. He was wearing a pair of very faded jeans and an orange T-shirt with a Clemson Tiger logo on it, which was so old the hem of one sleeve was completely torn out.

J.P. noticed things about Caroline, too. He liked it when she maintained eye contact even when talking about trivial subjects like vacation destinations or basketball tournaments, or interesting characters like favorite comedians. J.P. tried to focus on things she said to him, but he found himself wanting to sit back and look at her. Caroline's long, straight brown hair had been pulled back into a ponytail, but shorter loose strands of hair hung down around her face. It didn't look like she wore make-up, with the exception of light mascara, but she really didn't need to. She had high cheekbones and a slender nose. She too, had a very nice smile, and J.P. could tell that she probably had braces on her teeth in the past, to straighten them perfectly. He sometimes had a habit of shifting his eyes to the floor when trying to talk with someone he'd just met, being shy but trying not to show it, but he couldn't stop looking directly at her. There was something unique about the golden color of her eyes, almost honey colored, and the way her lips were gently curved as she sat there attentively listening to him.

As they talked, she heard the sound of the turntable dropping another record in place and soon the sweet sounds of soft rock filled the room.

J.P. commented, "Bet you like that artist. Most women do. He performed at Littlejohn Coliseum a few years back."

"Yeah, I actually went to that concert. I was still in high school."

"Imagine that. You were in high school, and I was a Jersey boy, come down to sow my oats at Clemson."

"Sow what," she posed, with the words *you dog* popping into her consciousness?

"Just kidding," he said. "I got your attention."

As they talked on and on, and laughed endlessly, it seemed that the others in the room had faded away.

"Hey, Caroline, we need to get going," Emily said giving her a harmless little finger poke. "My momma is gonna have a hissy fit about us gettin' home so late. We sure don't want Momma 'n' Daddy to think you're a bad influence on me, draggin' me over here to a house full of reckless guys."

"Us, reckless," Butch asked?

"Well, yeah," she answered. "Okay, y'all are a little on the loony side."

Emily began to laugh, but Caroline simply stared at her, with her eyebrows raised. She felt embarrassed just like the day in fourth grade when she realized she'd left her baby doll pajama bottoms on under her mini skirt.

Emily added, as she winked at Caroline, "Anyway, I want you to be welcomed at Momma and Daddy's, in case you wanna come back to Summerville."

At that point, Caroline blushed and turned toward the door to gain composure. She thought to herself, *"Why is she talking about me wanting to come back like I'm gonna start chasing him or somethin'?"* Emily, shut that trap before you really embarrass me.

J.P. spoke up and asked Caroline, "How long will you be in town?" He seemed to lose some of his acquired drawl when he got serious.

"I have a big placement test at school on Tuesday, so Emily and I need to head out Monday. It'll take about four hours to get back to Rock Hill. If I study some on the way back and when I get there, I should be fine."

Emily intruded into the conversation and said, "Unlike me, Caroline's one of those studious types."

Caroline felt herself turn four shades of red with embarrassment.

Then J.P. suggested, country like for effect, "Maybe y'all can join us tomorrow night. We're havin' some friends over 'bout six for our annual oyster roast. We always pig out, drink a lot of beer, and have a good time."

Emily knew about the oyster roast but had forgotten to mention it to Caroline. Although she liked J.P. and Chris very much, Emily wasn't trying to set Caroline up with J.P. for fear that she might catch some flak from her family about J.P. being a Northerner. She didn't really know much about Caroline's family. Emily's own staunch Southern grandpa, in Anderson, still steeped in prejudice, told her once that if she ever married a damn Yankee, he'd cut her off for sure, giving her no prospect for future inheritance. Family attitudes in the South in the 1980's were still as important as church attendance every Sunday. In some families, one didn't step outside of certain boundaries or there would be a high price to pay for those choices.

Taking a risk on her own, Caroline answered, "Okay. Looks like I'll be gladly attendin' my very first Lowcountry oyster roast."

Emily was almost giggling, her body looking like she had a nervous tick, as she tried to suppress it because she knew Caroline had no idea that she'd be eating nearly raw oysters.

Caroline added brightly, "See y'all tomorrow night 'bout six. Thanks so much for invitin' us, we 'preciate it."

Feeling like the breath had been sucked out of him, something he'd never felt before, J.P. finally sputtered out, "It'll be great to see y'all again."

Caroline had a slight bounce to her step, and as she walked, her ponytail swung from side to side. As J.P. watched her go out the door, he thought to himself that she had a nice personality, cute mannerisms, and seemed like a decent girl. He could hear her asking Emily why she was laughing as they walked down the front porch steps, Emily's answer trailing off in the distance.

Although the girls had brought too many clothes to begin with, they still found an excuse to go shopping on Saturday morning to get something new to wear to the oyster roast. Some new T-shirts and matching flip-flops wouldn't break the bank. Around four thirty, they got showers, ironed their T-shirts, and slipped on shorts and the new shirts. Caroline dried her long brown hair and braided it into a single braid that she brought forward over her right shoulder. Mascara and a touch of blush was enough make up for her. Her basic sterling silver looped earrings were a bit tarnished from frequent use, so she cleaned them with toothpaste and a paper towel. Before putting on her flip-flops, she touched up the coral colored nail polish on her toenails which looked chipped. Primping had to make sense to her, had to be absolutely necessary; most of the time she saw no real need in much of it and was a bit annoyed when girls made a career out of getting all gussied up, as her granny would say. Her older sister, Rhonda, was like that as they were growing up; it drove Caroline crazy every time they were getting ready to go somewhere. She'd be sitting around reading a book waiting for Rhonda to get all dolled up for nothing.

"You ready to go?" asked Emily. "I think we'll be there at the right time if we leave now."

"Yeah, I guess I'm as ready as I ever will be, but what if I don't like roasted oysters?"

Emily continued, "Don't flip out. If you don't like 'em, stuff yourself with hush puppies and crackers to soak up the beer you'll drink. You don't want to be getting' goofy over there."

Caroline countered, "You're the one who gets goofy most of the time."

"True," said Emily shrugging her shoulders as if to say, oh well, and then she cackled like a hen.

Driving through the streets of Summerville, Caroline marveled at the old oak trees adorned with silvery, Spanish moss swaying in the breeze, nearly obstructing the views of some of the restored historic homes painted in a soft color palate of pastel pinks, yellows, and blues. Even the homes painted white had so much character, they were interesting. Emily took a couple of side streets just to show Caroline some of the large Victorian homes with elaborate ornamentation and surrounded by beautiful landscaping and smaller houses with wide front porches with post and spindle railings.

When Caroline and Emily arrived, J.P. saw them parking on the side of the road. He met them as they were getting out of the car and walked with them to the backyard. He and his brother had created a fire pit using concrete blocks. A large piece of sheet metal, with holes drilled in it, had been placed across the top of the pit. Oak logs in the pit were burning down to coals. Burlap feed sacks were stacked up on a bench next to the fire pit, and a metal wash tub filled with water was on the ground. Layers and layers of newspaper covered eight to ten picnic tables, and a cluster of oyster knives were placed in the center of each table. Chris and Butch were busy putting coolers of ice and beer at the ends of the picnic tables.

As they walked toward the grill, J.P. explained to Caroline, "Oak is the best wood to burn on a grill like this because it doesn't make too much smoke." Then he described the steaming process, with animation, his arms moving in swirling, spherical motions, "We'll place the oysters on the top of the sheet metal and cover them with wet burlap sacks to allow the steam to open the shells enough to slide the oyster knives into 'em."

Curiously, Caroline asked, in random fashion, with a quizzical look as she scanned the yard beyond them, "Where'd y'all get all those picnic tables?"

"Oh, we got drunk one night, and went out in the truck. We sort of borrowed them from the yards of rich people in town; stuck 'em in the back of the truck, one at a time, and hauled 'em home."

Unbelievingly, she said, "No, you did not."

"Sure we did; they didn't need 'em, so why not?"

Emily piped in, saying, "I declare, you caint believe nothin' one of these dudes tells ya."

"I wouldn't doubt it.," Caroline said as she looked at J.P., blinking and scrunching her nose like an adorable bunny rabbit.

"Okay, but we really did borrow 'em from our friends," he admitted. "So, are you ready to have your first roasted oyster?"

"I guess so, but I'm still not sure of the way it's done."

"Just sit next to me," he said. "Watch what I do with an oyster, but don't let yourself get grossed out. It might take a little getting used to. I always say to slurp and then chug some brew."

Caroline was still in the dark with that statement, slurp what, she thought.

A couple of the wives and girlfriends were coming out of the kitchen with packages of crackers, bottles of hot sauce, and baskets of hot hush puppies. One girl put two jugs of sweet tea on the table, next to a stack of tall red plastic cups and a small cooler of ice.

Butch announced, "The first batch of oysters is ready. Let's get started!"

By that time each person had taken an oyster knife from the center of the table. The oysters were scooped up with a wide, old fashioned, coal shovel and dumped on the newspaper covered tables. J.P. made sure he got started right away so Caroline could see how to open and eat an oyster. Caroline watched, observantly, as he slid the oyster knife blade to slit the shells and pried them open, using the knife to cut the oyster at the points of connection to the shells.

She had a rather shocked look on her face and realized why there were no other utensils on the tables except the oyster knives.

Then he looked over at Caroline smiling and said, "This is the part I call slurp and chug." He put the oyster shell to his mouth and took a big slurp of the oozy oyster, holding the oyster in his mouth chewing to savor the flavor and then swallowing. He then chugged some of his ice cold beer.

She grimaced.

"That's how you do it," he said to Caroline.

Caroline sat there for a moment munching on a hot hush puppy. She leaned over to J.P. and whispered, "I'm not exactly sure I can pull this off, but I'm going to try if you'll help me open the oyster. Here goes..."

Caroline despised the texture of the roasted oyster as she slurped it from the shell, smelling the briny smell of the sea. She thought she was going to be unable to swallow the viscous thing. With it still in her mouth, without haven't chewed it, she looked at J.P. smiling at her and nodding his head trying to coax her to swallow, but being careful not to let other people see him secretly coaching her. Then she tried to chew it, finding that she actually liked the flavor, but feeling the slimy and chewy texture was about to make her shudder; she finally had to take one big gulp of beer to get the oyster down.

"What do you think of our regional cuisine," J.P. asked after another big gulp of beer? "I don't think you can beat it."

"It took a little getting used to, but now I think I can actually enjoy the taste of oysters without worrying that I won't be able to get the slimy things to slide down my throat." She and J.P. just smiled at each other. He appreciated her unadulterated honesty. After a couple of beers, Caroline felt as if she'd had enough, because she didn't want to get too polluted and say something to embarrass herself. She got up from the table and went to pour herself some sweet tea over ice.

She sat back down and J.P. teased her, saying, "I'll bet you had sweet tea in your bottle as a baby."

"I wouldn't doubt it. My family drinks sweet tea like water, always have and always will."

Eating, drinking, and chatting went on for a while. Caroline was feeling the effects of the beer, as well as the sweet tea she'd consumed.

She quietly excused herself to go into the house to use the restroom. As she carefully crept up the creaking steps to enter the back of the house through the kitchen, she could hear Sebastian whining. It sounded as if the poor mutt was trapped in the bedroom nearest the kitchen. She was troubled to hear him scratching on the back of the door and making such pitiful sounds. Her intention was to open the door and pet the lonely dog in hopes that he would be consoled since she was an animal lover, too. What an asinine mistake! When she cracked the door, he stuck his snout through the opening and twisted his head with great force to get the door open. He seemed to have the strength of three or four dogs and bolted out the bedroom door, almost knocking Caroline down. She was horrified as he flashed out the screen door and leapt over the steps. The screen door slammed with a loud clap as he ran into the backyard. She peeked out the kitchen window and wanted to die when she saw Sebastian terrorizing the female quests.

She could hear Chris saying, "Oh, no! The mangy mutt got out." After locating the restroom, she felt too embarrassed to go back out and start apologizing for letting Sebastian out of the bedroom. Frustrated and thinking she was going to be in tears any minute, she really didn't know what to do next.

Caroline ambled through the living room and went out to the front side of the wraparound porch to get it together. Hanging from the ceiling in the corner of the porch, was a Pawley's Island rope swing. She got into the swing, which automatically made her spine curl to sit in it, and began to turn herself in full circles until the chains were tightened up. Then she picked up her feet from the porch floor and began to spin, listening to the creaking of the rusted chains as they unwound, and praying she wouldn't have another catastrophe like the swing falling. As her momentum finally decreased, she caught a glimpse of J.P. standing on the porch grinning from ear to ear. By the time she came to a stop, she was feeling quite woozy and was almost ready to puke.

"So, you thought you'd help ol' Sebastian out. He's a con artist with pretty women, so watch your back and don't fall for his tricks."

Caroline felt like her face was on fire from embarrassment. She said with genuine sincerity, "I'm so sorry for letting Sebastian out to pester the daylights out of everyone. I felt sorry for him, you know?"

"No problem!" Then J.P. held out his hand for Caroline to help her out of the swing. She was still dizzy from the swing and the beer and almost bumped into J.P. trying to plant her feet on the worn planks of the porch floor. As he patiently steadied her by holding her arm, she could feel his strength, and for a fleeting moment she allowed herself to feel that she needed him. Reality gripped her and she felt like such an idiot. How could she screw up so royally? She felt like a big, fat baby. Her flip-flop was awry, and as she bent over to center her foot on it she tipped over an empty beer bottle. As it rolled toward the end of the sagging porch floor, they both got tickled and laughed. The tension had let up, and she was at ease. J.P. had done that for her, really made her feel comfortable.

"Let's sit out here on the porch for a while and talk," he said. The conversations in the backyard were starting to get pretty loud. "I like sitting here at night and listening to the cicada's shrill song. I wish we could hear 'em now, but it's not quite late enough in the evening." He started laughing and then commented, "It always sounds like some entomological orgy to me."

She smiled and thought that she liked the fact that he was witty and smart, with a good vocabulary. She liked to think that she was the same. They both sat down in the weathered rocking chairs and just relaxed. Caroline was starting to sense that J.P. was demonstrating more than acquired Southern hospitality. She was thinking, how can this guy be a Yankee? He's not a pain in the butt at all. She was enjoying his company so much, she was secretly wishing the evening wouldn't have to end too early.

As the guests started leaving later that evening, there was one couple who seemed to linger a little longer than the others, Clayton

Jeffery McMahan III, a young local attorney, and his beautiful wife Anne. They chatted with J.P. for a few minutes until Butch stepped in to take over the conversation, to actually diffuse what could have become an uncomfortable situation for J.P. The couple left rather abruptly and Butch turned and walked behind J.P. and Chris mumbling, "Wish she'd get over it. For Pete's sake, she's married." He slapped J.P. on the back and said jokingly, in a low tone of voice, "Anne's a real piece of work, ain't she buddy? Bet you're glad you don't have to contend with her."

Caroline couldn't make out what Butch said to J.P. and was basically undiscerning of anything out of the ordinary. J.P. was smiling at Butch but stood silent for a moment; then he moved closer to Caroline, and asked, "How'd you like to go down to Charleston with me tomorrow morning?" He realized she'd have to leave on Monday to get back to school, but he wanted to show her some of the local sights, and to get to know her better.

Thinking to herself that Emily wouldn't mind, and she could spend some time with her family, Caroline replied, "I'd like to do that. I came to Charleston once when I was a kid, but the only things I remember beside the days at the beach, were visiting Middleton Place and riding over a huge bridge to look at some gargantuan military ship."

Don't expect a nice autumn breeze in Charleston, like you'd have up in the Blue Ridge Mountains." Then he added, slowly like a good ol' boy, "It's still pur...dy dang hot down there."

The next day, Sunday morning, she dressed in beige linen pants and a loose fitting, long sleeve cotton top. She loved to wear those 'free flowing' shirts made in India. Her hair was pulled back into a ponytail, and she put on a pair of large, looped, white earrings. She wore flip-flops thinking they would be easy to slip off and on if they went to the beach.

J.P. rang the doorbell at precisely 9:00. When Caroline got into his Toyota, she could smell the aroma of bread and cinnamon.

"I stopped by the bakery this morning to get us some fresh hot cinnamon buns," he said. "I hope you like them."

"Oh, shut my mouth. Hot cinnamon buns are my favorite. Man, you're some kinda guy." She felt a bit flushed after saying it, but felt it was a well-deserved comment.

"It won't take long to get down to the city," he said. Charleston is a beautiful place, with more charm and mystery than any other city I can think of. Thanks for coming down with me."

"Well, thanks for ask…in' me to come," she replied in a cute drawl.

Caroline relaxed and savored the last bite of her cinnamon bun.

J.P. took the exit to get to East Bay Street to show Caroline Rainbow Row. She was in awe of the rich colors of the old buildings. They drove down to the Battery, parked the car, and strolled along the Battery looking at the grand old mansions, symbols of Charleston's aristocracy.

"Let's take a carriage ride through the city", J.P. said.

"Perfect," responded Caroline.

She'd never ridden in a horse drawn carriage before, but she didn't want to make comments to disclose that fact and expose herself as being so naïve, so uncultured. They had to walk a few blocks to begin the carriage tour and were able to find a beautiful white carriage drawn by coal black horses. The carriage was draped with silk rose garland, covered in red roses; it almost looked like a special carriage for newlyweds on a honeymoon.

The carriage driver gave the normal tour description of the landmarks and historic places. J.P. had worked in construction in the city, and knew a lot of things the carriage driver didn't mention, things that some of the local old timers had told him, some of which would curl your hair with tales of ghostly nature, but he stuck to the historical characteristics of one of the most fascinating cities in the country.

As they rode through the streets, J.P. put his arm behind Caroline on the seat back, and quietly added to the driver's words, so as not to distract the other anonymous couple sharing the carriage. Often, she had to lean toward J.P. to hear him over the noisy clopping of the horses' hooves on the cobblestones of some of the streets, her shoulder brushing his chest as she moved in closer. Many streets on the tour were very narrow, so there was little noise from street traffic. There were still tourists on foot viewing the sights at their leisure with brochures and guides in hand, even though it was not a peak tourist season. They completed the fascinating fifty minute tour near Market Street.

"I'd like to show you the Market next," said J.P. "Don't know if you know much about the market building, but everything here is chock-full of history."

"Do tell," she said, with genuine interest.

"Over two hundred years ago, a wealthy family willed the land to be used as a public market.

The building has survived tornadoes, hurricanes, and a major earthquake. During wartime, even fires and bombardments didn't take it down. You'll find it amazing when you see it," he said, oozing enthusiasm.

"I'm sure I will. I can see that you like history."

He nodded in affirmation.

As they entered the Market, Caroline asked, "What kinds of stuff do they sell here?"

"They sell just about everything, fresh fruits and vegetables, jewelry, and crafts. You'll probably find the sweet grass baskets interesting.

Caroline was indeed intrigued to see a woman weaving a sweet grass basket with a plethora of completed baskets surrounding her, displayed on an old tattered quilt, spread out upon the sidewalk. She stood there watching the withered woman as she worked, leaning against the back of her old worn ladder backed chair, beads of sweat on her forehead making her dark skin look shiny and slick. She looked up occasionally with a pleasant smile on her face. She would then turn to her friend, a buxom woman, and say something almost unintelligible to Caroline.

He noticed her looking at some tie-dyed T-shirts, which were tastefully displayed by a young man with dreadlocks, probably from the Caribbean, not a typical sight there in the Charleston area. She moved on through the market looking at other things, and he decided to get a shirt for her. In the crowded pathway, she turned around to say something to him and didn't see him for a moment. In the middle of a knot of shoppers, he popped into view, holding up a small shopping bag, tied at the top of the handles with a sheer pink ribbon and smiling at her to let her know he'd bought something for her. They inched their way, through the shoulder to shoulder crowd of tourists, to the end of that section of the market.

He handed her the shopping bag and said, "I thought you might enjoy this and have something to help you remember this little day trip."

"Oh, J.P. you shouldn't have done that," she said displaying sensitivity, "but I'm sure glad you did," she added with her most alluring smile, the trademark of a Carolina girl when her beau presents her with gifts. "This will look good with my favorite pair of jeans. I love to wear T-shirts. Thank you so much!" She was thinking how different J.P. was; she could think of no one else who had ever been so considerate and a nostalgic kind of person like he was. Could he be for real?

They continued looking at the merchandise in the third section of the market, and came out of the end of the building on East Bay Street, near the waterfront, a surge of warm air blowing the gift bag held tightly in her hand. From the Market, the two walked down to St. Phillips Church and graveyard. He told her a little about the supernatural sightings of bizarre happenings and ghosts. Just as he had Caroline going, thinking she seemed gullible, he said, "People in the city and on the islands thrive on ghost stories. It's a part of the culture and the tourist trade." He grinned and started singing a popular song about superstitions.

He asked, "You do believe in ghosts, don't you?"

"Now I hear tell of it all; you and Emily both believing in haints."

"You don't believe."

"Ain't nevah seen nary haint, Mr. Andersen, so don't know if I bl'eve in 'em or not," she said, having no intention of acting prim and proper. "I reckon if you do, I'll go along with it, to a point." She smiled warmly and touched his arm with her elbow, just a little gesture to let him know she liked him.

As they strolled Caroline admired the houses in the area, many of which had beautiful courtyards with gardens, with statues she could see through the wrought iron gates and creeping fig or ivy clinging to the brick walls, still as lush and green as the ferns in the courtyards. Climbing roses and Confederate jasmine hanging over arbors and hydrangeas, chaste trees, and yaupons were repeated in garden after garden. Window boxes decorated many homes filled with colorful petunias and asparagus ferns. Flickering gas lamps gave the streets a warm glow. She was enraptured. Charleston had to be the most beautiful and romantic city in America.

He pointed to sloping long porches overlooking the courtyard gardens, with rocking chairs, stretched across the sides of the homes. Hanging baskets with huge ferns hung from the porch beams and black painted pots filled with pink geraniums graced the porch floors. Even the upper stories had balconies overlooking the gardens with camellias, nandinas, and clematis climbing trellises.

They continued to walk back toward Waterfront Park as J.P. shared what he knew of the history of the slave trade in Charleston. "The culture of this area was defined by the slave trade. Most enslaved Africans were brought through the port. They were sold at public auctions to Lowcountry planters. They have stories to tell of the dreadful persecutions, killings, and ghosts, if you can understand the Gullah they speak," he said opening his eyes wide to appear frightened.

She interjected, "I suppose Gullah would be the mixture of African languages with English. Where I'm from, the people use a mixture of sayings of the English, Irish, Scottish, and German, and make up a lot of their own funny sayings. I guess we can be a little hard to understand at times if you're not used to some of our expressions."

"I'll vouch for that. I never knew what I was gonna get from some of the locals around Clemson and Seneca, when I asked a question."

"I reckon you hear...d uh answer," she said jokingly and with a forced drawl, more exaggerated than her own.

Caroline had been required to take South Carolina history in college, which bored her out of her gourd having a professor who was so old he must have fought in the Civil War himself, but J.P. could make the history come alive for her as he shared things he'd learned while living in the Lowcountry. She was impressed with him and thought he was very intelligent. She wanted him to know that she was intelligent, too, but she didn't want to hold back with her accent, because she was actually proud of it in many ways and used it with humor to captivate someone as she conversed. (There's nothing like turning the head of a Yankee with a drawl; usually they're fascinated but sometimes mistake dialect for stupidity, unfortunately.)

Caroline was tired of walking by the time they reached the park near the harbor. She teased, "You 'bout wore me slap out. I got to set a spell now." She felt sweaty and parched.

He laughed and said, "Country girls don't last long sightseeing in flip-flops."

She commented, "I'll have you know, I'm not a country girl."

"You can't be a city girl unless you come from a city of two million people or more."

"Bet you I could hold my own in your big city," she stated confidently, as she sat erect and unmovable upon the park bench.

He just smiled back at her and shook his head, knowing full well she had no concept of a metropolis like New York, which he claimed as his city.

They found a park bench in a shady spot and enjoyed seeing children run from the statue to the cannon. A warm moist breeze blew the long palmetto fronds, oscillating like great pendulums, and they shared a few quiet moments just watching, with fierce concentration, as the ships would come and go."

"You feeling hungry yet," asked J.P.? "We can drive over the Cooper River Bridge to Shem Creek and have some lunch."

Caroline suddenly had a frightened look on her face as she looked toward the huge bridge in the distance. "That bridge? You expect to take me over that high bridge? I'm terrified of bridges." She was serious, but he thought she was just joking about being utterly terrified.

"Okay. Just close your eyes, and I'll tell you when we're on the other side. Don't open your eyes or look down."

"Do whut?" Just his warning was making her stomach churn, like a mixture of cream and cider vinegar. "Thanks for that tip, but I really do get anxious on bridges. I'm not teasing. I know it sounds silly for me to feel that way, but I do." She knew that she'd already gone over that bridge as a child when on vacation, and probably did so with her eyes closed to keep from throwing up.

Stepping up to the sidewalk, still nearly hot enough to fry an egg upon it, J.P. and Caroline stood beside the Toyota. It was so warm in Charleston that time of the year, it took a few minutes for the steamy car to cool with the air conditioner on full blast. Both of them perspiring, they looked at one another with anticipation of a few more hours to spend together.

Feeling bashful and tryin' to be funny to cover it up, she said, "Ah'm 'bout to burn up." Even though she'd 'written off' men for the time being, she found herself captivated with J.P. He was so down to earth and definitely not like the Northerners her sister Rhonda had bellyached about.

J.P. drove on down South Battery and through many side streets to show Caroline additional homes that she'd not seen that day and to try to divert her attention from the Cooper River Bridge. Then he turned in the direction of the bridge. As they approached the ramp to the bridge, Caroline was silent, her legs stretched out and stiffened. She was trying to cope with the situation without looking like a six or seven year old child in front of J.P.

"You okay?" asked J.P. as he glanced over to see her with her eyes closed and her hands firmly pressed together, looking as though she was praying with the same fervor she would if caught in the middle of a war zone. She remained silent as she took long deep breaths, trying to stay calm.

"You can open your eyes now. We're over the bridge."

"Thank goodness, I didn't get sick in your car." I think a nice lunch, and maybe a shot of whisky, would settle my nerves after travelin' over the bridge."

J.P. drove to Shem Creek to find one of his favorite water front restaurants. The restaurant was crowded, and they had to wait about twenty minutes to get a table by the dock. As they waited they talked and read the menu. Caroline was not quite sure about the taste of some of the seafood dishes on the menu. She made her decision to have her old favorite, scallops, and absolutely no oysters. He ordered shrimp and grits.

It was well worth the wait, to sit by the window overlooking Shem Creek as they enjoyed scrumptious meals. Several boats were docked there next to restaurant. The water rippled as a trawler slowly prepared to dock. A lone brown pelican was perched on one of the dock posts preening. They talked about everything from horse racing to the impracticality of false fingernails. She'd never felt free to converse with someone so easily before, and neither had he. Curiosity killed the cat, and Caroline asked J.P. about Clemson, about why he decided to leave before graduating.

"My parents and grandmother had dreams for me in a field that I really wasn't completely devoted to. To tell you the truth, I've always had a dream to own my own business rather than work for someone else. I'm sure that will take some time, so I'm doing construction, actually inspection now, as I try to save some money. I want to own a restoration company of my own one day. That's why Butch and Chris share the house with me and we live like paupers, so we can all save money."

"I guess I'm not much of a risk taker," she said. "I probably wouldn't make a good entrepreneur."

He teased her saying, "You might be more of a risk taker than you think you are, spending the day with me."

"You don't seem like much of a risk," she said with her head cocked toward her shoulder, looking at him intently to see if she'd stirred some thoughts within him. "I wish I had the guts to venture out on my own and be self-employed, but I've already decided to play it safe and become a teacher. I don't want to be workin' for someone else either, as bull headed as I am, but I'm too chicken to step out of my comfort zone. Momma has always been a cautious type of person. That's had an influence on me, but I think I'll always have the desire to do somethin' noteworthy with my life, somethin' that'll have an impact on others, somethin' people will remember me for after I kick the bucket.

"You'll make a difference in the lives of many people," said J.P. encouragingly. "From my first impressions, you seem to have the capacity to be empathetic and giving. Teaching is a noble profession, and you're the kind of person who can change the course of history one student at a time." J.P. sounded profound and prophetic as he commented on the qualities he'd already seen in Caroline. He was using both hands for body language, like he was conducting an orchestra.

Caroline felt attraction toward J. P. but she tried to resist it. It seemed to be stronger than she was able to control. How could this be, she'd only known him for three days? Only a fool would start falling for some guy, and a transplant to boot, after spendin' just a few hours with him. Could what they say about oysters be true? Had she polluted herself over the weekend? She wasn't thinking straight. She snapped back into the conversation.

"Well, I'm not sure how successful I'll be as a teacher, but I always try to work hard at anything I do. Thanks for your vote of confidence."

"Are you rested enough now to go down to the beach?" asked J.P. We could go to either Isle of Palms or Sullivan's Island."

"How 'bout Isle of Palms," she asked because she liked the name?

They walked into the parking lot. Ocean breezes blew Caroline's long hair; even in a ponytail she had to brush the loose strands of hair from her face and tried to tuck it behind her ears to keep it from blowing in her mouth and eyes. J.P. looked at her and thought about the way she conducted herself, hoping he was seeing her true personality, a girl who appreciates the things done for her, and a girl who's honest and open. As he looked at her, he wanted to believe that she possessed a beautiful soul in addition to having natural physical beauty. One thing he knew for sure, she had spunk and a sense of humor. If nothing else ever developed than this friendship, Caroline seemed like she could be a friend for life, fun to be around and the kind of person you could turn to when you need to be listened to. It didn't matter to him that they'd just met; sometimes you just know a person is special, and you have to keep them in your life somehow.

"Okay, let's get down to Isle of Palms."

"I've always loved going to the beach," she said. "I've nevah had the opportunity to go to the beach in September. I'm so fair skinned, I don't do well in the sun for long; I guess I was supposed to born a redhead. But I absolutely love to walk on the beach early in the morning or late in the afternoon."

"Well, I think you'll be fine today with your long sleeved shirt and pants. I've got an extra pair of sunglasses in the glove compartment you can wear." The thought of her wearing something belonging to him made him feel a little more connected to her. He'd not yet touched her, but he wanted to reach over and take her hand. He didn't want to make her feel uncomfortable in any way, so he'd be content to go to the beach and enjoy her comments about the seascape and wildlife.

When they got to the public access parking area, Caroline rolled up the legs of her pants. She took the ponytail holder out of her hair and ran her fingers through it several times. Then she braided her hair in one long braid down her back and used the elastic band to secure it. She put on the extra pair of sunglasses, and J.P. couldn't help but think she looked cute. He wondered what she looked like, on the beach, as a little girl, probably sunburned and sandy.

Having gone to the beach many times in the years he had lived in Summerville, he came prepared with a gallon of water in his trunk so they could rinse their sandy feet before going home. He even had some sunscreen in his bag for Caroline since he had noticed the evening before that she was fair skinned.

"I'm surprised that you're so prepared for the beach today," Caroline said. "Are you always this prepared for your activities?"

"No, not when I'm with the guys. They'd think I was crazy. We usually just make sure we have plenty of beer and gas in the car," he said laughing.

They kept their flip-flops on as they moved down the grayish weathered wooden boardwalk toward the beach. The sea oats on the sand dunes next to the boardwalk danced in the ocean breeze. The boardwalk ended in a few steps down to the dry sand. As soon as Caroline got to the bottom step, she got barefoot, jumped off the step, and ran as fast as she could through the scorching sand. J.P. followed her, doing the same thing. They both raced to the cool wet sand and let the water cover their feet.

Up until this time, neither Caroline nor J.P. had talked about their families. Caroline said, "My momma and my grandparents used to bring my brother, my sister, and I to the beach in the summertime."

"What about your dad?" J.P. asked

Caroline looked down at her feet in the water and felt the sand washing out around them as the water receded. She couldn't say anything for a few seconds. She tried to allow the serenity of the ocean waters washing over her feet calm her spirit. Then she said with a tremble in her voice, "Daddy died when I was just seven years old. Momma nevah remarried, so she raised us by herself. Grandpaw and Granny tried to help her so that we could enjoy some vacations, like a lot of families were able to do."

"I'm sorry. I didn't mean to pry. Your mom must have been a very strong person to go through that."

Caroline couldn't respond to J.P. She had to calm herself and gain her composure, taking deep slow breaths. She remembered as a child the good feelings she had when she was on the beach just as she was at that moment. With each ebb and flow of the waves and the water washing over her feet, she could feel some comfort when painful memories overwhelmed her, memories of the horrible thing she'd seen as a child.

She hadn't worn mascara that day, so she took off the sunglasses and wiped her tears with her sleeves leaving no marks on her white shirt, as it dried instantly in the coastal breeze. She leaned back and then twirled around, with her arms outstretched, allowing the wind to blow through her sleeves.

This was a place where she could let go and leave her troubles behind, almost as if she wanted her pain to go out with the tide, to cleanse and refresh her emotionally. This would always be such a place for her.

CHAPTER 2

LEARNIN'

Caroline had been back at Winthrop for four days after the weekend she met J.P. She usually went to her mailbox, at the student center, about once a week. She didn't expect mail, but she checked just in case there was something from her momma or sister. Much to her surprise, there was a large card in a light blue envelope in her mailbox. She was ecstatic to see the return address with Summerville, S.C. in the corner of the envelope and a small sticker of a sea gull. She couldn't wait to open the card; it would be too much suspense to go all the way back to her dorm. So she went outside the student center and plopped herself down on the grassy hill, beneath a shady oak.

The card was an unusually nice thank you card, with swirling pastel designs and glittered flowers. J. P.'s note inside was succinct but most sincere; he was thanking her for the opportunity to spend time with her and get to know her. Caroline was moved that he would thank her in such a way. After reading the card several times, she pulled out her pen to date the card, and placed it back in the blue envelope. She just had that feeling that this card should be a keeper.

The rest of the week went by quickly for Caroline. This was her weekend to work in the dorm office Friday, Saturday, and Sunday nights from five p.m. until midnight. On Saturdays, she usually went for walks, listened to music, read for pleasure, or wrote in her journal in the afternoon before going to work at five. She'd study as much as she could at work to pass the time, but usually by eleven o'clock she'd get so bored she'd take a break from her studies and start verbal fist fights with some of the drunk jocks trying to lure girls to their rooms.

After trying to call most of the weekend, and starting to wonder if she were seeing someone else, J.P. decided to write her a letter, not just a card, and share things in his letter that he hadn't had the opportunity to do when she was in Summerville, to tell her more about the way he'd grown up in Jersey and things that had happened to him in Manhattan. He wanted to keep the lines of communication open and let her know that he was indeed thinking about her often.

The next time Caroline checked her mailbox, she was pleasantly surprised to see another light blue envelope in her box. She knew it had to be a letter from J.P. She took the letter out of her box, along with her usual junk mail, and tucked it in her backpack. She didn't have another class that afternoon, so she went down to a lake near campus to relax and read her letter from J.P. The weather was getting cooler, making it a sublime day to spend outside, no more sweltering heat and humidity. Before opening her backpack, she sat there a few minutes watching the swans swimming gracefully in the water and contemplating the new relationship she had with J.P. He was four hours away in Summerville, yet it felt like he was there with her in that serene place. She had to admit, the cards and letters made her feel important to him. She'd never gotten written communication from a guy before.

On Friday night Caroline went to the movies with one of her former roommates, Cathy. She got home around ten P.M., ready to shower and collapse. She took off her jeans and paraded around her room in her long white T-shirt, while searching for her navy gym shorts, when the telephone rang. Assuming it was Ida, the dorm mother, letting her know there was some disturbance on the fourth floor, she answered the phone with weariness in her voice.

A male voice asked, "You ain't been rode hard and put up wet, have you?"

Caroline said, "I can tell right off the bat it's you J.P." Drawling profusely, she said, "I declare, it's gooder'n grits to hear from you. You don't sound like no Yankee at all. 'Least you lernt how to tawk while you was livin' in Clemson."

He chuckled heartily, and spat out, "How in the heck are you, Caroline?"

"I'm good but just a little worn out. I'm really glad you called though."

"You're a hard one to get on the phone," he said. "That's why I wrote you a couple of times, but I'm not much of a writer."

"This is a good time to get me, except when I'm working in the dorm office. I only work one weekend a month."

"So you just worked last weekend, right?"

"Yeah! I won't have to work again until the second week in October."

"Drew told me that their family was hosting a big party the third weekend in October in Charleston. He said Emily would be coming here for that event. So, I was wondering if you'd want to come to Summerville that weekend. What do you think?"

"Sure, I'd love to do that, but I guess Emily will need to talk to her parents."

J.P. responded, "If it's not convenient for you to stay with Emily this time, I could put you up in a motel for two nights, unless you'd feel uncomfortable being alone at night." He explained, "There's something very special going on that weekend. A friend of mine bought some theatre tickets, but now he has to go out of town on business and can't use the tickets. He gave me two tickets to see *Porgy and Bess* at Dock Street Theatre in Charleston. I've never seen it, mostly 'cus I didn't know anyone to ask to go with me, who'd appreciate it. You seem like the kind of person who enjoys all kinds of artistic expression. Does that sound like something you'd enjoy doing after a good meal in a nice Charlestonian restaurant?"

"You're right, I'm a very creative person myself. I love to go to plays," said Caroline.

"You talk to Emily, and then let me know if you want me to reserve a motel room for that weekend. I'll call you back in a few days to finalize the plans."

They chatted on for a while, until Caroline was exhausted. She stretched out across her bed, and reached up to turn on the radio. She was absolutely elated about the invitation to come back to Summerville. She called Emily right away to tell her about J.P.s phone call.

Emily said, "I expected him to make another move soon. I already knew he was a good guy. J.P. is a hard worker, and he does a lot of nice things to help other people. He's active in the community and has made a lot of friends in a short period of time."

Caroline replied, "I can tell he's very thoughtful, and it was so easy to make friends with him."

"Looks like he may want to be more than just your friend."

"I might want to be more than friends, too, but maybe not. Let's go to lunch together tomorrow."

"If your family won't give you heck 'bout him bein' a Yankee, go full speed ahead," said Emily, trying to slip in some encouragement. "Now you find a good fella for me. See you tomorrow."

Caroline could feel the emotional brick wall inside of her being constructed brick by brick. She had created such defenses for so long, to keep from getting hurt, to avoid feeling loss when it was over; she didn't realize that she did this. But this time she was aware of what she was doing, and something wonderfully different didn't want her to do it. As Emily told her that J.P. might really be interested in her, she could feel herself slapping mortar on each brick of the wall. She tried to keep the next brick from being placed on top and wanted to tear down the part of the wall she'd already built, but she was feeling helpless to do anything about it. Why couldn't she just feel normal? Why couldn't she be like some of her friends who loved and were loved back? Why did she always want to hide herself behind her family, her schoolwork, her job, or her humor?

Caroline and Emily couldn't get down to Summerville until Saturday. It would be a rushed trip this time, but Caroline suspected it would be a good weekend. J.P. had made the arrangements for her accommodations since Emily's family members were in town. After Emily dropped her off at the motel, she felt exhausted from the long ride, so she turned on the television, lay down, and drifted off to sleep for about thirty minutes. She woke up when J.P. called.

"We're going to have a great night tonight, Miss Carter," said J.P. "Hope you got a little nap so you'll feel good when we go out. You know you've committed to a real date with me."

"Oh, is that what it is, a first date?"

"Well, that's what I planned it to be. Can I pick you up about 5 P.M.", he asked? "I made early dinner reservations at 82 Queen Street. We'll have a couple of hours for dinner and strolling in the city before the performance at Dock Street."

"I need to get busy so I'll be ready on time," she said. "Okay, I see you soon."

J.P. responded, enthusiastically, "We'll have a great time! See you."

He was mesmerized by the way Caroline looked, all dressed up, when he arrived to pick her up. She wore a mid-calf length black skirt. Black eyelet trim around the bottom of the skirt allowed a hint of her lightly tanned legs to show through the skirt. A white sweater, with a low cut v-shaped neckline, exposed her shoulders. The three quarter length sleeves of the sweater accentuated the delicate silver bangles she wore on her wrist. Earrings were also silver to match a serpentine chain around her neck. Her heeled black espadrilles had grosgrain ribbons that she'd wrapped around her ankles, very feminine looking.

J.P. had borrowed Butch's Volvo sedan, which was more comfortable than his Toyota. As they drove to Charleston, he told Caroline more about his family in Jersey. He explained that all his grandparents were of European or Scandinavian descent, that they'd immigrated to the United States, married, and started their families in the North. A cultural organization, for Danish immigrants, bonded the families together, so J.P.'s parents had known each other since they were children. Living so close to New York had afforded J.P.'s family opportunities for fine dining and entertainment.

J.P. said, "My brother and I grew up getting exposed to the Arts. I guess that's why I wanted to share tonight with you."

"I'm so glad you're taking me out tonight", Caroline said; "I can't imagine wanting to be anywhere else right now."

With that comment, J.P. felt it was the right time to take Caroline's hand in his as they drove down the monotonous stretch of highway from Summerville to Charleston.

They talked so much as they drove, they were in the city before they knew it. Once in Charleston, while navigating through the city, he explained that the restaurant was in the French Quarters and told her some of the history behind the building that had been converted into the restaurant.

As they entered 82 Queen, it was almost as if they were stepping back to another era, seeing the original brick exposed where a façade of concrete had been eroding for ages. Inside, she could hardly believe her eyes; the soft glow from an abundance of miniature glittering lights, illuminating green plants everywhere, created the most romantic ambiance. She was even more taken aback that J.P.

had requested that they be seated at the table in the gazebo in the corner of the courtyard. The round table was beautifully decorated with a crisp white table cloth, napkins decoratively folded, and delicate candle holders shimmering with light surrounding a glass bowl of floating flowers and lotus luminaries. It was so dreamlike to be there with him in such an enchanting place, and she didn't want to wake up from that phenomenal dream.

He had eaten at 82 Queen Street before, with his parents, when he first moved to Summerville, so he knew it would be a great place to bring Caroline on their first "real" date. He wouldn't always be able to bring her to nice restaurants like this, but this night had to be special. She had some kind of hold on him making him more and more curious about her as time went on.

They started the meal with fried calamari for an appetizer. Caroline decided to have a Lowcountry shrimp dish and J.P. enjoyed a delicious seafood stew. They limited themselves to one glass of wine each to accompany the meal.

He asked her, "Did you know that Dock Street Theater was the first theatre in America?" She shook her head, indicating that she was unaware of its history. "It was built around the mid 1730's," said J.P. "Ford's Theater, where President Lincoln was assassinated in Washington, D.C., was modeled after Dock Street Theatre."

Caroline was not intimidated by J.P.'s historical knowledge; rather she found herself becoming more interested in the history of this beautiful, but mysterious, city.

When the waiter arrived with their entrees, J.P. asked, "Am I boring you with this conversation?"

"Not at all; I'm intrigued." Caroline replied. "I love the way you share the history of the city with so much enthusiasm. You've really learned a lot about this place and probably know much more than most locals do. I've learned from you already."

Caroline looked at J.P. and admired his maturity and strong character. She'd told herself for so long that she needed to be independent, but she found herself wondering what it would be like to have a man to depend on; someone to help share both the good and the bad. What was she thinking? Her momma had always told her to be prepared to fend for herself. She had to snap back to reality.

She wanted to lean over and hug him, but instead, she put her hand on top of his and thanked him for showing so much care and concern for her.

He smiled and placed his other hand on top of hers and said, "Good relationships always start with good friendships. I'm glad I met you."

J.P. had made arrangements to leave the car in the restaurant parking area so he and Caroline could have a leisurely stroll to the theatre. As they walked down Queen Street toward Church Street, they could hear a jazz band playing in the distance. A few other couples were enjoying the walk. He took Caroline's hand as they strolled down the sidewalk. It was a delightfully cool October evening, just right for a walk. The light from the full 'Hunter's' moon illuminated the buildings and the street, and they could see moths gathering near the dimly lit street lights.

Caroline had worn her long hair down, and J.P. thought how naturally beautiful she was as her hair blew in the coastal wind. It felt so good to be with her, and he'd never really felt that way before.

Inside the theatre, she checked out every visual detail. Dock Street Theatre was very small by modern standards. Their excellent seats afforded them the opportunity to see the facial expressions of the characters as they sang the beautiful songs in the Gershwin musical.

J.P. kept looking at her during some of the most moving songs just to see how she was reacting. At that moment, Caroline felt just a little shy to look back, so she kept looking toward the performers, but she could tell he was looking at her. She felt J.P. put his arm on the back of her seat, so she leaned toward him to indicate that it was okay. When one of the most moving songs was being sung, she got the courage to look over at him, and he at her. He raised her hand to his lips and kissed it. He didn't care if anyone was watching them, and neither did she.

She opted to stay out a little later with J.P despite the fact that she'd have to get up fairly early the next morning. Emily worked part-time in a restaurant in Rock Hill and was scheduled to work on Sunday afternoon, so they'd need to leave Summerville early. She didn't care if she'd be exhausted or not because she wasn't driving back, and after she'd answer about a hundred of Emily's inquisitorial questions, she'd take a nap.

"Why don't we go back down to the Battery and see if any ships are in the harbor," asked Caroline? "I love to feel the cool breeze at night and see the water glistenin' beneath the light of the moon and stars."

"That's a great idea. It would be a bit of a hike to walk there in your dress shoes. We can go back and pick up the car and drive down to the Battery and stay as long as you want."

Charleston had always charmed J.P. Everything about it radiated sophistication. One was willing to put up with the grueling heat and humidity to have the opportunity to enjoy the magic of The Holy City. As he stepped out of the car and held out his hand to assist Caroline in a gentlemanly manner, he could visualize himself in another era with this lovely belle, although it would not have been acceptable at this late hour, by the Battery listening to the water splashing against the concrete seawall. The salty sea breeze was blowing through strands of hair surrounding her face. She smiled at him so sweetly. He could hardly believe he was here with such a beautiful, sweet girl. New York was spectacular, but it was nothing like Charleston, and he doubted that there was any other city as romantic as this one. There, next to the Battery, the gentle wind, the sounds of the lapping water, and the dim lighting served as the perfect backdrop for the start of their liaison.

They made small talk about the theatre, the delectable meal and ambiance they'd enjoyed at 82 Queen, and the ships in the harbor visible by the light of the moon. Eventually, they walked across the street to sit on a park bench, in White Points Garden, the same park bench they'd occupied they day he'd brought her there for the first time. He put his arm around her, and she seemed to melt into his embrace. They sat there looking across the harbor for some time.

Then she turned to him and said, "You're such a wonderful person."

He responded, "So are you," and with that they kissed for the first time.

What a beautiful night Caroline had to describe to Emily the next day on the trip back to school, so her umpteen questions would be simple to answer. Maybe, just maybe, she could give him a chance if she stopped looking at him in the same way she did guys in her past. At this point he was dreamy. Would that prove to be so down the road? Oh stop it, Caroline! You're bein' you own worst enemy.

CHAPTER 3

WONDERIN'

After spending time in the Lowcountry, Caroline found it difficult to return to campus life. Thank goodness she and Emily were friends, and she had someone to talk to who knew how the Lowcountry could beckon her. Emily was the kind of friend who could understand how J.P. might be sweeping her off her feet.

During a leisurely lunch, she asked Emily, "Can you believe I had an actual date with J.P.?"

Emily responded, "Of course I can. He seemed to like you from the 'get go'! I thought y'all would click. Caroline, he's a lot like you in that he's very intelligent, but he's also different in terms of being more of a risk taker than you are. After all, it's more risky for him to watch you return to school where you're around guys all the time. Heck, you even live with guys, being a resident assistant in the dorm."

"Oh, come on, Emily. You and I both know that those jocks living above me are not my type. There's no one at school who even comes close to J.P. I don't know if it's possible for two people to fall in love so quickly; maybe that's just infatuation. Last night, as we sat on the park bench by the Battery, motionless, looking across the harbor, I felt a strong bond between us, but I'm not sure what that feeling really was. I never believed people when they claimed to fall in love at first sight."

Emily listened carefully to Caroline, and then she said, "Love is what you believe it to be, and what you make it become. At least that's what I've read someplace, because love hasn't happened for me yet."

Meanwhile, in Summerville, J.P. was as awestruck as Caroline had been as she talked to Emily. He, of course, had kept his thoughts and feelings to himself, because he didn't want Butch and Chris giving him a hard time about a potentially serious relationship. With Caroline back at Winthrop, J.P. wanted time to himself, so he got in his car and started driving down the highway toward Charleston. He rolled the windows down to feel the cool wind all around him. He'd always thought of himself as being too young to get serious with a girl especially since another relationship hadn't panned out in the past; yet he wasn't quite sure about his feelings toward Caroline. She wasn't the drop dead gorgeous kind of girl, but Caroline typified beauty, intelligence, kindness, and sensitivity. Was he fooling himself that a girl like her would want a long distance relationship? Could she be having positive thoughts about him at this moment, he wondered? Maybe he just gave her something interesting to do to break the monotony of campus life. Why was he thinking so much about her when he really didn't know her?

He continued to drive toward Charleston, crossed over the Cooper River Bridge, and then on to Sullivan's Island. Before he got to the beach, he stopped at a convenience store and bought a beer. He got down to Sullivan's Island and sat in the Toyota with the windows down and slowly drank his beer. Then he got out of his car and walked down a sandy path to the beach. The moonlight illuminated the beach dotted with Palmetto trees, and he could see the sea oats swaying in the wind. He took off his shoes and went to stand in the water's edge. The water was chilly, but the breeze was still relatively warm. The roaring sound of the ocean waves made him feel calm, and the canopy of twinkling stars above made him feel hopeful for love, family, and a good life in his future. Could it be with her? Should he continue to stay aloof with women and keep his options open?

Standing there at the edge of the vast ocean, he began to question his readiness for love. The water from the incoming tide covered his feet. He sensed the water pulling the sand away from under his feet, over and over again, until he felt like he was losing his balance. He regained his equilibrium and looked up toward to moon, almost spellbound, and realized that it was time to grow and mature. It was time to let go of his reservations, time to step up to the plate, and start being the man he'd been intending to become.

Back in Rock Hill, Caroline had to really buckle down to finish necessary coursework before the end of the semester. She would be doing her student teaching next semester, her final semester of school. She knew the student teaching would be demanding, and she wondered how she would find time to spend with J.P. should their relationship continue to grow.

J. P. found the next week at work requiring more of his time. The company he worked for was doing some restoration work in Savannah, so he was on the road longer during the week. He felt the urge to call Caroline every night but was afraid he might make her feel pressured, so he didn't call at all. He had lunch with his buddies on Wednesday at a restaurant near the waterfront in Savannah. He went his own way after lunch to find a card shop to look for a card to send Caroline. Most of the cards just didn't say what he thought she needed to hear from him, so he opted to get a blank card with a beautiful coastal scene on the front. As he wrote to her, he was at a loss of words to convey to her how he really felt about their first date, but he wanted her to know that it meant a lot to him.

Saturday evening, Caroline's phone rang around eight P.M. She was so excited to hear from J. P., and they managed to have a conversation for about an hour. Caroline tried to be careful about the time spent on the phone, on a long distance call, because she really didn't know what J.P.'s budget was.

Toward the end of their conversation, he asked her, "Are you planning to spend Thanksgiving with your family?"

"Yes, we always go to my granny's house, in the country, on Thanksgiving Day."

J.P. said, "When Chris and I both went to Clemson, we couldn't go to New Jersey to spend Thanksgiving with our parents. There just wasn't enough time to make such a long trip and have ample time to visit. Sometimes we spent the holiday with Butch and his family in a 'podunk' town called Holly Hill down in the lower part of the state, or we'd go to Summerville to visit with my friend Roy's family. The food was always different from a Northerner's meal, but it was great."

Caroline asked, "Do you usually see your parents at Christmastime?"

"Yes, we still drive up to Jersey and spend Christmas with our folks."

"You know," she said, "I'm sure my momma would like to meet you. I've written her letters about how we met, not every detail, but I told her how great you made our first date. If you're willing to go with me, I'll ask Momma if you can celebrate Thanksgiving with us."

J.P. replied, "That sounds good to me. I bet a lot of good country cooks will be preparing the Thanksgiving meal."

"Oh, J.P., you can't imagine how much food they make on Thanksgiving. There's definitely plenty to go around. Let me talk with Momma this week, and I'll let you know about the details. My brother, Troy, lives in my aunt's old house, and I'm sure you could stay with him a couple of nights. We could do the family stuff on Thursday, but Friday we could go to the mountains. There are lots of places with beautiful panoramic views that I'd really like to take you to."

The next three weeks were filled with anticipation that the two of them would be together again. On Sunday, Caroline was going to study in the library all afternoon. As she walked across the campus, in the cool autumn air with the sun shining, she felt refreshed, but she wasn't looking forward to being cooped up in a library all afternoon. If she didn't have to do some research, she'd study outside, but she needed to find some information in the archive rooms.

On her way to the library, she decided to stop by the student center to get something to drink. She was standing in front of the drink machine, digging for change in her backpack. She realized that she didn't have correct change for the drink machine and was about to gather up her things and go to the library, when suddenly, she heard a guy with a deep voice say, "I have plenty of change. Would you let me buy you a drink?" She looked up and saw a tall, thin guy with an unusual, but nice, haircut.

He said, "I'm Joost Van Ness." Caroline noticed his accent with that introduction.

She said, "I'm Caroline Carter. It's nice to meet you. Are you a new student here?" She knew she'd never seen this guy on campus before. If she'd seen him, he would definitely have stood out in her mind. He wasn't the athletic type; he didn't look like the typical Winthrop jock. He was over six feet tall with shaggy blond hair, like a lion's mane, and deep blue eyes.

He said, "Yes, I'm fairly new here. I started in the fall. I'm an international student from Holland. So, are you going to let me buy you a drink?"

Caroline said, "I guess so, if you don't mind. I'm going to the library to study, and I'll probably get thirsty if I don't drink something before I go."

Then Joost said, "Good, I'm going to the library, too. What kind of drink would you like?"

"Oh, I'm a cola kind of person," she answered.

"Me, too," he answered.

It was obvious to Caroline that Joost had been speaking English for a long time. Although he had an unmistakable accent, he seemed to have an excellent command of English. Caroline was about to pop the tab on her soda can when Emily walked around the corner of the mailboxes and saw her standing there with this nice looking European guy. All of a sudden, Caroline remembered J.P. and the nice things he had done for her the previous weekend. In a most convivial way, she thanked Joost for the drink, told him her friend Emily was waiting for her, and said she hoped to be seeing him around campus.

She briskly walked over to Emily and asked, "What ya up to today?"

"Not much," Emily responded, "until five, when I have to work. Who's that nice looking guy you were talking to? I haven't seen him around here before."

"His name is Joost Van Ness. He's an international student from Holland. I didn't have correct change for a drink, so he offered to buy me a drink. He seems like a nice guy; maybe I'll introduce him to you and you could get to know him better."

"Right, Caroline," Emily commented. "That's just what I need, a foreign student who I know nothing about. It doesn't matter how good looking he is, it's risky because no one here knows his history. Ya know what Momma says about a person's history; ya gotta know where someone comes from. Actually, Momma says that pedigrees matter."

"My momma would probably say that, too, but she wouldn't call it a pedigree like your momma," said Caroline, laughing.

Caroline left the student center and went to the library. She studied for about two hours, but then she needed a break. She went over to the magazine section of the library and picked up a couple of magazines to peruse. That was kind of a reward she gave herself.

She was leafing through a home and garden magazine when she looked up and saw Joost Van Ness smiling at her. She smiled back, slumped in her chair, and buried her head behind her magazine. She felt a little like a cheat, enjoying the attention of another good looking guy, even though she rationalized that she had just met J.P., and had not entered into a committed relationship with him. *How could she have gone so long, doing her thing, and suddenly starting attracting men? Joost was more her age, right here to be friends with, and J.P. was so far away.* She had to stop thinking about such nonsense and focus her attention to schoolwork – besides, she was supposed to be asking her momma soon about J.P. coming for Thanksgiving. She sure couldn't do that while thinking about some Dutchman with a dazzling smile. You never know what lurks behind a smile like that, she thought.

Caroline wanted to call her momma right away, before she had any more chances to run into Joost. She figured he didn't have a lot of friends, being fairly new at Winthrop, and she was afraid he might sort of 'latch onto' her, since she was the kind, friendly, and compassionate type of person. If she'd already made plans with J.P., she'd be better able to resist Joost if he tried to get friendlier. He was a very fine looking guy, like the kind of guy you might see in an advertisement, a model. Caroline had never met an international student before who wasn't from a well-to-do family abroad, so he was probably 'loaded' too.

Early in the week, she called her momma to ask if J.P. could visit them over the holiday. On Wednesday, she'd received another letter from him. In the upper left hand corner of the envelope he'd drawn two eyes, with one winking. He wrote J.P. next to the eyes, and his address below. That little gesture brought a smile to Caroline's face. She sat down on one of the comfy sofas in the student center, propped her feet up on the coffee table, and read her letter. The words he'd written made her feel that he was mature enough to desire a committed relationship as he'd expressed that it made him feel good that she wanted him to meet her family and to spend a holiday with him.

Caroline held the letter close to her heart for a few seconds and tucked it back into the envelope; she looked at the winking eye next to J.P.'s initials, and felt happier than she had for a long while. When she got back to her dorm room, she read the letter again and again. Could it be true that absence does make the heart grow fonder?

The next morning, Caroline went to the school cafeteria early to have breakfast. She had a pen and notepad with her. She put a muffin with strawberry jam and a glass of milk on her tray and proceeded to a table. She took bites of her muffin and pondered how best to respond to J.P.'s letter. As her mind trailed off into thought, it was interrupted by a conversation behind her in Spanish. Her Spanish professors had spoken Castilian Spanish, and she noticed that one of the people behind her was speaking with a Castilian accent. She turned, just slightly, and could see that it was Joost. She turned her head back around before he could see her, she thought.

Caroline had just about finished with her breakfast when Joost walked around to the opposite side of the long, rectangular cafeteria table and stopped right in front of her.

He sat down and said, "How are you, Caroline Carter?"

"I'm fine, if that's possible at 6:30 A.M. I've never been in here this early before."

Joost continued the conversation, "During the week, I usually come in here early in the morning. It takes quite a few cups of coffee to wake me up in the morning. I like to take my time eating breakfast, reading the newspaper, or talking to friends." Looking down at her milk glass he said, "It looks like you're not much of a coffee drinker."

"Well, sometimes I have coffee," she said. "By the way, did I overhear you speaking Spanish? I thought you were from Holland. I'm a bit confused."

He said, "I was born in Holland, but I grew up in Spain. Both of my parents were Dutch. My father was a top executive for company in Spain. We moved there when I was four years old."

Not thinking about the verb tense Joost had just used, Caroline questioned, "Do your parents still live in Spain?"

Joost looked very somber, suddenly, and said, "Both of my parents died."

"I'm sorry, I didn't mean to pry," she said in a soft spoken voice. She knew that she, unintentionally, had made him answer something very painful, so she paused from the conversation and drank her milk, to give Joost time to settle himself after having to say that his parents were both deceased. Of all people, she could understand the devastating effect that the loss of a parent has on a child, teenager, or young adult.

There was no doubt that Joost was a very good looking guy with a wonderful speaking voice like that of a ring master in a circus. With his father having been a top executive with a thriving company, he was probably just another spoiled rich kid whose older siblings all wore expensive watches and sailed on the Mediterranean aboard yachts. It must have been obvious to him, in her tattered jeans and cheap little T-shirt that she wasn't from a similar economic background.

After having a few minutes to calm himself, Joost stood up and said, "I was wondering if you might be able to proofread one of my papers for an economics class. I've heard, from a mutual friend, that you're good at that type of thing. I'm prepared to pay you well, but you don't have to commit yourself now."

A mutual friend, Caroline questioned; who could that be? Maybe that was all he wanted, and why he had approached her in the student center as the knight in shining armor bearing gifts of coins for the drink machine. He needed a proofreader. Maybe there was no mutual friend at all, but it sounded good. Possibly, the fact that he needed help made him go out of his way to have a conversation with her.

Joost excused himself and got up from the table. He carried his tray over to the conveyor belt that led directly into the dish washing area of the cafeteria. Then he came back to her table to pick up his text book. He said to Caroline, "I'll probably see you in the library this week."

She politely responded, "I hope I'll see you again, and thanks for taking the time to chat with me this morning."

She called her momma again on Friday afternoon to see if it would be okay for J.P. to join them for Thanksgiving. Mrs. Carter said, "That's fine. He can stay with Troy. I reckon you better warn him about the ways of country folk."

"Oh, Momma, J.P. went to Clemson. He knows how people talk there. You'll be surprised at how country he can talk sometimes; he's practiced so much you don't even know he's a Yank."

During the course of the following week, J.P. and Caroline finalized the plans for Thanksgiving. Although Caroline had a few distractions, with Joost, she was looking forward to spending time with J.P. She'd been thinking a great deal about the perfect mountain spots where she and J. P. could go the day after Thanksgiving. She knew she wanted to take him to see an outdoor chapel on the side of a mountain which had the most breathtaking view.

Joost had approached her in the library one day that week, asking if she had considered helping him out with his term paper. After all, he was very nice and polite, and he needed to make new friends. She decided to help him by proofreading his paper, in the library of course, and making suggestions as to how he might word his paper differently. She told him before she started that she wouldn't accept payment for helping him; that she was willing to do it as a friend, and she could help him in the future if he needed her to. Being quite surprised about the fine job he'd done on his own, considering that English was not his native language, Caroline had very little to do by way of error corrections to his work.

She had no idea that Joost was sizing her up and tried very hard not to do the same with him, worrying that she might somehow betray J.P.; so she concentrated on the task at hand in helping Joost with his writing. With his looks and good manners, she found it a difficult to stay on task. J.P. was also good looking, in a different way, but he was in Summerville and Joost was sitting there gazing at her and smiling. She thought again, why now? Why are two guys taking interest in me? And not only that, but two nice guys seemed to be taken with her, or maybe she just thought so; nevertheless, J.P still had the upper hand. He'd already shown his affection for her in the way he treated her in Charleston, in his calls, and in his correspondence. All of these thoughts were just weighing her down until she finally said to Joost, "I'm hungry, so I'm going to eat. See you later, friend."

With Thanksgiving approaching soon, Caroline wanted to go shopping to find something cute to wear when she and J.P. would have their day together. She'd have to work one weekend before the holiday, but she still found time to go to the mall with Emily. As they traveled to Charlotte together, Caroline kept her business, about helping Joost, a private matter. She and Emily were friends, and Emily and J.P. were friends, so Caroline didn't want to get any drama started between the three of them.

Caroline rode home to Greenville with Jean Scott, one of her friends from school, on Wednesday morning. J.P. called her at her momma's house when he got into town. Her brother, Troy, took her down to meet J.P. at the pancake restaurant near the interstate.

Troy asked Caroline, "You really like this guy? Momma said he went to Clemson. What's he like?"

"Troy", she said, "You'd never know he's from New Jersey because he sounds like he's from here, most of the time. He's really a nice guy. You're going to like him."

As they drove into the restaurant parking lot, Caroline saw J.P. leaning against the side of his Toyota waving at them, with a big, friendly smile on his face. Troy and Caroline got out of the car to greet J.P. He and Troy shook hands as Caroline introduced them.

Caroline said to Troy, "We're going to Momma's house now. I think she said you're comin' to her house to eat at seven, right?"

Troy answered, "Yes, I'll be there. I told Momma I'd take us all out to dinner, but she insisted on makin' fried pork chops with rice and gravy. I can't pass that up. See y'all later."

As soon as Caroline and J.P. got to her momma's house, Mrs. Carter came out to the car. She gave J.P. a welcoming hug and said, "I'm so glad y'all are here. I hope you brought a good appetite, J.P. Troy and Rhonda, my older daughter, will be here at seven."

He quickly responded, "Oh yes, ma'am, I brought a very good appetite with me. I think good Southern cooks are some of the best cooks in the country.

Yep, J.P. had just made a hit with Mrs. Carter, thought Caroline. Her momma took great pride in her cooking. Even though she hadn't fed J.P. yet, it sounded like he had a positive attitude toward good country cuisine and wouldn't be finicky.

Caroline and J.P. followed Mrs. Carter into her house. The honey colored, paneled walls of her den were covered with pictures of her husband, her three children, nieces, nephews, parents, and siblings. A small television set rested on a metal stand in a corner of the room. The couch was covered in tan and brown fake velvet with orange flowers decorating it. A well-worn recliner was on the other side of the room in front of a 1950's television cabinet with a record player on top of it. To the right of that dated cabinet was an old bookshelf with numerous record albums stacked on the shelves.

After telling J.P. to make himself at home, Mrs. Carter excused herself to return to the kitchen to continue breading the pork chops. He went around the room looking at all the old photographs of Caroline, teasing her, until she blushed, about how cute she was when she was a little rotund girl. Then they sat on the couch. The coffee table in front of them was covered with stacks of newspapers and magazines. On the underneath shelf of the coffee table, J.P. spotted several photo albums. He teased Caroline, as he reached for one of the albums, saying, "Let's see more photos of little cutie pie."

Caroline said, "You just wait 'til I see all of the pictures your momma has of you in her house." She suddenly realized she had just assumed that J.P. would be inviting her to New Jersey. Feeling a bit embarrassed, she quickly changed the conversation to photographs of her daddy. She said, "You know, J.P., I don't remember much about my daddy. I don't know what I'd remember without these pictures." She had tears streaming down her cheeks, and J.P. searched the room helplessly for a box of tissues. He finally located the tissue box on the bookshelf holding the record albums.

"Thanks, J.P. I never seem to be able to stop these tears, no matter how many times I cry. I guess that's just something I'll always have to live with." She became silent as she thought of Joost telling her about the death of both of his parents. She forced herself to think of the compassion J.P. had shown her on those occasions when she spoke of her daddy. *Why was she having thoughts about two men at one time?* That was something so out of character for her. Was she feeling a need to connect with J.P. on some level, wanting him to understand something that he had never experienced? He had not lost a parent, but Joost had and could understand the depth of sorrow that was all too familiar to her. Then she felt the warmth of J.P.'s hand on her shoulder and she changed the subject again.

Just before seven, Caroline's sister Rhonda arrived at Mrs. Carter's. Rhonda was the boisterous type; a pushy female who knew no strangers. Caroline was friendly, but in no way was loud and aggressive like Rhonda. They seemed like such opposites. Rhonda, a cosmetologist, was always trying to give Caroline a makeover. Caroline didn't like the feel of make-up, so she was always turning Rhonda down when she offered to give her a new look. Caroline hugged her sister, and introduced J.P.

Rhonda asked rather abruptly, "I hear you're from New York, or is it New Jersey?"

J.P. said, "I'm from New Jersey, but it's very close to Manhattan. Have you ever been to New York?"

Rhonda said, "Lord no, I'd be scared to death to go to New York unless I was with someone who lived there and knew how to navigate in that huge city. We're small time city girls here."

"Oh, you mean a small time city of less than a half a million people," asked J.P.?

Rhonda said, "Yes, our city isn't the largest city in the South, but we're not the smallest city either."

Troy arrived shortly after Rhonda, and dinner was served. While listening to the Carters discuss various topics over dinner, J.P. suspected that a great deal of learning had always taken place in this home. He was aware that Caroline seemed to display a more distinct local dialect here, with her family, than she did at other times, and he thought she was cute and she chattered to her family members.

When the meal was finished, J.P. and the Carters lingered at the table for a while to talk. Caroline was impressed with J.P. as he withstood Rhonda's direct questioning. Mrs. Carter was very gracious when conversing with J.P. Troy stayed on equal ground in the conversations. Based on first impressions, Troy liked J.P. He had been the only male in his immediate family since he was ten years old and appreciated having another guy around. He planned to make J.P. feel very comfortable while staying at his home for a few nights.

Before the evening was over, Caroline suggested that she and J.P. go for a walk together. This gave Caroline a chance to share things she did growing up, without her older siblings telling the stories different ways. She put on her fleece lined hooded jacket. They walked about a quarter of a mile and then walked down a dead end street.

Caroline told him, "This is the street where the neighborhood kids came to make out, when I was a teenager."

"So you've been here before," asked J.P. with a ridiculous grin on his face?

"Well, I led us here, didn't I?" questioned Caroline. She smiled and took him by the arm. The street was illuminated by moonlight, but there were no street lights.

The two found a log bench at the end of the desolate street. They sat down holding hands and simultaneously looked up at the stars. Caroline snuggled up close to J.P. like she was cold. At that point nothing needed to be said, and they took full advantage of the opportunity to be alone. J.P. put him arm around her, kissed her cheek, and told her how much he had missed her. Caroline kissed him back, leading them to engage in a long, tender, yet passionate, kiss. For Caroline, at that moment, there was no thought of anyone except J.P., and she felt the same contentment she had felt after their very first kiss.

J.P. picked Caroline up early on Thanksgiving Day. She was wearing her new jeans and top she bought on her shopping trip to Charlotte. Her blouse was made of crushed gauze, light green in color, decorated with embroidered designs. She wore a turquoise gauze scarf around her neck like an ascot. Its color matched the embroidered designs on her blouse perfectly. Her hair was neatly braided in a single plait to the side, rather than down the middle of her back. Because her hair was pulled back, it was easy to see her silver and turquoise earrings.

Caroline wanted to take J.P. to her granny's house via scenic back roads. As they drove down the narrow, winding roads, they saw beautiful white houses with weathered barns, surrounded by fields. Long dirt driveways, flanked by rows of Bradford Pear or Live Oak trees gave picturesque vistas. Many fields, enclosed with barbed wire fences, contained horses grazing contentedly, with their stables in the background. Other farms were encircled by paddocks filled with cattle who watched them drive by as they cropped the long grass. Some of the far meadows seemed to be blanketed with patches of early morning fog that hid their features from view as they passed by on the roads.

J.P. said to Caroline, "Thanks for guiding me down these country roads with such fantastic views." He looked to his right and saw a sign that read 'Pumpkintown 10 miles'.

Caroline said "The folks around here call that place 'Pun...kin Town'. In the fall the town sponsors a pumpkin festival with crafts, blue grass music, food, demonstrations, and activities for kids. I love to be here in the fall to see the leaves change on the trees.

J.P. said, "I suppose you found autumn in Summerville to be quite different from that of the foothills of the Blue Ridge Mountains."

"Yes, I did," she said, "but the Lowcountry has a beauty all of its own. I so enjoyed the oyster roast and the coastal breezes as we walked in Charleston in October. The beach, the sea birds, and looking out across the ocean are breathtaking sights, too."

"Well, your next venture should be to see New York City at Christmastime," hinted J.P.

Caroline felt excited that J.P. wanted to take her to see his territory. She said, "Oh, I'm sure there are things I'll see there that are unlike anything I've ever imagined before."

He said, "I want to share that with you as much as you wanted to share this beautiful part of the country, and your heritage, with me."

Caroline noticed a small sign to an original covered bridge. She suggested to J.P. that they stop and spend a little time there. She knew her momma and Rhonda would arrive about eleven o'clock to help out with the meal. Troy would drive himself and would probably get there just in time to eat.

As they drove up to the old covered bridge, Caroline asked, "What do you eat up north at Thanksgiving?'

He responded, "We eat turkey with stuffing, mashed potatoes and gravy, creamed onions, Brussels sprouts or asparagus. We have rolls, purchased from the local bakery on Wednesday afternoon.

We have yams covered in sweet, thick brown sugar syrup, and jellied and whole cranberry sauces. For dessert we have pumpkin and mincemeat pies, topped with fresh whipped cream."

Then she asked, with a titter, "Good Land, what is a mincemeat pie?" All she could think of was shepherd's pie as she asked that question. Then she added, trying not to embarrass herself, "We have a big spread at Granny's, but you'll just have to wait and see it. I can tell you right now, you ain't gonna see no turkey and stuffin', cause we eat turkey and dressin'."

J.P. started to laugh, and said, "Okay, that's enough cus I'm gettin' hong...ry."

Caroline and J.P. timed their arrival at Granny's house just perfectly. Mrs. Carter and Rhonda had gotten there first, and Rhonda had warned everybody about Caroline's Yankee. Did the War Between the States ever end? They drove up on the grass near the house next to Uncle Bobby's old truck with the Confederate flag bumper sticker.

The old white house looked like it had many additions over the years, and the original structure was marked by an enormous rock chimney. The wide, screened front porch of the house sat very close to the road as if the road had been cut many years after the house was built. Several of Caroline's great aunts were sitting out on the porch talking with one another. She warned J. P. that people living in that country community had the habit of waving at everyone who passed by the house whether they knew them or not.

"You'll have to watch out for my great aunt Eula Belle. She's as crazy as a loon, and she may get you flustered. She thinks all young men are her late husband, Arthur, when he was in his twenties, and in his testosterone prime. Don't let her corner you somewhere."

Lots of younger cousins were running around the yard, chasing the weary dogs, and already dirty as little pigs. The men were sitting in shabby straight backed chairs outside under the enormous enveloping oak with their feet propped up on the knobby roots of the tree. Some of them were smoking cigarettes, chewing tobacco, or dipping snuff, and most of them were already drinking bourbon, including Caroline's Grandpaw Pritchet.

Caroline introduced J.P. and then said, "I'm sure Granny is waitin' to meet J.P.," trying to get J.P. out of there as soon as she could before an embattlement began, precipitated by the men making crude redneck comments about Yankees.

Granny Pritchet was as sweet as she could be, and made J.P. feel very welcome. She said, "Howdy, J.P. A little bird told me Caroline was brangin' a handsome feller. I'm sure glad you come. You make yersef right at home, you hear?

Caroline whispered to J.P., "You can go back out with the men, or you can wait for Troy to get here." Troy was Southern to the core, but not a redneck at heart, and he didn't' treat J.P. any differently from his local friends.

"Can I help with something?"

Caroline explained, "I'd love for you to help, but remember that they think this is women's work. They're so used to the men gettin' half-drunk from bourbon, they don't expect for a man to do much in the kitchen." She knew he was stalling, not really wanting to go back out to the old oak tree.

Caroline's aunt Josephine was still making her special potato salad, made with potato chunks, green peas, chopped onion, mashed potatoes, salt and pepper, and a whole jar of mayonnaise.

Momma Carter was helping her sister, Betty Sue, make more sweet tea. From the looks of the amount of sugar they dumped in the pitcher, it was sweet, sweet tea. They had already made five gallons, stored in plastic milk jugs.

Aunt Betty Sue looked up at Caroline and J.P., and for lack of confidence to introduce herself to an outsider, said, "You can nevah make 'nough sweet tea when yer havin' this many people git together."

Caroline tasted some of the tea and said, "Glory be, y'all musta put four cups of Dixieland Sugar in that gallon. It's so sweet, it makes my teeth sting." Then she kissed her aunt Betty Sue on the cheek and said, "Luv you!"

She introduced relatives to J.P. and mingled for a few more minutes so as not to seem uppity. Then she gave a big hug and holler, "Hey, Flora Mae, how you doin'?" She turned to J.P. and whispered to him that Flora Mae wasn't all there, mentally.

"Good, good, I reckon, and you?"

Caroline answered in rhyme, "Fine as muscadine wine."

Flora Mae giggled in response.

Rhonda was being her usual blabber mouth self, while struggling to get the cranberry sauce out of the cans, having no idea that opening both ends of the cans would help.

Caroline and J.P. washed their hands at the old, porcelain kitchen sink since the only bathroom was occupied. And despite what might be thought about J.P. helping, he and Caroline began putting ice in mismatched jelly jars used as glasses, about forty of them that Granny Pritchett had been collecting for many years.

When Troy got there, the kids came in hollering, "We're hong... ry." The men followed tossing their cigarette butts on the ground outside the back door and spitting tobacco juice, reeking of smoke and bourbon. The screen door slammed as the last man stumbled past the slop bucket for the pigs, located on the old back porch. The room was now extremely crowded and smelled like a tavern, and the kids were fussing in the bathroom, next to the kitchen, trying to get washed up like their mommas told them too. The youngest crying because her cousin had stepped on her tiny foot.

"Baby, cupcake, wassa mattah," her momma drawled? She picked her up, and the little girl screamed, dramatically.

When the kids got next to their mommas, it got very quiet, and the men took off their hunting caps. Granny gave Grandpaw a nod, and he asked Caroline's Uncle Doyle Earle to say the blessing. He was one of the few men who had not been drinking bourbon. He'd been a deacon in his church most of his adult life and was the obvious choice to say the blessing each year. J.P. thought the bless-ing would never end and silently counted Doyle Earle saying, "Dear Lord, we just wanna thank ya" about twenty three times before the prayer was finally over. He prayed so long his own two little boys were whining to their momma about being so hon...gry. Standing so close to Caroline, J.P. felt her shifting her weight from one foot to the other, like she had ants in her pants, or maybe she had to pee. He got tickled in the middle of the prayer. Caroline looked at him and saw his shoulders jiggling.

When the prayer of all prayers was finished and the entire clan said amen in unison, Caroline and J.P. wandered to the back of the serpentine serving line. Uncle Doyle Earle's wife was in front of Caroline. She said to her boys, "I'm uh gonna tan your butts when we git to the house; y'all know you'uns don't tawk when your diddy is prayin' to Jesus."

By the time they got up to the food table, some of the others were already seated and eating. Caroline said, "This is Aunt Betty Sue's sweet potato casserole. It's to die for, loaded with butter, brown sugar, and chopped pecans, and covered with tiny marsh-mallows before she bakes it. I know y'all eat yams, and they don't look like this casserole at all, do they?"

J.P. shrugged his shoulders, smiled, and said, "Sounds like it could be a dessert to me."

There was a whole table of casseroles. There was green bean casserole with French fried onions and cheddar cheese, broccoli casserole, and vegetable casserole. There were three types of potato salad, and two large pans of sage spiced cornbread dress-ing. Bowls of squash, butter beans seasoned with bacon grease, macaroni and cheese, and mixed vegetables covered one small table. About eighty deviled eggs were arranged on a couple of platters, sitting next to a pot of boiled corn. There were bowls of fruit salad, blueberry and lime congealed salads, and plates of jellied cranberry sauce.

As they stood before huge bread baskets filled with biscuits and cornbread, Caroline commented, "Granny's the expert on making breads. She's cooked fresh biscuits and cornbread two times a day, every day since she married Grandpaw, when she was seventeen years old." A tub of Granny Pritchett's hand churned butter was next to loaves of homemade bread. The bones of one turkey and a half of another sat next to huge bowls of mashed potatoes, chicken gravy, and creamed corn.

Trying his best to speak with a drawl, J.P. said to Caroline, "I nevah seen so much food at one time. A Southern Thanksgiving definitely 'ain't' like a Northern meal." He patted his belly and said, "I'd be a swine if I ate this all the time."

With his large oval plate full, he headed toward the table to sit down and eat. Caroline's cousin Danny said to J.P., as he passed by the long dessert table, "You orta come back to get nanner pudding, sweet tater pie, and pun...kin pie."

J.P. glanced over and saw chocolate, coconut, red velvet, carrot, and pound cakes and well as sugar cookies for the kids. Some of the guys were filling entire plates with desserts. J.P. couldn't imagine having enough room to eat that many servings of dessert. He was already wishing he hadn't eaten a bite of breakfast that morning.

Caroline sat down next to J.P. at the men's table, and tried to help him participate in the conversations. Since he wasn't into huntin', fishin', and going to the stock car races every weekend, J.P. didn't have a lot to contribute to the male conversations. He was like a fish out of water until Troy got his loaded dessert plate and sat down next to him. They had no problem talking together, Clemson football of course, so Caroline wandered off to talk to some of her cousins and make sure Rhonda wasn't over there talking about her. She loved her sister, but Rhonda just never seemed to know when to stop, and she really didn't care. She never let someone's opinion of her dictate her behavior; Caroline secretly admired that quality in her sister and wished she could be more like her in many ways.

Caroline knew that some gossip would take place, but she told J.P. that they'd be able to sneak away after the meal. She wanted to take a walk down to the old barn and creek. They walked across the cotton field, and through a patch of woods and, looking down toward the ravine, they spotted the creek. Dry leaves made Caroline slip and slide down the hill on her butt. J.P. decided to slide down too, for the fun of it, and to keep Caroline from feeling embarrassed. Caroline told him, "When Momma was a little girl, they used to put the watermelons in this creek. Caroline jumped over the creek, followed by J.P. and walked up the incline toward the sight where the old farmhouse once stood.

Autumn leaves of red, orange, and yellow dappled the landscape behind the old barn. Whirlwinds of dried leaves spun over the ground in front of the barn doors. The barn appeared to be leaning, as if the planks were warped and the old structure was almost ready to topple to the ground. There was nothing much left of the old home place except part of the chimney and some of the stone foundation. Ivy vines covered parts of a stone wall that had been erected behind the house to separate the yard from the woods. Remnants of a smokehouse and a rock walled well stood between the house and the barn. To the right of the structures were apple and peach trees that hadn't been pruned in years. To the left of the barn spanned rows of pecan trees loaded with nuts. In front of those trees, thirty or forty blueberry bushes, nearly barren of all their small leaves, had been planted in rows for ease of harvesting.

"Can you imagine my momma and her brothers and sisters growing up in this gorgeous spot? I love to come here and try to visualize their lives."

"Well, if this is the opposite of what you've known as a child living in Greenville, can you imagine me growing up where the homes are side by side and the trees are way down the street at the park," he asked.

"I loved spending a week here in the summer. It was hot, but that very spot where we slid down the hill was always shady and cool. It was fun to come here in the summer, but fall has always been my favorite season, and I preferred to come here in October or November."

J.P. said, "I can see how different your mother's life was from that of my parents', growing up in New Jersey." J.P. was also keenly aware of how different their mothers were. He hoped his mother's mannerisms wouldn't make Caroline uneasy when they'd eventually meet. His mother probably had different social expectations from those of Mrs. Carter. All he could do would be to warn Caroline of these differences, but try to do so in such a way that she wouldn't fear meeting his mother. He had definite plans to invite Caroline to New Jersey over the Christmas holidays.

The next day Caroline and J.P. spent time together as planned. The delightfully cool air and the bright sunlight made the weather absolutely perfect for a day trip to the mountains. The views of the Blue Ridge Mountains were magnificent. It was a world away from the hustle and bustle of New York as J.P. remembered it. Of course, NYC had its own appeal, but Central Park in all of its autumn splendor was no comparison to the natural beauty of this part of the country.

As Caroline and J.P. drove toward Asheville, N.C., the display of glorious fall colors of thousands of deciduous trees overshadowing evergreens made them feel as if they were being transported into an artist's rendition of the scenery. The shadows of clouds passing overhead, interspersed with sunlight, alternately muted and brightened the brilliant hillsides. Passing the hillsides and valleys to the left and right of them, afforded Caroline and J.P. the opportunity see patches of mist hovering over tributary streams flowing into small rivers.

"Caroline," said J.P. "I can't think of a more perfect place to spend the day with you." When he thought of her with her with her brown hair, golden eyes, fair skin and rosy cheeks, her beauty seemed to blend in with the beauty of nature all around him. "I know you've been thinking about some places you wanted to show me, but I was wondering if you would like to see the Biltmore House today."

Caroline was thrilled at J. P.'s suggestion. "It would be wonderful to be in Asheville all day. I've always wanted to go to Biltmore. Even living this close, we never had the extra money to go there. I've heard it's an astonishing sight to see. Have you been there before?"

"No, when I was in college I never had the extra money to go either. My parents struggled to pay out of state tuition for me to attend college. I haven't been able to take you out lately, so I say let's go and have a good time. It's exciting to go somewhere together that neither of us have ever been before."

"It's only about an hour from here, and I'm sure it'll be a beautiful drive," Caroline said.

They drove on to Asheville enjoying every bit of the scenery and telling one another little things from their childhood years. Once in Asheville, J.P. asked Caroline if she was hungry. Neither of them had eaten breakfast, and by that time it was already after ten o'clock, too late to stop for a sausage biscuit. Caroline suggested they stop and indulge at a breakfast bar.

They took their time eating breakfast and felt relaxed because there were no time constraints on their day. As they ate, they entertained one another's questions, both of them being keenly curious about the little details of their lives. She wanted to know all about what it was like for him growing up in a metropolitan area. He wanted to know what it was like growing up in a smaller city at the foothills of the Blue Ridge Mountains.

When they arrived at Biltmore, the two of them were very impressed with the acres and acres of interesting trees and plants. Caroline said, "The Vanderbilt's must have had many of these trees and shrubs imported from other countries, because they're not native to this area." She was savvy about botanical species since she had taken several botany courses in college, including one summer course taken at Boone, investigating plants indigenous to western North Carolina. As they drove through part of the grounds Caroline opened the brochure and read that Frederick Law Olmsted had done the landscape design.

She continued: "I know you've heard of Olmsted, since he designed Central Park in New York City, and you've been there so many times."

"Yes, I have. Does that brochure mention the number of acres on this estate?"

Caroline reviewed the brochure and answered, "Yep, looks like it has eight thousand acres,"

"Wow, that's hard to believe that one man can build a home on eight thousand acres of land. I'll be lucky if I ever have one acre of land."

They were directed to park their car in a sloping parking lot and had quite a walk on a trail from the parking area to the house. When the chateau was in sight, they both turned toward each other with the look of amazement. They were fascinated by the enormous house, the autumn flora, and the majestic mountain views.

J.P. said, "I've heard it's considered to be a castle, but I had no idea such a magnificent home would be here in North Carolina."

Caroline responded, "It's hard to believe that anyone, other than royalty, could live in such a grandiose home. I can't wait to go in and see the extravagant furnishings."

"Well, let's go and just imagine ourselves as the owners today," said J.P., smiling from ear to ear.

Caroline couldn't help but notice what a romantic J.P. was. She'd never met anyone else like him before. Oh, she'd met plenty of guys who tried to pretend to be romantic, but J. P. was genuine. He held her hand as they entered the house. Since it was the Thanksgiving/Christmas season, the huge mansion was decorated in its Christmas glory. They walked slowly through each room, taking in every detail. Each room contained, not only its usual period furnishings, but a fully hand decorated Christmas tree, and there were hundreds of wreaths and garlands displayed throughout the house. Caroline thought the dining room was unbelievably grand, especially the beautifully decorated thirty-five foot Fraser fir tree.

She said to J.P., "The fireplaces would make a person look small standing before them. I think the area of the formal dining table might be greater than the area of a beachside bungalow on Sullivan's Island."

"You might be right about that. It could be as large as a California bungalow that sells for a half a million dollars."

"Can you believe the height of this ceiling in the dining room," asked Caroline?

"We need to come back here and take the evening candlelight tour," he suggested.

"I've heard about that," said Caroline. "It sounds delightful."

"It's hard to fathom the immense wealth these people enjoyed," said J.P. "I'd love to have enough money to live comfortably, but I don't think I'd want to live in something this elaborate. I don't see how a family could experience intimacy living in such a gigantic place."

They were able to go out on the huge second floor back porch to view the colorful fall scenery, against the backdrop of the higher Blue Ridge Mountains. The fair weather cumulus clouds above the mountains completed the picturesque view."

J. P. said, "Now, this I could enjoy at the back of my home, of course on a much smaller scale, but I don't think the mountains are for me at this stage of my life." They stood there resting their arms on the huge concrete banister, looking out and admiring the landscape. J.P. put his arm around Caroline's shoulder and pulled her close to him and said, "This beauty makes me think of you and smile."

"Thanks," she said blushing. "You always say things to make me feel good about myself. You're something else. I'm glad you suggested this day trip; we needed to escape from our responsibilities by coming here. You done real good, Mr. Andersen." Her smile told him that she really admired and appreciated him.

There were so many things to see in the elaborately decorated house, but Caroline was also looking forward to going to the gardens and conservatory. Once outside again, a grand view of the garden could be seen as they stood upon a platform with vine covered pergolas. They walked down the steps and entered the garden filled with innumerable varieties of grasses and mums of every fall color. They wove their way through the formal display directly in front of the conservatory. The cool breeze blew through Caroline's long brown hair just as it did through the fall colored grasses in the garden. J.P. found even more pleasure in watching her than he did looking at the grandeur of the garden. Caroline turned back toward J.P. before she opened the door to the conservatory. He'd always been a gentleman and held the door for her. He sauntered toward her so she would not have to wait for him. As he opened the door, both of them noticed the warmth and humidity in the conservatory. There seemed to be specimens of hundreds of different kinds of plants gathered from all over the world.

Caroline and J.P. came out of the conservatory and strolled through the remainder of the gardens. They took their time walking and making little stops along the way to sit on benches and talk. He suddenly thought to ask her when her birthday was and tell her when his birthday was, too. She responded that her birthday was, on a Friday this year, and his was April thirteenth. The conversation continued until J. P. began to feel very hungry.

"Would you like to go to downtown Asheville," asked J.P.? "I think there are a lot of shops and art galleries. We could probably find a good restaurant before we head back to your mom's house."

"That sounds like a good idea."

Surprisingly, parking downtown was easily taken care of. They went in a number of gift shops and galleries before spotting a Thai restaurant.

"Do you like Thai cuisine," asked J.P.?

"I've never eaten Thai food before. Isn't it pretty spicy?"

"Most of the Thai restaurants I've been to, in New York, give you a choice of mild or spicy dishes."

"Okay, I'm willing to try it."

Caroline couldn't help thinking how different J.P. was from the good ole boys around home. All the things he had been exposed to living in a large city gave him a lot more knowledge than other guys she had dated in high school or college. Some of them were decent guys, but they just weren't very interesting to her.

J.P. was thinking about Caroline's attitude toward everything he'd suggested they do on dates. She was easy to please and seemed so enthusiastic about doing things she'd never done before. He really wanted to invite her to New Jersey for Christmas, but he was afraid she might decline because she wouldn't be with her family. She didn't know it, but he was sometimes reluctant to ask girls to do something like that, out of fear of rejection. Over dinner, he got up the nerve to ask her if she'd consider going with him.

"What would you think about going to see New York City during the Christmas holidays?"

"Going to stay with your folks, you mean?"

"Well, yes, you'd have to endure a visit with some more Yanks, with all of their questions and opinions, but I think you'd love to see the city at that time of the year."

"It sounds exciting, but I'm wondering if I would freeze my hiney off. I'm not used to being in the cold climate of the North like you are."

He resisted the urge to laugh about her frozen hiney and calmly said, "If you have a heavy woolen overcoat and winter clothes you can layer, you'll probably be okay. It's cold there, but it's not Siberia. But you've never been to Siberia before either," he said with a chuckle for release.

"So, if I were freezing on the streets of New York, you'd take me to a department store?

He laughed and responded, "I'd keep a good eye on you to make sure you weren't turning blue from the cold. I might have to take you into an Irish pub to get you warmed up, if that happens."

"How will your parents react to you bringing a Southern girl to visit," she asked? "Sometimes no matter how hard I try to control my dialect, I still sound like a country bumpkin. The more nervous I get meeting new people, the more grammatical mistakes I make. I might accidentally say something like 'he don't... or she ain't...' and embarrass you."

"Caroline, my parents have their own dialects, too. They're both sharp people, but they're not formally educated like you are. As a matter of fact, they'll think I 'tawk more cun...try' than you do."

"Thanks for the reassurance."

"You'll be okay. If I didn't think it would be a good experience for you, I wouldn't ask you to go. Just think about it; no need to answer right now."

She sat there in the restaurant eating slowly, but paused to say, "Okay, I'll think about it." What she was really thinking was: *why is he asking me to spend time with his family? Then she answered herself mentally, 'You wanted him to meet your family to see where you were coming from.' That just makes it easier to spend time with one another, if you can be yourself. Being a city boy is what he's all about.* She'd miss seeing Troy, Rhonda, and her momma, but she'd be back for New Year's Day with them, before having to start second semester at school. And it was time for her to be grown up, on her own, learning more about the world. What better place than NYC with all the different ethnic groups living there. It really did sound like an intriguing proposition. She'd always wondered about those dazzling window displays done by the big NYC department stores at Christmastime. Caroline knew if she stayed in her own state and was scared to venture out upon opportunity, she'd be losing out on a lot of good experiences. She needed to give this invitation a lot of consideration.

CHAPTER 4

DREAMIN'

Caroline had been invited to stay Saturday night at her friend's house on Lake Wylie, twenty miles south of Charlotte. The dorms were abandoned for the holiday weekend, so Susan planned to drive Caroline back to school on Sunday morning. When she found out that J. P. was bringing Caroline to her house, she suggested that he spend the afternoon with them on Lake Wylie. Her boyfriend, Ross, was coming over to take them out on the lake in his boat. The unseasonably warm weather they had been experiencing would enable them get out on the water if clad with warm hooded jackets.

Unlike J.P., Susan's beau appeared to be a very formal kind of guy. I guess you could say he looked like a preppie from an affluent family. Of course he was rich; he brought his boat over, his toy. Ross's jeans looked like they had been dry-cleaned. The sleeves of his navy blue jacket were tied around his neck, and he wore a long sleeved, button down, cotton shirt tucked in at the waist. At least he wasn't wearing a belt. He did have on a pair of navy blue leather boat shoes, sockless.

Good ol' J.P. was standing there in his ragged jeans and faded long sleeved T-shirt, with the bottom of the sleeves pushed up just below his elbow. He was smiling at Caroline as he stood there with his thumbs tucked into the pockets of the threadbare jeans. When he noticed that Susan and Ross were distracted, he winked at Caroline and then nodded his head to let her know he could handle the situation.

The lake house had a huge deck on the back of it overlooking the lake. Due to the many warm days and lack of rain and winds, vestiges of autumn leaves clung to the oak and maple trees around the lake. The two couples sat on the deck drinking warm apple cider, eating boiled peanuts, and chatting to get to know one another. Then the guys took the boat down to the nearby landing, and the girls walked and met them there. J. P. helped Ross launch the boat from the ramp and get it tied to the dock; then, the four of them got aboard the boat and put on life jackets.

The air was warmed by the bright sunshine, so there were quite a few boats out on the lake that day due to the beautiful weather. As they navigated on the lake that late afternoon, Caroline looked out across the water, which appeared to glisten as a gentle breeze caused tiny ripples on its surface. The sun, shining through the high clouds, made the sunset take on shades of blue and pink, a superb view with the autumn leaved trees reaching up to touch the pastel sky. Caroline looked back at J. P. and sensed he was admiring her as much as he was the fabulous sunset. At that moment she felt so close to him, as if they shared the same feelings, thoughts, pleasures, and possibly dreams. Could this be the soul mate experience? Cautiously, she resisted that thought.

She moved closer to J.P. trying to snuggle up to him as if she were freezing. He slipped his warm hand into hers and pulled his arm in close to his side, affectionately stroking her hand with his thumb. She put her head on his shoulder and whispered to him, "Thank you for being who you are."

He squeezed her hand and said, "Thank you, too; you're one heck of a special girl."

It wasn't easy for the two of them to part that evening, but Caroline knew that J. P. had a four hour drive ahead of him to get back to Summerville, and she hoped he would get there before midnight. The dorm resident assistants had to be back before most of the students were back, just in case there were any problems to attend to. Putting her laundry away, which she had done at her momma's house, Caroline thought of her great weekend with J.P. He'd been so wonderful, and she felt badly about the occasional reservations she'd been having in her mind.

When she arrived on campus, she went down to the school cafeteria alone, as her other friends were not back to campus yet. As she was standing in line to order her favorite plate of eggs, bacon, grits, and buttered toast, she heard that low, radio announcer type voice behind her welcoming her back to school. She knew it was Joost Van Ness, so she turned around to acknowledge him.

"Hey Joost, how are ya," she asked? "I hope you had a good weekend."

He responded, "I did have a good weekend. I went to visit my brother in Asheville, North Carolina."

"I was in Asheville on Friday, sightseeing at Biltmore Estate," she said.

Then he asked, "Would you like to join me for brunch? It looks like there're very few students in here."

Caroline felt like she should make up some excuse, instantaneously, but why couldn't she eat with Joost? As she said, "Sure, Joost, that sounds great," she was feeling like she was betraying J.P. somehow, but she dismissed the thought and told herself it was just a friendly meal with a fellow student who possibly had very few friends on campus since he was new to the college. Come to think of it, she had very few friends on campus because she was always busy working and studying. Joost stepped away from the drink counter first and guided them to the other side of the cafeteria to an alcove.

He asked, "Will this table do? It seems a little less intimidating than the center of the room full of empty tables."

"Yes, this is fine. Thanks for asking me to eat with you. I dreaded coming in here by myself, but I'm starving this morning."

She noticed how polite Joost was, waiting for her to be seated before he sat down. His radiant smile made her feel at ease as they began to eat. Lord have mercy, he could take her breath away if she let him.

"So, your brother lives in Asheville," she asked?

"Yes, he's my oldest brother. He married an American woman about ten years ago and moved to the United States. I enjoyed spending time with my nephew during the holiday, playing with his elaborate train set. I had an amazing train set when I was about his age, so it brought back nice memories."

"I guess you got to enjoy a grand American Thanksgiving feast," Caroline said. "Is your sister-in-law from Asheville?"

"She's from Hendersonville. Her mother still lives there, so we had our Thanksgiving meal there."

"How did you get up to your brother's house?"

"When I came to the states, my brother helped me find a used Volkswagen van to buy. When I finish school, I'd like to ship the old VW to Europe because that would be cheaper than buying a new vehicle. Everything is so expensive there compared to the United States. I could have the van restored and keep it. It would remind me of my college days here in the states."

As he spoke about his plan to ship the van to Europe, Caroline realized he was quite a frugal person. If he did have plenty of money, he didn't flaunt it. Even his clothing was modest, in that it was well worn, and he proclaimed no great pretensions.

Caroline said, "I don't have a car yet, but I wouldn't mind having a VW 'bug' when I start teaching. I know it would be great on gas. My best friend drives a bug."

"Do you plan to remain in South Carolina when you begin teaching," he asked?

"I'm not sure. I'll have to apply for teaching certificates in other states if I wish to apply for jobs. Even though my mother and siblings live in Greenville, I don't think I'll return there to teach, because I want to venture out and find out more about other places." She felt strange and a little fake to refer to her momma as 'mother', but he seemed so proper and she was trying to make a good impression for some reason.

"I think that's a good idea."

"So, what's your plan when you graduate," she asked, curiously?

"I'll need to go to graduate school to earn a MBA in international business. After graduate school, I'll probably return to Spain. Spanish is my dominate language, although I've improved greatly in English since I've been here. Speaking English well will be a great advantage in international business."

"Sounds like you'll always lead an interesting life," she said with just hint of envy. She wondered what it was really like for him growing up. His parents were probably well established financially before he was ever born, so he'd had every opportunity afforded him. She was surprised that he wasn't pompous or egotistical.

After they finished chatting and eating, Joost cleared his throat and asked Caroline, "Would you be willing to edit one more of my papers? The paper is the last major assignment of the semester and the professor is very demanding."

"Yes, Joost, I'll help you. You need to be more confident about your writing. The last time I edited one of your papers, you'd done an excellent job on it."

"Since the sentence structure of Spanish is sometimes the opposite of English, I fear I'll make errors and never realize it."

Caroline replied, "I would nevah notice trepidation, or fear, when we're having a conversation."

He smiled at her with a look of contentment. Then he asked, "Would you also let me take you to an Indian restaurant in Charlotte, to say thank you for helping me?"

Now, that question shed a whole different light on the situation. *Caroline heard Joost say the meal was to say thank you, but was that what it really was? If J.P knew she was going with Joost, would he feel that it was a simple gesture of gratitude?*

Then Joost added, "If you'd feel more comfortable, you can ask a friend to go, too. As a matter of fact, I'd like to invite my room-mate to go. He's from Indonesia, a really nice guy. Please consider the invitation."

As Caroline listened to Joost speak, she was impressed that he had such a good command of English and used contractions in conversation. So as not to commit to the outing, yet break the awkward silence, she asked, "What's your roommate's name?"

His name is Santoso. He's a very quiet and peaceful person; he's a very good person to share an apartment with."

Caroline thought for a minute how it might be quite interesting, an educational venture in a cultural sense, to go to an Indian restaurant with a Dutchman and an Indonesian.

"Well, I don't have any friends who are international students," Caroline said, "but it sounds like it would be fun to go eat. I'll get back to you later on that answer."

"Santoso and I have a female friend from Greece. If you'd like, we could invite her, and you'd have a cultural experience from several different countries."

Caroline wanted to mull it over rather than decline the invitation. She'd always wanted to learn how people from other countries conducted their everyday lives. When they finished their meals and the pace of the conversation slowed, Caroline and Joost got up from the table and took their trays to the conveyor belt. Caroline told Joost she would help him with the editing in the library on Monday afternoon, after her last class of the day. She thought that would be enough time to make her decision on how to respond to his invitation to dinner. This had to be a decision she'd make; it was a tough call to make.

It was always a drag to go back to school after a holiday, and Monday morning was no exception. Caroline barely woke up in time to get to her class. As she sat in the auditorium where her large class was held, she found it difficult to concentrate on the education lecture and began to daydream about J.P. The entire weekend, she felt the push and the pull of intimacy with J.P. She believed he was a sensitive guy, but that was no guarantee that things would work out between them. When she was with him, she felt a positive energy flowing from him to her, but she started to doubt when they were apart, dealing with their own lives. Suddenly, the focus of her reverie switched to her conversation with Joost. Knowing that she'd see him in the afternoon, she allowed herself to further escape to the thought of what Joost's world, his life in Spain, might be like. In her mind's eye she could see him walking the beach of Costa del Sol, all tanned and with sun bleached hair. She could see him sailing on the Mediterranean for hours, eating paella in the evening and drinking sangria. Just as she caught herself in these thoughts and tried to refocus her attention, she realized her class was being dismissed. She got up from her seat and walked to the exit. She saw Emily standing by the door, looking eager to speak to her. She knew what was coming.

"How was your weekend," inquired Emily?

"I'll have to tell you 'bout it. Wanna eat lunch with me at noon?"

"Sure, where do you want me to meet you?"

"Meet me in the lobby in front of the cafeteria," said Caroline. "I've gotta go now so I have time to get to the student center to check my mailbox before my next class starts."

"Okay, I'll see you at noon."

The next class was about as boring for Caroline as the first one of the day had been. Waking up late that morning, she hadn't had time to eat breakfast, and she felt the intense pangs of hunger as she survived the hour long class under the tutelage of the most humdrum Spanish teacher on the face of the planet. No wonder she didn't understand a thing he said when he gave oral exams, he hadn't taught the class in an organized manner at all. She sat there pondering whether or not to ask Joost to help her prepare for her final oral exam. Her professor had studied in Spain, so she figured that Joost would be an excellent choice for a tutor for test preparation. With that in mind she knew she'd accept his dinner invitation with Santoso and their female Greek friend.

She left the Spanish class quickly so she could run back to her dorm room and take a shower and still meet Emily at noon. As she got dressed, she gave a little more attention to the way she'd look for the remainder of the day, opting to wear jeans and a T-shirt. Her hair was still damp so she decided to French braid her hair and wear her large looped silver earrings, wanting to look casual but very cute.

Emily had been waiting a couple of minutes for Caroline to get to the cafeteria. She hadn't told Emily about J.P. coming up to her momma's for Thanksgiving, but Summerville was a small town, so she knew news traveled fast. She and Emily chatted in general terms as they stood in line to get hamburgers and fries. Caroline devoured her fries in a flash because she despised cold fries.

Just as she was about to take a bite of her hamburger, Emily piped up and said, "I went by to see Chris and Butch on Saturday night, and they told me that J. P. had gone up to spend Thanksgiving with you and your family."

"Oh, I guess you're wondering why I didn't tell you beforehand," retorted Caroline.

"Yeah, I guess I do. What was the big secret?"

Caroline countered, "I didn't want to be embarrassed if he didn't come."

"You wouldn't have had to have been embarrassed with me. I know how much he likes you and wants to be with you, even when it's not feasible because of the distance."

"So how do you know so much about his preferences," asked Caroline, curiously?

"Butch and Chris started saying that you've captured all of his attention because he's not the same as he was just a few months ago."

"In what way," Caroline asked?

"They said he's like driven, you know, focused and he won't sit around and relax like he used to. He's turned them down for partying when he planned to call or write you. In other words, they don't want their buddy to grow up until they decide to do the same."

Caroline laughed and said, "They'll probably be thirty five years old before they decide to get serious about life."

Emily asked again, "So, how did your weekend go?

"It worked out fine. Even my redneck uncle Bobby was nice to him; he's the one who drives around with a Confederate flag bumper sticker on the back of his pickup. At least there weren't any fist fights," she said laughing.

"He seems really interested in you." Being nosy, Emily asked bluntly, "Do you feel the same?"

"I think he's a wonderful guy, but sometimes I have reservations about letting this go any further. At times, my heart says yes, but my mind reminds me that I haven't had the chance to do things that a single adult would have the freedom to do. I'm afraid if I lock myself into a committed relationship, I may close the door on other opportunities to learn about life."

"Well then, maybe you haven't really fallen in love yet," speculated Emily. "He might be in the same boat, but he does seem awfully fond of you. According to Butch, there's only been one other girl he seemed serious about several years ago, but that didn't work out. It was a bad deal from the get go."

"Oh, neither of us has mentioned any past relationships to one another. We don't need to be bogged down about the things in our life that didn't work out; that just breeds negative thoughts."

"Okay Caroline, I see what you mean. Everyone deserves to have a fresh start in a new relationship, unless they've done something in their past that really was really destructive to someone."

Emily was glad Caroline was such an open minded person and knew she was right about resisting the temptation to judge someone based on someone else's perceptions. She wished she was as mature as Caroline seemed to be."

One more class that day and then Caroline needed to meet Joost at the library. The class was entitled: Diagnostic and Prescriptive Teaching of Reading. Even the title made Caroline bored. She was a highly creative person, an artist in a sense, so excessively structured classes stifled her creativity. Caroline realized that her first few years of teaching were going to be rough, but she had confidence that her creativity would pull her through; her students would need her to pull from every source to have the knowledge to teach them effectively.

Finally, the hour was over and Caroline left Tillman Hall and walked across the street to the library. The clouds appeared dark and heavy, warning of an impending storm. Having no umbrella with her, she was unprepared for rain and had only a light hooded jacket. Joost was standing outside the library smoking a cigarette. As she walked up the steps toward him, he promptly extinguished the cigarette and popped a breath mint in his mouth.

As usual, he was very polite, thanking her for taking the time to come help him. They entered the library, Caroline trying not to think of the stench of cigarette smoke, and then she excused herself to go to the restroom. Once alone, she thought of J.P. and the fact that he had never smoked around her. The only time she ever saw him drinking beer was the very first weekend she met him, when they had the oyster roast. Even that night he only had a few beers along with his meal. Caroline was no idiot, she knew J.P. drank in the past. She remembered the first night she went to his house with Emily, when the beer bottles on the porch were being knocked over by J.P.'s dog, Sebastian. She figured all the guys living there liked to drink their brew and in excess on occasion.

A jolt back to reality, made her realize that she'd been in the restroom for some time; she got finished in the restroom, and went to look for Joost in the library. He was in the periodical and magazine section reading a sports magazine, an article about an international soccer match. Caroline decided to get a magazine and sat down in the comfortable chair next to Joost.

He looked over at her, seeing the magazine she had selected, and asked in a whisper, "Do you mind taking a few minutes to relax and read your magazine?"

"No, I think I need to unwind from my classes. I always enjoy comin' in here to read the magazines, the ones I nevah have the money to subscribe to." Both of them were whispering, trying not to disturb other students in the library.

Then he said jokingly, "I didn't know you had a home and garden, yet."

"Well, one day I will, and I want to have lots of ideas about decoratin' it; besides, this magazine has a bunch of good recipes."

"I thought grapes came in bunches, not recipes," he said sprightly. "So you know how to cook," he inquired?

"Believe it or not," she whispered back, "I've been cookin' since I was a little girl. I make casseroles, soups, salads, and lots of fattenin' desserts," she replied. "I come from a family of good cooks. I'm not too good at bread bakin', but I can make biscuits and cornbread."

"What's cornbread," Joost asked?

"Cornbread is bread made from cornmeal."

He still looked puzzled. All he could think of was a corn tortilla he'd eaten in the Mexican restaurant.

"You'll just have to taste it to see if you like it. My momma makes delicious cornbread. She and her sisters can cook up a storm, but everythin' they make is very fattenin'," she said still whispering.

"I never heard 'cook up a storm' before," he said teasing her.

She whispered a response, "I reckon you ain't hear…d dis neither: Don't let yer mouth overload yer tail."

He chuckled as quietly as possible and asked, "What does that mean?"

She was giggling and responded, "It means you talk too much."

Trying not to make excessive noise, he arched his back and pretended he was laughing profusely, hugging himself as if he couldn't stop laughing. Caroline just smiled and went back to reading her magazine. Meanwhile, Joost was thinking how cute and funny she was; he liked her personality.

She liked him, too, but she knew she needed to keep it platonic.

They were in the library about an hour reading and editing his paper. When they came out of the library, it was pouring rain. Fortunately, Joost had come prepared with his large multicolored umbrella, which he'd left outside propped up against the side of the building, near the ashtray perched upon a metal pedestal.

Having no umbrella, Caroline would've gotten soaking wet if Joost hadn't offered to walk her back to her dorm, on the other side of the campus. The rain was splashing off the umbrella with such force, they had to walk very close to one another to keep both of them fairly dry; however, there was no way to keep the legs of their pants dry. Surprisingly, Joost didn't ask her to eat with him in the cafeteria, even though it was time to eat, and her dorm was right next to the cafeteria.

They parted and Caroline went to her room to get out of her wet jeans, lie down and just think, but who, was she going to think about?

CHAPTER 5

THINKIN'

Caroline's dorm room was always gloomy because the window only provided a ghastly view of another high rise dormitory rather than trees, blue sky, or clouds. It was particularly dreary coming back to her room when it was pouring rain outside and the evening darkness was soon approaching. Feeling exhausted from the long weekend of travelling, she fell upon her bed and looked out the window at the torrent of rain falling between the two buildings, the rain pelting against the window pane. She wanted to just fall asleep, but she'd never been the kind of person who could sleep at the drop of a hat, and usually she could never sleep before eleven. Her mind was always packed with thought after thought, leaving her in a state of tension. That mental preoccupation had been a defense mechanism for her as a child, after her daddy passed, for if her mind was filled with many thoughts, she wouldn't dwell upon those things that hurt the most.

Caroline spent a lot of time alone and liked having a private dorm room; she could be who she wanted to be and not have to contend with a silly roommate. She had friends at school but relished the daily solitude she'd become accustomed to. She thought of J.P., the outings with beautiful scenery, the letters and cards, and the phone conversations. Thoughts of his tenderness as he held her hand, or embraced her and kissed her, made her feel happy. She thought of the funny faces J.P. made at her when he was feeling nervous about meeting her family and transported herself in thought to the old home place near her granny's house and to the stroll in the gardens of Biltmore. Caroline wasn't used to thinking about a certain guy in her life, and these thoughts excited her and scared her. She wondered if she was capable of love; if she could allow herself to care and relinquish fear. She was starting to sense that J.P. was interested in her exclusively. Why would he drive so far to spend time with her? If he just wanted to date, for the heck of it, he could do that in Summerville or Charleston.

Maybe Caroline was unable to see that she impacted others in a very positive way; she considered herself to be plain and simple, and to some she might be boring or dull. She couldn't compare herself to the gorgeous, flirty girls who seemed to attract men like yellow jackets to ripened figs. She wasn't, and never could be, anywhere near that category and couldn't even remember a time when she'd tried to flirt with a guy.

Then there was Joost, nearby and popping up in her life all of the sudden. She kept telling herself that he was lonely and needed friends, and she certainly couldn't begin to ignore him. It seemed bewildering to her that someone with his background, a life of ease, could desire to spend time with her. Rich foreign students were notorious for the 'love em and leave em' scene, and she wasn't about to get caught up in that. Caroline suspected that Joost would appear soon, because she'd never given him a definite answer about dinner out in Charlotte with friends. She wanted to go but didn't want to betray the trust of J.P.

Caroline got up and turned on her radio. Cranking up the volume, she wanted to hear a keyboarding genius. Music was a universal escape for people, and she took the time to get absorbed by the sounds. She imagined seeing the artist in concert, in a front row seat, watching him run his fingers from the bass to treble clef and back again never missing a note. Going to concerts at Littlejohn Coliseum, at Clemson University, had been a big part of her life as a teenager.

She sat there on the edge of her bed, taking her French braid down to brush through her silky hair, and she was reminded of the freedom that she had experienced by not having a steady boyfriend. So many beautiful cheerleaders and homecoming queens, those that were on the top of the list of popularity, got married because they were pregnant, and some of those marriages had already failed, leaving a good looking woman plump and miserable. She had steered clear of serious involvement with anyone, even the smooth talkers who could make you swoon. Song after song, reminiscent of the 70's, playing on the radio, prompted her to recall images of her old friends, acquaintances, and the flings of her past. With the music still resounding, she fell back on the bed, stared at florescent stars she'd stuck to the ceiling, like a teenager, and felt self-pride in her accomplishments, the future being illusive at the moment.

Hump day had arrived, Wednesday, and she'd knocked out three days of classes, the rest of the week would be coasting downhill. She had to work in the dorm office that night, boring as it was, but that would give her the time to study. One of her friends, another resident assistant, was going to the pizza parlor and told her she'd bring her a small pizza since Caroline had to work the evening shift in the office from five o'clock to ten. She was sitting there at the office desk, pigging out on pizza and drowning in cola, with pizza sauce on her chin, when Joost stepped in through the office door. Caroline was utterly shocked to see him there, and found it hard to know what to say, afraid the blithering idiot syndrome would resurface. She didn't even know that he was aware of her job in the dormitory; she couldn't remember having told him about it.

It seemed a little creepy that he knew where she was. Like a bolt of lightning striking her mind, she suddenly remembered that he had indeed seen her with Emily the first day she met him, and maybe he'd asked her. That thought made Caroline concerned that Emily might jump to conclusions if Joost had asked her where she was. *Was she trying to write script for a daytime drama, or what?*

Gulping her last bite of pizza, with no thought of chewing it, Caroline looked up at Joost. She had no idea that a tiny string of mozzarella covered with sauce was dangling from her bottom lip.

"Hey! What's up with you? I'm surprised to see you here because I didn't think you knew I worked in the dormitory office," she said, fishing for a lead to her informant.

"I saw your friend Emily during lunch. I didn't mean to startle you, but I was coming by for a specific reason. My friends and I are definitely going out for dinner on Friday night at the Masala in Charlotte. Since I'd already mentioned it to you, I wanted to give you the opportunity to agree to go or to decline. So that's why I made it a point to find you tonight and hope that you'll agree to go."

Suddenly, feeling a tickle on her chin, she felt the sauce and cheese on her face and quickly wiped her face with her stain covered napkin. "That's certainly considerate of you," she replied. "I've thought about it, and I'm sure I'd have a good time going with you and your friends."

"Good, I'm glad you decided to go with us. I do want to express my gratitude for the help you've given me on editing my papers. Dinner is a small token of appreciation for what you've done for me as a friend. This world would be a much better place if there were more caring people like you."

"That's enough; you're gonna embarrass me in a second. I'm not used to a lot of flattery," she said, almost blushing.

"Caroline, es verdad; I'm sincere about my thankfulness. Foreigners in any country are often treated as though they can't fit in with the locals. Yet, you were willing to give me a chance to become friends with you and help me. I believe one would say that you're a 'diamond in the rough'."

"Well, I'm glad you consider me your friend, and I'll look forward to dinner on Friday night." *A diamond in the rough, she'd never been told something like that before.*

I'll call you on Friday afternoon to give you details?"

"Sure." *Ooo wee, he's good looking, she thought.*

"Okay, from now on I'll remember you as the pizza girl," he said, trying to tease her. "I'll call you later."

As he walked out the door, she couldn't help but think to herself that she liked him, but he was too much of a risk to consider having anything other than a companionable relationship with him. It's too bad that he's some rich dude from Spain, she thought. On the other hand, could that be part of the attraction in addition to his good looks, his personality, and his kindness? Of course it was; after all, she'd grown up struggling in a single parent home with limited resources compared to most of her friends. Could her life become less difficult if she let something get started between them?

She wished she could stop thinking about guys for now; she'd always gotten tired of hearing other girls talk about the same thing she was doing in her thoughts. At least she wasn't boring any of her friends, or pumping them full of information that was none of their business, sharpening their claws to make them dig into her soul.

After a couple of dreary, rainy days, Thursday brought warm sunshine and cool air. The autumn days were soon to leave and the near barren oak and maple trees scattered across the campus told Caroline that winter was approaching. She had only two morning classes that day, so she and Emily met at the student center to sit and talk while gorging on some junk food from the canteen. Crunching some chips in her mouth, Caroline jumped up and said to Emily, "I'll be back in a minute; I wanna check my mailbox while I'm thinking about it."

Emily sat there and filled her cheeks with candy until she looked like a blasted hamster. To Caroline's astonishment, she actually had three letters in her mailbox, one from her momma, one from Rhonda, and the third from J.P. She went back over to sit with Emily and tried to unobtrusively slip the letters into her book bag before Emily started hammering her with questions about them. It was too late because Emily had already spotted the baby blue envelope and assumed it was from J.P.

"Aren't you gonna open it," Emily asked?

"Not right now. I love to keep my letters to read when I have quiet time to myself."

"Okay, I was just curious. Can you at least tell me if it's postmarked from Summerville," Emily probed?

"You know it is. Who else, beside my family members, would be writing me right now? It's not like I have a steady boyfriend writing me from Greenville."

"Well, you do have a couple of guys who seem interested in you. Who knows how many more there are," said Emily.

Caroline knew what was coming next. Emily was like most girls and wanted to know everything about the love life of her friends. Much to her chagrin, Caroline engaged in the conversation about men.

"A couple of guys," Caroline asked?

"Yes, a couple of guys; you already figured out who told Joost you were working in the dorm office last night."

"Yeah, I did, and I forgive you for that," she said with a teasing smile.

"Oh, come on Caroline; you're not gonna tell me anything else about him? I know it must be tough for you to stick with just one of those men, both bein' so good looking and nice."

"Emily, don't start. It's not like that with Joost. We've become friends, but just friends," responded Caroline.

"That's hard to imagine; however, I realize that he's risky, being a foreigner."

"I don't think he's looking for more than friendship," said Caroline. "He'll graduate in the spring, be off somewhere for graduate school to get his MBA, and go back to Europe in a couple of years to start his business career. His brother will probably introduce him to some rich girl, and the rest will be her fairy tale, not mine."

"You're probably smart to keep things on a friendly basis with him, so you don't get burned in the end," said Emily, with a note of concern in her voice.

"Don't worry 'bout me, Emily. You know I think a fairy tale is just that, a tale; but it's okay to dream once in a while. Listen, I gotta go so I have time to do my laundry."

Outside, she noticed the sunlight streaming through the near barren trees making the campus grounds seem to glow and longed to have one more beautiful sunny day, before the chilling days of winter arrived. The air was cool, but she wouldn't be cold in her faded Winthrop sweatshirt and well-worn corduroy pants over knee socks. She walked over to the main campus, where the stately old buildings stood, named after famous men of historical significance, and sat on a bench on the sunny side of Kinard Hall, a beautiful old Neo-Georgian-style building. Retrieving her letters from her backpack, she decided to read Rhonda's and her momma's letters before reading J.P.'s. On the back of the envelope of his letter, he'd drawn a simplistic depiction of ocean waves rolling up on a beach and an inscription of, "Thinking of you...." The scene beckoned her to open the letter and allow herself to read and imagine in a dreamlike state, a dream of the Lowcountry. She had no reservations about the kind of person he was, a true romantic; only a romantic would take the time to make his letter so personal. Slowly tearing the envelope open, in an attempt to preserve the envelope as she would the letter, she felt a sense of deja vu of his prior expressions of affection. *Could he have been showing her all along, in all of his actions, that he's falling in love with her? Had she been blinded by her own fear of intimacy to see that?*

As she read his sweet words, he told her how much happiness that she'd already brought into his life in the few quiet moments they'd spent together. He said that she was a beautiful person and made his heart skip a beat, but he admitted that writing such words seems rather foreign to him. Much to her delight, he asked her to go to Jersey at Christmastime to meet his parents and said that he wanted them to know how much she meant to him.

Caroline was almost blissfully numb after reading his letter. She read it over three times before tucking it back in the envelope to hide it away from all others. These expressions were very personal for both J. P. and for her. She knew that Emily would want to know what J.P. had to say in his letter, but Caroline felt she should be the only person privy to reading something so unfeigned.

She felt humbled by his display of affection through his words, and as she walked alone back across the campus a range of emotions flooded her soul. Although she was apprehensive about meeting his family in New Jersey, she wanted to go with him, to see his world, to experience some of his joys. She would write back to him while she was doing her laundry.

The washing machine must have been stopped for a while before Caroline realized she needed to put her clothes in the dryer. Almost robotically, she transferred the clothing from the washer to the dryer as she continued in thought. Tomorrow night would be the night to go eat dinner with Joost and his friends. She felt like an insect caught in a spider's web, with no way to change her plan at the last minute. She certainly didn't want to be impolite or cause Joost to be uncomfortable around his friends if she cancelled the excursion. She'd just received the most romantic letter of her life, and she'd already committed to spend the following evening with some other good looking guy. She knew that she'd done nothing intentionally misleading and didn't want to continue to beat herself up over it. Rationalizing the situation, she'd given her time freely to help Joost and deserved to go out, she was determined she'd go to dinner, meet new friends, and enjoy herself.

J. P. had Friday afternoon off. He'd worked four, eleven hour days and Friday morning, and his boss agreed they all needed a break. He drove down to the Battery, parked, and with his brown sack lunch and bottled water in hand, walked across the street to the park. The wind blowing across the water was chilly, but the sun was bright. He was wearing his jacket and thought he'd be comfortable to sit on the park bench and eat his roast beef sandwich. Purposely selecting this spot for lunch, alone, he needed to have the time to think about things in his life. Looking to his right, he saw the bench, next to the fountain, where he'd kissed Caroline for the first time. Reminiscing about a date with a girl was not his typical afternoon off. Ordinarily, he'd be in a grill, with his buddies from work, having a good hot Philly cheese steak sandwich and washing it down with a cold dark beer; but that scene was getting a bit old and leading him nowhere. He'd soon be twenty eight years old and felt like his life might be stagnating, while many of his friends were already married and having kids. He had every confidence that Caroline was a special girl; he could feel assurance when he was with her.

When they dated and showed signs of affection, he couldn't see her being the type to be playing around with guys, getting what she wanted, but not really caring. That wasn't the Caroline he'd seen; she was kind and considerate. He thought he'd done the right thing by writing the letter. They'd been dating several months even though the dates were intermittent, and he'd made sure he contacted her in some way every week. Wondering what she thought as she read his letter made him anxious to hear from her, and if she wrote back it would be several days before he'd receive a response. So many thoughts were crossing his mind as he sat there eating his lunch, watching the ships in the harbor and listening to the sea birds, and he wished he could be sharing the afternoon with her.

After her class at Rutledge Hall, Caroline took off to mail her letter to J.P. She hadn't sealed the envelope yet because she wasn't one hundred percent sure she'd written the right things. Since she'd started the letter, and rehearsed the situation in her mind over and over, she wondered if she should put something in the letter to let him know about her friendship with Joost. The tone of his letter and her response to it didn't lend itself to a discussion about her college friends. She'd have to find a time later to explain the situation with Joost and assure J.P. that it was nothing more than a friendship.

As expected, Joost called her in the afternoon to let her know where the group would meet on campus. It was agreed upon they'd all meet at the student center at six o'clock and Joost would have his Volkswagen van in the parking lot ready to go to Charlotte.

When Caroline got to the student center, Joost introduced Santoso, his roommate, and Helena Theophilus. On the way to Charlotte, Caroline sat in the back seat of the van with Helena. With a thick accent, she asked more questions about Caroline's cultural background than Caroline asked her, but the conversation was quite productive, and Caroline felt she was getting to know Helena and her culture better.

Once inside the restaurant, Helena and Caroline, neither of whom had ever been to an Indian restaurant before, were overwhelmed by the beautiful décor of ornately carved wood, figured arches, and bronze light fixtures with brightly colored glass inlay. The tables were arranged in such a way to provide privacy, being divided by screens decorated with lacquered colorful images of lovely Indian women, flowers, and fruit. The walls were adorned with brocade wall hangings, with designs of large lotus flowers or copies of what appeared to be cave paintings. Dim lighting and Indian sitar music created a uniquely intimate milieu. This was obviously a very classy restaurant, one that Caroline would never have been able to afford, and she was positive about her choice to take advantage of the experience. In her thoughts, she was sure J.P. would understand her decision about coming here with Joost; she'd explain that it was a group event and not a date.

Joost had frequented this restaurant with one of his Indian friends, Ranjiv, who lived in Charlotte, so he was very familiar with the menu. After their drinks were ordered, he took the liberty of ordering a bread basket filled with poori, naan, and paratha and made sure the waiter brought mango chutney with fried papad, a crispy wafer, and coconut soup for their appetizers. After some discussion of the menu items, vegetarian and non-vegetarian thali and curry dishes were ordered.

The conversations that evening were very interesting to Caroline. Each person in the group described the geography and seasonal changes of their own country. Family was also a topic of conversation; Caroline having two siblings, Joost having three, Helena having four siblings, and Santoso being one of seven children. Each of them told how old they were; Caroline mentioned that she would soon be twenty four years old. At that juncture, Joost asked Caroline specifically when her birthday was. Her birthday was only one week away, and she really hadn't given it any thought. They all continued to share on topics of food, religion, government, and architecture. Caroline had never seen Joost in a group setting. She saw a different person, so gregarious, enjoying every minute of his social life; he was remarkably irresistible to her, but she suppressed it.

Although still very impressed with Joost, Caroline wouldn't let herself start fantasizing about him. *Could her letter from J.P. be a sign, a confirmation that he's the man she should be thinking about, in a more realistic way?* No doubt, Joost possessed charisma, but Caroline couldn't let herself get carried away with him. She needed to resolve to make this her only outing with Joost but do so in a way that didn't make him feel rejected.

Once back to campus and settled in her dorm room, Caroline's phone rang. A kind gentle voice said, "Hey, young one! You must have been out on the town tonight. I hope so, 'cus I wouldn't want you to feel cooped up in that dorm room night after night. Your time in college is a time to enjoy."

Caroline felt some relief to hear J.P. speak to her in a tone of understanding and acceptance. Sometimes, he seemed too good to be true. She replied to him, "Yes, I've been out with friends to an Indian restaurant."

"Maybe an early birthday celebration," he asked?

"I can't believe you remember when I told you when my birthday was."

"I may not remember everything I should, but I do remember some things," he said with a jocose air.

"J.P., I'm so glad you called me. I know you wouldn't have gotten a letter from me yet, cus I just mailed it this morning, but I want you to know how happy I felt when I read your letter."

Then J.P. responded to her, sounding as if a heavy load had just been taken off his back, "I'm really glad to hear that; I was afraid I had scared you off by moving in too fast. You're such a great girl, and I didn't want someone else sweeping you off your feet before I decided to get off my butt and get a broom."

Caroline started to laugh, "J.P. I know you're being serious, but I can't help but laugh."

He was laughing, too, and said, "At least you're laughing with me and not at me."

"You're a silly goose, too, sometimes. Besides, I'd only laugh at you if you were wearing a clown suit at a kid's birthday party."

"Don't say that," said J. P., "I might be doing that one day."

"For a part-time job," she asked?

"No, I might get sucked into being a clown for my own kid's birthday party one day or worse yet, get asked to play Santa Claus."

Caroline wanted to giggle, but he sounded like he was trying to tell her something with his silliness. She paused for a moment to get her urge to giggle under control and said, "I think the kids would like you as a clown or Santa. I like you, and I'm just a big kid. You make me laugh a lot."

"I like you, too, little cutie pie," he said. "I'd rather make you laugh than make you cry."

"I'd rather laugh," she stated.

After an hour of phone conversation about this and that, J.P. could tell Caroline was getting sleepy when he teased her, and it took her a while to come back at him. She'd already told him that she'd been awake since five thirty that morning to study her notes before her test. Before she hung up, he asked her if she was going to be working this weekend, but he didn't question her too much about it. At midnight, he encouraged her to go to sleep and have sweet dreams. After he hung up, he thought to himself: *You knucklehead, you've been trying to have a conversation with someone almost comatose for the last half hour, and now you have to pay the big fat phone bill. But she's worth it, just to hear her faint responses.*

The weekend and the following week were fairly uneventful. Caroline had studied hard all semester and exempted her exams, for which she was very grateful. She called her momma and told her about her plans to go to New Jersey with J.P. over Christmas and then spend New Year's Day at home. Mrs. Carter already knew it was coming, so she tried not to sound disappointed; her baby bird was leaving the nest. Her momma said that she and Rhonda had planned to drive up on Saturday afternoon and take Caroline shopping for her birthday. They'd stay in a motel in Charlotte on Saturday night, have breakfast out the next day, and take Caroline to her friend Susan's house on Sunday for a little birthday celebration she'd planned. Caroline was thrilled about that; she'd been thinking about how cold it might be up north expecting to freeze her butt off. She had a heavy woolen overcoat, but not many other warm clothes. She'd saved some money from her campus job, so she'd be able to get new clothes for winter but a little help with money wouldn't hurt.

Before work on Friday, Caroline walked to a local ice cream shop and treated herself to a banana split with all the toppings and whipped cream she thought she could stomach. She stopped by the pharmacy on the way back and splurged on three magazines to read during work. The dorm office was always very boring on Friday night, until eleven or twelve, because everyone went out on Fridays, and Caroline had no intentions of studying on her birthday. She hated to work those late hours, having the onerous task of contending with a bunch of drunks, mingled with a pack of idiots, so she was glad Beth was going to be taking over at eight.

At six o'clock, Caroline was still feeling stuffed from her banana split and couldn't imagine eating dinner. She was leaning back with her feet up on the desk, reading one of her magazines, when she heard 'that voice' say from behind the door, "I thought I might find you here." Joost peered around the door and with enthusiasm yelled out, "Happy Birthday!" He was holding a gift wrapped in colorful paper with a multicolored curled ribbon bow, which immediately reminded Caroline of the bold colors of a Picasso painting.

"Come on in and set a spell," she said, cheerfully.

"I just came by to wish you a Happy Birthday and offer to go out and get you some food.

She chortled and then said, "I feel like a hog after eating a banana split. Thanks, but I couldn't pack in another bite."

"What's a banana split," he asked?

"You've been in the United States for several years and never had a banana split? Poor thing! It's bananas with three flavors of ice cream, sweet toppings, nuts, and whipped cream with a cherry on top. Eating a banana split almost guarantees that you will have a stomach ache, and you'll gain five pounds, or a couple of kilos, in your case."

"It sounds sinful. I'll have to try it."

"By all means do so, but get ready to feel sick afterward. It gives a new meanin' to the words: sugar high."

Silently, but with a bright smile, he handed her the beautifully wrapped gift, and it brought a smile to her face, being stunned that he'd thought of her on her birthday. She asked, "Can I open it after we talk a few minutes; that will spur my imagination as to what on earth you would've gotten for me?"

"Not really knowing any of your preferences, I did the best I could, but the gift does have some significance to me," he said trying to heighten her curiosity.

Joost looked like he was about to ask her something when suddenly Caroline looked up and saw J.P. standing in the doorway with pastel colored balloons in one hand and a dozen coral colored roses in the other. He'd not seen Joost yet, who was seated slightly behind the door of the tiny office. She started coughing; feeling like her throat was swelling; she grabbed her water bottle, and sucked down several ounces of water in one big gulp.

"Surprise;" with a million dollar smile, he started to sing, "Happy birthday to you, happy birthday to you…"

She felt as though she was seeing some phantom or was hallucinating. He was still standing in the doorway and had not stepped forward to enter the room. She sat there motionless and tried to think of something to say to him before he noticed Joost. In a split second, she leapt from her seat and ran to hug him. He then stepped forward to receive her embrace and saw Joost sitting there with eyes wide open.

She thought, *"Good gracious no, this can't be happening on my birthday. What have I done to deserve this?"*

"Oh J.P., I can't believe you drove four hours to surprise me like this," she said still hugging him as he made every effort to reciprocate, with his hands full of flowers and balloons.

Joost suddenly realized that this guy seemed to be in love with her, and she obviously knew him more intimately than just as a friend. He wanted to somehow make this awkward situation more comfortable for all three of them. He came up with a plan almost instantaneously.

As Caroline turned toward him, grasping for an explanation of his presence, Joost stood up to greet J.P. Caroline turned back toward J.P. and took the balloons and flowers, with a cheerful smile, and made a comment on the beautiful roses to stall for time.

Gallantly, with the finesse of a seasoned diplomat, Joost extended his hand to J.P. and said, "Hi, I'm Joost. Caroline attended an outing with some of the members of the international club, and I came by to extend birthday wishes from some of her new friends. Unfortunately, two of those friends are at work tonight. We were just chatting, but I need to excuse myself to be able to pick up my date on time."

"Liar, liar, pants on fire," she thought, *"but thank God, he smoothed everything over."*

Without hesitancy, J.P. shook Joost's hand and introduced himself. Caroline was standing there, dumbfounded that Joost had been able to come up with just the right words to get her off the hook and save all of them from embarrassment.

Joost nodded his head once and said, "It was nice to meet you, J.P." He turned to Caroline and said, "I hope you enjoy your little birthday gift from Helena, and Santoso. Have a great time on your birthday!" J. P. stepped aside to allow Joost room to briskly exit the small office.

Caroline said with a bubbly disposition, "Thanks Joost for delivering the gift from Santoso and Helena, and tell them thanks."

As he exited he said, "Da nada," in his romantic Castilian Spanish, and she stood there nearly swooning from the excitement of two very different suitors.

J.P. looked a somewhat puzzled and said, "I didn't think he sounded like he'd speak Spanish; his Anglish is purdy good," trying to sound like a good ol' boy again to make Caroline laugh.

She let herself get very tickled at him to have some think time about what to say next. Then she said, "I reckon yur Anglish is purdy good, too, since you's a fur...ner yurself."

"Y'all still think everyone north of the Mason Dixon Line is a foreigner," he asked?

"Yes, you'uns is jest fur...ners to us, cus y'all ain't learnt how to tawk or eat right," she retorted, hoping to keep the conversation silly a little longer to ease her own tension. "Well, since yer here, why don't you set a spell. Sorry we ain't got no rockin chairs in here, like them shabby ones on yer porch."

Still laughing at her exaggerations, he said, "Honey, I'd set any...whur with you and feel like I wuz in hawg heaven."

The glass vase filled with the beautiful coral colored roses was placed on the old massive oak desk. Caroline took the helium balloons and tied the ribbon around the spindles on the back of the old, swivel office chair. She invited J. P. to pull up the other chair, which Joost had been sitting in behind the door, and move it closer to her. She sat in the oak office chair on the other side of the desk ready to answer the outdated, black, rotary dial phone, if needed.

Then Caroline said in her more familiar dialect, "I think, with some polishin', you could sound like an authentic hillbilly. You might enjoy the people who live in the Blue Ridge Mountains. There's quite a rich cultural heritage there; it's not all about fiddle playin', makin' moonshine, and loadin' a shotgun, you know."

"I think Asheville is one of the most beautiful places in eastern part of the country, especially in autumn," he said. "You never know, I might end up there one day. I don't think I'll ever go back to live in New Jersey. I can't imagine paying the exorbitant taxes they pay up there. That's why my parents never bought a home in Jersey; the property taxes would've made it impossible for them to afford some of the opportunities we had going to Manhattan, like to restaurants, Broadway shows, and sports events."

"I assumed that you liked the Charleston area well enough to stay there."

"Oh, I probably will stay there, 'cus I love being near the beach. But the Blue Ridge Mountains might be the way to go when I finally get to retire. Maybe I'll have a modest home in both places. That's some big dreaming, but dreaming is good."

Caroline suddenly became cognizant of how fast time can slip by and one's life can be over. She sensed that J.P. may have been thinking about those kinds of things, too, and he might be ready to stop his 'party days' with his buddies and get down to doing the things that would bring meaning to his life and prepare for his future.

Snapping back to give attention to the conversation, she said, "It was a huge surprise to look up and see you tonight. I was overcome that you'd take the time and energy to drive four hours to see me on my birthday. No one has ever done anything like that for me before."

He said, with genuine sincerity in his voice, "Caroline, I wanted to be here with you. It was nothing to drive the distance to have the opportunity to help make this a special day for you. I'm glad you're here in the office, so I'd be able to find you."

"I'm glad I already made arrangements with one of my friends to take over this job at eight o'clock."

"Would you like to go to Charlotte after you get off work? I think we'd be able to find somewhere descent to eat in the city. I decided to come when I found out when your birthday was. I was glad to discover it would be on a Friday, since it's fairly easy for me to take off in the afternoon and drive up. I called Emily to find out what you were doing for your birthday, and she told me you had to work. I thought I could at least surprise you here and keep you company."

"You mean, you drove up here planning to spend the evening in this gloomy office watching me deal with all kinds of lunatics all night?"

"Yeah, if that's what it took to spend time with you on your birthday."

As they conversed, they continued to catch up on the little details of their everyday lives. She was curious about the restoration projects he was working on in Charleston near Queen and King Streets and wanted to know about the architectural details of the buildings and precisely how they were being restored.

He could tell from her comments that she thought Charleston was a romantic city. He wondered if she'd be interested in living there when she finished college.

J.P. didn't like girls who acted jealous all the time, and he didn't want to seem that way to her. But he couldn't help but wonder about Joost, seeing what a good looking guy he was, but he tried to focus on facts and not get carried away with doubt. He wanted to know if Caroline had received her assignment for student teaching and how she was going to manage transportation. Not knowing if she'd have the money to buy winter clothes for the trip to Jersey, he wanted to know if he could help her with some cash for shopping. Maybe he could just give her cash along with her birthday present he would give her later that evening.

Caroline looked down at her watch and it was only seven o'clock. J.P. said, "I think I should go down to the motel and get a room since we may be late coming back to Rock Hill. What time do you have to be in your dorm?" He thought she'd still have to be on duty even though she got someone else to work in the office.

"I should be back by twelve, since that's when the office will close. Sometimes, all hades breaks loose after midnight with the inebriated jocks on the second and fourth floors. Especially on the fourth floor; I guess they think I can't hear them that far away from my room, but most of them are too brainless to realize that the girls on the third floor are going to call me and complain. There are perks with this job like a little extra spending money and the luxury of a private room. It has been a good experience for three years. I'm not so naïve about college life, now. When I first came to Winthrop, I thought everyone came to college to study and get an education, but I soon learned that most of the students use it as an escape from their parents to become wild and free."

J. P. laughed at Caroline's remark and said, "I guess I was naïve, too, until I did the same things as the other students at Clemson and got wild for quite a while. I'm starting to settle down a little."

Caroline agreed with J.P that it would be better for him to go and reserve a room. She was thankful to have met a man who didn't just show up and expect to stay in her room and put pressure on her. She admired J.P for his self-restraint, because he could've moved in on her already, but hadn't done it. It was a rare find to meet a man who didn't try to sleep with you right away and expect you to be there to satisfy him all the time, while he did who knows what. That's what had happened to those cute little cheer leaders and beauty queens in high school, whom Caroline had been a bit jealous of, girls now divorced with a couple of kids to raise or having to put up with husbands who still think they're Peter Pan, floating around from girl to girl or call-girl.

What had started out as a pitiful excuse for a birthday, working in a dorm office and being alone, looked like it was going to be an interesting birthday after all. She was still bewildered by Joost's quixotic actions and wanted to have the opportunity to thank him personally for making a potentially volatile circumstance manageable for her. She didn't want to dismiss his actions as simply good manners, for her heart told her that he really did care about her and didn't want to put her in a stressful situation on her birthday. She didn't believe for a minute that he had a date for later that evening. Was her attraction to Joost based on a bond of friendship, a mutual respect for one another's emotional hardships, or just the fact that he seemed desirable? She'd never experienced a time in her life when two great guys were showing her so much attention at the same time, and she didn't quite know how to handle it gracefully. She couldn't admit to herself that she was definitely falling in love with either of them, but J.P. and Joost were both special to her, and she had a strange awareness that maybe both of them satisfied some emotional needs she had. Confused and fearful that she was going to hurt one of them or both of them, Caroline knew she needed time after this weekend to contemplate her feelings.

But it was her birthday, and she was going to enjoy it.

Finally, eight o'clock arrived and Beth came in to relieve Caroline of her office duties. They left to go to Charlotte without knowing exactly where they'd eat. J.P. was completely unfamiliar with the city, so he had no suggestions about a good restaurant. Driving north on the interstate, Caroline suddenly remembered a little Vietnamese restaurant, near the Plaza and Sugar Creek, she'd gone to with Susan. It was nothing fancy, so casual dress would be fine, but it did have an interesting ambiance and fabulous food and service.

On Sunday morning, J. P. picked Caroline up at nine o'clock so they could go out for breakfast. Sitting in the restaurant, J. P. studied Caroline intently as she looked at the menu. She was so beautiful, he thought, so naturally beautiful. With the weather beginning to get chilly, she no longer wore her hair in a ponytail or a French braid. Her hair was down, straight and parted down the middle. She had her hair tucked behind her ears, with just a few strands left hanging down revealing her silver earrings. Her slightly chapped cheeks were pink. He could tell she'd used just a little mascara to define her golden colored eyes and had applied a hint of brown eye shadow on her eyelids that gave her eyes depth. She was wearing faded overalls with a cream colored knitted sweater, and an earthy type of brown leather boots. The pockets of her overalls had a stuffed appearance, with her set of dormitory keys bulging in one and a bunch of tissues in the other. She seemed to have the sniffles that morning, and the sleepy look of her eyes made J. P. wonder if she was feeling bad.

"Are you feeling okay today," he asked?

"I'm not feeling too bad, but I'm not feeling great. I guess I've picked up a little cold."

"I hope you get to feeling better soon, our trip to New Jersey is only a couple of weeks away."

"I'm sure I'll be fine by then. I can drink all the orange juice I want in the cafeteria, so I'll plan to drink lots of fluids and get some rest. I'm looking forward to going up there. How many hours will it take to up to get to New Jersey?"

"From here, it may take about ten or eleven hours, depending on the weather and traffic. I'll go ahead and make a reservation here at a motel. That way Chris and I can drive up from Summerville to Rock Hill, on December 21st. We can get some decent rest in the motel and pick you up very early the next morning. We always try to leave several days before Christmas because the weather may be bad up north."

"You haven't told me much about your family, yet."

"Maybe I should warn you a little bit. Most of the people in my family are loud. They seem to have no restraint when it comes to comments or questions. My best advice would be to smile and forget about it."

"Oh, that bad?"

"I'm afraid so. They just speak their minds."

"I'm not really worried about it. It's not like I'm staying there forever."

"I don't imagine you'd want to. The South is a great place to be, and I don't think I'd ever be happy to live up north again."

"That's good to hear," she said with a grin.

Before he left to go back to Summerville, J. P. gave Caroline some extra money for her shopping trip. Mrs. Carter and Rhonda arrived just before noon. They agreed to have lunch in Charlotte and then go to the mall for an afternoon of shopping.

Rhonda tried to keep her comments to herself, but she finally tried to warn Caroline. She said, "Sistah, you have no idea how rude they can be up north."

Caroline just smiled at her, remembering how J.P. had already warned her about his family. "Remember when I went up north to meet Rinaldo Rommano's family? They gave me absolute hell about being a Southerner, like we're all dumb and as slow as old hound dogs. Rinaldo turned out to be no count, for sure."

Mrs. Carter tried to remain neutral in the conversations, as usual, and said, "Now, Rhonda, Caroline's experience could be completely different from yours."

Rhonda had to come back on that one, saying, "They're loud, in a hurry all the time, and say exactly what pops into their minds whether it's polite or not. They just as soon yell in your face, and then knock you out of their way, and mumble 'Geeze, what an idiot.'"

Then Caroline interjected, "Maybe I'll get lucky and his family will show me some respect."

"Good luck," Rhonda chimed in, "you'll probably be calling us, just bawlin', after your first day there. You'll be so miserable, you'll be begging J.P. to take you down to the bus station and have a thirty-six hour ride home between every teeny-weeny town b'tween Jersey and South Carolina."

Caroline asked jovially, "Is that what happened to you, wherever you were up north with Rocky Ricardo?"

Rhonda just looked at her with a scowl on her face. "No, I did not leave on a bus; that butt wasn't gettin' away with that, and his name was Rinaldo, you goofy thing."

Caroline was really sniggering, knowing that she'd gotten Rhonda's dander up.

Mrs. Carter said, "Maybe they'll realize that you actually have more of an education than some of them do and that you're a pretty sharp cookie. Now, don't you worry one itty biddy bit 'bout your accent. I've always taught you to use it to your advantage."

Rhonda added, "When they ask you what you want to drink, don't say gin and tonic, because some jerk will tell you that's a summer drink, and don't ask for a peach daiquiri because they'll tell you to go back to Georgia or wherever the heck you're from down south."

Mrs. Carter said, "Oh, Rhonda, behave yourself."

"Momma, Caroline's always gonna be your baby but we gotta quit shelterin' her," said Rhonda.

Caroline thought, sometimes Rhonda could be like sandpaper on a delicate antique. But Caroline suspected, from her psychology training, that Rhonda masked some deeply suppressed suffering.

Then Caroline said, "I'm not as sheltered as y'all think I am. I'll have y'all know, I could find my way around Atlanta and get home safely."

Rhonda had to say, "In your dreams, little girl. Manhattan has a lot more people than 'Et...lanta." Then all three of them laughed for a while.

Caroline loaded her shopping bags with turtle neck shirts, sweaters, and corduroy pants. She found a cute scarf, hat, and glove set. She also bought a pair of fur lined boots, and some woolen socks. She thought she was ready to handle the cold of the North, until Rhonda started again by saying, "No matter what you wear, you're still going to be freezing your butt off in New York at night."

"Well I guess we'll find some place to go where I can get warmed up," said Caroline, confidently, "or J.P. will keep me warm."

Rhonda said laughing, to get the last word in, "Yeah, right, the two of you are going to walk the streets of the city like Siamese twins."

CHAPTER 6

TALKIN'

In a few days, Caroline would be finished with her final academic semester at Winthrop. In the second semester, she'd be overrun with student teaching tasks, leaving her with very little time for relationships.

Monday afternoon, she went to the library, to turn in some books and also see if Joost was in the library. She wanted to thank him and tell him more about her relationship with J. P. She didn't want guys to play around with her feelings, and she didn't want to do the same thing to J.P. or Joost. She didn't see him anywhere on the main level of the library, but as she got to the top of the steps, she saw him sitting at a table leaning over a textbook. He looked up and saw Caroline coming toward him and gave her a warm smile indicating that he was glad to see her again.

She had no idea how she was going to bring up the events that had occurred on Friday night, but she knew she had to acknowledge his courtesy. After saying, "Hey, Joost!" she took a deep breath, and asked, "Are you doing okay?"

"Sure, I'm fine; how about you?"

"Oh, I'm good."

Then he asked, "Did you have a good birthday weekend?"

"Yes, I did. I wanted to explain a few things."

"Don't feel like you owe me explanations," he said.

"Well, I do feel like I want to talk to you about it if you have the time."

He smiled and nodded his head in approval. He stood up and pulled out a chair for her and waited for her to sit down. Then he sat back down and looked up at her smiling and said, "Okay, it's your turn if you want to tell me something."

"First of all," she said, "I want to thank you for helping me in a sticky situation. I had no idea that both you and J.P. would be coming to the office that night. You were so kind to make it easy for me in that predicament."

"Caroline," he interjected, "I like you, and I wouldn't want to cause any problems for you. I never asked you if you were dating anyone, so you owe me no explanation."

"Well I'm going to tell you anyway, if you want to listen," she said gingerly, not wanting to force herself on him.

"Okay, sure I'll listen to you," he responded.

"I met J.P. when I went home with my friend Emily to a small town near Charleston. He was very friendly and asked me to go sightseeing, have lunch at a seafood restaurant, and go down to the beach. Since that first weekend I met him, we've written letters and talked on the phone. In October, I went down to visit again, and he took me out to dinner and to the theatre. I asked him to share Thanksgiving with my family, since his parents live so far away."

Joost interjected for a moment and asked, "Are you sure you want to tell me all of this? You really don't have to. I could tell on Friday night that he seems like he's in love with you, and there seems to be a close bond between the two of you."

"I think you're right, but I still want to share it with you, because I'm trying to deal with emotional conflicts right now. You've told me enough about your life that I think you could understand how losing a parent, when you're young, can affect your relationships. That's what I'm going through right now, I think."

Joost looked at Caroline, noticing that she had tears in her eyes and asked, "Are you in love with him, too, or are you scared to fall in love with anyone?"

She looked at Joost with a penetrating gaze and said, "I knew you'd understand how I feel. I don't know if I can let go and love anyone for fear of losing that person. The thought of love scares me."

He reached out and put his hand on her forearm and said, "Let's go get something to eat so we can talk a little more freely." He knew if he didn't get her out of there she might break down at any moment, and he didn't want her to feel embarrassed in front of other students in the library. She was so emotional, she couldn't answer him, but she nodded her head indicating that she wanted to go, and then she reached into the pocket of her jeans to retrieve a tissue.

They made a rapid exit out of the library and headed across the campus. The trees were barren on campus, and the dormant grass was tan colored. It was so late in the day, the dismal cloudy sky made it seem dreary. As they walked down the cement paths in front of the classroom buildings, a large flock of Canadian geese had congregated in the grass, as if searching for green grass, and on the walkway. They warily watched as Caroline and Joost approached them. There were so many birds, they had to walk around them to continue toward the parking lot where Joost's VW van was parked. Suddenly, they heard the sound of flapping wings as the geese took flight and turned to get a glimpse as the birds formed the V shaped formation. Standing there for a moment marveling at the acts of nature, Caroline turned to Joost and said, "I've always thought it was incredible how birds instinctively know how to fly in that formation. They just seem to know exactly what they must do in life. We, as human beings, are clueless about what we need to do to make it through life."

Joost noticed how the beauty of nature seemed to calm Caroline down. He had sought that peace so many times when he was upset about his parents; when he experienced the serenity of nature it helped him to find the joy of life again. He had found that joy standing on the beaches of Spain watching the sea birds feed on the fish in the Mediterranean.

He looked at Caroline and said, "When I feel lonely, I find a place to watch the birds, to distract me from the nightmare of lost loved ones. It helps me feel that maybe life goes on, and I can be happy again."

He did understand how she felt, how tumultuous her emotional life had been. He'd experienced the 'roller coaster' of life, the ups and the downs, the good and the bad. He knew what it was like to feel paralyzed by the loneliness caused by the sting of death. He knew how approaching holidays brought both excitement but also spawned the grief of missing family members.

When the birds had all but vanished from their view, Caroline and Joost turned toward his apartment building and walked slowly and silently for a few minutes. I'm going to take you to a neat little sandwich shop that serves Bavarian style sandwiches, potato salad, and German beer," he said.

"Okay, that sounds good," she said even though she had no idea whether or not she'd like Bavarian food.

When they reached the van, Joost politely opened the door for Caroline. He walked around the front of the van, Caroline watching him unobtrusively, and then opened his door and hopped in the van being careful not to hit his head. The old VW, with the gear shift lever on the steering column, took a couple of attempts to start after Joost pushed in the clutch and turned the key. He explained that the ride might be rather bumpy since he needed to replace the tires before leaving to visit his brother's family in Asheville over Christmas. That statement opened the doorway for Caroline to tell Joost that she had plans to go to New Jersey with J. P. and his brother. She explained that his family lived very close to New York City and that she'd never been there before.

Once inside the restaurant, they ordered their food and beer. Caroline had a dark beer with a sauerbraten roast beef sandwich and potato salad. They continued trivial conversation until she switched the tone of the conversation and said, "Thank you so much for understandin' what was goin' on with me in the library and getting' me out of there so I could breathe and think."

"I've been there more than once, and somehow my friends would rescue me from my own thoughts and cheer me up." He went on, "I think you needed me to be that kind of friend to you today."

"You're right, I did," she said. "That's why I came to the library in hopes of finding you. I had to explain the situation with J.P. to someone who could understand me. Don't get me wrong, J. P. is a great guy and has been very kind to me, but I'm not sure he could understand the depth of my pain. That pain has stayed with me for so long, I don't know if it will ever leave me. I don't know if I can feel normal."

"I know that my pain has kept me from reaching out to others who need to be loved and want to love me," he said. "I have no problem socially, meeting new people, making friends, or entertaining, but I never let it get any further than that. I don't want to love either, only to lose that loved one in the end."

They both sat there looking at one another until they simultaneously refocused and sat pensively for a minute or so. Caroline was feeling so emotionally overwhelmed, she changed the conversation just a bit and asked, "So, you're going to visit with your brother's family?"

"Yeah, I need to leave here before the college near Asheville gets out for the holidays," he said. Caroline had no idea why he brought up that tidbit of information. She remained quiet but attentive in case he wanted to elaborate on that topic a little more. She felt she had no right to pry with questions, but her curiosity had been sparked and she was wondering why he was mentioning another college.

"For my first three years of college, I went to a school near Asheville. Last spring, I got caught up in some scandalous hearsay about an unfavorable situation with the daughter of a school official. It was all rumor, but the girl didn't deny it because she was obsessed with me, I was kicked out of the college for a whole semester. My brother was able to get me into Winthrop, so that I could continue to take my classes, but my time here is almost over. I'll need to return to school in North Carolina in January so I'll be able to graduate in the spring."

Caroline started to have a sickening feeling about what Joost had just told her. But, why would she let that news bother her? She wasn't dating him, and it would be possible to remain friends even with some distance between them. She remembered what Emily had said about foreigners and the "love 'em and leave 'em" syndrome. But Joost didn't love her and neither did she love him, or did she? No, she couldn't let herself love someone who was obviously the 'off limits' type, a rolling stone. If she let herself fall in love, it should be with someone who seemed to adore her, someone grounded on her own soil, someone like J.P. She halted her thoughts and tried to come up with something to continue the dialogue between herself and Joost.

"Oh, I'm sorry to hear you're leaving."

"I like it here; it gets very cold in the mountains and I don't want to go back there," he said. "I need to graduate this spring and start graduate school in the fall to continue to qualify for the money I receive from Holland, because I'm a Dutch citizen. If I stay at Winthrop, I won't have enough credits to graduate in the spring."

Caroline felt envious for a moment, but she came to her senses, reminding herself that Joost had lost both of his parents. What amount of money could make up for losing both of your parents?

Empathetically, she said, "I can only imagine what you went through. I'm so fortunate to have at least one parent still with me."

Both of them sat there thinking as they ate slowly. Joost thought about Caroline wanting to share with him, coming to the library to find him. He thought about the fact that Caroline wouldn't say that she was in love with J.P. He thought she'd never be forward with him even if she was beginning to care for him, or care more for him than she did for J.P. He liked her and realized that it was more than just a superficial friendship that he'd had with girls in the past. He could feel her intense emotions as she talked to him, and he began to feel again as she listened to him. He'd refused to feel anything for anyone for a long time, since his mother's tragic accident. Here was this sweet girl, able to understand his feelings, and he felt touched by her spirit. He liked to spend time with her; she could keep him laughing, and he stopped focusing on his grief with that laughter. He shared his grief with her because she understood which seemed to ease the sting of it. He wished that he could stay at Winthrop, but he knew he had to return to school in the cold mountains and leave his warm hearted friend.

In deep thought, Caroline found herself wishing that Joost wouldn't have to leave. There was something about him, a magnetic force, drawing her to him for friendship, companionship, or maybe a relationship. She felt confused by her own thoughts and unsure of herself. That wasn't what she felt earlier as they walked across the wintry campus and shared the excitement of watching the Canadian geese fly away. That wasn't what she felt in the library when he tried to console her. That wasn't what she felt when he showed up at the dormitory office on her birthday. Why does he have to be so wonderful and still have to leave before she finds out what could be between them? Maybe this is another sign - her momma would believe it to be a sign from God - that she should steer clear of this foreigner. She hated to have to think about these kinds of things, stigmas, attitudes and fears. She'd much rather go through life excited by one serendipitous experience after another. Life had to be too safe, too predictable, for her, but she wished she could let go of that and truly feel free to live and enjoy her fate.

She washed down a bite of her sandwich with a swig of dark beer, and looked up at Joost. He was nursing his own bottle of dark beer but stopped drinking when he noticed she was looking at him again. She had a flashback to the night of her first date with J.P. when she wondered what if felt like to be in love. Her emotions were churning inside of her, but she wanted to forget about everything except the events of the moment.

When they got back to the campus, Joost asked Caroline, "Would you like to come see some photos of my family? Our apartment has a little sitting area next to the kitchen where we could visit. Santoso is probably there studying at the desk in his room."

Caroline told herself that this was no different than going to J.P.s house the first night she met him, and she had a strange fascination that this might be one of those serendipitous events she'd been wondering about. She asked Joost, jokingly, "Are you sure you'll behave? Or better yet, are you sure I'll behave?"

Joost laughed heartily and said, "I'm not sure about you."

She knew from the look on his face he was teasing her, so she had no qualms about going. They parked the van, entered the building, and began the ascent to the second floor of the old apartment building. The stairwell was narrow and felt damp and chilly; their voices reverberated in the passageway. Once they got to the hallway it was warm and quiet. She looked at Joost, a tall and exceptionally good looking European, and she felt like she was a thousand miles away, not at Winthrop at all.

As Joost opened the door, Caroline could see the starkness of the kitchen and sitting area. She was quite surprised to see an immaculate kitchen. There was a small round dinette table with two matching chairs separating the kitchen from the sitting area. There was also an ugly gold upholstered sofa, an avocado colored vinyl armchair, and a simple coffee table, all of which were dated. The walls of the apartment were painted with the same dark beige paint used in the hallways, a sickening color. At least her dorm had some color, even if it was green.

Joost called out to Santoso to see if he was in his bedroom, but he got no answer. For just a moment, Caroline felt a little strange being there alone with Joost. She sat down on the sofa, and Joost offered to get her a cola. He filled two tall plastic tumblers with ice and poured the drinks from a two liter plastic bottle. He then set the tumblers on the coffee table, but he accidentally bumped the tumbler closest to Caroline, overturning it. Within a matter of seconds, the contents flowed over the side of the table and soaked the right leg of Caroline's jeans. His face turned so red, he almost looked like a sunburned Scotsman. He ran to the kitchen to grab the roll of paper towels as the drink continued to spill onto the floor. It was so obvious to Caroline that he was more than embarrassed, but she felt the overwhelming need to laugh. She tried to hold back her laughter to the point that her shoulders were moving up and down, and sounds were coming from the side of her mouth and her nostrils, as her breath tried to escape. He noticed her effort to conceal her sniggering. He suddenly started laughing, and they were howling together.

When all of the mess was cleaned up, he excused himself to get his photo album from his bedroom. As Caroline watched him walk out of the room, she thought of her first visit to J.Ps house, with Sebastian's dog hair all over the sofa and a big mess in the kitchen. What a contrast between his place and Joost's. The thought made her want to giggle again to herself, but she remained composed. She didn't want Joost to think she was excessively jovial and misconstrue her mood as mocking him in any way.

Joost came back holding a leather covered photo album and a pair of worn, brown corduroy pants. He looked at her, a deep penetrating look, as if he could read her mind, and she felt like he could. He sat down on the sofa next to her and set the photo album on the opposite side of the coffee table. He handed her the pair of his pants and said, "You can go in bathroom, just off Santoso's room, and put these dry pants on, if you'd like to. I feel terrible to have made such a mess and gotten your pants wet."

"Don't," she exclaimed!

She did, in fact, go into the other room. She held up the pants and wondered if she could fit her butt into them. She peeled off her wet pants and put on Joost's pants. It felt bizarre to be wearing his pants, the legs being about five to six inches too long. And there she was, coming out of the bathroom and standing in the middle of some stranger's bedroom looking in the mirror, how uncharacteristic of Caroline Bethany Carter!

She went back into the living room, nearly tripping on the long legs of the pants. He was smiling at her with her every step. She sat back down next to him. She pushed her back to the sofa, exhaled loudly, and said emphatically, "You're one skinny butt man, 'cus I'm 'bout to die in these tight pants."

He understood enough of what she said to get the drift, and the roaring laughter began again. He went over to the kitchen and said, "Let's try this again," and he started to refill the empty tumbler with soda.

As he slowly opened his photo album, she felt connected to him.

"I feel honored that you asked me to see your pictures," she commented. She was thinking what each photo must mean to him, a simplistic commemoration of his parents that he could no longer interact with, at least not in an earthly realm, images to keep their memories alive, as though they'd vanish in a mist.

As Joost turned the page of the album, she could see a large photo of his father, obviously a distinguished businessman, accepting an award from his company. She thought to herself that Joost must have gotten more of his mother's physical traits, because he seemed to show little resemblance to his father, a dark haired mature man.

The next page of the album brought tears to Joost's eyes. It was a picture of his mother holding the hand of four year old Joost with his sun bleached hair and a cute little smile on his face. He commented, "This is the day we left Holland to move to Spain with my dad. My mother was both excited and scared. She didn't speak Spanish at all and had reservations about going. As a matter of fact, she never learned much Spanish, just enough to communicate to her maids and garden caretakers. She had to keep a Spanish dictionary in her purse at all times."

The following pages of the album were filled with pictures of special events of the family, weddings, births of his nieces and nephews, special award's banquets, etc. Caroline confirmed her awareness that Joost had grown up in an affluent European lifestyle. An uncomfortable thought struck her sensibility, knowing that her upbringing was so different; there were no formal affairs in her childhood.

The back of the photo album was filled with pictures of Joost at different ages and in various locations. Caroline liked the photo of him at about the age of sixteen, tall and tanned, his hair bleached by the sun, standing next to his brother's catamaran resting on the shore of the Mediterranean. What a life, a life that she'd never know.

It was getting late and she finally told Joost that she needed to get back to her place. Walking back to her dorm, the night air was brisk and cool. Joost had his hands tucked into the pockets of his jacket and the collar of his jacket turned upward to keep the air from making his neck feel chilled. By the time they reached the dorm lobby, their noses and cheeks were pink. He gave her a big, brotherly type hug as they said goodnight and parted before she went up to her room. She used the restroom, and got undressed, being careful to hang Joost's pants over her chair. She turned her radio to her favorite local station and put on her headphones, before crawling under the soft comforter on her bed.

Caroline woke up the next morning, with the headphones on her pillow, to the sound of a mellow folk song. She sat up in bed and began her morning ritual of brushing out the tangled mass of hair at the nape of her neck. She rose from bed to stumble to her bathroom, the lyrics of the song fading as she moved further away from the headphones. As usual, she brushed and flossed her teeth before getting in the shower. The shower of warm water flowed over her shoulders, and the lyrics of that song replayed in her mind. The past months had given many of those days she'd like to experience again with both J.P. and Joost. A flood of emotions overwhelmed her as she came to the conclusion that she wasn't in love with anyone at this point in her life. Life is like a dream, played out day by day, she thought, and one never knows exactly what the next day will bring. The events of life can't be controlled. She'd been all wrong by trying to plan and plan, hoping that a clear course of action would assure her of having little or none of life's disappointments in her future. She'd be out on her own in a matter of months and had a choice. She could suffocate herself with fear, or she could really live, serendipitously.

The phone was ringing, but she didn't try to answer it. Instead, she took time drying off using her thick, terrycloth beach towel, wrapped it around her, and went to unplug her headphones so she could hear the music on the radio. She sprayed her hair with detangler and started the arduous task of drying her hair with a travel sized blow-dryer on its last leg. The blow-dryer just made her static problem worse, and she thought she looked like she'd just touched a Van de Graff generator every time she finished drying her beautiful long hair. After surveying her new clothes and deciding she had more than enough for her trip, she selected a comfortable pair of sweatpants.

Caroline came back to her room after her classes. She didn't want to go to the library to study because she thought she'd see Joost and wouldn't keep her mind on her studies. She didn't want him to think she was pursuing him. About four o'clock the phone rang. Wondering who would be calling, she made sure she got to the phone this time. It was Emily, saying that she'd tried to get her that morning, and she wanted to come over and talk to Caroline. She told Emily to come on over, thinking something must be up with her or she wouldn't have called her early in the morning.

About ten minutes later, Emily knocked on the door. Caroline opened the door and said, "Hey, what's up with you?"

"Not much, I just wanted to talk to you," Emily said. From the tone of Emily's voice, Caroline thought she might be in a serious mood.

"Well, just in case you or some of our friends saw me walking across the campus with Joost last night, I want to assure you that it's not a big deal with him."

"So, tell me more about that," said Emily.

"It's sort of a long tale."

"Oh don't tell me you had some big mess happen on your birthday with your admirers," Emily said, with curiosity.

"Actually, it was not a big mess at all, but it sure could've been."

"I already know J. P. showed up because I stopped by their house, and Butch said that he'd taken off to surprise you for your birthday. So what happened?"

Caroline walked over to her tiny refrigerator and said, "I think we're both going to need something cold to drink while we talk about this one." She then proceeded to tell Emily the entire story about J.P. and Joost both coming to the dorm office at the same time. She looked over at Emily, started laughing and said, "You better close your mouth before flies get in there." They both giggled like two sixth graders.

"So when Joost left, what did J.P. say about all of it," Emily asked?

"He really didn't say much because Joost's performance was enough to put his mind at ease if he was wondering if something was going on. To tell you the truth, I don't think guys are suspicious and jealous like women are."

Emily responded, "I bet they can be, but they don't want to show it."

Caroline asked Emily, "So, what's so important that made you call me twice today?

Emily reached in her bag and pulled out a small neatly wrapped gift and said, "For one thing, Goofy, I wanted to give you this and wish you a Happy Birthday, belated of course."

"Emily, that's awfully sweet of you," She opened the gift to find a nice key chain. "Now, I can keep my own room key separate from the dorm keys. Thanks, so much."

"You're welcome," responded Emily. "I did come to talk to you about something else."

Now Caroline's curiosity was aroused, noticing that Emily had more of a serious look on her face. She said, "Okay, let me hear it."

"I know you're planning to go up to New Jersey with J.P. for Christmas. I don't want to gossip, but my brother told me something I thought I might need to tell you.

"So, what on earth is it, Emily," asked Caroline?

"He said that J. P. was engaged to a girl when he was a student at Clemson. Apparently, the wedding date had been set, and he took her to Jersey to meet his parents. His mother had planned an engagement party, but the girl didn't know anything about it. She was overwhelmed with the pressure involved with dealing with a bunch of rude acting people, who were all strangers, and none of her family present. She was bombarded incessantly with questions and was totally unprepared to deal with it all. To make a long story short, there was a big break up later on.

I didn't want you going up there and get caught up in some kind of drama about something you knew nothing about."

"Well, my relationship with J. P. is not at that level, so I really don't think I'll be that uncomfortable. I do appreciate you telling me and trying to spare me from possible confusion and embarrassment," said Caroline. She guessed as far as dark secrets are concerned, this part of J. P.'s past was not a major concern to her, unless something about the break up was really strange. To change the subject, they spent a while talking about how to mix and match Caroline's new winter wardrobe followed by an early dinner together. Nothing was discussed about Joost because Caroline wanted to keep that to herself. Emily was her best friend, but Caroline didn't divulge any of her emotional issues with her, feeling like she wouldn't understand the inner conflicts that she struggled with.

Due to scheduling conflicts, Caroline called J. P. and asked him to plan to make a hotel reservation in Greenville rather than Rock Hill, and they would need to leave from there. As they talked, his enthusiasm lighted a flame again for her in terms of their relationship. Why had she been shying away from him and letting herself connect with Joost? Now she knew Joost would be leaving campus soon, and chances were she'd never see him again. She forced the thought of Joost out of her mind and expressed her excitement about the trip to J.P.

She saw Joost only one more time that week. They ran into one another in the cafeteria and ate breakfast together. He asked her for her mailing address, and she gladly gave it to him. She wished him well and let him know how much she appreciated his friendship, his warmth and understanding.

CHAPTER 7
TRAVELIN'

At last the day arrived for Caroline to leave with J.P. and Chris and travel north. They picked her up at eight o'clock that morning. Her momma handed her a Christmas card containing two hundred dollars. Caroline left her momma smiling, wishing them a safe trip and encouraging Caroline to see as much as she could of New York City. Getting in the car, J.P. noticed Caroline looking a bit teary eyed. Once inside the Toyota, she looked at J.P. and said, "I'm okay. I just wish my momma had the chance to do this, too. One day, I'll take her to see NYC."

"Sure you will," he said reassuringly.

Within minutes they were driving north on Interstate 85. It would have been a little less driving if Caroline had stayed at school, but J.P. and Chris certainly understood that she didn't want to stay there any longer than she had to and wanted to see her family for a few days before she left with them.

Chris spoke up and asked her, "Caroline, have you ever been away from home at Christmastime?"

Rather embarrassed because she suddenly felt like a baby, she answered, "No, I haven't been away from my family before, during the holidays."

J.P. started laughing and said, "Don't start picking on her just cus she's a girl."

Then he said to Caroline, "He's never been away from his family before either, cus he's always with me."

Chris turned as red as a beet and, with his best attempt to speak with a drawl, he said to J.P., "Alright, dog breath. Looks like we gone be gettin' even with each other the whole time we on this trip."

"Who are you to be talking 'bout gettin' even with me," asked J.P? "You look like a tree boa, all curled up in that little back seat with your gargantuan legs and that hideous green sweater you have on."

"Are y'all gonna act like two birds in a cock fight all the way to Jersey," Caroline asked, and sniggering between the phrases in the sentence?

All three of them started laughing hard, just like they were family, and Caroline began to feel comfortable.

"Me and my brother and sister used to fight like cats and dogs every time we got in the car," commented Caroline. "It got so bad, my momma used to keep a hickory switch under the car seat, and she'd whip it out to pop our legs."

In earnest, Chris asked, "What in the world is a hickory switch?"

Caroline started laughing louder and asked, "You been to Clemson, and you don't know what a hickory switch is? It's a thin branch from a tree that kids get their butts tore up with if they don't behave. My granny calls every butt whuppin' switch a hickory switch, no matter what tree she gets it from. You don't mess around where Granny can hear you, 'cus she can sting some butt."

"Oh, I don't know how I missed that information when I was at Clemson," responded Chris.

"I do," said J.P. "You missed a lot of things, little brother. You spent too much time getting' drunk."

"Look who's talking," said Chris in his own defense. "You were found passed out on the couch most of your college career. You didn't even need a bed."

J.P. chuckled and said, "I guess you got me on that one. I had to sleep close to the bathroom, in case I had to hurl." Then he said to Caroline, "I know I just grossed you out, but you might as well know that side of me, too. Hope you're ready to listen to some music instead of all this mudslinging? I'm not sure what he's going to tell next."

They drove on for about an hour and a half, listening to music and chatting intermittently, while Chris snoozed in the cramped back seat of the tiny Toyota Corolla. Caroline hadn't eaten much that morning because she didn't want to have a nervous upset stomach.

When they got past most of the exits in Charlotte, she said, "Maybe we should stop on the other side of Shawlet if we see anywhere we can get some bald p-nuts and grape soda? I'm pretty hungry now since I didn't eat much before we left."

"Bald p-nuts," questioned J.P., just to tease her?

"Yeah, you know, bald p-nuts, goobers, hot boiled peanuts.'

"I know what they are. I was just picking at you," he said, as he thumped her leg with his middle finger.

She hollered at him to quit and woke Chris up.

They did see a tourist trap, with a little portable cart housing a large steaming pot of boiled peanuts in the parking lot in front of the store. When Caroline got out of the car, she said, "It's cold as all-get out." They rushed into the store, and quickly located the restrooms. The country store was filled with jars of homemade preserves and local honey, antique bins filled with hard candy, salt-water taffy, and a variety of nuts. There were tables, like the ones found in a vegetable market, covered with toys, like pop-guns and sling-shots, and coon skin caps. Caroline walked back to the drink cooler and found a bottle of grape soda. J.P. and Chris both got bottles of root beer, one bag of chips, and one bag of pork rinds. *Caroline was thinking that pork rinds are so nasty.*

Caroline said, squinting and causing her nostrils to flair just a bit, "I can't stand to drink root beer.

J.P. commented, "And you don't like to eat Brussel's sprouts for breakfast."

"Good memory," she said. "Now let's go outside in the artic wind and get some hot bald p-nuts for me."

She was quite satisfied with her snack, and as J.P. drove on the interstate, she slept for a while until they came to the exit for Oxford, North Carolina. As J.P. started to pull off the interstate, she was trying to wake up. She noticed old tobacco barns, junked trucks popular in the fifties, and a rooster farm, probably used to supply birds for illegal cockfighting. They were able to find an old gas station next to a greasy spoon café'. They stopped for lunch. Oddly enough, all three of them ordered country fried steak, with rice and gravy, green beans, and biscuits. The waitress automatically brought out a pitcher of sweet tea and ice filled glasses.

She asked, as she smacked her chewing gum, "All y'all drank sweet tea, don't ya?"

Caroline told her tea would be just fine.

Then the waitress asked, "Where y'all from?"

Caroline laughed and said, "I'm from Greenville, South Carolina, but these two carpetbaggers are from New Jersey. They sort of migrated south and ended up at Clemson. You might as well serve 'em because they do love our Southern style food."

The waitress just stood there, smacking that gum and looking bewildered, probably because she had no idea what a carpetbagger was.

The guys were about to crack up listening to Caroline make small talk with the redneck waitress. J.P. was sitting right next to her and nudged her in the side with his elbow. She really started giggling, tried to take a swig of her sweet tea, and almost strangled on it.

The country waitress screamed, "Oh no, she's choking her brains out." She was slinging her hands and saying, "We gotta do something, Lord have mercy."

Caroline was able to shake her head from side to side and wave her hand dismissively to indicate that she was okay.

Finally, a little dumpy man called out from behind the counter, "Norma Jean, settle down and come get this order of fried catfish 'fore it gets cold."

Chris said, "This is about as funny as an episode of Gomer Pyle. I love it. Are you going to put on this kind of drama when we get to Mom and Dad's house?"

Caroline replied immediately, "No way! They're gonna think I just graduated from Vanderbilt."

J.P laughed, with an infectious kind of laugh, and said, "They'll never believe a woman with a degree from Vanderbilt would be spending Christmas with derelicts like the two of us."

The three of them had a blast together, eating, talking, and telling redneck jokes, Caroline being a ringleader in the joking but trying to keep the guys from getting too loud. They were absolutely stuffed by the time Norma Jean came back to their table and asked if they were ready for some fresh apple cobbler.

J.P. spoke up, trying his best to act like he was a local, and said, "Cain't do it. I'll bust for shore iffin I eat one more bite. Just brang me the check, darlin'. And fix us up some of 'at cobbler to go."

They chuckled all the way out the door of the café.

Chris took over the driving. Caroline sat in the back seat to give J.P. some leg room since he'd been driving several hours. The sky turned gloomy grey, and J.P. predicted that they might run into some nasty weather further north. As Chris drove, J.P. fell asleep quickly in the passenger's seat. Caroline pulled out her journal and started to write about the antics of the day. It felt good to be away from the pressure of school and work on campus. She was just having a good time. By tomorrow, she'd be smack dab in the middle of Manhattan, astounded by the skyscrapers, subways, and millions of people. What excitement she felt! She'd have so much to tell Momma, Rhonda and Troy on New Year's Day.

By the time they reached the point to take Interstate 95 north, Caroline was getting pretty restless even though they'd already made a long pit stop in Virginia. From what J.P. had told her about the trip, she knew they were about half way to their destination. It was raining when they took a break at a rest stop; the air was getting colder and the late afternoon seemed like nearly evening. After their break J. P. took over driving, and Caroline reclaimed the passenger's seat to be able to talk to him.

"Have you thought about what we would do in Manhattan," she asked?

"Actually, I haven't given it any thought yet. We usually just go over and do what we feel like at the time. I'm not very experienced as a tour guide for someone who's never been there before. I've only taken a couple of Rebels to the city." He paused. "What do you think you'd like to see first?"

She laughed and asked, "Do you mean Rebels or Rednecks? I think it would be cool to see the Statue of Liberty and the World Trade Center," she said. "You'ont to go there?"

He loved how her language fluctuated between correct grammar, everyday speech, and colloquial sayings. She was cute and kept him laughing a lot.

"That's in the same general area of the city. We can go down and see the statue from the park. We won't be there long cus it's gonna be colder than a witch's tit," he said like a redneck. "I still think we're going to run into some snow in the next couple of hours."

Snow at Christmastime sounded thrilling to Caroline, but she had no idea that she was about to be in the coldest weather she'd ever experienced. As she was growing up, there might have been one or two snow storms a year. Most of the time, there were ice storms rather than snow storms, the type that weighted the branches of the pines causing them to break and hit the power lines. Her mother always kept flashlights, candles and matches, and snack items and other food that didn't require cooking. Losing electricity in a storm was expected, although many people didn't take heed and ended up unprepared.

She asked J.P., "Were there any winter storms when you were at Clemson?"

"Yeah, we got the biggest kick out of seeing how the people down south react to winter storms. You go in the grocery store to buy beer and peanuts, and the entire community is in the store buying supplies, long lines at each register, people standing there with a loaf of bread, a gallon of milk, some eggs, and cookies. I never understood why they were buying eggs."

Caroline laughed and asked, "Don't you know when a storm is comin' you boil eggs? We love boiled eggs, deviled eggs, egg salad sandwiches, or sliced boiled eggs on white bread with mayonnaise. It's better than peanut butter and jelly sandwiches or cold cereal."

"Didn't know that," he replied, smiling. "We just stuck to peanuts and beer."

Then she asked, "Didn't you ever lose power in winter storms when you were growing up in the north?"

"Occasionally, we did. I guess we just ate what was there in the pantry, sardines and crackers, canned fruit cocktail or applesauce, nuts, those kinds of things."

"Sardines," she asked? "How could you eat sardines? I'd feel like I was eating someone's pet fish."

He laughed at her and said, "We ate our pet fish, too, if we ran out of other food."

"Oh, you did not just tell me that," she said as she pinched his arm.

"You better stop or we'll have a wreck and be stranded on the side of the highway when the worse winter storm of the year arrives." He had her spooked for a moment, and she sat there quietly. "Oh, I'm just kidding. We'll be fine."

As the hours of driving passed, Caroline noticed the mixture of urban and rural scenes along the highway, but it was difficult to see much in the darkness. By the time they were bypassing Baltimore, the snow was falling rapidly, and it began to blanket the ground to the left and right of the highway. Chris was driving. J.P. was sleeping in the passenger's seat. Caroline rested her head on her travel pillow, snuggled up under her warm overcoat, and fell asleep.

She was awakened hours later, in the wee hours of the morning, to the sounds of transfer trucks surrounding the Toyota in the middle of a traffic jam. J.P. woke up and said, laughing, "Welcome to Jersey." Horns were honking and truckers looked irritated. She'd never seen so many trucks before in her life. She'd always wondered how so many people living in such a small geographical area got necessary goods.

"This is a daily occurrence up here," said Chris. "Don't think we've ever come home before, at this hour, and not gotten caught up in a traffic jam, with lots of eighteen wheelers trying to rush into the city to make early morning deliveries. Traffic is just a part of life in a heavily populated metropolitan area. You can't really avoid it."

They were stuck in that traffic jam nearly an hour. For the first time in days, she thought of Joost. She was glad to know he was with his family, enjoying the company of his nephew. What would it be like for her to be with him right now? As the holiday approached, could he comfort her with the understanding he felt from his own loss? She better hold her horses and stop thinking about him; it was just going to get her all depressed. J.P. had been as sweet as he could be to her, and she was going to see New York City. She wanted to be distracted by things she'd never seen before. She didn't want to have old pain resurface as it had done most of her life at this time of year.

Finally the traffic started moving, and they crossed lanes to the exit. Within minutes, they were driving through a crowded residential area and J.P. said, "We got about three more blocks." The tall houses were sandwiched side by side with nothing but tiny walkways between them. The snow on the streets had already been plowed, and a salt and sand mixture covered the streets. Mounds of snow pushed over by the plows were covered with a spray of the sand, making it look nasty to Caroline. The street lights illuminated the snow covered sidewalks and steps leading up to the houses, and she could see light snow still falling. Caroline had never seen houses so close to the streets, with absolutely no front yards, room only to plant a few shrubs next to the steps.

They pulled off to the side of the street. J.P. said, "Here she is, Home Sweet Home. Stay here just a minute." He got out of the car and jumped over a mound of snow, almost falling when he landed on the other side. He walked to the side of the house and got a large flat aluminum shovel, with a rather short handle. He walked back to the mound of snow, probably covering the walking path to the house and shoveled enough snow to create a narrow path for Caroline to walk safely to the steps. He knew Caroline needed to get into the house as quickly as he did since they'd been sitting in the traffic jam for such a long time. He figured Chris' bladder was about to explode, too.

J.P. went back to the car to help Caroline get out and held her hand as she navigated up the front steps to the house. He retrieved the key from the family hiding place, unlocked the door and then directed her to the bathroom. Once relieved, she looked in the mirror and thought, Oh man, I look like I've been on a three day drunk. Although she needed to spruce up a bit, she didn't stay in the bathroom long so the guys could use it.

A lamp had been left on to light the living room. Caroline went in and sat on the sofa waiting for J. P. while he and Chris unloaded the car. The furnishings in the living room were purposefully sparse, a crisp clean look. The sofa had been covered with an egg shell white slip cover, with its straight modern lines marked by fabric covered piping. Blue and white needlepoint cushions rested on the arms of the sofa. The sleek end tables and coffee table were designed with the base made of metal and the top made from a blond colored wood, probably Beech. A single fluted glass bowl filled with hard candy was on the coffee table next to a few magazines, perfectly fanned to make them look decorative. Two large portraits of J.P. and his brother, with white wooden frames, were on each side of the entryway, and she couldn't help but notice how cute J.P. was, in what looked like his high school senior picture. His dirty blond hair, wire rimmed glasses, and winter paleness made him look like a Scandinavian youth. He must have been wearing contacts since she'd met him because she'd never seen him wearing glasses.

J. P. soon joined Caroline, reading a note left by his mom, giving them instructions about where to sleep. Mrs. Andersen had also written that she'd prepare brunch and awaken them about eleven o'clock.

J.P. laughed at Chris as he came into the room and said, "Looks like mom started writing the holiday agenda. As usual, she'll be ticked off at us if we don't abide by it."

Chris questioned, "So, what else is new? I hope she doesn't tell us we're expected to be here for dinner at a certain time. We usually end up making her mad at us the first day we're here cus we're over at an Irish pub, getting so drunk we can barely get back to Jersey by train."

Caroline commented, "Y'all are awful; better show some respect for your elders."

J.P. said, "We don't mean anything by it." In a whisper, he said, "Our mom's just the type of person that manages everything. We finally assured her last year that we were old enough to buy our own underwear." They all wanted to laugh but didn't want to wake anyone up.

Caroline scanned the living room and then asked J.P., "Where's the Christmas tree? Danish people do have Christmas trees, don't they?"

"Well, that's always been a big secret around here," he replied but gave no more explanation. "Let's all go upstairs and get a little sleep before mom rouses us in a few hours. I'm beat."

When Caroline got to the top of the stairwell, she was sure a roaring lion was in the next room. She looked at J.P. with horror on her face.

"Sorry, I forgot to tell you about Dad's snoring, but I did bring you some earplugs. I'll get them for you."

She went to the upstairs bathroom to get ready for bed. When she looked in the mirror, she put her hand over her mouth to muffle her laughter, but wasn't sure whether to laugh or cry. What had she done? She was far away from home, in a house with no Christmas tree, and sleeping next to a roaring lion. She might as well be a foreign missionary. She brushed and flossed and headed for her room. By the time her head hit the pillow, with her ears stuffed with soft rubber, she was out.

Later that morning J.P. came in to awaken Caroline at five minutes after eleven. The smell of sausage and bacon and fresh baked goods made her realize how hungry she was. J.P. told her he'd be back in a couple of minutes to get her. She went into the bathroom to wash her face and brush her teeth. Then she went back to her room and got started dealing with the tangled rat's nest of hair at the nape of her neck. Once her hair was detangled, she slipped a cream colored turtleneck sweater over her head, brushed her hair once more, and braided it in one long braid secured at the end with a satin covered rubber band. She wished she had time to get a shower before brunch, but she didn't want to keep everyone waiting if the meal was prepared. What pressure she felt to display her best manners, self-imposed pressure. Little did she know that her best manners might not measure up to that of some Yankees who seem to take pride in making all Southerners look inferior and think that even university graduates are nothing more than glorified hillbillies.

J.P. knocked on the door to see if she was ready to go down to meet his parents. Simply the fact that she was far from home and in a stranger's house made her feel nervous. As she opened the door, he thought she looked awfully pale. With genuine concern he asked, "Are you feeling okay?"

She answered, "Feels like I'm making ice cream."

J. P. looked at her with a puzzled look but smiling because he already knew she had a good sense of humor, too. "Making ice cream when it's this cold outside," he asked, to play along with her?

"Yeah.....churning some cream, sugar, vinegar and motor oil with gastric juice."

"Yuck, Caroline," he said with his face contorted. He put his hand on her shoulder and said with consolation, "They're different, but they're just plain people, too. Mom might put on airs a little, but don't think anything of it. Southern women are a lot more realistic and compassionate; that's why I like y'all so much."

She raised her shoulders, neck and head and asked with sass, "What do you mean by y'all?"

"I don't mean y'all, literally. Let me rephrase that statement," he said. "That's why I like you so much; you're such a cutie pie. You're strong, intelligent, beautiful, and compassionate."

With his admonition, she felt she could hold her own with anyone, even his parents. She stepped back and looked at herself in the mirror. She stared intently, while J.P. watched her, and said to herself, "You're about to embark on a new adventure, Miss Priss."

Then she turned to J.P. and said, "Let's go do this, 'cus I'm hon...gry." She was stretching her words out like stretching a well chewed piece of bubble gum.

They began the descent down the wide stairwell with large bulky handrails covered by numerous coats of paint over the years. When they entered the small kitchen, Chris was sitting there with a cup of coffee and said, "We've got a real Southern belle for y'all to meet."

J.P. leaned his head through the doorway, putting his arm around Caroline, and said to Chris, "You wish you had one like her, too." He then took Caroline by the hand and leaned in the opposite direction to kiss his mother. She then kissed both of them and welcomed Caroline to their home but never managed to make eye contact with her. As J.P. had said she would, his mom called him Paul.

His father rose from his seat, kissed Caroline first, and gave J.P. a strong hug. He turned back to Caroline, and said, "We're glad you made it here safely, dear," seeming much more genuinely friendly than did his wife.

Caroline longed to feel a true sense of relief. She'd been thinking she was about to devoured by a school of piranhas. So far, it was tense but tolerable.

The kitchen was extremely small; there were only two chairs at the little round breakfast table. Mrs. Andersen said, "We're going to eat in the dining room, of course." J.P. knew hell would freeze over before his mother would ever let a guest eat in the kitchen, even if there had been sufficient space. Formality was the order of her life.

J.P. turned around and led Caroline into the other room. A large formal antique dining table, draped with a white lace tablecloth, was covered with glass and silver bowls and plates of food. Caroline could tell that much of the brunch, such as the cheese plate and bowl of ambrosia, had been prepared ahead of time. Croissants and a variety of bagels were beautifully arranged on a glass tray covered with a white paper doily. A loaf of nut bread had been placed next to several small bowls filled with softened cream cheese, butter, jam, and marmalade. Dainty juice glasses and a crystal pitcher full of orange juice had been placed at the end of the table. There was also a brilliantly polished, silver platter of deli cold cuts on the table. The table was set with lovely glass plates and white linen napkins exquisitely folded into triangles standing upright on the plates. Ornate stainless steel silverware had been meticulously placed to complete the table setting. Mrs. Andersen walked into the room holding a silver plated bread basket full of hot rolls, and Mr. Andersen brought in a tray of freshly cooked breakfast meat.

Caroline was seated and looked up and noticed an impressive display of Danish Christmas plates on the wall above the massive antique sideboard topped with tall silver candlesticks, blue and white Danish figurines, and several German figurines. Looking at Mrs. Andersen, Caroline commented, "The plates and figurines are beautiful."

Mrs. Andersen explained, "We started receiving the plates as gifts from family and friends when Ejnar and I got married. We've been married for thirty years so the collection is large now."

Caroline was thinking how different this was from how her family entertained guests and felt a little homesick for her momma's crab dip, fresh homemade ham biscuits, and greasy hot sausage balls, placed on a table covered by a red vinyl tablecloth with a poinsettia in the center of the table. There was no fancy décor, but it was beautiful to her, and the aromas brought back memories of past holidays.

She looked around and noticed that everyone started serving themselves and eating without saying a blessing. With her eyes wide open and a smile on her face, she said a silent prayer, *Thank you Jesus for helping me keep my foot out of my mouth, so far, and thank you for this food.* She partook like the rest of them and listened to the conversation hoping that a question would not come soon. Mr. Andersen was quiet while his wife told her sons the latest local news of engagements, marriages, births and deaths. Caroline endured the discussions, eating each bite of her ambrosia as slowly as she could. She figured no questions would be asked while her mouth was full. She noticed one glass plate on the table filled with some meat that looked totally alien to her. J.P. held up the plate and asked her, "Would you like to try some pickled herring?"

Heavens no, she didn't want pickled herring today when she had a hankerin' for sausage balls and ham biscuits. She smiled sweetly and said, "No thank you. I might try some at another time."

When she was jam-packed and couldn't hold another bite, the inevitable occurred, and Caroline was bombarded with questions. "Where does your family live? How many siblings do you have? Your mother is a teacher, isn't she? Are your grandparents still living? Caroline answered each question as politely as she could. She would no sooner spit out the answer to one question before another one would be asked. What are your interests and hobbies? Where do you attend college? Do you have a lot of friends? What is your major? She was relentless. What kind of social interaction do you have with your peers? Do you belong to a sorority? When will you graduate? What are your plans after graduation?"

With each question, the content began to get more and more personal, and Caroline felt like she was target of some inquisition. J.P. spoke up to break the cycle of questions, and Caroline thought, *Thank you Lord, he's goin' to shut her up.* She breathed a sigh of relief, slowly and restrained, never showing the rise and fall of her chest, never letting J.P.'s mother see that she made her feel like a cat on a hot tin roof.

He said, "Mom, once again, you've outdone yourself preparing a fabulous brunch. Can we help you clear the table and clean up the kitchen before we head over to the city?"

"Oh, no Paul, your father and I will take care of it. You two boys go show Caroline the sights in Manhattan. I have to warn you though; it's going to be very cold outside today."

Caroline was hoping she wouldn't freeze in the blustery wind in the city. She excused herself to go take a shower and clad herself in the warmest clothes she owned. By the time she was fully dressed, she felt like a two ton cow in a leotard. She could barely move, and she had no idea how she was going to walk once she put on her heavy woolen overcoat. She cautiously descended down the stairs hoping that J.P. would be waiting for her in the living room. No such luck, his mom was sitting there reading and looked up at her, with her head tilted down peering over the top of her tortoise shell reading glasses. *Lord, help me to answer her meddlesome questions and get out of here ASAP, and please never ask me to move to New Jersey. No hot grits this morning, or homemade biscuits with sausage gravy, and I feel so homesick.*

"You look like you're ready to battle the bitter cold," commented Mrs. Andersen. "Have you ever been up north before in the winter?"

That woman can talk so fast, there ain't no separation between her words. Caroline finally deciphered the question and answered her. "No ma'am, I've nevah been up north at all; hope I'm ready for the cold," she said, as she looked out the window to see that more snow had fallen while she slept earlier in the day, and J.P. was out clearing the pathway again.

"I'm glad to see that you have nice warm boots to keep your feet dry."

Caroline responded, "You know, boots aren't a necessity to have in your wardrobe, in my neck of the woods. Fortunately, for my birthday, Momma and my sistah, Rhonda, came up to visit me and took me shoppin' for winter gear. Rhonda was in Philadelphia one Christmas, and like a Floridian travelin' from Miami to Asheville in winter, she came back tellin' horror stories about being colder than she'd ever been in her life. She described her boyfriend's mustache as lookin' frozen and his breath as lookin' frosty as soon as he exhaled." After rattling on, Caroline suddenly stopped speaking having realized that she, in no wise, sounded like a cultured graduate of Vanderbilt. In fact, she sounded more like she'd just fallen off the back of a watermelon truck.

"Well it may not be as cold as Siberia, but the wind whipping through the alleys between skyscrapers can be chilling, especially at night," she responded, looking at Caroline with a nondescript facial expression. Finally, she smiled and said, "If you feel like you're frozen to the bone, make those sons of mine take you into a department store. They'll probably try to get you to go to the pub instead." Finally, she's speaking to me without playing the part of an interrogator.

"I wouldn't doubt that!"

Suddenly, she heard the heavy front door creaking as it was opened, and J.P. peeked around the corner and said, "I hate to break up this little pah...ty, but are you ready to go, Miss Car...o....line," he asked trying to perform his pseudo drawl in front of his mother?

"Why of course, Paul," she said rolling her eyes, but not letting his mom see her.

"Chris is out in the car, warming her up. You've never been through an underwater tunnel before, have you?"

"Now, Paul," she was still making silly faces at him without his mother's knowledge, "you know the only tunnel I've been through is in Asheville, which isn't underwater."

"Frankly, my dear," he said, trying to imitate a Southern gentleman, "you're in for quite an experience."

She giggled and got out of there as fast as she could but politely told Mrs. Andersen she hoped she would have a good afternoon.

As they exited the house J. P. told Caroline they would drive to Manhattan only once and then take the train the next day. "The traffic is insane and parking in the city is an expensive nightmare, but I want to drive over this time so you can experience the tunnel."

"I reckon ah'm 'bout ta have the ride of my life." *Please don't let me flip out inside this tunnel. Why do I imagine the worst that could possibly happen? I'm gonna need a sedative before this day is over.* She tried to act enthused for his sake, but she was already shaking in her boots. She didn't want to go in that underwater tunnel and feel like she would if trapped inside a car, sinking in the Chattahoochee River. They stood next to the car and he kissed her on the forehead. He was so excited about taking her to the city for her first time. She was feeling like she had taken a heavy dose of castor oil.

They took Route 3, toward the Lincoln Tunnel, to get to Manhattan from New Jersey, slowing down only to drop tokens into the receptacle at the toll booth. Once inside the tunnel, the muffled noise of traffic gave Caroline a creepy feeling. She started imagining strange things happening, like the yellow wall tiles coming off one by one until water gushed through large cracks and ultimately flooded the tunnel. Dark puffs of diesel exhaust made her feel like she was suffocating inside the tunnel, as the traffic rapidly moved through, and the tunnel lights were hypnotic as they rushed past them. She could see why J.P. wanted to drive her over, for at least one day, for the experience.

Once through the tunnel, she felt some sense of relief as they took the curving exit ramps to Port Authority for parking, and she was flabbergasted by the enormity of the tall buildings. She put her hand on J.P.'s arm and said, "Wow, I can't believe this place. I could never have imagined it like this, even from seeing it on television."

He responded, "It is pretty amazing. I'm glad I grew up here, but I'm glad I live in the South, now."

"I'm glad you do, too. But it's nice to be able to come and visit this place, even though the trip north was long and uncomfortable," she said. "Where did you say we're goin' now?"

"To Port Authority to park, then we'll take the subway down to the park to show you where Miss Liberty is. You've never been in a subway before, have you?"

"You know the answer to that."

He'd been right about how cold it would be once they came out of the subway and walked toward Battery Park, where ferries depart for the Statue of Liberty, at the waterfront. The chilled wind blowing over the New York Harbor made Caroline's teeth chatter and her cheeks were already getting chapped and rosy. They walked close enough to get a view of the patina covered statue and then rapidly made their way to the World Trade Center, walking as fast as they could to stay warm. Her layers of corduroy and wool were no match for the stinging coldness; her cheeks and nose felt numb.

On the way back to New Jersey, she was talking a mile a minute about how awesome it felt to be viewing the city from the observation deck of the South Tower, as she described the delivery trucks and automobiles looking like an army of ants in a convoy on the bridges below. She was still so pumped full of enthusiasm, J.P. couldn't help smiling to himself and feeling so good that he had been able to allow her to have this experience.

The following days were chocked full of happenings and her spirits remained high. She soon lost her anxious feelings about meeting family members and friends and found herself enjoying everything about the day trips to Manhattan and the cultural enrichment she was having the opportunity to gain during the stay. By the time the visit was near to a close, she found herself wanting to have the chance to come again in the future.

CHAPTER 8

RETURNIN'

Caroline was now on the home stretch, ready to do her student teaching and would need to be tenacious to get everything done on time to graduate in the spring. Several new students were coming in to study for the second semester, mostly graduate students. Checking her new roster and resident information sheets, Caroline noticed that one new graduate student, Debra Hembree, had attended Clemson as an undergraduate, but she had completed her undergraduate work several years back. Caroline immediately thought of J.P. and wondered if they had any mutual friends. That wasn't likely since Clemson had such a large student body, so she let that thought go.

Having just seen J.P. and her family, Caroline didn't expect any mail to be in her mailbox. She went to the campus book store and decided to go upstairs to check her mailbox anyway, just in case she had any mail pertinent to her student teaching assignment. To her surprise, there was a letter in her box. There was no name in the upper left hand corner of the envelope, but she noticed a postmark from Asheville, North Carolina. *No, it couldn't be Joost,* she thought.

Would opening this letter get her all stirred up again? They were just friends, weren't they? So it should be no big deal for her to read his letter.

The letter was from Joost, and as she read it, Caroline felt that her emotions were like a leaking faucet, turn on and turn off, turn back on and try hard to turn off again, repeatedly. Joost told her that he was planning to come to Charlotte in February to see one of his friends, and since it was so close to Rock Hill, he'd like to come to Winthrop, also. He wanted to spend time with her as well as see his old roommate, Santoso.

Caroline felt bad for Joost, but knowing he was coming to visit in February and that he wanted to see her made her as nervous as frog legs fryin'. She started fantasizing that Joost would come back and want to get close to her, and she wouldn't know how to handle that without making him feel worse. As usual, she suppressed all emotion and wild ideas, tried to use her reasoning, and told herself that Joost was well aware of her relationship with J.P. He was the one who told her that it was clear that J.P. was in love with her. He'd be seeing her to keep their Platonic relationship going, wouldn't he?

Caroline spent the next few evenings hovering over her portable sewing machine making some clothes to wear during a semester of student teaching. Thank goodness her momma had made sure that both of her daughters learned to sew at an early age, although Rhonda wouldn't be caught dead wearing homemade clothing, and she sure wouldn't subject herself to looking like a plain Jane student teacher. On the contrary, Caroline wouldn't be caught period wearing makeup, slathered on an inch thick, and her hair teased until doubled in size and glued down with hairspray, like a translucent helmet. She and her sister were like night and day, the teacher and the cosmetologist.

J.P. called that night and talked incessantly about how special it was to have her visit up north with him. She could tell how eager he was to find out how she felt about his family and their Danish cultural traditions. Having the utmost respect for him, she would never tell him how much she missed the traditions from her own childhood. She'd been so naive to think that everyone who believes in Santa expects him leave the North Pole on Christmas Eve, arrive to deliver gifts in the wee hours of the next morning, and then children wake up early on Christmas Day to find their presents. If she hadn't already known J.P. fairly well before spending the holiday in Jersey, she'd have sworn that his family was a bunch of coots.

To encourage him, she made it a point to tell him all the things she liked about the visit and the holiday celebrations. She commented on the experiences of seeing the Statue of Liberty and the fabulous views from the observation deck of the World Trade Towers. She told him how neat it was to look at authentic dinosaur bones in the Museum of Natural History. She spoke of the wonderful aroma of fresh baked Christmas cookies on Christmas Eve and her astonishment at how beautifully the tree had been decorated while they went skating with his cousins. Saying all of this with excitement in her tone of voice, she hoped he felt that he'd done a good job helping her have a great holiday.

That conversation was their last for nearly a week. Caroline suddenly began to worry that she had offended J.P. in some way. She was sure he would've written or called if something was not terribly wrong. She decided to call him but got no answer. Trying to contact him several times, she began to get anxious and had difficulty sleeping. The next night at approximately eleven o'clock the phone rang. Even though she was exhausted from doing her student teaching and emotionally drained, she answered the phone cheerfully, sure that it was J.P. calling her. She could tell immediately that it was Butch.

"Caroline, this is J.P.'s friend, Butch."

"Oh hey Butch, how you doin'? I'm surprised to hear from you," she said. "Whut's up?"

"Durn, I hate to call you like this, but I was checkin' the answerin' machine when I got back from visitin' my folks and noticed several calls from you. I'm callin' to let you know that J.P.'s grandmother passed away suddenly, about five days ago. J. P. and Chris flew to Jersey to be with the family."

Caroline knew how close J. P. was to his grandmother and was aware of the devastating effect that her death would have on him. Whenever she learned of the loss of a loved one, she would feel a frightening and sickening feeling.

"No wonder he hasn't called me. He must be torn all to pieces," she said with compassion in her voice. "He's been so close to her his entire life. When we were up there for Christmas, it appeared that his relationship with her was much more comfortable for him that it was with his mother."

"Yeah, he's always been very close to her, and I know it's killin' him to lose her so unexpectedly. She came down to see him and Chris several times while we were at Clemson and seemed like such a sweet little lady."

"What on earth happened," Caroline asked?

Butch responded, "Poor J.P. was so messed up about it he couldn't even call me. Chris called and told me about it. I don't know if you went there, but she lived in an apartment above her son's home. The stairwell was rather steep. She was comin' down to get her mail and fell from the top step all the way down the stairwell. Her daughter-in-law heard thumpin' and bumpin' sounds and tore out the door to check on her. She found her unconscious at the bottom of the stairwell and got an ambulance there right away. Unfortunately, they found that she had suffered a cerebral hemorrhage and died a few hours later."

Caroline felt breathless at that moment and couldn't say anything to Butch. She had a horrible flashback to the time of her daddy's accident, execrable scenes never divulged to anyone other than her momma. It all frightened her so severely she couldn't stand the thought of J.P. having to experience it now.

"Caroline, are you okay," asked Butch with concern in his tone of voice?

She remained speechless and Butch repeated his question.

Caroline began crying and tried to say something, but she couldn't get it out at first. Finally, she got a hold of herself and said, "Butch, that's awful. It just breaks my heart to think about findin' her that way and knowin' she died so soon after the accident. J.P. must be in total shock."

"He is Caroline," Butch said. "If he couldn't get it together enough to call either one of us, I know he's in bad shape right now."

"I wanna reach out to him," she said with desperation in her voice. "Please give me his parent's number so I can call tomorrow. I feel so helpless to comfort him. Just sayin' I'm so sorry can't penetrate that shell of grief surroundin' him."

"Caroline, he needs you now more than you'll ever know. He loves you, and from what he's told me, you can offer the most sincere sympathy. Of all the people in his life, you understand what he's goin' through right now. Just hearin' your voice will calm him. Don't worry about what you're gonna say, it'll come. I can tell you love him, too. So do I; we've been like brothers for many years now. I regret that I can't be there for him now. He's a Yankee boy with a Southerner's heart, the kind of guy who's not too busy to feel."

"I know you're right. I'll make every effort to calm down and stay calm for him. I'll call him tomorrow. Butch, I know you hated to call me with this bad news, but I'm glad you did. Since I hadn't heard from him for days, I was startin' to worry about him. Thank goodness he has a friend like you to help him get through the rough days when he gets back to South Carolina. I know this is gonna kill him. I really regret that I'm here in Rock Hill and he's goin' to be there in Summerville."

"It must be hard to have a long distance relationship," Butch said. "I've nevah met anyone who meant enough to me to try to do it. But J.P. was crazy 'bout you from the first time he met you. He hasn't acted like himself since you first came to Summerville with Emily. He stopped wantin' to party with us and got all serious about his job. The more I've gotten to know you, I see why he's fallen in love with you. You seem to be the perfect person for him, you know, you can bring out the best in him."

"I do respect him and appreciate all that he's done for me. I'm not sure at this point what love is, maybe because I have so much goin' on, tryin' to finish school and find a job for next year."

"I can understand that. You need to find yourself in the adult world, and I know J.P. realizes where you are. We've been there ourselves not to awfully long ago, even though we may seem old and decrepit to you," he said with a chuckle. Okay, Caroline, I'm gonna let you go."

"Butch, thanks again for callin' me to let me know what happened."

"You betcha, kido, goodnight!"

She cried herself to sleep that night. She cried for the pain she knew J.P. and his family were experiencing, she cried for the loss of someone special she'd just met, and she cried for the deep rooted feelings of anguish that she'd felt for so long.

The call to J.P. the following day was unbelievably difficult for Caroline. He answered the phone at his parent's house, but when he realized it was Caroline calling to express her condolences, he had no words to express himself. For the very first time, he became keenly aware of the depth of her pain, and she instinctively knew it. No explanation of his near silence was needed for she felt the same burden that he was feeling, that burden of a heart ripped apart by grief, his recently induced and hers experienced most of her life. She asked no questions because she knew he would be unable to answer, but as she tried to comfort him her voice quivered. He sat there at the table in his parent's kitchen and wept, until the phone fell out of his hand and snapped him back to his call from her.

Their conversation was not long that day, but Caroline told him she would call again the following day. Somehow J.P. was able to manage to tell her about the funeral arrangements. The family had put it off as many days as possible waiting for his grandmother's brother to arrive from Canada. He had immigrated to Canada in 1952 from Scotland and was her only living relative of her generation. The family felt that she would've wanted her brother to attend her funeral as they were so very close growing up.

Caroline ended the conversation gracefully, but hung up the phone feeling horrible. It was almost dark outside because she'd waited to make the call after her day of student teaching. Ironically, Joost called Caroline that evening, which was a complete shock to her. Knowing the situation J.P. was in at that time, she felt wrong to even talk to Joost, but something within her compelled her to want to tell him about the circumstances that had occurred over the past week. Of course Joost said just the right words to make Caroline feel better as he sensed she was at the brink of tears as she told him about J.P.'s poor grandmother.

They had talked for almost an hour before she realized what time it was. Without thinking about the possibility that she might sound eager, she asked him if he was still planning to come to Rock Hill to visit his friends. As soon as she asked, she felt like it was a mistake to open a can of worms.

The big dilemma still existed for her. Did she really want to see Joost or forget about him completely and focus only on her relationship with J.P.? The answer to that question wasn't going to come without a lot of soul searching. Since she met Joost, she'd been telling herself that he could understand what it felt like to have a deceased parent, but that might not be the attraction, but simply an excuse for her to continue feeling connected to him somehow. After all they weren't friends for very long before he left to go back to school in North Carolina, and in most cases it would be pointless to concern yourself over a foreign student who very soon would be out of her life completely. In her own comparison of J.P. and Joost, she would say to herself that Joost understood a part of her that J.P. couldn't in the past. But now J.P. could understand the secret part of her, even though he didn't lose a parent, he'd lost a special grandmother who had done things for him that his parents couldn't do.

After her chat with Joost, Caroline sat there pensively, mulling things over and over in her mind. She was physically exhausted and emotionally drained. Before she retired for bed, she went to the closet to determine what she'd wear for teaching the following day. She looked up on the shelf above the hanging clothes, and low and behold she saw the unopened birthday gift that Joost had given her before the Christmas break, the one with the beautifully colored paper. She retrieved it from the shelf and opened it ever so carefully, trying to preserve the multi-colored wrapping paper. Inside she found two objects of the same size wrapped in colored tissue paper. She opened the first one to find a cassette tape of a British band. Assuming the other gift would also be a cassette, she opened it to find a tape of Spanish music by a group from the South of Spain. She popped that one into the cassette player and went into the bathroom to get ready for bed. The sound of the music was so romantic, she began wondering what it would be like to see the Mediterranean coast of Spain, and for a fleeting moment, she imagined herself there with Joost. She quashed the scene in her mind and instead thought of standing next to J.P. as they looked out across the Charleston harbor. She found the Spanish music to be a bit much at the end of that difficult day, and decided to put in one of her own favorite tapes instead and soon drifted off to sleep.

CHAPTER 9

WRESTLIN'

The remainder of January was extremely cold for the South, with temperatures in the teens for nearly a week. On the very last day of the month, it snowed. Caroline was up at 5:30 that morning and ran down the hall to look out the large window at the end of the hall. The street lights illuminated the shapes of the walkways next to the dormitory which were covered with a blanket of snow. Creeping back to her room, shuffling her feet in her pink fuzzy slippers, she wanted to shout for joy, but remained quiet while the rest of the residents slept, like homeless drunks in the middle a city. Pressing the palms of her hands together with her fingertips touching her chin and praying for a day off from school, like she did as a child, she then tuned her radio to the local station. Minutes later, she got in the shower in case she'd have to go teach that day but was hoping the schools would be closed. Good news of school cancellations came in around 6:00 A.M. As usual in an upstate South Carolina snow storm, everything seemed to come to a halt, until school authorities made sure the roads were safe for school bus travel, particularly in areas closer to the mountains where the winding snow covered roads can be quite treacherous. Caroline did a jig around her room, still wearing her white terry cloth bath robe, and said to herself, repeatedly, "Woo hoooooooooooooooot, no school!" She dried her hair and put on some gray, ratty old sweat pants and a red Winthrop sweat shirt with the cuffs and neckline cut off, leaving a raw edge. She sat upon her bed and reached for a pad of paper and a pen, feeling compelled to write a simple poem to comfort J.P. She wrote:

For Our Loved Ones

Clouds form and rain pours
Day turns to night
But hope for what good will come
Gives us strength and light

Life is so bitter
And yet so sweet,
Never to truly end
And never quite complete

Days on end
We lament those dear
Failing to remember
That our strength is near

For it is within us
We must not let go
May pain and suffering
Help us to grow

Anguish and anger
From us now flee
Open our eyes wide
That we may see

That death will not be
The final end
Malleable and willing
To change and bend

To cope with the
Journey of life
Without resentment
Fear or strife

Until the day
We see God from above
Showering us with infinite
Comfort and love

May His peace
Give us rest
In the storm of
Life's test

And give us
Hope for the day
When His plan
Makes a way

To unite and
Bind and seal
Making our families
Eternal and real

Finishing the poem and rereading it a couple of times, she felt like a greeting card author wannabe; but, she thought her poem was adequate and rubbed her halo for giving it her best shot. She knew it sounded very religious, but it came from her "Bible Belt" version of dying. To think that our spirits would go to an alien planet, Mother Earth, or be reincarnated in the form of an animal was not Caroline's view of the afterlife. Her upbringing focused on a spiritual paradise, a beautiful heavenly place where loved ones would be seen again one day. She had no idea what J.P. really believed, spiritually, but she hoped that he did have some way to gain inner peace during the trials of life.

She rose from her bed, shuffled across the tile floor in her warmest socks, and opened her desk drawer to retrieve a box filled with colored and printed paper, tiny unusual fabric scraps and ribbons, and vintage buttons. She proceeded to create a sympathy card and planned to mail the card and her poem to his home in Summerville. As difficult as it would be, she'd have to bite the bullet again and call him within the next day or so. It wasn't that she didn't want to do it for him, but it was so hard for her; it took so much emotional energy. She was twenty four years old and had never gone to a funeral before. Momma Carter didn't push her to attend her own father's funeral, giving her a choice, and she could never force herself to go to a funeral over the years. It made her feel abnormal as a young adult to let other people know that she'd never gone to a funeral, so she always kept that fact to herself.

Caroline was getting emotionally exhausted at this point and wanted some diversion from everything going on with J.P. and Joost. She decided to call Emily to see what she was up to.

Emily answered the phone and said, "Caroline, I haven't heard from you in days, but Lord, girl, it is so early to be callin' me."

"Sorry. I guess I got over excited that I have a free snow day."

Emily said, "I have been tryin' to getta hold of you, but don't ever get an answer when I call. You don't have some other good lookin' guy after ya, do ya? You always seem to have much better luck than I do."

"No, no one new, but I'm completely worn out from the ones I already know."

"What do you mean," Emily asked?

Caroline sighed and said, "I got a phone call yesterday from Butch, and he had some bad news to tell me."

"What on earth did he tell you?"

Caroline proceeded to tell Emily the entire scenario with J.P.'s poor grandmother.

"Caroline, that's horrible. I'd be devastated if my grandma passed away, wouldn't you?"

"Yes, I'd take it very hard if Granny died. I know one day it'll happen, but I hope it won't be for a long time. I've been upset for J.P., but I also feel a loss even though I didn't know his grandmother very well. She seemed to accept me more than anyone else did while I was in New Jersey. She was such a sweet person."

"I can only imagine how hard it is for you and for J.P. I guess you're worn out from the stress of hearing bad news like that. So, I take it that J.P. and Chris went up to New Jersey."

"Yeah, I feel so helpless in the situation because I'd rather be with him than have to talk on the phone about all of this."

"Well, not to make light of the things you've just told me about, but maybe you need a break from all this morbid stuff. What about those other fellows?"

"Fellows? You make it sound like I have a line of guys outside my dorm, like hounds with their tongues hangin' out," she added with laughter.

"Maybe they're waiting for you with genuine concern or just waiting around to see what you're gonna do with your other fellars."

"Stop Emily," she responded. "Don't be jokin' around right now. Save it for later, cus I'll really need it."

"So, is it Joost who may be shakin' ya up a bit?'

"Emily please don't betray me on this."

"Caroline, have I ever betrayed ya," Emily asked with sincerity?

"Well, no you haven't, and I really didn't mean to imply that you had, but I feel awkward to tell you about Joost callin', since you know J.P. so well, and I don't want you to breathe a word to another soul."

"Joost has been callin' you?"

"He hasn't been callin' me regularly, but he did call last night."

"You haven't heard from him since he left Winthrop, and he just calls you out of the blue?"

"I got one letter from him, which had and incomplete return address, so I couldn't write back. In his letter, he told me he planned to come back here to visit friends next month."

"Maybe he called you last night to see if you had plans for the middle of the month, around the fourteenth."

"Stop teasin' me, Emily. You make me feel like we're still in high school. He didn't write me or call me to try to get me to go out with him. He's been havin' a really tough time feeling lonely back in his old school since most of his friends have already graduated."

"You need to lighten up, girl and get out of that depressin' dorm room and do somethin' fun. You wanna go to ladies' lock-up tonight and have a few beers?"

"Not really, I don't need to get inebriated and have one big pity party, but it would be fun to go out in the snow sometime today. Maybe we could walk down to the grocery store and get a box of doughnuts and some hot chocolate."

"Caroline, it sounds so wholesome, I'm not sure I'll be able stand it," Emily said, laughing. "Besides, we'll freeze our tails off."

"I have a good pair of boots I bought before I went to Jersey, and two pairs of warm mittens if you need to borrow some. All we did up north was trudge through the street side mounds of nasty snow to get up to the porch or out to the car, no fun at all playin' in the snow. There wasn't enough space in the yards to play in the snow. I don't think those Yanks appreciate the snow like we do here in the South."

"Of course not, snow is just a frequent nuisance to them."

"I'm glad it's still mystical to us. I've probably seen snow a lot more than you have, comin' from the Lowcountry."

"Oh yeah, I'm sure you have. I can only remember one snow from my childhood, and that one little inch of snow seemed like a blizzard to us. The dwarf snowman we made was gross looking, all covered with pine needles, but we had fun."

"That's sad! I guess we've had more ice storms in the Upstate than snowstorms. Let's not waste this one. Meet me around the corner, at Margaret Nance, at one o'clock."

"I'll be there."

The brilliant sunlight, reflecting off the white snow and making the campus grounds light up, nearly blinded Caroline, and she wished she'd worn her sunglasses to frolic in the snow with Emily. After walking to the store and playing outside until their noses, fingers, and toes felt like they had frostbite, they came in to thaw out, listened to music, warmed up a couple of doughnuts in the dorm kitchen, and made hot chocolate.

They talked about this and that and relaxed until it was time to head to the cafeteria for supper. As they were coming out of Caroline's room, Emily got a glimpse of Debra Hembree, the new grad student on the hall. Recognizing Emily, because she'd met her once while visiting her brother Drew at school, Debra, a portly girl with a pug nose, came over to Emily and started inquiring about some former Clemson students. Caroline stood there, silently, wondering if Debra might also know J.P. As Emily made small talk with Debra, Caroline got the feeling her friend might not be too fond of the new coed.

Debra headed toward the other end of the hallway as Emily opened the door leading to the stairwell. Nothing more was said until they got to the bottom of the stairwell, ready to enter the hallway to the cafeteria, and Emily muttered, "Durnit, get me away from that girl. She's bad news."

"What in tarnation are you talkin' 'bout," Caroline asked, looking as innocent and bewildered as a preschooler?

Emily just about snorted she got so tickled at Caroline, but she held back her laugh and said, "Drew introduced her to me at Clemson, durin' the last homecomin' weekend he was there, but he cautioned me to be wary of her. She's notorious for stirrin' up trouble but nevah gives you an inklin' that she might be up to somethin'; she's sneaky. You don't need a busy body 'round here with all the things you're dealin' with right now."

"Amen to that, sistah. I've 'bout had all I can take, and you know I don't like a busy body, period."

"She uses a kickstand to park her broom at night," snorted Emily.

Laughter spewed from Caroline like opening a soda shaken in a saddlebag during a long, hard, bumpy ride.

They dropped the subject altogether and went to get in line to be served their meals. The background noise in the cafeteria was so loud they didn't even try to discuss anything until they found a spot at an empty table, the very table where Caroline and Joost had sat together eating a meal. Before either of them spoke, she thought of him and started feeling so shameful; wishing deep down that she could keep both guys in her life, more than simply as friends, but not hurt either one of them. Her momma used to say, "If wishes were fishes, there wouldn't be room to swim in the sea." Obviously, it wouldn't be possible to go on like this, thinking about Joost and wanting J.P., too. She couldn't help feeling that relationships were just too difficult to maintain, too complicated, too emotionally draining, but oh, so much fun. Much to her chagrin, she knew she'd have to make a choice and stick with it, never to look back.

"Caroline, snap out of it! You're goin' to end up needin' Valium if you don't let some of this stuff go. Try to concentrate on yourself right now. You've got a lot of irons in the fire with teachin', graduatin', and relocatin' to find a job. You've been so doggone good since you've been here, I think you might need to go a little crazy when you graduate. I think I'm goin' to go a little crazy when I get done with school."

Caroline looked at Emily, rolled her eyes, shook her head and said, "Emily, you're full of it. You know good and well I can't afford to go crazy and get wild. Remember, I don't know how to do that. You're the one who hog tied me into goin' to visit three guys, the night I met J.P."

"Don't be a prude."

Caroline retorted, "Don't get too big for yer britches, missy."

They both sat there laughing at one another for a while, and it felt good to Caroline, a much needed stress release. Emily was right about the fact that she needed to make time to enjoy herself. She'd always tried to grow up so fast, perhaps because she felt she had to help her momma by being the hard working type, so she wouldn't be thought of as the baby of the family. Rhonda had been telling her for years, just as Emily was, to let go and have some fun, but she'd resisted and kept pushing.

"Emily, what are you gonna do when you graduate?"

"I don't really know what I'm gonna do for sure. I've thought about rentin' an apartment close to Charleston," Emily said. "My parents said they'd help me out if I'd get a part-time job and go on to graduate school. Maybe you could find a teachin' job there and share the apartment with me."

"We'd probably drive each other up the wall if we lived in the same apartment."

"I doubt that. If I get a job in the daytime, I'll be gone a lot at night goin' to class and studyin' in the library. I know I'm gonna take some time after graduation just to have fun, if I'm gonna have that kind of a schedule in the fall."

"You're blessed to have your parents to help you. I know Momma would help me if she could, but that's not possible. She'd let me stay with her if I got a job in Greenville, but it's not an option for me to go back to there. I need to move on."

Emily continued to talk, but Caroline got totally lost in thought. If she moved to Charleston, she'd probably see J.P. a lot; it would be a committed relationship. Is that what she really wanted, tied down before she had a chance to be on her own, making all of her own decisions? Part of her wanted to be autonomous and part of her wanted to be with someone she could depend on.

"Caroline, you're gettin' kinda spaced out. Don't analyze things so much. When you try to plan everythin', somethin' invariably happens to mess things up."

"Well ain't that the truth, girlfriend?"

"A lot of things can happen between now and May. Maybe you'll get a teachin' job up north."

"Oh no, movin' up north will nevah happen because I couldn't handle livin' up there. I don't think I wanna leave South Carolina, with its gorgeous beaches in the east and incredible views of the Blue Ridge Mountains in the west." She was as country as cornbread, black-eyed peas, and fried okra, knowing she always would be, and she had no intention of ever trying to live where she had to be someone else, including Europe.

Melting snow during the day and a drop in temperature, after the sun went down, made a thin layer of ice over the snow. For teachers and students, the following morning was 'hallelujah' time again, and Caroline planned to make the best of another day off. She ventured out of her dormitory, trudging to the campus bookstore to buy a cheap paperback, planning to get lost in some recreational reading the rest of the day. Hearing the crunching sound as her boots penetrated the ice covered snow, while walking over the white drifts, refreshed her memory of years gone by and the wonder of snow in the South.

The steps up to the student center, on the south side of the building, were still covered with snow. The stoop, at the top of the steps looked like it had been cleared, but Caroline nearly busted her butt as she stepped up and her foot hit an icy spot and shot out from under her, like an old lady kicking a wild goose attacking her grandchild.

Caroline was a lone shopper in the bookstore. There wasn't a great selection of paperback novels, so she chose a book quickly and then looked for a card to send to J.P., but didn't find one she was satisfied with. She wondered how he was doing. Of course he hadn't called her, and she just assumed that things were too hectic and too emotional for him. Little did she know that he'd always turned his pain inward and became reclusive. She certainly didn't know he had a history of doing that to cope with the difficult circumstances of his life, none of which she knew about. Caroline had already placed him upon a pedestal, thinking he was the perfect kind of guy, which was not a smart move on her part. After all, most guys his age, and many a lot older, were very good at trying to fool women, to get what they wanted. Were all men dogs, or were there truly a few good ones on the face of the earth? She thought of her brother, Troy, and could imagine him thumping her in the back of the head for having such bad thoughts.

When she got back to the lower level of the building, Caroline decided to stay there a while and read her new book. She sat down on one of the sofas, pulled off her boots, rolled her blue, down filled jacket into a pillow, kicked back, and began to read. A few minutes later, her reading was interrupted by an unrecognizable voice saying, "If ya wanna know more about a juicy story, I prolly have one that's better than 'at book."

It seemed freaky for a stranger to say something like that to her, and she questioned whether or not to even acknowledge the person speaking to her. When she looked up, she saw Debra Hembree, heard a humorless little laugh and had a flashback of Emily's description of her as a meddling trouble maker, or even a pit viper. Not being quite sure how to handle the situation, she mumbled, "I'm sure you might have a story, but I'm really engrossed in this book at the moment. Maybe we can talk about it some other time."

She felt no shame to have been cold because she really didn't want to be involved with this girl.

Debra said in a sarcastic tone of voice, twanging, "Wel...l, I'd wanna have someone tell me the truth 'bout the person I was a datin'."

Caroline was stunned by Debra's comments and wanted to slither, like a snake in a flower bed, to the nearest exit and get back to her room before the busy body told her something she didn't want to hear. How in the heck did Debra know she was seeing J.P., assuming that he was the one she was referring to? Knowing that Debra was an acquaintance of Drew's at Clemson and Drew was tight with J.P., she had to be talking about him. But what was the purpose in inundating Caroline with details of J.P.'s past? You bet this girl was trouble! She didn't even give you a chance to get to know her before she started gettin' all up in your business. This kind of mudslinging garbage was exactly why Caroline stayed to herself so much, not wanting to be bothered by nosy girls. As for Debra, Caroline figured she didn't have a life, a typical scenario for an unattractive grad student at Winthrop, probably didn't have a man and didn't want anyone else to have one either. Without a doubt, Caroline smelled a dead rat!

She stood up, towering over Debra who was no taller than five feet. Debra looked up at her with a sheepish grin while Caroline was thinking, *you remind me of a Shih-tzu, with that pug nose of yours.* With a look of disgust, she said, "I thought I told you I wasn't interested in this conversation. What part of that did you not understand?"

To avoid a cat fight altogether, Caroline sat back down and began to put on her boots, never looking at Debra as she stood there with her hands on her hips. Out of the corner of her eye, she saw Debra stamp her foot and whirl around to face the door. Caroline sat, motionless, for a moment to let her get out of her sight and then proceeded to remove her boots again, feeling quite sure that Debra wouldn't return.

The next day meant back to the grindstone in the confines of an aged school building. The day seemed long to Caroline because she had so much on her mind; the disturbing conversation with Debra, the recent call from Joost, and the overload of emotions spurred by the passing of J.P's grandmother was weighing upon her, like a bag of bricks in her arms. By two o'clock, she was fatigued to the point of tears, but she remembered it was Friday, and she'd have a couple of days to get herself together.

She tried to contact J.P. in the evening. His mother answered the phone and told her that her sons had already returned to Summerville. Nothing more was really said, and Caroline was shocked by her distant tone of voice. She expressed her most sincere sympathy but felt strange when Mrs. Andersen hung up the phone. It seemed to Caroline that death might be handled differently in their family, almost like you live and you die and that's it, end of discussion. She didn't get that from J.P. on the day she spoke with him, but why didn't he let her know when he would be leaving Jersey. Here she was, concerned beyond all measure about his feelings, but she felt so out of the loop not really knowing what was going on with him.

A week passed and still no contact from J.P. Caroline tried to call him, but there was no answer. She was worried that something had happened to him but reasoned that Butch would have called her if there had been some accident. By the weekend, her nerves were shot, and she wanted to take Emily's advice to go out and have a few beers, but she was so embarrassed to tell her that she hadn't heard a word from J.P. She called her anyway and asked her to come over.

When Emily arrived, she was dressed much more risqué than Caroline would ever dare to attempt to pull off, with tight fitting jeans, a low cut sweater, high heeled boots, and looped earrings large enough to wrap around a peanut butter jar.

"Emily, you look pretty good tonight," said Caroline, trying to be polite. She much preferred to see her friend wearing jeans, a T-shirt, and flip-flops like they did in Charleston, but it wasn't summer and they sure weren't in the Lowcountry.

"I haven't put on make-up yet, but I brought mine. I thought it might be fun to fix one another's make-up."

"You trust me to put make-up on you to go out. Are you kiddin'? My sister Rhonda says I couldn't put make up on a mannequin if I was about to be handed five hundred dollars to do it."

"Caroline, your sister's a professional cosmetologist. That's the one thing she does better than you do, so she's not about to boost your confidence. What's the harm, if I don't like how I look when you're finished, I'll wash it off?"

"Emily, why do you mess with me so much? You rarely give me a break."

"Deep down, I envy you. You're a beautiful person and you don't need to cover up to be attractive, but tonight you need to be someone else for a while and take your mind off some of the things that have been botherin' you."

Emily pulled out the chair in front of the desk, the seat of which was covered by a navy blue cushion, and as she plopped herself onto the chair said, "Go to it! Gimme some big ol' lips. Oh yeah, and we're gonna find two fine young bucks and dance our butts off."

"You wish. What we'll prob'ly find is a slew of drunks from the jock jungle in my dorm, waitin' like hungry piranhas."

"You're actin' grotesque and have no vision."

"Yes I do, I envision us getting eaten alive if we drink too much."

"Okay, do as you wish. I'll designate you to be the one to get us back home safely stumblin' back 'cross Cherry Road."

"Smart move on your part," said Caroline just before she giggled.

When they finished applying make-up and Caroline got dressed, nicely, but not quite as sexy as Emily, they locked the door and then carefully crept down the stairs.

Passing the dorm office, Caroline made the comment, "I'm glad I don't have to work tonight."

"Me too, cus I definit'ly wouldn't go to the bar alone."

"Why not, are you catchin' a little bit of prudence from me?"

"I hope not. One Caroline is enough to take care of us both. I love you, my friend."

They began to cross the street in front of the two high rise dormitories and could see a crowd of guys standing outside next to the entrance of the bar. Caroline looked at Emily and asked, "Do you think these guys are gonna leave us alone?"

"I doubt it, but just ignore what they say with their slurred speech. They've been boozing it up for a while, right above you in your dorm."

"Emily, I wanna make this clear: this is gonna be a once in a while kind of thing to do. I've been brought up to do better," she grinned and giggled, like she'd seen a naked old man dancing in the street.

"Sometimes, nothin' keeps me out of trouble except the thought of sittin' in a cell at the county detention center," said Emily. "Okay just kiddin', here we go."

Caroline felt like she just eaten a greasy possum and began to feel a bit queasy."

Before they could even cross the street, they could hear some of the guys making rude comments, and Caroline felt like she and Emily should tuck their tails and run straight back to the dorm. Just as she was ready to turn around, standing on the concrete median, Emily took her by the hand and yanked her to the other side of Cherry Road.

Meanwhile, the guys outside the bar were acting like animals, or fools, and Emily smarted off, yelling above the sound of the music, "Y'all need to shut your faces and get out of our way."

All Caroline could think about was the potential rare form that Emily could get into if she drank alcohol. She was the kind of girl that acted out when she got stressed, and something unspoken was bothering her.

Needless to say, the half-cocked guys did nothing constructive, and continued to block the entrance to the bar with their presence. Fortunately, a bouncer exited the building and asked the young men to vacate the premises until "ladies lockup" was over. They protested a little, all of them together were no match for the muscular bouncer.

The girls smiled at each other and then sashayed into the bar. They scanned the room to search for a place to sit, but the only vacant table was covered with empty beer bottles and dirty plastic cups, some of which were partially filled with stale draft.

After they drank a couple of beers each, Caroline vowed that she'd drink no more that night. Emily started to really loosen up and questioned Caroline about her encounter with Debra in the student center.

"How did you know about that, were you a fly on the wall," Caroline asked?

"No, I just happened to go to the library yesterday to work on my project, and I ran into her, unfortunately, just after she'd approached you. She was mad as an old wet hen and went ahead and let the cat out of the bag."

"What do you mean by that?"

"She blabbed, but better me to get an ear full, than you. She was dyin' to tell her big story, so that's when she spilled the beans. Because she's a gossip monger, she found out, from her old friend who lives in Charleston that J.P. was datin' someone here at Winthrop, someone that I'd introduced to him. Apparently, her connivin' friend met you at the oyster roast last fall, so when Debra saw us together, she just assumed that you were the one. I'd nevah do the asinine things I've heard she's done."

"I can already see that she's somethin' else. What real pleasure can she possibly get from gettin' into everyone else's business?"

"She'll prob'ly always be that way, and if she does find a man and get married, she'd be divorced within five years cus the poor man won't be able to take it."

"So what did she tell you?"

"Lord, Caroline, I don't know where to start. I need another beer, before I can tell you."

"Just go ahead, and let me draw my own conclusions when you finish." A multitude of thoughts flooded her mind as she sat there, pensively, while Emily was ordering another brew, trying to think of which girl she'd met at the oyster roast who would have been the one to spread gossip. She had no clue. They all seemed polite, but she was probably oblivious to any indicators of jealousy or contention.

Emily wished she'd never starting telling Caroline about any of this tale, but what if there was truth in it, and she needed to know the details? She thought of the game she'd played as a child where the participants sit in a circle, and one person whispers a secret to the person to his right. By the time the statement has been told over and over, it's nearly unrecognizable when it comes around, full circle. What if this rumor about J.P. has been told so many times, it's not the same story? These questions plagued Emily until her third beer was brought to the table by a buxom cocktail waitress with bleached blond hair so dry it looked like she'd burst into flames if a cigarette lighter was lit too close to her. She must have had three pieces of gum in her mouth as she mumbled to Emily to pay up. Her long acrylic nails, with tiny little flowers painted on each nail, clanked on the bottle as she handed it to Emily.

Caroline tried to break their silence by commenting, "Mercy, did you see all them rings on her fingers? Man, her boyfriend must be the king of costume jewelry."

Both of them laughed until the sound of disco music blasted from the stereo system. Emily nursed her beer as Caroline wondered if she should just stop her from divulging any information or hearsay about J.P's past. Knowing what he was going through with his grief, she felt uneasy and feared she would regret pursuing the conversation any further. She stood up and said, "You finish your drink. I'm gonna run to the restroom."

Caroline looked at the mirror wishing she'd see the image of her father standing behind her with his hands resting upon her shoulders, leaning his head to the side as he whispered to her the answers to all of her questions, the advice that only a father could give. Instead, she saw girls coming out of the stalls looking like they were totally blasted from excessive alcohol consumption. It occurred to her that she and her friend were definitely in the wrong place and needed to leave before Emily got plastered. She felt somewhat nauseated again and looked flushed, so she leaned over the sink, turned the water on, and splashed her cheeks. She resisted the urge to vomit and tried to calm herself. She had to make a difficult choice here.

When Caroline got back to the table, Emily was about to order her fourth drink, and it was evident that she was trying to forget the whole conversation about Debra Hembree's insinuations. Caroline stepped over next to Emily, gently tugged at her arm and said, "Let's just forget about all this and go back to campus. You don't need to get polluted and have a terrible hangover tomorrow. Don't worry about it. I choose to just let it go. Come on."

The bulk of the story was not told that night.

CHAPTER 10

WAITIN'

For the next couple of days Caroline began to doubt her relationship with J.P. She knew he'd been through a traumatic experience and must be grieving terribly, but she felt so left out. She had a need to nurture, but he had a need for solitude. They just didn't understand one another, and she was getting unnerved, to realize their differences.

She made arrangements fairly quickly to get a ride to Greenville, and left Friday after school. When she got home, Rhonda was over at her momma's house doing Mrs. Carter's hair. Caroline walked into the house and asked her momma, "What you getting all gussied up for?"

Mrs. Carter replied, "Before we heard you were comin' home, we'd planned to go to Asheville for the day. Rhonda wanted to spend some time in those hippie shops. I wanted to go in some of the craft stores to look for beeswax to make my own candles. We'll prob'ly freeze cus the high there today is supposed to be thirty nine degrees. After we shop for a while, we'll have lunch at a Bavarian restaurant on the Weaverville highway. Rhonda says their German potato salad is somethin' else."

"I can't imagine any potato salad tastin' better than Aunt Josephine's," commented Caroline.

Rhonda chimed in, "But this is the best German style potato salad I've ever eaten, and their kraut is good, too."

"Why ja haf to say that? You know I can't stand sauerkraut."

"Well, me and Momma love sauerkraut. You can just be the oddball at lunch."

Mrs. Carter added, "Mercy me, if we'd acted like the two of y'all, Momma would've told us she'd cut a hickory and tan our hides. Y'all caint be together for two shakes of a lamb's tail before you'll start that squabblin'. When are y'all gonna act like young ladies?"

The two girls looked at each other and simultaneously said, "Nevah!"

"Jinx, buy me an ice cream."

"No way, you're buyin' me one."

The two of them got the silly giggles and their momma did, too. They laughed until they could laugh no more.

Rhonda said, "Momma, you're gonna look so good, the men will swarm to you like flies to molasses."

"I hope not, that might mess up our girls' day out."

The conversation switched to a topic familiar to Rhonda, hair. Mrs. Carter and Rhonda both knew that something was up with Caroline, since she came home so abruptly, but they didn't want to question her about anything. (Well, Rhonda, being so nosy, did want to grill her, but she wouldn't do it in front of their momma.) They were aware that J.P. had lost his grandmother, but didn't know that he'd shut himself off from Caroline, and she'd become very unsettled about the situation.

Rhonda rinsed her momma's hair, cut, and styled it. It looked something like a wedge with layered bangs swept to the side and some lift on top.

"Momma, your hair is so cute," exclaimed Caroline! I caint believe Rhonda knows how to cut it like that.

"Just hush Caroline before you stick your foot and your leg in your mouth again and choke on your knee."

Suddenly, a spray of saliva filled the room as all three of them began laughing again. It made Caroline feel so good to laugh. She looked up and saw Rhonda sticking her tongue out at her, and she roared with laughter. They laughed so hard, their sides were hurting and Rhonda yelled as she was running out of the room, "Now, I gotta pee, bad."

When morning came, Caroline crawled out of bed looking like rats had made a nest in her hair. She'd failed to braid it, so the hair at the nape of her neck was one big wad of tangles. She stumbled into the bathroom, used the toilet, brushed her teeth, and washed her face with mild soap. She sprayed her tangled hair with detangler, got the comb with the jumbo teeth, and went to work on the mass of tangles. It took her about five minutes to get enough tangles combed out to be able to wash her hair in the shower. When she finished her shower, she put on a crocheted mauve sweater and a pair of jeans. The warmth of the blow-dryer felt good to her as she dried her beautiful long hair. Just a bit of blush and mascara was all she needed to look great. There was no way she could wear a lot of foundation like her sister and feel like she had a plastic mask on her face. She wanted to look and feel fresh, but the blush and mascara helped her to look a less plain and might save her from the taunting that could be dished out by Rhonda.

When Rhonda arrived, she was wearing tight fitting, black jeans with high heeled boots. Her purple sweater, with a huge cowlneck, was belted at her waist by a belt of interlocking metal circles secured by a hook and chain. Several long strands of beads swung from her neck as she leaned over to zip one of her boots securely.

Caroline thought, but would never say, Rhonda was way overboard and would look so out of place in a city like Asheville, a hippie haven. She looked at her sister and said a silent prayer, "Please Lord, don't let me ever be like my sister." Not that her sister was bad, but Caroline was earthy, and she intended to stay that way. Caroline would rather be wearing overalls and hiking boots, with her hair braided and essentially no makeup. To be dressed up would be wearing a cute long sleeved T-shirt, faded jeans, and clogs with just a bit of a heel.

The drive to Asheville, with blue skies turned to smoky gray, warning of an impending winter storm, was still a beautiful sight to Caroline. The silhouette of the Blue Ridge Mountains and valleys looked like crests and troughs of rolling ocean waves far out to sea. She looked over to her left to see barren deciduous trees and sparse evergreens. Sheer rock faces on the side of the mountain seemed to be glaring back at her. Looking over to her right, she saw enormous homes, nestled in the trees, looking like they were hanging from the side of the mountain. As they passed an excavation site for fill dirt, the soil was light brown, not nearly as reddish as the soil in the Upstate of South Carolina.

At the back of a country store, Caroline saw a couple of enormous trees, so overgrown with kudzu, they had the shape of an elephant. She allowed her thoughts to trail off to the time she and J.P. had made this trip in the fall. She missed him; his smile, his stories, and his interest in her. Even though she understood loss, like a familiar sad song ringing in her ears; it seemed senseless that he'd withdrawn from her. Her self-esteem began to plummet, and she felt the tears coming. She tried to turn off the emotion as she heard Rhonda's loud voice above the hum of the old Honda Civic's engine as they ascended the mountainous highway and the faint sound of music on the radio. Rhonda was asking her a question, but what?

Caroline scrambled to answer but knew she had to respond with, "Sorry, I didn't get that. It's purddy noisy back here."

Rhonda repeated her question, "Caroline, you're a million miles away from us in that backseat. Are you okay?"

Caroline was stunned by any display of compassion from Rhonda. Clearing her throat, she said, "Oh, I guess things have been stressful lately. I was just drifting off in tranquil thought." Bull hockey. She felt flushed and wondered if Rhonda was looking at her in the rearview mirror.

Mrs. Carter, with her keen insight, quickly changed the subject to neutral ground, the weather. "You girls know it's gonna be real cold today."

"Now Momma, you know we've both been up north in the dead of winter. We know what cold is," Rhonda interjected, trying to be savvy of all things.

Now collected, Caroline said, "I can't imagine Asheville feeling colder than New York was in December."

"Well, I've nevah been up north," Mrs. Carter said, but it can get pretty dadburn cold in these hills."

Rhonda added, "I reckon that's why there are so many moonshiners up here. They're all boozing to try to stay warm."

The three of them giggled, and Caroline felt some relief.

⇥⇤

Back in Summerville, Butch noticed how sullen J.P. had become. He was aware that J.P. had not mentioned Caroline at all. He knew Caroline had written J.P., as he was the one who found her letter in the mailbox and had given it to him. Butch wasn't the kind of person to beat around the bush, so he just opened up a very personal conversation with his friend.

"I know you're still hurting a lot about your grandma, but what's really going on with you? What's up with you and Caroline?"

"I don't know," J.P. responded. "I guess I'm just screwed up in the head. I haven't contacted her in a while."

"J.P., don't be a butthead with this girl. I think this is more than just your recent circumstances. I think you're tryin' to avoid intimacy with another person."

"Who made you a shrink while I was gone," J.P. said in a sarcastic tone of voice. "And who are you to tell me anything about intimacy? J.P. was furious, but then he calmed down a bit and tried to lighten up the conversation. "Man, I didn't mean to lash out, but you just got on my last nerve."

"I didn't mean to," Butch admitted, "but I thought you knew you had a good thing goin', and you're gettin' old."

"Butch, you're older than I am, you buffoon. We need to grab a beer and sit on the porch a while. I guess I should call her tonight."

J.P. started trying to get in touch with Caroline around six P.M. He called the campus switchboard to get the phone number to the dorm office just in case she was working. Around eleven thirty P.M. he finally convinced himself that she was out with some guy for the evening. As ridiculous and unfair as it was, he began to doubt her sincerity toward their relationship. Feeling full of regret for not having contacted her for so long, he couldn't really blame her. Why should she sit in her room alone, waiting for him to call her? He'd been wrong to shut her out after she'd been so open with him. He realized he had to get a grip on things and make a genuine effort to get connected with her soon or he might lose her all together. She was a natural beauty, intelligent, motivated, and sensitive. Obviously, he wasn't the only guy who'd go after her.

J.P. knew he wouldn't be able to sleep. He went into the kitchen to retrieve another beer from the refrigerator and went back out on the creaking wraparound porch and sat down in one of the weathered rocking chairs, munching on pork rinds. Sebastian, the crazy mutt, came bounding out the screen door, causing it to slam loudly behind him. Then Sebastian leapt up onto J.P's lap and began licking him in the face. How loyal he is, thought J.P., one could scold him or ignore him and he'd still keep coming back with loyalty and affection. Not so with women. Had he been unmindful to Caroline's needs and desires? Had he been expecting her to have the same loyalty to him as his old buddy, Sebastian?

Suddenly, he started feeling like a real jerk. No, he never pushed Caroline to sleep with him and then ignored her, so could he be a true jerk? Maybe he wasn't a jerk, but maybe he'd been a fool. He had to do something about this situation between them. After making himself a roast beef sandwich and some steak fries, he sat down to write her. Before Caroline Carter came into his life, he'd never even dreamt of writing a girl. He tried and tried to write, but he couldn't write a single word. His was a dried up well of words, or a wounded heart trying to mend. And it was easier to simply stay in his shell.

Finding a parking place in the city of Asheville wasn't going to be too difficult, like it would be in warmer weather. Caroline noticed few people out shopping as she looked up to see the temperature of thirty four degrees displayed on a sign in front of the bank building. Seeing a North Carolina flag wildly flapping in the breeze told Caroline that the wind chill would probably make that thirty four degrees seem like it was in the low teens, so she advised her sister and her momma to put on their scarves and gloves, as well as their winter coats, before facing the cold. She almost felt foolish to make a trip here in the dead of winter when most people were hunkered down in front of their fire places or wood stoves, eating hot soup or stew. Still, for a girl born in the foothills, there was a magical feeling about being in the mountains in winter. She would love to visit when snow was on the ground, but she knew better because neither she nor Rhonda knew how to drive in those conditions on the treacherous mountainous roads.

Just as they were getting out of the Honda, a strong chilling gust of wind whipped down the street, and Caroline immediately was carried away in thought to one of the days she'd spent in New York with J.P. She looked over at Rhonda, who was already complaining, "Durn, I'm ah freezin' already. Let's find a shop to browse in, fast." Caroline switched her thought right back to New York to feel J.P. take her arm and gently guide her into the warm pub the day they'd gone to the World Trade Center, as she instinctively hooked her arm around her momma's and guided her into the nearest shop.

It was a gift shop filled with handmade items like soap, pottery, chocolate, and hand knit scarves and mittens. Caroline roamed over to the jewelry counter to admire the earrings made from polished stones and silver, while Rhonda was drooling over the handcrafted hair accessories. Mrs. Carter was inspecting aprons, made with coordinating, brightly colored, cotton fabric in paisleys and floral patterns, as she contemplated the purchase of a gift to save for Granny Pritchett on Mother's Day. The room was filled with the scent of pine, Caroline's favorite, and the sound of water was calming, coming from the display of ceramic fountains filled with layered river rock for the illusion of small waterfalls. In the background, you could hear the mountain music of a dulcimer, banjo, and psaltry. Caroline found herself in front of shelves filled with all types of hand dipped candles, interesting pewter candle holders, ceramic incense burners, and handmade, Moravian style, wooden lanterns with glass panes, the type used in Winston Salem. The mixture of the aroma rising from a burning scented candle and pine from the boughs decorating the banisters leading to another level in the store, made for an earthy smell of rich soil covered with leaves and decomposing sticks and pinecones, one would expect to find when visiting the Blue Ridge Mountains.

With all the treasures upstairs and a book and card shop downstairs, the ladies managed to spend about thirty minutes in the gift shop. An inviting refreshment area was set up in the corner of the book room, with hot apple cider, tiny sugar cookies, and cinnamon twists. They enjoyed a couple of dainty cookies and warmed their bodies with small glass cups of hot cider, while lounging on comfy chairs upholstered with old patchwork quilts.

They decided to brave the cold and briskly walk down the street to the vintage clothing store. Rhonda tried on a 1960's, form fitting, short dress.

Caroline commented, "Rhonda, that dress looks so cute on you. It fits you to a tee. You look great in this vintage stuff."

Rhonda remarked, "I thank I'm gonna git it to wear to the salon one day. It's all about lookin' good when you're workin' in a nice salon, but I like to look different, too, don't wanna look like I went to the mall over the weekend, like everyone else."

Caroline thought to herself, *"You're different, alright. I've never met anyone else like you, and prob'ly never will. You're usually a rude pain in the butt, unless you are gettin' somethin' you want."*

Then she actually responded, "Rhonda, you do look good in that dress, get it," hoping that the encouragement would help her get out of the vintage clothing shop and on to one of the shops that sold the gauze type muslin shirts she loved, the ones made in India. She knew there was one of those shops right next to a mountain craft supply store where her momma would find beeswax sheets for candle making. They got back in the car and drove to that part of the city; there they popped into a coffee shop to get hot chocolate since the hot apple cider had whet their appetites.

A couple of hours of shopping drained them, and they had to save money for lunch at the Bavarian restaurant. It was a few miles from the city, so they raced to the car as quickly as possible as the cold wind nearly took their breath away.

The Bavarian restaurant was quaint. The building looked like a log cabin surrounded by gnomes, which seemed to Caroline to be a little on the tacky side. The small patch of dry, lawn was covered with barren tables, reminding Caroline of eating alfresco by the dock in Shem Creek with J.P. As a matter of fact, almost every destination that day reminded her of J.P., but the painful reality that he'd withdrawn himself from her made her melancholy.

Inside the restaurant, Caroline was shocked when she was greeted by a large boar's head mounted on the wall right in front of her in the entryway. Moving on inside the dining area, she found herself being entertained by the décor of cuckoo clocks and ceramic and pewter plates on the walls.

Rhonda piped up and said, "Law, law, law look at all these critters hanging up here a lookin' at us. The owner of this place must moonlight as a taxidermist." Momma Carter and Caroline got a bad case of the silly giggles just as the host came over to seat them. They got so silly, Rhonda had to take over and tell the host to seat them.

There were a variety of deer heads and antlers on the walls, a stuffed ring necked pheasant on top of a shelf, and a wolf skin hanging over the fireplace. All kinds of German steins were hanging from the beams overhead, which made it seem very cozy because the ceilings were so low. There were flowers in every window sill, giving the place a little bit of a feminine flair to an otherwise very masculine décor.

The three ladies were seated in the dining area near the bar. There were two other rooms with dining areas. Caroline could hear laughter and group conversations coming from the other rooms. It was such a small restaurant, even the noise from the kitchen could be heard in the dining rooms. Fortunately, the host had seated them next to a window, and Caroline was able to look out and up at the billowy clouds in the sky. Even that made her think of Charleston, looking out over the water at the Battery and up at the clouds overhead. She had one bad case of yearning for J.P and the Lowcountry.

Why had she let herself get so tangled up with J.P. that she hardly had fun with her friends and family? If their short lived relationship needed to end, she had to let it go and get on with living. Her momma noticed her pensive look and tried to cheer her up. Even Rhonda tried to help her snap out of it by offering to buy her a beer served in a stein. Mrs. Carter went along with it saying that she'd pass on the beer but be willing to drive back if needed.

"Momma, I said we planned to have a beer but not sit here all afternoon drowning our sorrows with brewsky," said Rhonda.

"Momma, I'm sure one beer is all I can take," added Caroline. "Beer makes me feel like a bloated hog." She cracked a slight smile but still had a look of sadness about her.

"Well, I was just telling y'all that I could drive back home if y'all need me to," Mrs. Carter said.

The waiter came to take the orders. Along with her dark beer, Caroline ordered cheddar cheese bratwurst and German potato salad. She asked to replace the weinkraut with spaetzle, with no thought to the load of carbohydrates and how that would make her feel with the beer.

Having had no breakfast, she was feeling the effects of the one big dark beer even though she made sure she ate bread and butter before her entrée came. Rhonda was also feeling the effects of the beer and asked Caroline to go to the restroom with her. They both got up from the table and walked toward the back of the restaurant where Rhonda asked the bartender to direct them to the ladies' room. Caroline was following behind her. As they walked past an entryway to another dining room, she heard a man speaking in another language. Assuming he was speaking German, she paid no attention and continued on to the ladies' room. Suddenly, the same man spoke in English and she froze. That voice sounded so much like Joost. She took two steps back to peek into the dining room and saw his unmistakable mane of hair. She nearly gasped as Rhonda turned around to see what had captured her sister's attention. Caroline all but leapt into Rhonda's path to get into the ladies' room. By that time Rhonda knew that something was up, and she went along with it, not saying a word to Caroline until they were both in the restroom.

"What," she asked Caroline?

Caroline looked at her sister with a puzzled look. "I think I just saw Joost."

"Joost who," Rhonda questioned?

"Joost Van Ness, that's who, and I wasn't expecting to see him here."

"Caroline, you've nevah mentioned anyone named Joost. What kind of name is that?"

"He's a guy I met at school."

"You must have 'cus there ain't no Joost Van Ness 'round home. So you met some foreigner at school, and now you've seen him in a restaurant. What's the big deal? Are you friends with this guy, or is there more to it than that?"

"I'm honestly not sure how to answer you."

"Come on, you know if he's just your friend or if he's interested in you, or if you're interested in him."

Caroline started feeling uncomfortable with Rhonda pushing her, trying to find out about her own personal affairs, so she steered the conversation away from Rhonda's questions.

"I can't believe he's out there. I don't know what I should do."

"Use the toilet before you pee in your pants, and then wash up, said Rhonda in her older sister tone of voice and laughing. "Momma's gonna wonder what's happened to us in here."

"Oh no, poor Momma is sittin' there all by herself. Rhonda, you get back out there to Momma, and tell her I'm sorta in a predicament."

"I have no idea what kind of predicament you're in, but we'll iron that out later, when I get the truth outta you. Get yourself together girl, you look like you've seen a ghost. Pinch your cheeks or somethin', get some color goin'."

Rhonda went out of the restroom while Caroline stood there looking in the mirror. She mumbled to herself, "Yuck, I look like I'm high on something, not good." She tried to run her fingers through her hair to comb out the tangles. She took a moistened paper towel and cleaned the mascara smudges from under her eyes. Then she turned on the water and cupped her hands to get some water to rinse her mouth, thinking she must smell like a brewery. She wanted so badly to speak to Joost but didn't know how she could do it without looking silly, interrupting his family time. She was about to exit the ladies' room when she remembered why she'd come in there in the first place. She went into the restroom stall contemplating making it a hiding place until she could get the nerve to go back out to the dining area. She stayed there long enough to get her gumption up, as Granny Pritchett would say, and then she made another stop by the sink to wash up. Now she was ready to exit the restroom and try to approach Joost's table.

Caroline took a deep breath and opened the door. Joost was walking through the entryway to the restrooms, ducking a little because the arch was so low. He looked up to see her standing there with her eyes wide opened.

"Caroline, what a pleasant surprise to see you here," he said, smiling. "Small world."

She was caught off guard because she was planning what to say if she went up to his table. Now she felt awkward and shy.

"Back at cha," she said, nearly stuttering, but smiling sweetly. Suddenly, she realized that he might not be familiar with that saying so she explained, "Oh that means same to you."

"Are you visiting Asheville for the day," he asked?

Both of them moved away from the restrooms and into the area next to the bar, not visible to her momma and sister.

"My sister and I came with our momma to get outta town, girls' day out."

"That's nice. I'm here with my brother and his family. We frequent this restaurant because the food is so *wunderbar,* saying the word in German.

"I'm enjoying the food, too," she said, not really knowing how long to keep conversing. She wanted to leave her momma and sister alone in the next room and steal him away from his family to find a small table in the room, away from both families. Shame!

"Caroline, can I call you next week?"

She felt excitement and responded quickly in the affirmative. She thought of the words, *serendipitous moments* and also remembered that she'd had no contact from J.P.

He reached out to shake her hand and said, "It's really good to see you again." He pulled her forward to him and hugged her, patting her on the back. Then he arched back a bit and kissed her from cheek to cheek three times. "I'll look forward to speaking with you next week."

"Me, too," she said, feeling like a dope for not thinking of something charming to say to end their conversation.

He turned to walk back toward his family, but turned his head back toward her and smiled, *his million dollar smile, to boot,* she thought. Then he added, "I still want to visit the campus in February, and hope I can see you." He laughed profusely and said, "The Rock Hill paper mill smell is getting into my nose again, and I can't stay away."

She giggled but she was really stuck for something to say, out of nervousness, so she just waved, smiled her most enticing smile, and turned to walk back to her table, with her heart feeling like it was going to pop right out of her chest. So, she turned back to find him still watching her and said, "I'll wait for your call."

Mrs. Carter was looking at her with a hint of worry and asked, "Are you alright, honey?" The cheek pinching color was gone, and she was as white as a sheet.

"Yeah, Momma, I'm fine."

"It took you so long in the ladies' room; I was starting to get concerned that you weren't feeling well."

"No, Momma, I'm not sick. After I came out of the ladies' room, I was actually talkin' to a friend of mine from school. I met him at Winthrop, but now he goes to school up here."

"That's nice you ran into him."

Rhonda was sitting next to Caroline and gave her a nudge with her knee. She was determined to get some answers to her questions, later, and Caroline knew that her sister would be relentless until she found out every detail of her relationship with Joost.

CHAPTER 11

WISHIN'

Despite Rhonda's incessant questioning, Caroline enjoyed the rest of her weekend at home. Coming back to school with mixed feelings toward J.P. and Joost, she felt like she was right back in a state of confusion. She wished she could make a firm decision about one of them or refrain from having a serious thought about anyone, but she wasn't ready. It seemed expected of her to at least have a steady boyfriend when she graduated, probably another antiquated idea that all girls should be serious about someone by the time they reached her age or they'd be labeled 'Old Maids', like school teachers who'd been expected to remain unmarried, in the past.

Student teaching was so demanding, Caroline sometimes doubted that she'd be able to cope with the demands of a real teaching job. How had her mother done it? She was already feeling drained of energy, and every weekend she dreaded the week to come. She had to refocus on school, lesson plans, reviewing materials, completing reports, all of the things she hated to do. She wanted to be creative, but it seemed that teaching actually stifled her creativity and left her wondering why she'd chosen education for her major. Certainly, her decisions about becoming a teacher were greatly influenced by the fact that her mother was a teacher. But Caroline had a giving spirit about her, and she wanted to make a contribution to society, change the human condition, if you will. There would be little money, little accolades, long grueling hours of preparation, and lots of attitudes, but somehow she'd make it and hopefully make a difference.

Sunday night was a nightmare back in the dorm. The basketball players on the floor above her sounded like they were having a full court game around eleven o'clock that night. She desperately needed sleep, as did all of the girls on her hall, who'd called her complaining, so she got her pen and fine pad ready. She ran up the stairwell to get her adrenalin flowing, jerked the hallway door open with such force it hit the wall of the stairwell, making a loud sound, and met the crowd of mindless players with the loudest and most cruel voice she'd ever used. She yelled, "Who wants the first fine tonight? Y'all are completely nuts if y'all think I'm going to put up with all this racket up here. Now, get those basketballs in your rooms and get quiet up here or I'm going make history at Winthrop for being the R.A. to have written the most fines in one night." Oh, she felt so empowered and actually felt very good about herself and her assertiveness.

The next morning, at five o'clock, Caroline hit the floor feeling like she'd pulled an all-nighter. Between the hullabaloo upstairs with the jocks and the myriad of thoughts about J.P. and Joost, she felt like she'd barely slept and knew she was in for a rough Monday. She hated going to school on winter days because she felt like she was leaving the campus in the middle of the night, in the dark, and wouldn't even see daylight until after lunch, at recess. She longed for the spring, daylight savings time and a break from the dreariness of winter.

On the way to school that day, Caroline was deep in thought. She had been so excited about graduating, but now she got depressed, at times, realizing that her life was going to continue to be hard. She had to make it on her own, and the profession she'd chosen was going to be constantly demanding and would arrest her.

When she got to school, she was thankful that she hadn't been student teaching long enough to take over the class for the entire day. Today was going to be interesting because her supervising teacher was giving her the opportunity to explain to the students the historical significance of the term Redneck, and she wondered what the comments would come from a group of third graders.

Sure enough, it was a real hoot listening to some of the little Rednecks trying to ask questions and make comments in the midst of the social studies lesson. One little dirty faced, ginger kid, with a big smile on his face, spoke up and said, "My grandpaw's a Redneck. He works out in the field all day till his neck gets plumb blistered and sweaty." The little boy drawled so it took him almost a minute to say two sentences. Needless to say, the entire class roared with laughter and Caroline lost control of the class for a while.

When she got back to campus late that afternoon, she turned on the radio and fell upon her bed, too exhausted to do anything. Listening to one of the tapes that Joost had given her, she was asleep in two shakes of a lamb's tail and woke up about fifteen minutes before the cafeteria entrance was scheduled to close. With her hair all mussed and her clothes wrinkled from napping, she ran down the stairwell, her rubber soled shoes squeaking on the painted concrete as she turned the corner. Fortunately, the entry gate to the cafeteria was not closed. She managed to get some greasy meatloaf with mashed potatoes and green beans, and sat down to eat.

Emily was about to leave the cafeteria when she spotted Caroline trying to inhale her food like she was in an eating contest. Emily walked up behind her, tapped Caroline on the shoulder, and Caroline nearly choked. She took a swig of sweet tea to wash the lumpy mashed potatoes down her throat. Emily was laughing, but

Caroline wasn't amused, feeling like she was going to gag on a big lump of potatoes.

"Ooh wee girl, ain't you a mess? I was wondering where you were all weekend," Emily said.

Caroline cleared her throat and said, "Oh, I had to get outta this crazy place for a while."

"Where'd you go," asked Emily, being nosy?

"I went to see Momma. I saw Rhonda, too, but Troy was in Atlanta visiting my cousin Jimbo."

"I didn't know you have a cousin named Jimbo," she commented, laughing again.

"I guess you don't have any relatives with stupid nicknames."

"At least not on Momma's side of the family, but Daddy's clan is a different story. I didn't mean for you to get your panties in a wad."

"Sorry, but I'm in a foul mood cus I didn't get much sleep last night."

"I figured. You look rough right now."

When I got home from Gastonia, I was give out. I fell asleep right away. I just woke up from my cat nap, and now I have to cram my food into my mouth, like I have to do at school every day, so I won't be hungry all night."

Caroline tried to get a few bites of food down while Emily responded, "I didn't get much sleep either. I had a project due today, and I didn't start working on it until yesterday morning."

After another swig of sweet tea, Caroline asked, "How long had you known about the project?"

"My professor told us about a month ago."

"I don't feel sorry for you, Emily." I would nevah procrastinate like you do."

"I know Caroline, that's why you haven't had much fun in college, and I've had a blast," Emily chortled, as she spat out the last line.

Caroline kept on chewing her food and rolled her eyes at Emily.

"I guess I better let you eat before they close the place."

Thank the Lord she didn't ask about J.P., thought Caroline. There was no way she was going to complain about J.P. or tell Emily about seeing Joost. She wanted to keep intimate matters to herself and make her own judgments about the men in her life, without having two cents' worth, or five dollars' worth of advice from Emily.

Tuesday at school was not quite as bad as Monday had been. Caroline thought, tomorrow is hump day and Friday will seem a lot closer. She hated feeling that way, having a bad attitude about school, but many of the teachers were saying the same thing in the lounge as they ran in to snatch their food out of the refrigerator and check their mailboxes, complaining about this and that report that was due.

Caroline didn't get back to campus until five o'clock. To avoid having to inhale her food again, she made sure she went straight to the cafeteria when she got home. After dinner she dragged herself up the stairwell, being fatigued from a long day and sluggish from a full stomach.

As she was fumbling with her room key, she heard the phone ringing. She rushed to get the door unlocked, but the harder she tried to hurry, the longer it seemed to take her. Finally successful on the fifth ring, she darted for the phone and sounded out of breath when she answered the call. In a flickering moment, she wished it was J.P. calling her.

"You must have jogged down the hall trying to get to your telephone."

She knew with the first word that it was Joost. She had to admit to herself that his deep, masculine voice always captivated her in a conversation.

"No, I didn't jog, but I was struggling with my key. I think it may have gotten bent somehow."

"Did you have a good weekend, away from campus," he asked?

"I did have a good weekend; I enjoy being with my family even though my sister drives me crazy sometimes; she can be so sarcastic and irritating. It was nice to run into you at the restaurant," she added.

"I'm glad I saw you there, too. Wasn't the food fabulous? I had a parfait with black forest cake, dark cherry ice cream, and whipped cream for dessert. It was so rich, it was sinful," he said.

"Oo...h, that does sound sinful. I was so full from the beer and the meal; I couldn't possibly have had room for dessert."

"Caroline, I mentioned to you that I'm still planning to come to the campus soon; I'll be arriving on the sixth of February. I wondered if you'd do me the honor of having dinner with me the following evening." His well-mannered formality always seemed to intrigue her, but sometimes she wished he could talk like she did so she could relax and not have to be mindful of her dialect all the time.

Given how excited he seemed to see her in Asheville, she'd anticipated the invitation, and she couldn't turn him down. He never mentioned a word about J.P. and she didn't either. Actually, she'd been so lonely lately, she was thrilled to be shown the attention. She responded quickly, "Sure, I'd love to have dinner with you."

"Do you have a preference in terms of cuisine," he inquired?

"Gee, I really don't know what to say. Anything you choose will be fine with me." She felt silly to speak so simplistically.

Joost was refined and cultured, born with a silver spoon in his mouth, and had grown up in the lap of luxury. Her background was the antithesis of his; she and her family had lived a plain and simple life, but it had been a good life.

"Okay, we'll decide later. Thanks for saying yes. I'll let you go for now. Take care."

"You, too, Joost. I'll talk to you soon."

Caroline hung up the phone. She looked around her dorm room – painted concrete walls, a full-length mirror on the back of the door, and makeshift book shelves made of more cinder blocks and unpainted boards. The two single beds in her room had been pushed together to make them look like one big bed, draped with a king sized comforter covered with tiny pink flowers and bumble bees. She felt secure in this room, but she knew that soon she'd be finished with school and out on her own. Perhaps prematurely, she'd thought that her relationship with J.P. was going in a serious direction. After all, why would he have taken her to meet his family if he didn't really care about her? But now, there was no communication between them; and what had she done by having agreed to go out with Joost? The excitement she'd felt just minutes earlier was diminishing rapidly, and she began to cry, in her isolation, walled in silence. She was allowing herself to continue some kind of relationship with a foreign student who would beak her heart when his season was up in the United States and it was time to go back to Europe. She cried even harder when she thought of J.P., because she missed him, too, and he already meant so much to her. But she feared that he'd break her heart. She cried for fear that growing up in sort of a dysfunctional family, with no father figure, was making her want guys in her life that she couldn't really have. She cried for her daddy, with incalculable grief manifested in great heaving sounds, wishing he could help her during this difficult transition in her life. For the first time in a long while, she had to admit that she didn't want to be an adult, she didn't want to have to grow up so fast. She cried, all alone in her room, for a long time that night and felt a loneliness so profound it seemed impossible to come out of. She finally wore herself out crying, changed her tear soaked sweatshirt, pulled off the purple, high top tennis shoes she was still wearing, and eventually fell asleep.

The following evening, Emily came by trying to entice Caroline to go to Daddy's Money and drink a beer or two. Emily didn't have to student teach, so she could cut class the next day if she didn't feel like going. Caroline didn't know how she did it, but Emily always managed to make friends in most of her classes who were willing to share their lecture notes when she decided to cut class. Unlike Emily, Caroline was restricted by the demands of her daily schedule, and too much party time would bring misery the next day.

Caroline begged Emily to share the cost of a pizza and stay and chat with her while she cut out laminated game boards, letters for a bulletin board, and some handwriting cards. It seemed to Caroline that teachers never had a moment to themselves; the work was never finished. It was going to be one heck of a job, but it was too late now to change that course she'd taken.

They ordered a large pizza and went downstairs to get two cans of orange soda out of the vending machines. Back upstairs, after the pizza arrived, they talked about random topics as they stuffed themselves; then Emily got down to business asking about J.P. as Caroline started cutting.

"So, how's it goin' with J.P.? Are y'all gettin' along good," asked Emily? She was unaware of the fact that Caroline hadn't heard from him at all.

"Emily, I really hate to tell you this, but J.P. hasn't called or written me for quite a while."

"Oh, rats. I had no idea. Sorry to hear that. From everythin' I've heard from Drew, he's crazy 'bout you. There caint be someone else. He hasn't dated anyone else but you, since he met you, or I would've heard 'bout it. Summerville is such a small town, word still gets out 'bout things, and some people don't mind their own business," she said as she cleared her throat a little and smiled and then shrugged her shoulders and rolled her eyes.

"Well, prob'ly won't work between us."

"Caroline, don't give up on him. He's really a good guy, and he has a good heart."

"Emily, I have a heart, too, and I don't want to let it get broken, over and over again."

"If you worry so much about gettin' your heart broken, you may miss love altogether."

"What is this - response from Dear Emily time?"

"No, I'm not tryin' to get all up in your business."

Caroline cut her off and said, "Well don't, then." She stuffed one more bite of pizza crust into her mouth and just looked at Emily, who was quite shocked to see Caroline almost have a Class A hissy fit."

CHAPTER 12

FORGIVIN'

Caroline was still standing next to her mailbox as she read J.P.'s letter that day. He admitted to her that he'd been alienating himself from everyone and that he was feeling like a real jerk for the way he'd been treating her, having no communication with her. She walked over to the seating area and sat down to read the letter a second time. Streams of tears started to roll down her cheeks, and she searched for a tissue in her backpack before her nose started to drip. She believed every word he'd written, realizing that he'd been grieving in his own way, alone. She even felt regretful to have given up on him, so to speak.

It suddenly dawned on her that he did want to see her soon. She was in a real pickle now, having planned to go out with Joost and knowing that J.P. wanted to see her, too. What if he showed up again, at the same time that she would be with Joost? If that happened, he'd never believe that they were just friends. But were they just friends? After all, she had accepted another dinner invitation and felt like Joost was asking her for a date. How was she going to deal with this now? Well, the answer to that would be to do it with charm, "Gracefully, of course, like any fine lady of the South would do."

The next day was horrible. Five blocks before Caroline and her friend arrived at school, they pulled off the street and into a parking lot because the car was pulling to one side as they drove. Caroline suspected a flat tire and got out to find that the tire was flat. It looked like the rim was sitting on the pavement. They must have been riding for miles on a slack tire, but now it was completely flat. Her friend started to cry like a big baby. Finally, she got a grip and said, "My momma and daddy barely have enough money to pay for the car payment and insurance. I can't destroy this tire, by continuing to drive on it and then expect my parents to pay for a new tire."

Caroline knew enough about tires to realize that it would destroy the tire to drive it any further. She also knew it was cold and her backpack would be heavy to lug for a couple of blocks, and her punctilious nature would make her ill all day being late to school.

Because the streets were well illuminated, the decision was made for the two girls to walk to school. Caroline's lower back was killing her from the heavy backpack, and the bottom of her slacks got wet when she stepped in a puddle on the way. What a miserable day!

The afternoon wasn't much better. Walking back to the car, helping her friend change the tire, and then waiting forever in a busy tire shop while the tire was patched, all proved to be draining and exhausting for Caroline. At least she learned how to change a tire that day.

When she got back to campus, all she wanted to do was find tomato soup and grilled cheese sandwiches in the cafeteria, but instead she had her choice of greasy fried fish, boring spaghetti, or corned beef hash, none of which she wanted to eat. She resorted to the same old nasty salad, which was never drained properly, with watery blue cheese dressing, a roll, and a slice of dry spice cake. She knew she should be grateful for what she had, grateful for the fact that she was even there at Winthrop, but this day was too much like the adult life that she didn't want to face alone, too soon in her future, a day filled with hassles, discomforts, and disappointments, another day just getting by.

Joost's days didn't seem to be like that, with plenty of money to do what he wanted, and J.P.'s didn't seem to be either, although he had to work harder for his keep. Caroline was feeling a bit of panic about graduation being only a few months away and no job yet because school systems don't start hiring new teachers until the spring and summer. Where was she going to live, what was she going to drive; what was she going to eat? If she just had her daddy, she wouldn't have to worry, but she didn't and these life issues were her own to deal with. She wanted to scream and holler, but she was in the middle of the cafeteria, eating crappy food and feeling very sorry for herself.

Once back in her dorm room, with the radio tuned to her favorite station, and having changed into her most comfortable sweat pants, she collapsed onto her bed and stared up at the ceiling. She reached over to the desk next to her bed and retrieved the letter from J.P. As she read it again, the tears started to flow once more and she said to herself, "I gotta do something 'bout this mess, before it gets messier." She lay there a few more minutes to think and to relax from the stress of a "pain in the butt" kind of day. She got up only to turn on the radio and then repositioned herself upon the bed. After listening to the music and meditating for a while, she came up with a game plan.

Finally, she pulled out some stationary and began to write to Joost. She had to distance herself somehow, but do it in such a way that he'd know how much he'd helped her through the rough times. The situation with J.P. warranted some explanation. She had to let Joost know how much she'd always treasured their friendship, but she definitely needed to let go of any chance of a relationship with Joost.

Okay, the letter was written, but would she have the guts to mail it. She had to do it; she had to stop feeling like she was playing two guys. Being flattered by the attention was one thing, but it was against her nature to ever intentionally hurt someone. She wanted to observe the Golden Rule, and treat others the way she wanted to be treated. She cared about Joost, too, but not in the same way that she cared for J.P., and she didn't want to lead Joost on. The letter from J.P. made all the difference. It had helped her to clarify her feelings and thoughts. If she had a chance at all with J.P., she had to go for it with him, she had to forgive him and forget about the way he dealt with things, accept his differences. She herself had to deal with her own tragedy in the best way that she could, so she had no right to judge him for the way that he dealt with his own pain.

Caroline waited several days before she mailed the letter to Joost, to be absolutely sure that she wanted to break the ties with him. He was a beautiful fantastic guy, and it was difficult for her to let him go out of her life. But J.P. was different, he made her hope for a future, and for months prior to the death in his family, he'd made her feel loved. She couldn't help feeling that Joost was really off limits, being a foreign student; and she didn't want to be in that trap of seeking attention from guys she could never have, avoiding true intimacy out of her own fear of losing someone. She was aware of these dynamics, yet it was hard to put into practice, emotionally, what she knew from an intellectual standpoint.

J.P. was equally as interesting as Joost was, but he was less formal. She had seen how popular he was when she was at his oyster roast in Summerville. He just knew how to deal with people; he knew how to entertain.

The more she sat and pondered over the good traits that J. P. had, the more she wanted to build an emotional bond with him and was willing to trust that his letter was truly a reflection of his character.

A couple of ordinary days passed and Caroline found it difficult to keep her mind on her student teaching assignment. She watched the other student teachers and their supervising teachers and wondered if they ever had a life. Everyone was so engrossed in their work, and it seemed that teaching was very competitive. She couldn't see the necessity of working on a bulletin board for a week, drawing, cutting, pasting, and taping one's life away. She was already sick of file folders and index cards. *Would she have to do this for the rest of her life? How on earth had her momma done it for so long? How would it be possible to have her own children, in the future, and still teach school?* Her mind was running a mile a minute and she needed to get off the treadmill.

It wasn't until she started to write J.P. a letter that she remembered she hadn't mailed her letter to Joost. As soon as she thought of Joost, she got up and put on her down filled jacket and clogs and headed out the door to go mail the letter. She had to do it, and it had to be final. A few minutes later she stood in front of the mailbox. She kissed the envelope and then quickly put it into the mailbox. Now it was finished. Her decision had been made, and she couldn't entertain thoughts of Joost other than fond memories of what they'd shared together. Now she could move forward.

Her letter to J.P. was rather short because she didn't want to sound like she was head over heels in love with him. She was still trying to sort out her feelings, but she had to respond positively to his letter. He seemed to have poured out his heart to her. She closed her letter saying that she'd love for him to come for a visit. Then she sealed the envelope and hoped that he wanted to see her near Valentine's Day.

Sure enough, J.P. called her and asked to see her on Saturday, February 14th. It was so wonderful to hear his voice. He sounded as cheerful as he had when they'd first met. The phone bill for that call must have been astronomical because they talked for at least two hours. It was as if they'd never been apart, let alone been at odds over a lack of communication. She was curious when he asked her if she thought she could get a ride back to Greenville, but she assumed he only wanted to have a better selection of restaurants than could be found in the rinky-dink city of Rock Hill. She assured him that she could get a ride home that weekend because so many girls would be going home to spend the holiday with their hometown beaus.

In the following days, Caroline felt insouciant, like a billowy cloud floating in the Carolina blue sky, having not a care in the world. Her teaching wasn't getting on her nerves; her mindless job in the school dorm wasn't driving her up the wall. Even the male idiots that lived on the floor above her weren't bothering her. What had happened to her? She'd never felt like this before. Maybe vacillating between J.P. and Joost only masked her true feelings. She'd been suppressing her feelings for so long she didn't know how to feel comfortable with the emotions that most people nonchalantly accepted.

Arrangements were made for travel home on Friday. When she spoke with her momma, she was bewildered to find out that J.P. had called Mrs. Carter and requested that she make sure Caroline was ready to go out on Saturday night no later than five o'clock. She knew he was up to something, and he would entertain her with finesse. Now, all she needed to do was relax and find a way to the mall in Charlotte so she'd have a beautiful outfit to wear on the special occasion. Fortunately, she'd built up a little nest egg from her earnings on campus.

Before she knew it Friday arrived and she found herself in Greenville awaiting his call. He'd stay in a motel for the weekend as Troy was out of town. He knew they would both be tired, so he called and suggested they go to the movies and pig out on buttered popcorn. It was an evening filled with a long awaited squeeze hugs and tender kisses.

Not having known whether or not she had the money for a new outfit, J.P. wanted to take Caroline to the mall on Saturday morning. When she realized what his intentions were, other than having a desire to spend time with her, she was touched by his sentimentality. She told him about having gotten a new outfit in Charlotte, but he insisted on buying her some very nice costume jewelry that she picked out. He told her that he wanted her to have a very memorable evening on their first Valentine's Day together.

Rhonda came over that afternoon to style Caroline's hair in an updo and also do her makeup. Caroline told her to be sure to apply about one quarter of the amount of foundation that she wore. Rhonda did do a great job on her eye shadow, and Caroline wore eye liner for the first time. Her hair looked fabulous, so much so that Caroline was paranoid about messing up her hair when she changed into her outfit. Rhonda had pulled her hair back, secured it, and curled it with a curling iron. Two loose ringlets touched her cheeks. She managed to get dressed without wrecking her hair or her makeup. She wore black dress pants. Her red and black silk top was sleeveless with the fabric gathered in the front and back to tie into a mock collar, buttoning in the back with four fabric covered buttons. She adorned herself with the gorgeous, flashy earrings and bracelet that J.P. had gotten for her at the mall. Rhonda had brought over her black dress shoes, which just fit Caroline, and her black woolen dress coat. When the makeover was complete, she could have passed for a super model, if only she were a few inches taller. Before she could leave her bedroom, the one the sisters had shared as children, Rhonda came in armed with a perfume bottle and began to mist Caroline until she almost lost her breath. They both squealed with delight until Caroline hollered, "I gotta get out of here so I can breathe." Caroline escaped, and Rhonda gave one more squeeze, more mist filling the room, behind her sister.

When J.P. arrived, Mrs. Carter welcomed him at the door. She set her instant camera on the top of the piano and was ready to take pictures of Caroline and J.P., just as she would if they were going to a prom, a photograph for posterity.

J.P. looked dashing in gray dress pants, a gray turtle neck, and a black sports coat. His squeaky clean hair was tousled, making him very handsome. It was apparent, from the sheen of his black shoes that they were brand spanking new. And talk about smelling good, his cologne wafted into the room. Mrs. Carter could certainly understand why Caroline was so taken by this young man; she would have been, too, if she were still in her twenties. He was very good looking and polite, very personable.

When Caroline emerged from the hallway and stepped into the living room where J.P. was chatting with Mrs. Carter, he rose to greet her and was again awe-struck by her beauty, as he had been on their previous date in Charleston. She came and stood facing him, the scent of perfume making her even more desirable, where they engaged in a warm embrace. Neither of them knew exactly what to say, with her momma in the room, so they simultaneously spoke saying, "You look great!" Both of them laughed when they realized they had the same thoughts and spoke nearly in unison.

He stepped back and said, "You look way better than great, you're absolutely beautiful."

She blushed, with her momma sitting there smiling in the winged armchair, and thanked him in her most appealing drawl. Then she lightened things up, saying that they both were a little overdressed to eat a hamburger.

Her momma chimed in and said, "It looks like you better make other plans." Caroline knew that her momma was well aware of J.P.'s plans for the evening, because she had told her to be ready by five, and she wouldn't say another word to spoil his surprise.

J.P. said jokingly, "Well, we'll have to go for a long drive until we find something suitable."

Caroline knew he was teasing her. He definitely had made reservations somewhere with it being Valentine's Day. Mrs. Carter realized they needed to go, to make their reservations on time, and asked if she could take a few snapshots of them all dressed up.

When he opened the door of his Toyota, J.P. had a single red rose placed upon the passenger's seat; the stem of the rose had been wrapped in cream satin ribbon. Caroline picked up the rose and turned to him and kissed him on the cheek saying, "You think of everything, don't you." She smiled at him, with her glossy lips parting to show her radiant white teeth.

He just shook his head, and said, "You are the loveliest creature I have ever laid eyes on," and he definitely meant it.

As they exited the neighborhood, he asked to be directed to Highway 25. Caroline knew there were no classy restaurants on that route. All of the really nice restaurants were in downtown Greenville or on the east side of the city. She expressed no thoughts to him, but promptly directed him to the highway.

When they got close to the highway, she saw the skating rink and said, "There's the skating rink I went to as a child and teenager. I got my first kiss there and my first broken bone."

He chuckled and responded, "I didn't know you could roller skate. I've never been to a roller skating rink, but I have tried to ice skate up in Jersey."

"I'm not very good in roller skates," she lamented. "I used to be very envious of the good skaters. After I broke my wrist, I was always afraid I would fall and break another bone, so I really didn't develop much skill."

"Well maybe we need to go try," he replied.

"You wanna go roller skating," she asked?

"Yeah, If we go skating, you're going to feel good about yourself, 'cus I'm going to stink at it and will fall and bust my butt a few times," he said as he laughed.

As he said those words, Caroline began to feel that feeling of love and concern he expressed for her. It was so strong she couldn't deny that he cared for her deeply, and it made her let go, even a tiny bit, to express emotion toward him. She said, "I wouldn't let you fall without me, 'cus I'd be holding your hand as we tried to skate together."

"Sounds like a plan to me. Tell me if I am going north if I take a right."

They were indeed going north, but Caroline saw the fairgrounds, churches, houses, gas stations, and strip malls. She was clueless about where they were going to eat. Maybe there was a nice place north of Greenville, which she wasn't aware of. After all, she'd been away from this area for four years. She didn't question him but tried to make conversation when she spotted the elementary school where her momma worked. Meanwhile, he'd dropped a cassette tape into the player, since the radio reception was poor. They traveled several miles and passed the exit to Traveler's Rest. It was at that point she realized that he might be taking her to Asheville.

"I guess now you know where I'm taking you since we're almost out of Greenville county, crossing over the state line to North Carolina," he said awaiting her questions.

"You're taking me to Asheville," she asked?

"I am taking you to Asheville, but I'm not going to tell you where we'll go once we arrive in the city. I want this to be a surprise to you when we get there."

"Okay, I'm not going to pump you for information," she said. "I know it'll be a fantastic place. You've always tried to make things special for me." She wanted to say that's why I love you so much, but she wouldn't allow herself to say what she felt at the moment.

With the car in fifth gear and no need to change it for a while, J.P. reached over and took her by the hand resting their hands on the tiny console between the two front seats. Then he shocked her in saying, "I want to do this because I love you."

She squeezed his hand, but she couldn't say what was on her mind and in her heart. She felt love but she was afraid to let herself continue to feel it. She was afraid to love a man and then lose him, abandonment issues. No, no she couldn't think about things like that right now. She couldn't ruin this wonderful night, such a special night. She didn't think seeing a shrink would help. For the past couple of years, she'd dismissed the whole thing, telling herself that Mr. Right hadn't come into her life yet. In retrospect, perhaps that was true, but was she still pushing the good ones away, trying to say to herself, they aren't perfect? Her momma would be quick to tell her that no human has ever been perfect, except Jesus himself. But Caroline didn't want to talk to her momma about things like this because she didn't want her to worry. She didn't want her family or friends to think she was nuts. She sure didn't want J.P. to think she was a loon. So, she sat there holding his hand and waiting for enough time to pass to change the tone of the conversation.

Then she said, "I can't imagine where you're taking me in Asheville."

"I'm sure we'll both like it. From everything I've heard, it's the kind of place you don't forget, but that's all I'm telling you."

"Okay, I don't want you to tell me, so no matter how much I beg you, you can't give it away," she said in a very sweet but juvenile tone of voice.

"Let's change the subject before you figure it out. How's your student teaching going?" he asked.

"I guess the student teaching part is going okay, but sometimes I wish I hadn't chosen education as my major."

"I know I couldn't do it," he said. "When I have kids one day, I'll be very glad to have them taken off my hands for a few hours."

"J.P., that's terrible," she said, almost giggling.

"My buddy from Clemson already has three at his house. He calls them little rug rats. His wife stays home with them all day, and he doesn't even have to deal with them until the weekend. Then they usually get a babysitter, and she takes them to church on Sunday with the grandparents."

"Is he a male chauvinist or what," she questioned?

He started to laugh on that one and responded, "I guess you could say that, but if you ever see him again, don't tell him I told you so. For now, his name will remain a mystery."

"What do you mean, see him again," she asked?

"I mean you met him already when you first came to Summerville, at my oyster roast."

"Who are you talking about?"

"I'll let you figure that one out one night when you're really bored working in the office of the dorm."

She said jokingly as she let go of his hand and slapped her hand on the console, "You're terrible."

"Well, I might be terrible, but I'm still taking the most beautiful girl I know to a very nice place tonight. If I have anything to do with it you're going to be with a terrible man for a long time."

She sat motionless and silent until he finally changed the subject.

Once in Asheville, they took an exit where the city streets were lined with small businesses and some small stone houses. A tiny unobtrusive sign guided J.P. to turn left into a residential area. The homes were large, some stone and others brick, in the well-established neighborhood with huge, old trees. Some homes were barely visible from the street with large plantings that covered the lower floors.

One fabulous Tudor style home looked especially expensive. Thinking back to earlier fantasies, Caroline could imagine herself living in such a grandiose home, beautifully decorated by an interior designer, with custom ceiling to floor floral drapes, silk pillows covering the back of the chintz sofa, and mahogany tables covered with strategically stacked books, tastefully selected foreign or antique trinkets, exquisite lamps with fringed shades, and silk floral arrangements in chinoiserie vases. She could see an image, in her mind's eye, of herself in the garden cutting fresh flowers to arrange in a crystal vase atop of an enormous oval dining room table, beautifully set with china, crystal goblets, the best silver, and napkins folded in the shape of a tulip.

As they were ascending the streets on the hillside, they could see more enormous homes. Again they saw a small sign directing them to a golf course. The inclined winding two lane road took them to the side of a huge stone building.

J.P. said to her, "This is the Grove Park Inn. Many famous people have stayed at this inn. I've spent years wishing I would come to this place, and I know both of us are going to love it."

Neither of them had ever seen such a mammoth stone structure. J.P. drove on up to the porte-cochere to take advantage of valet parking, not caring one whit about driving a Toyota rather than a Mercedes. Caroline felt pampered as J.P. opened her car door and took her by the hand, like stepping back into the last century to be assisted to exit her carriage. He couldn't take his eyes off of her, for that moment, and thought how beautiful she looked. She looked directly into his intoxicating blue eyes; she'd never had such an intense feeling toward anyone else. But she tried to conceal it by inhaling deeply and slowly and smiling as a belle, arriving at the ball, would do with confidence.

They walked between huge stone columns to the inn's far entrance. To the right and left, rows of handmade rocking chairs, created from twisted branches and vines, rocked back and forth in the crisp evening breeze. For a moment she could almost envision patrons sitting there, rocking back and forth. Suddenly, an image of a woman rocking a baby, flashed before her, but she quickly turned her head to see the beautiful black urns by the doorways that were filled with winter grasses, trailing ivy, and colorful pansies that J.P was commenting on. He opened one of the heavy pine doors, and held it open for her. They walked into the inn where J.P. checked with the concierge to get directions for the restaurant. As they entered the elegant lobby, they saw two massive stone fireplaces.

Moving toward one of the two-story fireplaces, J.P. softly said, "I've heard about these, and they're incredible. I bet you could fit a car in the inner hearth. They must be about thirteen or fourteen feet high," he said with the enthusiasm of an adolescent.

She smiled at him and winked. Caroline was spellbound at the sight of it all. She looked around the open room, one vast lounge with mission style sofas and tables and cocktail waitresses dressed in black scampering from patron to patron. A pianist was playing jazz on the grand piano, which was dwarfed by the surroundings.

Caroline asked J.P., "Can we sit here for a little while and listen to the music?"

"Of course we can," he answered, agreeably. "We aren't on a tight schedule. Our dinner reservations are for seven thirty."

Caroline glanced across the room seeing well-dressed couples in their thirties, forties, fifties, and many even older. She thought they all must be living the good life, being guests at the inn paying astronomical prices, spending the evenings at their leisure. She tried to refocus to give J.P. her attention, realizing she'd been bedazzled for several minutes, but her thoughts were racing. She managed to comment on the jazz pianist and simply told him that the place was so wonderful, she was without words. He'd been quite content as he marveled at the architectural details and the extraordinary stonework and sizable exposed beams above. Suddenly, their eyes met again, and he took her by the hand. He stroked her smooth skin and felt the contours of her fingers, especially her ring finger. She wondered what he was thinking as they sat there in silence listening to the pianist run his fingers over the keys from one end of the piano to the other. Their seating was facing the back of the room, and they could see lights through the windows.

His curiosity aroused, he asked, "Do you want to go outside for a quick view of the garden? I heard it's full of ornamental shrubs from many other countries. I'm sure it's superb, even in the winter." His real intention was to be alone with her, even if only momentarily.

"Sure," she responded as put on her woolen coat, not having checked it upon arrival, and the sleek, black kid leather gloves she'd borrowed from her momma. "But we'll have to make it very quick so we won't freeze."

"We may be in the mountains in the winter, but it's not as cold as Manhattan was with the gusts of freezing winds."

"Stop now," she said. "You'll make me so cold thinking about it, I won't go outside."

"We'll be okay for a few minutes."

He placed his hand on her back, gently guiding her toward the door. Of course when they exited the room, there were no other couples outside, in the cold. They looked down the wide stone steps to the well-lighted garden.

Then J.P. admitted, "I needed to be alone with you for a few minutes. You're so beautiful tonight." Before she could thank him for the compliment, he embraced her and kissed her. After he kissed her, he held her tightly; he put his head near her shoulder, taking in the essence of the fragrance she was wearing. Then he whispered, as if the garden was filled with spectators, that he was so sorry for putting her in a stressful situation when he didn't contact her. She reached up and stroked the back of his neck and whispered back that it was the past and they were going to have a very special evening. Without warning, her mind was filled with doubt, as if something sinister was trying to dampen her spirit, but she resisted the ill thought.

They walked hand in hand, back into the lobby and down the hallway. The walls were lined with mission style bookcases filled with all types of memorabilia of famous visitors to the inn, postcards, letters, and photographs, decades of reminders of the past. The two of them stood there reading articles written about famous authors, government officials, actors, and business leaders. After taking the elevator up a few floors, they meandered through the hallways of the inn, with her arm in his, until the restaurant was in sight. They stopped by the window to their left and looked out over the illuminated garden below. He so wanted to kiss her again, but he didn't want to give her the impression that he was all over her; she meant so much more to him than that. He opted to stand there quietly, thinking about the first day they'd spent together in Charleston and on the beach. She had no idea that he was being secretly sentimental and felt a little awkward standing there in silence.

It was not quite time to enter the restaurant. Outside the entrance to the restaurant, there were plush sofas and chairs placed strategically to promote conversation. They sat upon the chenille sofa sinking into the oversized cushions as J.P. described the cuisine of the restaurant as he knew it, using body language to depict something as small as one of the hors d'oeuvres or as large as the piece of pinkish beef from which prime rib was being sliced. One would think he was a French chef for all the enthusiasm he was displaying. She thought he was really cute. They chatted a few more minutes, and then he politely excused himself for a moment to let the hostess know that they'd arrived and wished to be seated a few minutes early, if possible.

As they followed the hostess through the lounge, they were both shocked to see enormous ice sculptures in various rooms containing buffet items, the first of which was salads and breads. The display tables were tiered and covered with elegant white linen tablecloths. The food was in large silver or glass serving dishes, with every dish looking scrumptious. Male servers wearing white jackets and chef's hats stood behind the tables ready to assist. The lighting of the buffet was fabulous, highlighting various culinary displays. They continued to follow the hostess through the buffet area and bypassed the room filled with meats and vegetables, to reach their table in front of a wall of windows, from which the view of the city lights was fantastic. A server soon came to them, filling goblets with water and then unfolded the linen napkin to place upon Caroline's lap. A faint sense of insecurity flooded her thoughts as she feared not knowing the proper protocol for fine dining. Her countenance must have exposed her feeling because J.P. asked her if she was okay.

"Yes, I'm okay," she said. "It's so nice here; I can't believe how wonderful everything seems." She knew that J.P. was big on the atmosphere of a fine restaurant. He loved to enjoy the ambiance and delicious food that fine dining offers. She reminisced back to their date to 82 Queen Street and Dock Street Theatre, and said, "You have a flair for entertaining me in the most fabulous places. I'll never forget our first official date, how special you made it."

"I want this to be equally as special for you tonight," he said. They were interrupted momentarily as their waiter wanted to know if they would be enjoying the buffet or wished to order from the menu, and J.P. ordered a bottle of wine. Then when alone again, he reached into his pocket and pulled out a small gift to present to her. Her eyes opened wide, and she began to smile as she opened the dainty gift. She lifted the lid of the black velvet jewelry box to find sparkling diamond earrings, not tiny earrings, but those of substantial size. She dropped her shoulders and exhaled before lifting her head to look at him.

Then with teary eyes, she said to him, "You are so wonderful to me. You've done so much for me in the past five months." Then she placed her hand over his, no longer being able to imprison her feelings, and said, "John Paul, I love you, too."

His face beamed with a smile as he leaned over to kiss her cheek and said, "I'm glad you do. It would be a tragic thing for me to love you this much if you didn't love me back."

For the first time, she didn't want to go back to her momma's house that night, but she would. *Lordy, Lordy, what would Momma think if she could read my mind right now? Thank God, she's not a clairvoyant."* She sat there smiling; she was at peace with the man she really loved.

CHAPTER 13

FALLIN'

After the date of her life at the Grove Park Inn, the defined start of her courtship in her thinking, Caroline found it almost unbearable to separate from J.P. as she had to return to Winthrop, and he had to make the long trip back to Summerville on Sunday afternoon. Although Caroline thought her big sister might have a nosy motive for doing so, Rhonda offered to take her back to school, as it was very tiresome for her momma to do the round trip and still have to prepare to teach the following day.

Rhonda had dated lots of men but refused to engage in a committed relationship and thought Caroline should do the same. But Caroline was not about to follow suit with her sister if she had a dog's chance to be with J.P. in a long term relationship. She thought Rhonda perpetuated that dysfunctional family excuse to avoid dealing with relationships.

"You're so quiet, Caroline," Rhonda said, trying to get the dialogue going between sisters. "What was it like last night?"

"You've never been to Grove Park Inn for dinner before, have you?" Caroline questioned. She thought if she kept shifting the conversation back to Rhonda, she might ward off Rhonda's constant questioning - no such luck.

"You know I've nevah been there for dinner or anything else," Rhonda answered in half sarcastic voice and half joking tone of voice. "The way your lips are as tight as two oyster shells, it must have been such a romantic date you don't want to tell me about it. What happened?"

Not wanting to give her family members too much information too soon, especially big-mouth Rhonda, out of fear that something dreadful would happen, and the relationship would fall apart, Caroline responded in general terms. "The Inn was breathtakingly beautiful; you know how I love nature. It's the largest stone building I've ever seen. Honestly, the buffet in the restaurant was more elaborate than I could have ever imagined; there were several rooms of foods, with elegant displays and ice sculptures."

"Yeah, I've heard about it from some of my married friends," Rhonda said. "J.P. must be crazy about you to take you there, cus I'm sure it cost him uh arm and uh leg."

"He took me to a beautiful restaurant in Charleston on our first date, and we went to Dock Street Theatre afterwards to see *Porgy and Bess.*

"Momma told me about that one cus you nevah tell me nuthin'. I don't know why you want to be so secretive about everything, like a cat's got your tongue."

"Rhonda, I'm scared my business would be all over Greenville if I told you about my love life."

"Caroline, I wouldn't do that. You're my baby sister," Rhonda said in a demure tone of voice, which was unusual for her.

Caroline responded, "I know good and well, you'd let something slip at that beauty shop, while you're teasin' and sprayin' hair, and it would be all over town in a matter of days."

Back to her outspoken way, Rhonda said, "Caroline, you're just paranoid. My friends and clients aren't your age anyway. Why would they want to spread rumors, or even the truth, about you? We don't gossip in there."

"To heck y'all don't. Every time I've ever been in that salon, all y'all talk about everybody in town. That's what women do when they go to beauty shops; they spill their guts or talk about anything they've heard about anyone else lately."

"Maybe you've heard a conversation or two, but as a rule, we don't gossip."

"Yeah, and my name's not Caroline Bethany Carter."

The sisters laughed for a moment. Rhonda knew that Caroline had no intention of giving her more information. Caroline changed the conversation to their brother Troy. From there on to Rock Hill, they talked about things they did when they were little and laughed and joked a lot. The two hour drive became much less tense and more enjoyable for Caroline, although Rhonda tried to mention Joost, but Caroline cut her off quickly saying that was over and done with. Rhonda didn't really believe her. Caroline distracted her by commenting on the wondrous sky, with whorls and streaks of pink and violet as the sun went down.

When they arrived on campus, Caroline did show Rhonda the diamond earrings that J.P. had given her for Valentine's Day.

Rhonda nearly squealed and said, "Lord have mercy in heaven baby sister, you got a couple of rocks. What did you say he did for a livin'?"

"He works for a company in Charleston that restores old buildings and private homes."

"They must pay well or he just went in hock up to his ear lobes for those beauties."

"Oh Rhonda, stop it! It's not about where he takes me or what he gives me, it's about who he is and what his heart feels."

"Your right, but it sure helps to know he doesn't have to slave in a cotton mill or work at a hamburger joint."

"Well, I guess I'm thankful for that."

Caroline entertained Rhonda for a while to give her a break before her two hour return trip home.

Monday was an unusually warm day for February, with highs in the 70's. Spring fever had Caroline, the other teachers, and the children on the playground trying to stretch recess out as long as possible. Most schools in the South had no air conditioning, and the classroom felt terribly stuffy. The playground had been well designed to preserve several enormous oak trees, with benches under the oaks, strategically placed to capture both the streaming sunlight and a hint of shade as the branches of the oaks blew back and forth in the wind. As a student teacher, Caroline was pretty much a loner, with the teachers being polite but not overly friendly. The well-seasoned teachers didn't want to talk about school all day, as they had already spent the better part of their lives in school; Caroline had so little experience outside of school, she didn't know how to switch the conversation to a different topic, from that of husbands and college aged offspring. She rose from the bench and started walking in the sunshine, encircling the playground and keeping an eye on her students. Her supervising teacher sat upon the bench with her colleagues. Caroline was trying her best to stay focused on the children as they frolicked on the grounds, but she was unable to keep the thoughts of J.P. out of her mind. There were so many uncertainties in her life, but she was convinced that he was in love with her, and she was without a doubt in love with him; she could no longer deny it. Still, that didn't guarantee her that everything else would work out in their favor. She resolved that she must get a job near Summerville if they were going have a chance to grow in their relationship, but she had absolutely no funds to purchase a car and had no idea how to get to work if she had no car. She knew enough about the city of Charleston, to know that most of the residents were either very rich or very poor, and she might not find affordable or suitable housing within walking distance of a school. She had a lot to think about.

For the next couple of weeks, Caroline's routine stayed generally the same - school, dinner, checking mail, school work, and writing letters to J.P. He'd called her the second night she was back on campus. He literally wore his heart on his sleeve during the last call as he tried to encourage her and let her know how he felt about her and how much he appreciated her for standing by him.

She found herself fantasizing about what her future could be like if they were together, filled with the earthy romanticism that only the Lowcountry has to offer. She envisioned strolls along the battery in Charleston like the belles of antebellum Charleston, sailing in the harbor, visits to Magnolia and Middleton gardens, moonlit nights on the beaches of Isle of Palms and Sullivan's Island, and oyster roasts with all of J.P.'s friends. She'd already fallen into the fairy tale trap and didn't want to escape from the allure of the Lowcountry.

Caroline made a copy of J.P's letter when she went to the library to check out books from the children's literature collection. She wanted to keep the letter with her each day, to reread it going back and forth to school, and she didn't want to take a chance on losing the only copy of it. When she got back to her room that evening, she placed the original copy of his letter in the bottom compartment of her jewelry box where she kept her beautiful diamond earrings and her most prized childhood possession - a very small piece of her own embroidery done when she was only four years old. The kit, to embroider a design of a little boy holding a baseball bat, was given to her by her daddy. He knew how creative she was, even at that early age, and wanted to encourage her to develop her talents. She surmised that the embroidery thread and canvas was for her and the baseball player was for him - a way her daddy fostered a father/daughter relationship. A relationship that couldn't be severed.

Caroline was writing to J.P. each evening and then going over to the student center after dinner to check her mailbox and to mail his letter. One evening she'd gone by the library to check out some South Carolina history books. When she went over to the student center, she placed her three ringed binder and the small stack of library books on the sofa, before going to check her mailbox. She went back to pick up her things and she noticed something tucked inside the front cover of one of the books. She pulled out an envelope with her name written on the front of it, in perfect manuscript. She thought it was odd that someone would leave something for her in those few minutes it took for her to get to her mailbox. She searched the student center, but no one familiar was in sight. Sitting upon the sofa, she opened the envelope, and started to read the neatly written letter enclosed. As she began to read the letter, she realized that it was about J.P. In almost a sympathetic way, the author was apologizing for writing the letter but felt it was necessary to do so.

As Caroline read, the drama unfolded about J.P.'s involvement in a sordid relationship with a girl, named Anne, while he was at Clemson. Once Caroline started to read it, she couldn't stop. *Was she being warned or informed in a way that J.P. had been unable to tell her?* She'd made herself clear to Debra Hembree, the slithering pit viper that she didn't want to discuss anything with her. Surely, she wouldn't have placed this letter in her book and scurried away. Caroline skeptically read on, with the image of a coiled cobra ready to strike in the recesses of her mind.

The girl, named Anne, was steadily dating J.P's good friend. Sometimes, Anne seemed like she was flirting with J. P., but he didn't want to be involved with her because of his friend, Clay.

One Friday night, Clay talked J.P. into going to a party on Lake Hartwell. J.P. had qualms because he was sure there'd be lots of booze at the party, and he didn't want Anne getting inebriated and coming on to him, which she had attempted to do before. She was stunningly beautiful, smart, and rich, but she drank like a fish, on her way to becoming an alcoholic.

Clay was insistent about J.P. coming, not having a clue that his girlfriend had flirted with him before. Reluctantly, he went to the party but drove his own car. Anne got drunk quickly that night, guzzling mixed drinks, and Clay's food and alcohol consumption left him spending most of the night hugging a toilet or passed out on one of the beds.

Clay was in no shape to drive Anne home. About one o'clock in the morning, Anne began begging J.P. to take her home; she was done with the party, and J.P. was ready to leave, having developed a horrible headache. Clay stayed at the lake house, trying to sober up so he'd be able to drive his car home, but asked J.P. if he'd go ahead and take Anne back to her apartment if she wanted to go.

On the way back to Clemson, Anne was seemingly passed out in J.P.'s car. He tried to arouse her to walk into her own apartment, but he ended up nearly dragging her in. When he got her to the bedroom, she livened up a bit and asked him to stay for a while, but he declined saying he had a headache; and that she'd had too much to drink. She told him to take a couple of aspirin with some water, both of which were sitting on her nightstand.

Taking Anne's remedy for a headache, not knowing what he was taking thinking it was aspirin, was a big mistake for J.P. because he woke up the next morning in her bed, while Clay was banging on the door, and Anne was prancing to the door in boxer shorts and J.P's t-shirt. Then all hell broke loose when Clay's rage overtook him as he rushed in and started beating the snot out of J.P., leaving him bruised and bloody.

It stands to reason that Clay and Anne broke up after the big confrontation, but she still tried to get her hooks into J.P. Several weeks later, she announced to J.P. that she was pregnant with his baby. He was torn up inside; he disappeared for weeks. His brother didn't even know where he was. Not a soul knew where he was; of course he wasn't attending his classes at Clemson.

When J.P. finally got back in town, he hoped that everything was somehow mistaken, that the distressing nightmare was not true. Anne heard that he was back and called him to let him know that she'd seen another doctor who also concluded that she was indeed pregnant. It was a terrible situation for everyone. It was especially terrible for J.P. because he didn't remember a thing about what went on with Anne that dreadful night.

Caroline knew what the remainder of the letter was going to say. It was very damaging for a baby to be born out of wedlock. Most of the time the parents of the two young people involved would insist that they be married before anyone knew that the girl was pregnant.

J.P.'s parents and Anne's parents agreed, when they found out about the pregnancy, that it would be best for the baby if J.P. married Anne. So, poor J.P. was trapped into a situation where he became engaged to Anne simply because she was pregnant. J.P's brother and friends say that he tried to make the best of things, but he knew he didn't love Anne and didn't know how he was going to follow through with marriage. He fell into a deep depression.

Weeks later, Clay came back into the picture. According to Anne's friends she had shown no signs of being pregnant, no morning sickness, no tiredness, no bloating. J.P. went to her apartment one night and found Clay and Anne both as drunk as skunks, sitting shoulder to shoulder on her couch. Anne started sniffling when she saw J.P. and told him, with slurred speech, that she had suffered a miscarriage, and that it was probably best for everyone. Clay chimed in, even in a drunken stupor, to tell J.P. he had no hard feelings.

J.P. was off the hook then, but the eerie incident haunts him to this day, like a never ending falling boulder on a mountainous road.

The author of the letter concluded saying that it was best if Caroline were told by someone who would tell the entire story, exactly as it happened. There was no signature at the end of the letter.

Caroline sat there in the student center, tears coursed down her cheeks as she tried to dry her eyes with the sleeves of her jacket. She folded the letter back up, stuffed it into her jacket, and in near-panic walked briskly to the bathroom. There in a bathroom stall, she started bawling. She was deeply saddened by learning about the obscure story but didn't feel betrayed by J.P. for not telling her. She could see how uncomfortable it would be to tell someone about such an unfortunate event. She finally came out of the bathroom stall, and ripped the letter into more than forty pieces, and tossed it into the waste receptacle in the corner. She stayed in the bathroom for a long time to regain her composure before making the trek back to her dormitory. She was falling in love, or had already fallen in love, with a man with a terrible secret, and she had no idea how to handle it. Her fairy tale couldn't end when it had just started. She had to try to be strong and give love a chance, to be empathetic and understanding. That's what he needed from her. His past was his past, and she wanted to be his future. Oh, how she wanted her daddy, right now, to tell her just what to do.

Days passed, and Caroline was receiving letters from J.P. on a frequent basis, some discussing mundane issues informatively, and others very sincere and heartfelt. How was she going to pour out her heart to him in her letters now that she had been told his dark secret by an anonymous writer? Deep down, she didn't want to think anything negative about J.P.; she was already in love with him and she wanted to proclaim that nothing would ever get in the way of love. But often the mind rules over the heart and constrains one from truly living and loving another unconditionally. As she had those quiet moments to think about him, she tried to bring to her mind verses of scripture, she'd memorized as a child, on the topic of love:

"Love is patient; love is kind...is not selfish; is not provoked; does not keep a record of wrongs...bears all things; believes all things; hopes all things; endures all things. Love never ends."

She had to move past this uneasy feeling about the anonymous letter, and give J.P. a chance to tell her about the circumstances, so flagrantly disclosed, in his own way and in his own time. She didn't want to be self-righteous and judge him for something that happened in his past; that wasn't her nature. And she didn't want to be judged for any of her own stupid mistakes.

After a tough week, the weekend finally arrived with unusually warm weather so Caroline gathered her spiral notebook, pen, and quilt and headed across campus to write, if the mood struck her. She spread the tattered, calico quilt upon the dry, dormant grass in such a position to catch the sunlight streaming through the barren branches of the deciduous trees that cast dancing shadows upon the ground as they blew in the wind, like dancers so distant they looked like stick figures. She reclined and felt the solace of the sunshine engulfing her body with warmth. With her eyes closed to block out the rays of the sun, she drifted into a semiconscious state, allowing herself much needed relaxation. For a span of twenty minutes or more, she managed to block out every worry from her mind and enjoy the beautiful day.

⇥ ⇤

"Man J.P., you gotta keep your mind on the job; you're getting a little too slap-happy to be up on the roof. You ain't no acrobat, you know."

"Okay Frank, I got you," J.P. responded. "I'm on my way back down. It looks like the flashing wasn't done professionally around the chimney."

"Prob'ly not," Frank called out, "More than likely, it was done by a grandpa, back in the 1920's, who didn't know much about sealing a chimney and didn't have much to work with either."

Frank and J.P. had been assigned to inspect an old house in Walterboro, which would be used as a gift shop when they finished, and determined what renovations needed to be made to bring it up to code to be used as a commercial building. The roof, on the old house in question, was steeply pitched making both inspection and future renovation hazardous. Frank, J.P.'s co-worker and old Clemson buddy from Walhalla, preferred to let J.P., who was not in the least acrophobic, handle the roof and chimney inspections of the antiquated structures of the Lowcountry, which they were responsible for as a team. Because of the possible danger involved, the company never sent out a single inspector, but always assigned a team of employees to inspect and refurbish the old homes and commercial buildings.

J.P. had the thoughts of Caroline tucked beneath layers of knowledge of his profession and everyday responsibilities. When alone, even if a minute here or there, he would think of her and imagine himself with her. He didn't want to admit it to his buddies and co-workers, but her spirit had touched his, and he had a sudden understanding of the words soul mate.

Frank's voice would cause him to tune in and attend to the task at hand and complete it as quickly, but efficiently, as possible.

When he came down from the roof, Frank asked, "What were you doing up there on the roof so long? You gettin' crazy on these roofs."

"I didn't realize I was taking any longer than usual to inspect an old chimney," he responded, "Sorry 'bout that."

"No problem," Frank said. "I was just getting a little concerned 'bout you up there on that steeply pitched sucker. You looked like you were kinda in a daze."

Frank was a licensed chimney sweep and was well versed in inspection of the soundness of the chimney structure and flue, both of which can be inspected from the fireplace. They entered the old house together to complete the inspection.

"Glad we're almost done with this day," J.P. said, just making small talk.

"Hey, why don't you come have dinner with me and Beth tomorrow night? I'm grillin' steaks, and I'm sure Beth would love to see you. She hasn't seen you since you had that oyster roast at your place, last fall."

His mind went back to the oyster roast, Caroline's first time at his house and her first time eating roasted oysters. Man was she cute trying to swallow the first oyster.

"Sorry, What did you say, 'bout Beth?"

"I said she'd love to see you, it's been a while since you had your oyster roast," answered Frank. "Are you alright, man?"

"Yeah, I'm fine. You know I always burn out the last couple of hours, on a Friday. We're lucky our cut off time is three today. There're a lot of perks with this job. The weather is so unusually warm, I'm going down to Edisto after we get done."

"You must have spring fever to drive all the way back down there when you live in Summerville. I'm headin' straight to Goose Creek when we get done."

"I'll have plenty of time to drive down to the beach. My kite is in the trunk of my car; I think I'll fly it today and have some time to myself to relax."

"My idea of time to relax is passin' out on the couch while I watch the sports channel," Frank commented. "Beth hates it, cus she's ready to go somewhere when I get off early. You're lucky you're still a bachelor," he said laughing. "I really didn't mean that; don't know what I'd do without Beth. We've been together a long time now."

"How long did y'all date before you got hitched," J.P. asked?

"Oh, I guess we dated about a year and a half. I think I fell in love with her after just a few months, but she'd been in another long term relationship in high school and was afraid to get serious for a while."

"I didn't realize I hadn't seen Beth since the oyster roast."

"You definitely need to have another one next fall. Man, you do it with finesse."

"Butch and I really get in to doing it. Chris gets solicited to help, but I think he'd prefer to keep it small. We had a yard full of people last time, didn't we?"

"You seem to have taken to the Winthrop girl, that night. Did you start datin' her?"

"As a matter of fact, I've been dating her since last fall."

"You don't say. You kept that one quiet."

"It's a little hard to do it long distance, but it's been good, really good." J.P. admitted.

"I'd imagine it would be hard. You haven't been gettin' serious 'bout her have you?"

"Don't know."

The fact was, he did know, but he wasn't ready to let Frank go home and tell Beth, who'd be up all night calling every mutual friend they knew. Gossip spreads in the South as fast as kudzu grows.

They walked up the creaking steps, and stood on the porch. "Speaking of the people at the oyster roast, I ran into Clay McMahan last week, at the court house. He said that he and Anne were expectin' a baby."

The news stunned J.P. for a moment and he abruptly changed the conversation. "Let's go on into the house."

"Frank, I think we better get this job done. I'm ready for quittin' time." He turned from Frank for a moment and walked on into another room that appeared to have been the dining room. He surveyed the empty, high-ceilinged room, with a chandelier missing half of the dangling crystals, and the filth encrusted heart-pine floors. He redirected his course and was again standing in the front parlor with Frank. Sunlight streamed through the tall dirty, clouded windows. He was in deep thought about the news that Anne was pregnant, but he didn't want to remain in that place of thought.

Almost mechanically, he mumbled, "Go ahead and take a look up in that chimney."

"Sure, let's finish it up."

⋙⊹ ⊹⋘

Emily and her friend Jason were sprinting across the campus grounds like an imp and a fairy. Jason was very effeminate, and Emily almost looked at him as the sister she never had, but of course, she didn't dare say it. Next to Caroline, he was her best friend at Winthrop. He enjoyed everything she did. They'd shared numerous art classes and went to artsy kinds of events together. Jason was majoring in art history and hoped to land a job as an art curator when he finished school, but he was super good looking and did some male modeling on the side. He was focused about his art career, but Emily didn't know exactly what she'd do with her art degree.

Emily spotted Caroline as she basked in the sunshine, as lazily as a gator sunning on the banks of a river. "Jason, that looks like Caroline over there crashed out on her quilt. We'll sneak up on her."

"Girlfriend, she may have a heart attack if we sneak up on her and scare her. We'll scare the crap outta her."

"Jason, don't be so crude, besides, you'd have a heart attack or convulsions, but not Caroline Carter. She's as tough as an old leather boot, but most of the time she seems to handle everything with grace and poise."

"You're so obnoxious to me, Emily; I mean almost abusive," whined Jason. "I don't, for the life of me, know why I adore you so much." He giggled, girlishly.

"It's because I do all of your dirty work for you, and all you have to do is stand around with that pretty boy smile and charm everyone," she replied.

"Oh, shut ……..up," he said, enunciating perfectly, like an irate old woman. "I can handle my own naughty work; thank you very much. At least I think I can."

They were too far away for Caroline to hear them, so they both roared and snorted, laughing until Emily's side hurt.

"Let's go get Caroline. She'll go to Charlotte with us to get some lunch."

They crept up on Caroline, as quietly and cautiously as two cats near a birdhouse. Jason felt bad about startling Caroline and nervously cleared his throat. Emily knew he'd blown it as Caroline started to awaken and stretch.

Still trying to alarm Caroline, Emily called out loudly, using a high pitched tone of voice and sounding as if she were an animal in some kind of danger, "Caroline, wake up."

Startled, Caroline sat straight up and barely opened her eyes in the sunlight, only seeing Jason through the slits in her eyes, with Emily now behind her. Still in a state of stupor, as she struggled to wake up, Caroline was unable to recognize Jason. She'd only met him once, as he was dressed and groomed immaculately that day. This guy had a two day stubble on his face and was dressed in a frayed Winthrop T-shirt.

Seeing her being utterly confused, he felt very uncomfortable and said, "Caroline, Caroline, it's me, Jason."

She responded, sounding curt, "Jason who, what in the heck are you doin', wakin' me up like this when I'm out here relaxin'?"

Then Emily said, laughing, "Just like I told you Jason, she'd handle it with grace and poise."

Caroline turned to get a glance at Emily and said, "No wonder poor Jason doesn't know what to say; you put him up to it at the last minute." At that point Caroline started smiling and went on to say, "Just wait Emily, what goes around comes around; you're going to get the pee scared outta you the next time, and I hope I have the pleasure of doing it."

"What put you in such a puny mood, Cow…line?" She flopped down on the quilt next to Caroline, putting her arms around her shoulders, as if to hug her, and said, "Don't be hostile, dear. We just wanted to ask you to go to lunch with us, and be blessed by your comp'ny. You can give us a little of your precious time, can't you honey," she asked, drawling like a west coast actress auditioning for a part in a screen play?

"Well, what a way to give an invitation," Caroline exclaimed, as she gave Emily a nudge with her elbow!

Jason chimed in, "Caroline, I'm so sorry darlin', you know Emily made me do it. Accept our lunch invitation, please, pretty please. We'll have fun going to Shawlett for the day." He was dramatizing, but it seemed natural using his Charlestonian brogue. As he spoke he slapped his hand downward in the air, with his arm stationary, classically effeminate.

"Emily, don't you ever take time to study," Caroline asked? Most of the time, the girl acted like she didn't have a care in the world, definitely a right brained kind of girl.

"Jason, tell her that you've seen me study." Emily's head was bobbing up and down, hoping that Jason would back her up.

He said, "Well, I have seen you study a time or two."

Emily dropped her shoulders and exhaled forcefully to release her frustration. "Do y'all think I'm a dumb butt, or somethin'?

"Emily, sweetheart, we don't think you're a dumb butt." Then Caroline asked, "Where are y'all goin' to eat in Charlotte?"

Jason answered, "We're not sure." He placed his long index finger toward his temple to indicate that he was still thinking. "Why don't we drive down near Queen's College, stop and get some subs, and have lunch at a little garden down there."

"Don't cha think that's a good idea," asked Emily? "Jason has offered to drive. Please go with us."

"Okay, I'll go with y'all, but I need to go back to my dorm and put my things away. How 'bout I meet y'all in front of Margaret Nance in thirty minutes?"

Jason stood there, lightly clapping his hands together under his chin and said, "Oh, goodie. She's goin' with us. Gracious, what will I wear?"

Emily rolled her eyes at Caroline, without Jason seeing her. Then she said, "Well, go on. See you in thirty."

As Caroline vigorously shook her quilt, to rid it of pieces of dry grass, she began to think. She'd spent very few Saturdays, in her four years at Winthrop, leaving campus for the afternoon to goof off and have fun with her friends. It seemed like only yesterday she'd started college. With dedication she'd worked and studied; she'd visited family and friends, and she'd met J.P. Her relationship with him had monopolized much of her thoughts for the past few months, and she'd spent a lot of time thinking about Joost, too, until she'd snapped out of it and let it go.

Now, she was ready to graduate, to make her own decisions, to make her own way.

Caroline wanted J.P. to be in her life, no matter what it would take to fully understand him. She had him on a pedestal. In her eyes, he was still a good ol' boy, not a cold Yankee. Her notions of him wouldn't be tainted by some incriminating story of his past. She wanted to live close to him, to have quality time with him, to be the adult he was and not just a silly school girl dependent on her family for support. She wasn't one hundred per cent sure about all of this, but her feelings were pushing her closer and closer to J.P.

With her quilt and spiral notebook bundled in her arms, she hurried back to her dorm and excitedly readied herself to meet Jason and Emily. She changed into a soft knit sweater, braided her hair, and put on a pair Navajo designed turquoise earrings. Then she searched her desk drawer to locate a twenty dollar bill and stuffed it into the top pocket of her blue jean jacket. She gave one quick glance in the mirror before dashing down the hall and rapidly descending the stairs to make it to the designated meeting place on time.

Jason and Emily were waiting in his yellow Mustang directly in front of Margaret Nance. Caroline hopped in the back seat. Jason drove conservatively to exit the campus and down Cherry Road, which was always crawling with cops. When they were safely heading north on I-77, Jason tore out like a bat outta hell, speeding up the interstate. Emily bellowed out a boisterous yee-haw turning around to find Caroline with a repugnant look on her face. Emily admonished her to stop being Miss Goodie Two Shoes and kick back and have a good time.

Several minutes later, the dreaded sound of a state trooper's siren whirred in their heads, and Jason was forced to decrease his velocity and pull to the right. The patrolman came to the side of the car, and Jason rolled down the window. He asked to see Jason's driver's license and registration.

Emily turned around and said to Caroline and said, "Oops! I guess we have a little delay here."

Caroline was freaking out, silently. What if this officer hauls us all to jail, thinking we're intoxicated or high on drugs?

After taking Jason's credentials to his patrol car, the officer again came to the driver's side of Jason's car. He asked Jason to step out of the car. They were standing at the back of the car, so Emily and Caroline couldn't decipher what the trooper said to Jason. After he spoke to him for a minute, the patrolman went and stood next to his patrol car facing Jason. Jason began slowly walking toward the state trooper.

Caroline said to Emily in near panic, "Oh Sweet Jesus, he thinks Jason is drunk or high. He prob'ly thinks all of us are high on drugs and will search the car next."

Jason got into the state trooper's vehicle.

"Caroline, will you stop fabricatin' the incident," said Emily, "and we don't have any drugs in here to get caught with, but I wish I had a sedative to give you. Since Jason is under twenty-one, and the car is registered in his daddy's name, the officer may be makin' contact with his daddy to see if he had permission to drive the vehicle."

"His daddy will prob'ly be furious at Jason, and tell the officer to haul us all away," Caroline said, fretfully, thinking about the worst possible outcome of getting arrested and then not being able to get a teaching job.

Emily retorted, "Stop bein' so negative. It'll all come out in the wash. Besides, Mr. Harrison is a successful investment banker down in Charleston. The family lives like royalty out on Isle of Palms. What's a little speedin' ticket to a man like that?"

"Emily, how can you be positive when you're involved in somethin' bein' handled by law enforcement?"

"Because I've been stopped and ticketed more than once," Emily answered, vexed by Caroline's paranoia.

"Well, 'it'll be cold day in …'", Caroline paused mid-sentence, "before I get caught speedin' and have to pay for a ticket."

Emily applauded Caroline.

"No need to worry 'bout me," Caroline said, 'cus you caint squeeze blood out of a turnip, and I know better than to get myself between a rock and a hard place."

Emily responded laughing but trying not to let the patrolman see her, "That you do, my little Miss Prissy friend. I love you when you're authentic."

In a few minutes, Jason got back in the car, with a ticket in hand, and started giggling like a girl. Rattling the ticket he said, "Daddy will love this story."

"You mean your daddy won't mind that you got pulled by a trooper," Caroline asked?

"Heaven's no, it's just a little sixty five-dollar fine. He'll prob'ly laugh and say, 'Good job son! You didn't even get locked up for DUI. Besides he deposits about nine hundred a month for me to have for spendin' money while I'm in school. The real trick though is not to act too sissified, as he would put it, around my daddy. He's as tough as nails, and he doesn't want the baby boy to shame the family. If he thought I was doin' anythin' kinky, he'd cut off my funds or cut off my toes."

"Yeah, during spring break, I'll have to go out the beach to visit Jason and act like I'm a little sweet on him," said Emily as she stroked the back of Jason's neck.

With a look of bewilderment, Caroline said, "Y'all are absolutely outrageous!"

Jason asked, "Don't you love us to pieces?"

With his statement about toes, she started feeling discombobulated. How on earth could a father be so sadistic? He had to be kidding. Or was he trying to make a statement about the condition of his relationship with his father; was he the progeny of a psychopath, and a wealthy psychopath, to boot?

"Earth to Caroline," said Emily, sarcastically but not offensively, if there is such a thing. "Are you back there spacin' out again?"

"Me, spacin' out; I nevah do that," Caroline said as she shot her one of those doubtful looks.

"Oh yes you do! Don't start readin' some Freudian stuff into any of our conversations," said Emily. She meant it, but she didn't want to hurt Caroline's feelings, and she wasn't even sure that Freudian was the necessary term to be used.

Jason waited until the state trooper drove off, crossed the median, and headed in the opposite direction. Then he cranked the car, pulled back onto the highway, and accelerated to the speed limit. They soon crossed over the state line into North Carolina, when Jason pushed the pedal to the metal, in an act of defiance, and Caroline nearly swallowed her tongue. Emily screamed for Jason to calm down.

He slowed down to about ten miles over the speed limit for N.C., and they cruised along.

"Lunch is on me, ladies," he said, jubilantly. "Let's go to Shawlett."

CHAPTER 14

PLANNIN'

The phone was ringing as Caroline fumbled to unlock the door. It was just after seven o'clock, and she'd already eaten her supper, disgusting sloppy joes smothered with ketchup and cold French fries dipped in mustard, washed down with sweet tea. She answered the phone with a queasy feeling in her gut trying to take the best of her, maybe nerves, and maybe sloppy joes and greasy fries.

"Hello," she said in a soft tone.

"How's my girl today," J.P. asked, blithely?

He didn't mention that he'd not been able to reach her; he wasn't the jealous type and didn't want her to feel like he was suffocating her. He felt that she needed time to spend with her college friends before those days were over, too soon.

"Oh, I'm good. I know I shouldn't complain too much about the sickening cafeteria food because soon I'll have to start fixin' my own food. I'm not much of a cook, you know."

"You don't like cooking much, huh," he asked? "I guess you can do what I do and live off cereal, salad, and sandwiches. It's almost a balanced diet."

"I thought y'all liked to cook," she said.

"Nope, don't like to cook. Butch and Chris like to cook. If they leave me something after they've had their fill, I eat well. If they're really hungry and devour the good stuff, I eat cereal."

"How do y'all decide who pays for groceries?"

"We don't; we just buy what we want at the grocery store, and we eat when we get hungry." Then he hee-hawed and said, "It all comes out the same in the end."

"Oh, J.P. you come up with some outlandish stuff to say."

"I do know how to cook a few things," she said trying to change the course of the conversation a tad before he said something else disgustingly boy like.

"Like what," he asked with excitement in his voice?

"Well, like fried chicken, country fried steak, rice and gravy, green bean casserole, sweet potato fritters, buttermilk biscuits, and pound cake."

"Oh yeah, I'm licking my chops right now. Sounds like good food like we had at your granny's house. You didn't tell me then you could cook."

"That's because I can't really cook in comparison to Granny, and Momma, and my aunts. Even my boy cousins and Troy can cook better than I can, grillin' barbeque chicken and smokin' pork ribs. The only person in my family who can't cook better than I can is Rhonda, but she thinks she can.

I wouldn't even ask her to make me a peanut butter and banana sandwich, or even a mayonnaise sandwich. Don't trust her culinary skills."

"Caroline, I think I have some news you may be interested in."

"Okay, shoot."

"I had lunch with one of my old friends yesterday, Clay McMahan. I believe you met him, and his wife, at my oyster roast. So, Clay and I had lunch downtown. Frank had already told me that Clay and his wife Anne are expecting their first baby. Clay reminded me that Anne has been teaching at Jasper Elementary School, on James Island, for the past couple of years. She never really wanted to teach, but Clay was trying to get settled in with a reputable law firm, in Charleston. She'd gone on to graduate school in Education when he was at The University of South Carolina School of Law. Now that she's going to have a baby, she has no intention of teaching next year. There should be at least one vacancy at that school, and Clay asked Anne if she'd be willing to tell her principal about you, if you're interested in requesting an interview for a first grade position."

"Gee, I don't know what to say except wow; that it sounds like a wonderful idea to interview for a job down there. I'd love to be so close to the beach."

"Is that all," he asked in a forlorn tone of voice?

"No, I'd love to be close to you, too."

"Glad to hear that. Well, there's more. Clay and Anne have been living in a small apartment on the bottom floor of a historic home in the city. The house is owned by a friend of Anne's father. I've never seen it, but Clay described it as being quite nice, with an intimate courtyard, separate from the main courtyard used by the family living on the upper floors of the grand house. The house is near the old Baptist Church, the one with headstones stacked up against the walls, and Stoll's Alley. Although the apartment has two bedrooms, the McMahans say that they'll be too cramped with a baby, when they're inundated with baby equipment everywhere. Anne is so spoiled by her father, she'd say that they'd be cramped in the White House. Anyway, they're planning to move out to Mt. Pleasant. Her father has purchased a cottage there and has had it completely restored for them to use temporarily. They plan to build a new house on the beach because she's not interested in living in the city anymore. Anne's too focused on herself to even be social."

"It sounds like you're thinking that I might be able to lease the apartment in the city when they vacate it. The problem would be financial, my dear. A first year teacher can barely afford to rent a single room in a boarding house."

"Listen to this. Clay's first cousin just finished cosmetology school in Atlanta. She's planning to take a job in a classy salon downtown, and her parents want her to live in the apartment that Clay is moving out of. Her daddy's a doctor, also a friend of Anne's daddy and the homeowners, and plans to basically foot the bill for the apartment. Her parents want her to live in Charleston, hoping that she'll find some suitable young man in the social ranks that they'd approve of. She's very young and doesn't feel comfortable living alone. She asked Clay and Anne if they knew of someone who would like to share the apartment. It sounds like she's a good Christian girl, having had some big conversion experience while she was in Atlanta. She might be someone you'd be compatible with."

"It all sounds like it's too good to be true. What about transportation to work? I know I won't be able to afford a car for a while."

"I'm sure the city transit can get you from downtown to James Island. It may be a hassle for a while, but you can do it while you're saving money to get a car. I'll help you look for a car, and you'll have one in no time.

Caroline, I want you near me. We've only had a long distance relationship, which has been the best thing in my life, but I'd love to have you closer to me so I can spend quality time with you."

"Sounds like you love me."

"I love the heck out of you. You're my sweetie pie," he said, so caringly.

Caroline needed time to hash things out and then move forward. She loved him, but something inside of her was making her afraid that she'd blow it with him in the end. Maybe it was that old unresolved fear that the ones you love leave you and there's no way to control it. She had to respond to him quickly so he would not feel that something was wrong, feeling the clock ticking timing her response.

She blurted out, "I'm so excited about all this and so happy to have you say you want me to be near you."

"Well, I guess you'll have a little resume writing to do if you think you want to go for it."

"There's a professional here at Winthrop who will help me get my resume written appropriately, and I'll have to complete the school district application before I can request an interview."

"Sounds good," he said cheerfully. "One more thing for you to think about, love, I know spring break is coming up soon, and I wish you could come down here. I realize you'll want to go see your family first, but I could pick you up in Greenville after you've had a few days with them. I could put you up in the motel again, right there next to the azalea park. This place is going to be magical then, but I don't want to spoil that for you by running my mouth too much. I'll have to work some, but my boss is letting me take some vacation days since it'll be the week before Easter. Maybe when I'm working, you could bum around with Emily or do school work you need to do during the break, go out in the park and stretch out on a quilt."

"Thank you from the bottom of my heart for offering to do so much for me."

"I'll call you back in a few days to see what you decide. I know it's a lot of things to throw at you at once. You get some sleep tonight. Night, night, have sweet dreams. I love you."

"Okay, I love you, too. Bye."

A zillion thoughts were swirling in Caroline's mind, like debris in the vortex of an Oklahoma tornado. She decided to take something to settle her stomach and then take a nice, long, bubble bath. She brushed her teeth, flossed, and then brushed her hair and twisted it up on her crown to place a large clip in it so her hair wouldn't get wet in the tub. A little mood music was in order.

After her bath Caroline dried herself with a fluffy, white towel, and slipped on her well-worn, flannel pajamas, with the puppy dog print, the ones with the hole in the left leg of the bottoms. She padded over to the bed, turned down the thick comforter and then wrapped herself in the tattered calico quilt of her childhood that had been laundered hundreds of times as she grew up, softening it with each wash, a magical quilt that had calmed her during eons of long restless nights.

As she lay there, trying to go to sleep, she tossed and turned until she was no longer cocooned in her quilt. She was thinking about J.P.'s enthusiasm, his voice ringing in her head, like the jubilant voices of children on a playground. She wanted to emulate that same air of excitement, but for some dread reason, her heart stood still. It felt as if a dark cloud hung over her alone, while others were enjoying life, a portentous omen.

She thought maybe some more music would help, so she picked up the tape Joost had given her, the Spanish guitar music. She desperately needed a distraction, an escape.

She got back in bed but was soon up again pacing the floor. Something wasn't right; a thought from her subconscious was trying to force its way into her conscious mind. *Was it her lifelong fear of losing someone you love? Was it some detail that she'd failed to remember? Was it those ghosts of Charleston that Emily and J.P. mentioned, coming to haunt her and tell her to stay away? No, it's not ghosts. That's as absurd as thinking a brown cow gives you chocolate milk, not gonna happen. It must be a combination of fear and failure to remember an important detail, a sort of temporary amnesia, the mind trying to rid itself of the poison of emotion. What was she doing, some kind of self-psychoanalysis?*

She couldn't call Emily, and she definitely couldn't call J.P. back, the situation revolved around him, and she loved him and didn't want to make him uncomfortable or make him feel that she was worry wart. She fell to her knees and asked for clarity and comfort as she'd been taught to do all her life.

Caroline slept but had disturbing dreams during the night. Most of the dream or dreams, she could not remember precisely, but one feature kept coming back to her, hauntingly. It was the faint image of a young woman with a baby in her arms.

CHAPTER 15

DECIDIN'

Caroline couldn't eat a bite of breakfast and was starving by the time her students had lunch at noon. She sat in the cafeteria that day, looking out over the nodding heads of the children as they ate, ravenously, and chattered like little monkeys. Through the series of windows, she had a clear view of the school's butterfly garden, with a beautiful weeping willow, several butterfly bushes trimmed back ready to begin another cycle of life, and iris and tulip leaves and stems springing up everywhere. Three crepe myrtle trees had grown large next to the brick wall, and the new growth of hosta, beneath the trees, had already popped up through the brown mulch. Creeping Jenny had begun the transformation from dull green to vibrant chartreuse.

"Miss Carter, Miss Carter, you alright," asked one little boy with olive complexion and dirty blond hair hanging down across one eye?

"Oh, I'm fine, Charlie, just fine," she answered in a daze.

"Miss Carter, can I ask you something?" He spoke so slowly he had long pauses between each word.

"Sure, Charlie, go ahead."

"Miss Carter, can I go to the bathroom?"

She laughed, brightly, dismissed the little boy, and tried to refocus her attention to her students. It was difficult for her to keep her mind on student teaching, with spring break just around the corner and the impending decisions she had to make, looming as assuredly as spring was about to arrive.

The days at school were even longer because she had the full responsibility of the classroom, the teacher simply serving as a tutor to some of the lower children and as a consultant and supervisor to her. Did she truly want to do this for the rest of her life, day in and day out? What could she do about it now? It was too late to change the course of her career.

Emily called Caroline right after she got back from school and asked, "You wanna go to dinner with me? We could drive down to the steakhouse, and have some sirloin tips. Your dinner is on me tonight."

"Hallelujah! I couldn't take another night in the cafeteria. I've actually gotten paranoid 'bout eating pork barbecue at school, there's no tellin' what's in it. I might as well buy it off the back of a truck from some guy called Bubba Joe."

"You're ready for spring break, aren't you?"

"Lord, yes, I caint wait. J.P. asked me to come to Summerville and said he'd put me up in a motel. He said there's something special goin' on, but he didn't want to spoil it for me by sayin' too much."

"He's right 'bout something special, but I'm not goin' to spoil it either"

"I'm so hungry I could 'bout eat a cow right now. See you in a few."

Caroline always got so tickled about Emily's slaughter of the language, since her mother was Debutante Deb, the daughter of a prominent attorney in Columbia, and the granddaughter of a judge.

She apparently married for love and not for money or social status, heaven forbid, when she wed Emily's dad, the son of a mill supervisor from Anderson. He'd been a handsome hunk on an academic scholarship to Clemson, studying forestry, when they met at a tailgating party. How ironic for a girl from Columbia, USC Gamecock territory, to be inebriated hootin' and hollerin' with the Clemson Tigers' fans.

Emily's mother always tried to put pressure on her to speak and act appropriately, to rear her properly, but Emily wouldn't be tamed. She'd drawl and use colloquialisms to the hilt, to emulate her daddy and his people, as well as Caroline did for effect. Both of them were sharp cookies and knew how to use their accents to their advantage. That's the way of a true Southern woman, to be unusual and witty, especially around the Yankees.

At dinner they talked at random about passing thoughts. Emily was bubbling with excitement about an upcoming trip to New York. Artsy Jason had asked her to go to NYC to visit the Guggenheim, The Museum of Modern Art, a number of small art galleries in the city, and anywhere else of their hearts' desires. His father was footing the bill for both of them to fly up and spend a few days there during spring break. They would definitely experience the subway system, international cuisine, Central Park during daylight hours and see famous shows on Broadway.

Caroline didn't tell Emily about her uneasiness the night before. She didn't relish the idea of Emily giving her advice on that one; the girl never put in two cents worth but hurled dimes and quarters worth of advice.

Caroline did, however, tell her about her unsettling nightmare of the young woman holding a baby in her arms. It was a nightmare because she had such an eerie feeling when she woke up, and there were unearthly sounds, like a howling sound meshed with crying and evil laughter.

"That would be some kinda wicked sound," Emily commented. "You may find that you bl'eve in those ghost stories after all."

"Emily, the dream was not about ghosts."

"How do you know for sure, Caroline?"

"'Cus I could tell that the young woman had on a short skirt and heels, not some garb from the nineteenth century."

"How interesting; maybe the ghost has been to Belk's for a mega sale, and updated her wardrobe."

"Very funny," said Caroline with the look of skepticism all over her face. "Well, I'm not gonna let some weird dream keep me away from Charleston. I'm gonna do exactly what Momma and Granny would suggest, pray on it."

"You do that, sister, but tell me if you have any more visions."

"Visions, are you for real? Forget this conversation. Let's eat that cow!"

Caroline did some soul searching as she tried to decide about moving to Charleston. Most girls her age would die to have the chance to live there. If it worked out for her to live with this room-mate, she would have it made, living as she never had before, one of her big breaks in life and maybe she should go with it. There was nothing else being offered to her right now, no offers to be a governess to the wealthy in Europe or a chance to teach at the top of the world in Tibet. And she loved J.P. and wanted to be near him. Somehow she had to break the cycle of emotional suffering, always fearing the worse to actualize. Was it a curse?

※

J.P. and Butch sat on the porch having a few beers and wishing they were drinking Heineken instead of Budweiser. They were going to regret it the next day, not so much from the effects of beer, but the pollen stirred by the wind would create havoc, swollen eyes and drip-ping noses. The weather had warmed considerably, in preparation for the floral explosion beginning to take place. Nature's miracle was about to happen again, and allergy sufferers would withstand it and marvel at the beauty of the blooming vibrantly colored azaleas and mystical purple wisteria.

They sat there in the old creaking chairs, rocking, drinking, and talking for a couple of hours until evening closed in signaling the mosquitoes to start their dance on exposed arms and the back of their necks. The fireflies looked like blinking holiday lights against the backdrop of the pines, and cicadas started their nightly serenade.

They'd talked about many things in the space of two hours or so, especially about their past days as Clemson students and the friends that both of them still saw from time to time, getting more nostalgic as the night wore on. Those were the wild, care-free days, the kind of days when a bad hangover would soon ease with plenty of coffee and aspirin, just in time to get to class and do assignments before the party started again. It was a perpetual cycle, lasting for weeks until the body simply said, that's enough, and a breather was needed to rejuvenate.

Before calling it a night, J.P told Butch about seeing Clay McMahan and about the conversation concerning the job and the apartment he hoped Caroline might go for. Butch liked Clay, but he didn't like Anne. He remembered the kind of things she did when she was at Clemson and wondered how J.P. could stand having to deal with her now that she and Clay settled in Charleston. Anne was beautiful, alright, drop dead gorgeous as a matter of fact, but she was a snake in the grass. Butch knew what good friends Clay and J.P. had been all along, and he knew J.P. wasn't going to turn his back on Clay because he married someone like Anne. J.P. was too good of a person to do that, and Butch admired him for it.

Butch was intensely fond of Caroline, and he could see she was no dummy. He thought she was perfect for J.P., and he hated to see her have to get tangled up with Anne, in any form or fashion, directly or indirectly. He didn't want to see trouble on the horizon. But he understood why J.P. wanted to tell Caroline about the job and apartment, wanting her to be close to him and wanting her to have the chance to live in the lap of luxury in downtown Charleston. J.P. had told Butch before, in so many words, that Caroline may be the one girl he has no intention of letting go.

Butch kept his thoughts and comments to himself, for some of those thoughts were so intensely private that no one should know them, but diverted the conversation with J.P. by saying, "Let's go inside and have another beer!"

Despite her conundrum, Caroline was finally able to decide about spending spring break in Summerville. It would be fun, and she could bask in the warmth of J.P.'s tenderness. He was a fabulous entertainer, too, and she desperately needed to detach herself from her responsibilities at Winthrop and go to the Lowcountry for some good times.

J.P. called her back, and she was beginning to show him signs of some elation about the forthcoming break. She could hear the thrill in his response when she told him that she'd be glad to see him when he came to pick her up for spring break. So plans were all set. He didn't push her at all for an answer to anything concerning the apartment or the job. He figured that she'd be able to see the apartment while she was in town and would probably fall in love with the whole idea, the romance and intrigue of Charleston, if the haunts didn't scare her away. It would be up to him to give her all the reassurances she'd need to make the other decisions knowing that he loved her and accepted her no matter what she chose to do.

He remembered back to the time in his life when he could no longer depend on his parents for financial support. It was a hard transition to make. He finally realized what he'd had growing up, all the things his parents had done for him to give him the best life they could possibly afford. It was a sobering realization to know that it would take him years to attain what his parents had over the years. He was willing to work and lately seemed to have more drive to achieve.

Caroline's situation had been different. She was no stranger to working hard. She'd always had to work for what she got, as a baby-sitter, working in a restaurant, or working on campus. J.P. admired those qualities about her. He knew that she'd succeed in any endeavor she pursued, and she seemed so dependable and compassionate.

When one is young, little of life's problems are dwelt upon for any length of time. The spirit is still so resilient, as Caroline's had been, not succumbing to darkness and depression. Time and circumstance have a way of making a person stronger, better able to handle the big bad issues in life. Although one tends to think that other people don't have problems, the reality is that pain and suffering are inevitable and most people have some type of cross to bear.

Neither J.P. nor Caroline would be expecting the events that were soon to follow.

CHAPTER 16

GLIDIN'

Time absolutely flew as Caroline finished her requirements for student teaching and projects for classes. She could hardly believe that soon after the break she'd be graduating. Winthrop graduates had excellent chances for employment because of the long time standing of the college as the primary school for education majors in the state. Her student teaching supervising teacher had given her an outstanding evaluation, of which she was quite proud, and she had a number of excellent letters of recommendation from her professors and advisors. Caroline felt very confident that she'd be able to land a job of her choice, in Charleston or any other place in South Carolina.

With all her reservations aside, her resume had been prepared and she'd contacted the school district to apply for the job on James Island. She and Emily had shopped in Charlotte and Caroline had found the perfect outfit to wear for her interview, a navy blue linen sleeveless dress with a coordinating light weight cardigan. She'd also splurged for some navy pumps and tasteful, dainty costume jewelry and matching large hair clip to complete her ensemble.

She planned to wear her hair down but pull the top section of her hair to the back, teased a little to give it a little poof, and secured with the large clip. When Caroline had dressed and done her hair to get an honest opinion, Emily confirmed that she looked perfect for a job interview for a teaching position.

A ride to Greenville at the onset of spring break was easy to get. Caroline arrived at her momma's house around six on Friday.

"Sweet Jesus, it's good to see your face," exclaimed Mrs. Carter as she came running out the back door to meet Caroline in the driveway!

"Momma, are you okay," asked Caroline, wondering why her momma was so overly excited to see her?

"Lord, I've been scared silly all afternoon. I heard there was a terrible accident on I-85 just south of the Blacksburg exit. The news said that it appeared that some college aged kids had been killed, but no names were given at the point of the broadcast. I been terrified. Thank God, you're here safe and sound, but someone's children have been killed in an accident involvin' four vehicles."

"Oh Momma, that's awful!" Caroline's eyes were already filled with tears for the accident victims and for her poor momma being so afraid that something had happened to her. "So many bad things happen over spring break when everyone gets excited about leavin' campus, and crazy nuts start their drinkin' binges."

"I know, baby. I'm so thankful you don't run with the wrong crowd."

"You know I have friends who like to drink a little beer, Momma, but I don't really run with any wild crowd," she replied, wincing, as she had a flashback of Jason racing northbound on I-77 toward Charlotte and being pulled by the state trooper.

"I been on my knees off and on for the past few hours, prayin' over you."

"Momma, it's been your prayers, as well as Granny's, that have kept me outta lots of trouble durin' the past four years. It's hard to misbehave if you think of your kin on their knees." She smiled sweetly, just as she'd done as child.

"Well, come on in the house. I made some fried chicken, pole beans, fresh biscuits, and a whippin' cream pound cake. I thawed some Georgia peaches and whipped some cream to smother that cake."

"Momma, my belly hurts just thinkin' 'bout it. I bet you seasoned those pole beans with some bacon grease, didn't ya? I can't wait."

A vase of daisies had been placed on the Formica top table in the den. The table was already set with the white Pfaltzgrafff dishes with yellow polka dot napkins laced through napkin rings of barnyard animals in matching white porcelain. One look at the table reminded Caroline of the simplicity and beauty of country life that her momma was so proud of, the life she had growing up. She gazed across the room to see a new bookshelf crammed packed full of small figurines, little baskets, and tiny decorative boxes.

She walked over to the new shelf and asked, "What's all this, Momma?"

"My whatnots. That's some of the stuff my students have given me over the years. You'll have your own little collection one day."

"Oh, interesting. I can't wait to get a shelf full of whatnots," she said with a hint of sarcasism. "Hey, Momma, are Troy and Rhonda comin' over?

"Yeah, they'll be here any minute. Listen, Troy got a new job. It's still masonry work, but now he's workin' on some real nice houses on the east side of town. That area used to be farm land, but in a couple of years, you'll see big expensive subdivisions where lovely old farms used to be. I know J.P.'s from New Jersey, and he's really different, but I can't help myself but to say that a lot of Northern folks are floodin' into town. Before you know it, the school system will be filled with Yankees, too. I know that sounds mighty prejudiced, but it seems like they come down here with the attitude that we're all stupid and need them to turn things around."

"That does sound prejudiced, Momma but I understand how you feel. I hope I don't come up against those kinds of attitudes if I teach in Charleston."

"Sweetheart, Charleston may have been the pinnacle of colonial life in the South, but now days I hear the school system is far behind Columbia and Greenville. People of means in Charleston send their children to private schools."

"Really, Momma, you think it'll be hard to teach there?"

"Baby, it's hard to teach anywhere."

"I think a lot of teachers are burned out. Pardon me, but it seems like y'all have too much crap to do that doesn't have anythin' to do with teachin'."

"Well, you're precisely right, and it gets worse each year. Now is not the time, honey, for you to make changes, but maybe one day somethin' else will open up for you. Pray for the Lord to deliver you."

"Yeah, like slaves comin' outta Egypt." They both laughed.

The back door creaked as it opened and Caroline heard a loud, "Howdy!" from Rhonda.

Caroline inched around the corner and said to Rhonda, "Look what the cat drug in."

"A mighty big rat, Cow…line, a mighty big rat,' said Rhonda, grinning from ear to ear apparently happy to see her little sister.

"You know I hate for you to call me Cow…line," she whined.

"Well, you started it, Sissy." replied Rhonda using her favored nickname for Caroline.

"I reckon I did. I guess it serves me right."

"How in the heck are you, Baby Girl?"

"I'd be fine if everybody would stop callin' me baby this and baby that. That's Cow…line, Sissy, and Baby Girl in less than sixty seconds."

"Well, ex...cuse me, Miss Grouch Puss. Can we switch to a party mood, here," inquired Rhonda? "I thought I came to pig out and celebrate."

"See, another name you find to call me." Caroline half-heartedly smiled at her, trying to stay on guard to ward off Rhonda's coming verbal assaults. Sometimes her sister was like a hungry gator in a Florida swamp, ready to attack.

Troy followed Rhonda and walked in reakin' with body odor from workin' outside all day in the heat.

He said, "Law me, hand me a glass of sweet tea, 'fore I pass out on this carpet."

"Mrs. Carter handed him the sweet tea, and Rhonda commented, "You need to head for the shower ASAP to get that stink offa you. Don't you know you smell like a polecat?"

"Yeah, little momma, I know I need a shower. No wonder, it's already hotter 'an a goat's butt in a pepper patch out there, if you're workin' out in 'at heat all day.

Caroline don't care," he said rising to the floor, setting the empty glass on the coffee table, and coming toward her with his arms open wide, "do you?"

"Too heck, I don't. Go get a shower, Troy, and then give me a big ol' bear hug."

"Women are so mean."

"Now, Troy, you been raised to know that women don't want a stinkin' man around 'em," reminded Momma Carter.

"Okay, I'm outnumbered again," he complained.

"I'll be glad when J.P. gets up here on Sunday, so y'all won't gang up on me."

Caroline said proudly, "You can bet yer bottom dollar J.P. won't stink."

"I guess not, little one," he added as he patted her on the head on his way toward the bathroom. "He's still tryin' to win you over, just wait."

Caroline balled up her fist and punched him in the arm as he walked past her. "My beau ain't nevah gonna smell like a hog," she said, defensively.

She loved being with her family, enjoying a great meal together and having a lot of fun as they joked and picked at one another. Everyone sort of sensed that this might be the last time they'd be together like this before Caroline ventured out into the adult world to seek her fortune, something like the youngest of the three little pigs leaving home. She was still green to what life would be like as an adult although they'd all lived through some tough times in the past. The joy of family, and Momma Carter's unwavering faith, had been the cement to bind them together during fiery trials.

Mrs. Carter got out the old Bell and Howell movie projector and folding screen to show treasured movies of the three kids on vacations and special events. No matter what their ages, Rhonda, Troy, and Caroline enjoyed seeing the old home movies. They especially loved playing the movies backwards to see the sand jump back into the buckets and water jump back up into the plastic containers or one of the kids come up out of the water and land on the diving board to resume a diving stance. They laughed and laughed until they were doubled over sitting on the imitation velvet floral sofa. In every picture, Caroline looked like a little peanut next to her older brother and sister. They still thought of her as a little bitty peanut.

Sunday morning came bright and early. Mrs. Carter got up at the crack of dawn to make meatloaf, potato salad, speckled butter beans, and sweet potato pie for lunch after she got back from church. She'd make some fresh hot cornbread, too. Southerners are famous for lots of starchy meals, and women are no strangers to getting up at the crack of dawn to prepare the bulk of Sunday dinner, eaten at noon, before heading off to worship at church and teach Sunday school. Mrs. Carter made no attempt to try to get Caroline up as she was totally exhausted. She'd spent all day Saturday, going to Sliding Rock with her old high school buddies. Caroline would've been obliged to go to church with her momma, but she was sleeping so soundly her momma didn't want to forcefully awaken her. J.P. wouldn't arrive until around three in the afternoon, so Caroline had plenty of time to look alive.

When Momma Carter got home from church, she heard Caroline in the shower. It dawned on her that she hadn't planned a decent meal for the evening meal since she thought J.P. and Caroline would already be on the road to Summerville. She made a couple of tomato sandwiches on white bread slathered with mayonnaise. She opened a small bag of sour cream and onion chips and got out a couple of ice cold orange drinks.

Caroline finished her shower and came bouncing out of the bathroom wearing Troy's old boxer shorts and a ripped Clemson T-shirt. Her wet hair was twisted up in a pink towel. She and her momma talked and agreed that they should eat the big meal of the day when J.P. arrived, as all hospitable Southern folk would, and that the tomato sandwiches would hold them over until he got there. Like clockwork, J.P. arrived at three. After a leisurely meal with Mrs. Carter, Caroline said her goodbyes with big ol' tears, hating to leave her momma but so excited to be going to Summerville.

Momma Carter was about to open the gate to go back into her yard when she turned around and said. "Y'all be good, y'hear. When the Lord comes a callin', he don't want to have to holler."

Caroline giggled, and yelled, "Love you, Momma, and they drove off.

The route from Greenville to Columbia was dull and uninteresting. Patches of wild flowers had blossomed, the stems of Queen Ann's Lace arched toward the sun, and the orange daylilies were just beginning to bloom. But the crepe myrtles were in the budding stage in the Upstate and midlands. Green leaves of the deciduous trees and kudzu vines were lining the highways, already making it impossible to see off into the distance.

Soda and sweet tea were now affecting Caroline, and she longed to see the rest areas that seemed so far apart. Both of them were so stuffed from the meal, especially Caroline, who had eaten twice in the span of three hours, that they found it hard to stay awake on the boring highway. She nearly drove him crazy blasting him with useless questions, trying to make sure he stayed awake. It seemed too hot to stop at a rest area and try to catch a few winks with the windows down. Everybody living in South Carolina knows that Columbia is the hottest place in the state, no mountain air and no ocean breeze, a bed for old Beelzebub, as Granny Pritchett would say, since she was a mountain woman.

The last thirty minutes of the trip were the worst for J.P. because Caroline had fallen asleep despite her efforts to stay awake and keep him company. Her hands were clasped and resting on her bloated tummy. Loose strands of hair were covering half of her face. J.P. kept glancing over toward her for quick glimpses, thinking that she was so pretty when she slept.

His hopes that she would remain asleep until they arrived in Summerville materialized. He had driven through the outskirts of town and made it down to the park before she woke up. This was the magic he'd waited for, a chance for her to wake up and see azaleas in colors ranging from the purest white to the deepest fuchsia, purple wisteria hanging in the trees, white, coral, and red camellias, and magnificent magnolia blossoms. It was like a fairytale, and she gasped when she saw the beauty of it all.

"This is your surprise, my dear. Welcome to Flowertown in the Pines."

"Oh, J.P., I've nevah seen any place like this in all my life. I assumed there'd be azaleas, but I had absolutely no idea Summerville would look like this in the spring. It feels like I'm dreaming."

They got out of the Toyota and took a stroll, hand in hand, meandering through the azalea park. They ended their walk at the white gazebo, stepped inside of it, and he twirled her around as if they were dancing to the most romantic music. Then he ran his fingers through her hair, tucking loose strands behind her ears, and kissed her tenderly. After the kiss, she rested her head upon his shoulder. They stood there motionless for a few minutes until the mosquitoes started their ravenous evening feed.

He checked her in at the motel and then drove her back through town to dine. It was almost ten o'clock when they left the restaurant, and they were both beyond exhausted.

As they sat in the car in front of the motel, he said, "I'm thrilled you're here. Now I have you all to myself for the rest of the week."

"Thank you, from the bottom of my heart, for driving so far to get me; that was eight hours on the road, for you."

"I'd do it all over again tomorrow if I needed to. Caroline, I love you, and I'm not here to say a bunch of things to you that I don't mean."

"We've got so much to talk about this week, don't we?"

"Yes, we do, but right now I want you to get a good night's sleep. I have to go down to Charleston in the morning to take a look at a private residence and give the owners an estimate. I feel sure that I'll be back by noon. So you can take your time getting up, and I'll be over in time to take you to lunch." He reached to the back seat and brought forth a box with one jumbo muffin inside.

"How on earth did you get this?"

"When you went to the ladies room at the restaurant, I walked over to the bakery section to get it. Then, I had to rush like mad to get it to the car and get back inside before you came out of the restroom."

"I musta been in there for a long time," she said laughing.

"You were in there for a very long time," he said grinning. "So the muffin and some coffee should fill you in the morning until I get back from Charleston."

"You think of everything."

"Well, for some people I do."

One more kiss for the night, and she was off to her room, like a good girl.

CHAPTER 17

SURVIVIN'

The EMT called the ER-triage nurse at the hospital. "I have a twenty eight year old, white male, well nourished. He has suffered a fall off a building roof which was witnessed by a co-worker.

The patient is oriented times 3 and is coherent, verbal in response. He reports that he is not on any medication at this time. Complains of dizziness. No SOB (shortness of breath) complaint of breathing, normal chest compressions. He has been immobilized on a spine board, and a cervical collar has been applied. B/P is 170/80. Pulse-120, He has been started on 250 cc of normal saline IV, O2-90cc. EKG started and patient exhibits normal NSR and has a heart rate of 120. His pupils are PERLA (pupils-equal, responsive, to light accommodation). The neuro checks show that he is unable to hand grip, and negative to pin prick and unable to move his upper and lower limbs. The patient has no visible signs of lacerations, puncture wounds, or fractures. He has some abrasions to his left arm. All vitals have been completed, and we're ready for transport."

Caroline was awake by eleven thirty that morning. She made a cup of coffee and had half of her muffin. She'd just gotten out of the shower and slipped on a pair of jean shorts and a T-shirt when she heard a knock at the door. It was nearly noon.

She called out, "Is that you, J.P.?"

"No, Caroline, it's Butch. I need to talk with you. It's very important."

She opened the door, forgetting about the privacy latch. She could see, through the opening in the door, that Butch had a very troubled look. He looked like his clothes were ready for a thrift shop donation, and his wiry hair was untamed. She guessed that'd he gotten ready in a hurry or had been working outside. She started getting anxious as she tried to get the door unlatched quickly, wondering why he was there rather than J.P.

"Please don't mind that I come in because I need to speak with you in private," said Butch, in a distressed tone of voice.

"Yeah, sure, I'm trying to get this dadgum latch undone. Okay, got it. Come on in and have a seat," she said as she pointed to the chair next to the small round table. "I'd offer you a muffin, but I eaten half of mine and don't have any more."

He was obviously upset. "Thanks, but I couldn't eat a bite right now. Caroline, I don't know how to tell you this."

"What, Butch, what is it," she asked, panicking?

"It's J.P. There's been an accident down in Charleston."

"Oh, no! Where is he? Is he gonna be okay?"

"Caroline, it wasn't a car accident. J.P.'s at the Medical University right now. Frank told Chris about thirty minutes ago, and he should be at MUSC any minute. I was s'posed to work on some design plans from home so I was there when Chris called me. I told him that I'd be here with you and to call us as soon as he could. All I know is that there's been a bad fall."

"Dear Jesus," she cried, with distress in her voice.

Butch assured Caroline that he would not leave her in the middle of the crisis with J.P. The plan was for the two of them to wait for Chris' call and then drive down to MUSC. Butch could offer some valuable advice to Chris about J.P. His older sister had been in a terrible car accident when she was nineteen years old and was a quadriplegic, so he was well aware of some of the procedures with trauma victims.

As they sat there in Caroline's motel room, Butch provided constant support to her as she worked through her own emotions. He had never met a girl as compassionate and sensitive as Caroline seemed to be, someone capable of loving deeply.

She sat at the table with her face in her hands, sobbing with great heaves, for a long time. When she finally lowered her hands to rest them upon the table, Butch placed his hands over hers and kept telling her that everything was going to be okay, although he was fiercely worried about his friend and didn't know what they were going to face when they got to the hospital.

After the EMT had called the triage nurse, she promptly notified the attending physician. When J.P. arrived at the hospital, the attending physician immediately ordered a CT scan and portable x-ray and requested a neurological consult. J.P. was intubated in case he had a seizure and/or difficulty breathing. He was also catheterized. A full blood panel, CBC, done, and blood type and cross were determined. A routine spinal tap was ordered to check the CSF (cerebral spinal fluid) to determine if there was pressure in the head, and/or possible bleeding or damage to other organs. The ER doctor recommended that a neurosurgeon be consulted should surgery be necessary.

Seeing edema on the CT scan and x-ray, the neurologist ordered a MRI. Upon reviewing the results of the MRI, confusion and edema from C3, 4, and 5 were noticed. There was minor confusion to C3/ incomplete. There was no dissection to the spinal cord noticeable on the MRI.

An IV of methylprednisolone was ordered to be run at 125ml-hour, and another bag of D5W (sugar water) was hung.

After several hours of painful waiting, the telephone rang. Butch warily answered the phone. It was Chris, but he really didn't know much about J.P.'s condition. He explained that J.P. had finally gotten out of the emergency room, where they had done a load of tests on him, and into his own room on the neuro floor. He was in and out of consciousness, sometimes asking to see Caroline, sometimes asking to see their mother. Chris said that he would be monitored every 15 minutes for the next 48 hours, a watch and see period of time. The nurses would be monitoring vitals, checking to see if J.P. was alert and oriented. They would check his breathing, O2 sats, blood pressure, and INO (fluid intake/ output). Routine labs would be run twice daily. The EKG monitor would still be attached for the first 48 hours and run every 12 hours during that time.

As soon as Butch hung up and relayed the conversation to Caroline, she packed her coffee colored backpack with some necessary toiletries, two changes of comfortable clothing, a couple of paperback books, a notepad and pen, snacks, some money, and her ID cards. She had no intention of leaving J.P. in the hospital alone. Responsibly, she asked Butch to keep her worn suitcase, with her other clothing in it, in his car or at his house. She told him that she was going down to the motel office to explain the unexpected situation to the manager and request that the reservations be cancelled until further notice, but gallantly Butch insisted that he do it for her. She was feeling so overwhelmed she was glad to relinquish that responsibility and let Butch help her.

Before they could exit the tiny parking lot of the motel, Caroline broke down again, crying so hard she made shrieking sounds between sobs. Butch knew that she was beyond the point of hearing any words of consolation, so he searched the car until he found a clean restaurant napkin, which was the best he could do. He handed her the napkin and then he tenderly patted her on the back until she could get a hold of herself again. He thought of the tremendous stress that she must be under.

They puttered through slow moving traffic on Main Street, in Summerville, to finally get to I-26. Once they got on the highway, Butch was flying past other vehicles, and they were in Charleston in less than twenty five minutes. In town, Butch knew the best route to get to the hospital with little to no waiting in the heavy traffic of the city.

By the time they got there, J.P.'s boss, Dave Westover, was leaving the hospital looking very distraught. He'd been there to make sure that J.P had the care that he needed and had told Chris to assure J.P., when more lucid and ready to deal with the issues at hand in the future, that his responsibilities at work were taken care of. He also said that his secretary would be filing necessary Workmen's Compensation, medical leave forms, and short term disability insurance forms that J.P. would need for benefits. He said that the company lawyer could work with Chris to obtain a limited power of attorney to enable him to sign the necessary forms for J.P. and get the ball rolling to get some money coming in for him as soon as possible.

The tall Scandinavian doctor had just made his rounds prior to the arrival of Butch and Caroline. Chris happened to be going to the canteen to get a cold drink when he saw Caroline and Butch near the visitor's lobby. He told them that the results of the tests indicated that J.P. was suffering from spinal edema due to the fall. There would be paralysis due to the swelling of the spinal cord, but since there was no dissection of the spinal cord, there was still hope that the paralysis might be temporary and he could have a full recovery if he responded well to intensive physical therapy. The doctor also mentioned there would be a team of professionals working with J.P. Members of the team would provide psychological support, neurological support, general medical support, and pastoral support. A patient advocate and social worker would be assigned to work with him, and he would receive occupational therapy as well as physical therapy. In addition, a respiratory therapist was already working with him. Caroline and Butch were really trying hard to remember all the medical details and were surprised that Chris had absorbed so much information.

Chris went to get a drink.

Butch looked over at Caroline. Tears streamed from her eyes, and he looked around the room to try to find a tissue for her. She looked rather pitiful with the loose strands of her hair already wet with tears she'd shed on their way to the hospital, no makeup, and a T-shirt so wrinkled that it looked like she'd slept in it. She was being so brave, and he was amazed that a girl, as young as she was, would be able to summon such strength from within to cope with this kind of tragedy. He knew she loved J.P., there was no doubt. And he also knew that the present circumstance made her personal situation even more uncertain and unsettling for her. J.P. had told him that Caroline had a job interview lined up for Thursday on James Island and had plans to meet Clay and Anne McMahan over the weekend to see the apartment and meet Clay's cousin, a potential roommate.

Frank, J.P.'s site partner, weary and exhausted, had arrived and stepped up to speak to them. Butch filled him in on the doctor's statement.

Already knowing Frank quite well, Butch introduced Caroline to Frank. Then he asked Frank, "What happened today? How did he fall?"

Chris got back from the canteen in time to hear Frank's rendition of the tragic event.

Frank said, "J.P. was up on the roof of a portico on one of them big ol' houses down on Church Street. He wasn't up very high, but might have slipped on some moss, with the house being all shaded by a huge Oak in the yard. When he lost his footin', he fell backwards. It coulda been damp and slick up there cus it rained last night, and those roofs have a slant. Anyway, he landed flat of his back on an old pathway with large protrudin' stones in the center and sunken brick on the sides of the stones. It looked like the mid-section of his spine hit a large stone, but thank the Lord, his head cleared the brick and hit the ground rather than the brick, or he prob'ly would be gone. At first he was totally unconscious. Dangnation, if I believed in spooks, I'd venture to say that somethin' supernatural got a hold of him and caused him to fall backwards, but I ain't gonna go there.

I ran up the steps to the house and banged on the massive door with both fists and started yellin' for help, not botherin' to find a doorbell. Fortunately, the owner of the home was there. She ran out in her fresh, white tennis garb and anxiously asked in her smooth Charlestionian brogue, 'What on earth has happened here?' Not waiting for an answer to her question, she ran back in the house to make a phone call an' got the paramedics out there. 'Em fellows were very careful how they moved him, not knowin' the extent of his injuries, an' all. They put him on some kinda board and put a collar 'round his neck. He was in and out of consciousness when the paramedics were takin' care of him, but he was able to answer some of their questions at times."

Chris went on in the room to check on J.P.

"Thank God you didn't have to leave him alone while you went to get help," Caroline said, still red eyed and sniffling. "You musta been terrified to see him lyin' there so helpless."

"I was still totally freaked out about it, but I headed down here as quickly as I could," Frank added. "By the time I got here he was already back in the 'mergency room, and I wasn't allowed to go in there. So, I left the hospital to find Chris. It took me 'bout twenty minutes to find him on a construction site down on East Bay. Lawt, it was so hard to tell Chris that J.P. had an accident.

Then I went back to the office to tell Dave and take care of findin' other crews to handle our jobs for a while. Dave has always treated J.P. like a son, and he flew down here to try to take care of things for him, but there wasn't a lot he could do."

Poor Frank told the entire story so fast he was almost panting when he finished.

"Yeah, we saw him leavin' just as we got here," mentioned Butch.

"Has the doctor been back in to see him," inquired Frank?

"Chris told us earlier that it looks like J.P. is sufferin' from spinal edema, a swellin' of the spinal cord, as a result of the trauma of the fall," Butch said, informatively.

"That's what we heard; so, what does that mean we're lookin' at, here?" There was no distinction between Chris, Butch, and Frank in terms of concern; they all seemed like blood brothers.

Butch explained further, "Dr. Nielsen thinks that there's still a chance that the paralysis could be temporary since his spinal cord wasn't severed. Everything is up in the air for the next 48 hours. They're gonna monitor him closely, checking him every 15 minutes, in fact."

Trying to be optimistic, Caroline spoke up and said to Frank, "I'm sure that it's goin' to take time and a lot of physical therapy. He's gonna need a lot of support from all of us to get back to where he needs to be." She wanted to sound like a young adult, but inside she felt like a scared little girl. She wanted to be strong and not fall apart when she went in to see him. Good gracious, how was she going to do it?

Still expressing himself so dramatically, Frank continued, "Lord have mercy, I've been so worried for the past few hours. The paramedics told me there was no tellin' what the extent of his injuries might be, hittin' that rock pathway the way he did. Shoot, he's been on much higher roofs and some with ungodly steep pitches. I still can't b'lieve he fell backwards. It gives me the heebie-jeebies it's so spooky, like it just shouldn't have been possible. He never has been wary of a roof like I am. I have to admit that I'm a wimp when it comes to heights. I don't get up there if I don't have to. He risks life and limb, and I stand back and write reports. Some site partner I am."

Butch said, "That's okay, man. Don't blame yourself for anythin'. It was clearly an accident. Besides, we're all wimps 'bout somethin', right Chris?"

"Yeah, right," Chris said as he shot him a look of disbelief, probably wondering why he'd admitted it in front of a girl, especially his brother's girlfriend. Then he gave Butch a wry smile because he was terribly afraid of snakes but never wanted anybody to know about it, and he wasn't about to tell Caroline.

Looking over at Butch and Caroline, Frank commented again, "Since y'all are here now, I'm gonna head on home and get a shower. Beth's gonna tell me I reek for sure, sweatin' from bein' so nervous all day and dealin' with this ungodly humidity. I'm sure that she'll wanta come visit tonight, but if he's still out of it, call us and we'll wait and come later. No sense in a whole battalion of comrades to be piled in this little room, bein' all loud and such 'cus Lord knows Beth caint be quiet fer nothing. We'd just be in the way of the nurses. Don't you think?"

Caroline stated, "You're prob'ly right. You have to be drained yourself, bein' with him when he had the accident, not knowin' what was gonna happen with him." Butch and Caroline entered the hospital room. Caroline first noticed the breathing tube where he had been intubated in the ER. The lights had been dimmed a bit, but she could still see all the monitors and dangling IV bags, which gave her a cold creepy feeling. She could feel the stress as it came over her whole body, a clear sense of deja-vu of scenes of her childhood. She wanted to start crying again, but she choked back the tears.

They were sitting next to the hospital bed waiting for signs that J.P. might become alert again. They'd look back and forth to one another, then look back to J.P. and allow themselves to scan the dreary sterile room. Butch noticed Caroline nearly shivering like she was cold, so he got a white towel from the bathroom and draped it around her shoulders.

Butch told Caroline, "I'm plannin' to ask my boss if I could take some vacation days this week. J.P. is gonna need me, and I think you'll need me, too. I'm gonna make sure you get to your interview and see the apartment on Saturday."

"That's awfully nice of you. You're another great guy. There're not many of y'all around. Right now, I can't even think about inter-viewin' for a job or lookin' at an apartment." She liked Butch and felt that he was always willing to help, a really good guy.

For a full hour after Frank left, J.P. continued to sleep. When Chris came back from the cafeteria, Caroline felt she needed to find a pay phone to get in touch with Emily. She didn't want to call Emily from J.P.'s hospital room for fear that she would get all upset talking to her, and she definitely didn't want J.P. to think that he was upsetting her.

Never having been to MUSC, she had no idea where anything was in the hospital. The place was crawling with medical students, some not much older than she was. She walked down to the nurses' desk to ask about the pay phone. Then she realized that all of her change was still in her backpack, so she had to go back to the room to get it.

Finally making it to the area housing pay phones, she slipped her change into the coin slot and waited to hear Emily, or her moth-er, answer the phone.

"Hello, Price's residence," Emily said.

Caroline was surprised. She tried her best to sound cheerful, and said, "Don't you sound formal, Miss Emily Jane Price?"

"Yeah, Momma did try to teach us some manners whether we use them or not, and you know most of the time I don't. I ain't heard from you in a coon's age, and I'm uh coming to find your haggard butt."

"Emily, this isn't an easy call to make."

"Whatcha mean," Emily asked with urgency in her voice? "What's happened?"

"It's J.P.; he's in the hospital, at MUSC. He fell off the roof of a portico of a big house in Charleston."

"Oh gracious Lord in heaven, Caroline, I'm so sorry. Can you tell me how it happened?"

She was about to cry then, but managed to get some of the beginning of the story out. "He and Frank were down in the city, doin' an inspection of a leak above the porch roof..." She couldn't say more.

"Oh baby, this is serious, isn't it?"

After a long pause she was able to say, "Yes, it's serious."

"What does that mean, Caroline? What has it done to him? God forbid that I ask this question, but is he paralyzed?"

"The doctor said there's swellin' of the spinal cord, causing paralysis. He said that J.P. may..."

Caroline broke down again before she could finish the statement.

Emily said, "Caroline, don't try to tell me anymore right now."

Caroline was sobbing uncontrollably.

"Listen, I'm comin' down there right now. I'll be there in thirty minutes. Don't even try to say bye to me. Just hang up and try to find a restroom to hide in a stall, and cry until you feel better. Cry your guts out. I'll find you when I get there. Love you, bye."

Emily heard the dial tone, hung up, and went to look in the kitchen for her car keys. She sat in the steamy car on the hot concrete driveway and cried, too, for a few minutes. She didn't want to be driving and find herself distracted. She'd take Highway 61 down by the historical gardens for the scenic tour, which always calmed her spirit and kept her out of some of the annoying traffic of Main Street in Summerville to get to I-26. She kept telling herself that she needed to be strong for her friends. She was feeling absolutely horrible about the whole unbelievable affair. How could this happen to him? How could something like this happen to poor sweet Caroline, who makes all the right choices in comparison to a lot of us?

Caroline did just as Emily suggested, found a restroom, and stayed in there crying a good fifteen to twenty minutes. Several times she heard sympathetic women in the restroom, asking her if she was going to be alright. She was unable to answer them and kept on crying. She finally came out of the restroom and got a drink from the vending machine before going back toward J.P.'s room. Butch and Chris were still in the room talking softly, but when Butch caught sight of Caroline, about to enter the room, her eyes red and swollen, he came out into the hallway to speak with her.

She dropped her head as if trying to hide her eyes, as she was sure they were beet red. Butch put one strong hand on her shoulder and gently lifted her chin with her other hand.

He asked, compassionately, "How are you holdin' up?"

She thought she was finished crying, having used a whole roll of rough toilet paper in the restroom to wipe her runny nose, what seemed like fifty times. She had stuffed some of the toilet paper into her pockets for emergency situations.

Butch pulled her head to his shoulder, much like her brother would, and she cranked back up, shaking uncontrollably and crying great tears. He reached to shut the partially closed door to J.P.'s room, and pulled the door shut. Then he just let her cry until she was ready to speak to him.

"No, I'm not okay at the moment and I feel like I'm nevah gonna be okay. I can't b'lieve that all this bad stuff is happenin' to us. We were supposed to have a wonderful week, but now, the love of my life is in there nearly comatose." Butch had no idea that this devastating accident was triggering all kinds of memories about her Daddy's fatal accident. It's a wonder that she could even breathe.

"J.P. needs to be zoned out sleeping right now so he's not flippin' out on us. He may have no idea that he's paralyzed. If he realizes that he may not walk outta here in a few days, he may need somethin' potent for anxiety. Worse yet, when he becomes aware that he has a catheter and can't even pee, his self-esteem is going to plummet, and he may get very depressed."

"I didn't even think of that. I know he's gonna feel embarrassed and humiliated; I'm sure I would."

"He really has no clue that you're here right now, Caroline. "Do you think it would do you some good to go for a walk with me? Chris is goin' to be here a while and can stay here with J. P. I know I may be freakin' you out tellin' you these things. It was really hard on my sister when she first realized that she was paralyzed. I saw her go through the shock and depression."

"Maybe we should go take a walk and talk some more," she conceded. "I'm not gonna turn my back on J.P., and I need to know what to expect and try to plan how to react to it. It could be helpful if you tell me more about your sister's accident."

"I have all the confidence in the world that you're the person he'll need most. You were brought into his life for a reason," Butch said with sincerity.

"I guess we both were, but I don't feel that confidence right now," she said sadly.

"Of course you don't feel it now, you're still in shock yourself, but the two of you are gonna grow closer together from this. Like your momma would prob'ly tell you, give this thing to God."

"Let's go take a stroll. The heat isn't too bad today, is it," she asked, unwittingly?

"You know it's hot as ten hells, like always and as humid as a sauna. But let's get outta the hospital for a little while and let you get yourself together. You've got a long night ahead of you if you're stayin' with J.P., and you need to feel some relief. Those nurses comin' in there every 15 minutes to check up on him are gonna drive you crazy and keep you awake all night.

She laughed for the first time in hours and said, "What I need is a jug of mountain moonshine and a cold rag."

"Moonshine, where would you get moonshine?"

"You don't know it, but I grew up near the Dark Corner."

"Where's that," he asked?

"Northern Greenville County is called the Dark Corner."

"How come?"

"All I can say is it's famous for the three m's.

"What are the three m's," asked Butch hesitantly?

Caroline answered, "The murders and mayhem caused by all the moonshining."

"Oh, you don't say. What's the cold rag for?"

"To put on my head when I feel like I'm gonna barf from chuggin' some moonshine."

"Girl, you would not," he said laughing at her seriousness.

"To heck I wouldn't." She suddenly felt quilty for enjoying herself with Butch while poor J.P. was in the hospital in such bad shape.

"You're a trip, Caroline Carter."

"You think we better go back in," she asked?

"Let's give it a few more minutes. Our laughter is good medicine for both of us; and I pray that J.P. will be laughin' in a few weeks, too. I can't see him down for long if there's that possibility that he can get better, and I b'lieve there is. I don't know how many times J.P., Chris, and I have sat out on that old porch, had a few beers, and tried to think of anythin' we could to make one another laugh. It just feels good," he said, drawling more than he had during the entire conversation.

"Lawt, I completely forgot to tell you that Emily is on her way from Summerville."

"Caroline, Emily will probably go straight up to the room and Chris is there to fill her in. We aren't staying away long, but you've already had a lot of emotionally drainin' stuff goin' on, and I think this little break is necessary."

Caroline secretly noted how protective Butch seemed toward her. They didn't know each other that well, but they did have lots of things in common just being true Southerners and being used to doing compassionate things for people in need. And both of them loved J.P. Butch had been friends with him for a long time and probably knew J.P. better than anyone else did, other than Chris. Would Butch be someone that she could always count on? Maybe he would.

CHAPTER 18

HOPIN'

When they got back from their walk, Emily was in the room with Chris getting the latest update from the nursing staff. J.P. was still sleeping. Caroline noticed tears coursing down Emily's cheeks.

She turned around to see Caroline standing there with Butch. Emily rushed over to hug her, and Caroline stood there in a daze, as if she didn't know what to do next. Emily suddenly sounded like a fundamentalist evangelical and said, "There's a reason for everything. God blessed J.P. or he wouldn't have a dog's chance to recover fully. This could've been one of those situations where all the outcomes would be permanent for sure. I b'lieve that God will make him walk again."

"I don't know when you got to be such a Righteous Rita, but I'm glad you're thinkin' 'bout him and prayin' for him," said Caroline. "We're both gonna need all the prayers we can get." She almost sounded mildly cynical, allowing her emotions to override and momentarily forgetting all of the religious indoctrination she had as a child.

Caroline pulled Emily's hand to indicate that she wanted to speak with her privately in the hallway, away from the guys. Emily followed Caroline's lead and stepped out of the room.

Once out of earshot from Chris and Butch, having moved down to the visitor's lounge, Caroline admitted wearily, "Emily, I love J.P., but I'm not ready to deal with this. First of all, I have to return to Winthrop to finish up the requirements to graduate. I want to free myself of all responsibilities at school. Secondly, I need to make sure I have a job and housing in an area where I can use public transit until I can save up for a car." Her voice was sounding shriller as she spoke to Emily. "I've gotta go somewhere in less than a month and have a job for the summer to tide me over until a teaching job starts. I know I can't go back to Greenville. Momma would be glad to help me, but I would be too embarrassed to move back home. I couldn't stand livin' with Rhonda; she'd send me to the nuthouse on Bull Street," she said in a panic stricken tone of voice.

"Caroline, Caroline, slow down. I don't see any reason why you should change your current plans to interview at Jasper Elementary and take a look at that apartment here in the city. J.P.'s situation doesn't have to change any of that. He has lots of friends in Summerville and at work. They'll all pitch in to help him get back on his feet. It will not all fall on you, darlin'. He's got up to 90 days in rehab with some of the most knowledgeable therapists in the state. Now calm down and take one day at a time."

Huge tears filled Caroline's eyes and she tried to wipe them away with her fingers, then wiping her fingers on her shorts.

Emily put her hands on Caroline's shoulders and said encouragingly, "Sister, it's gonna be okay. I know it seems awful right now. The happy day you're more than due for is just around the corner. Y'all just hit a gigantic speed bump going a tad fast."

Still fighting back the tears, she responded, "My life has always been filled with speed bumps and potholes." She tried hard to laugh, but she was still crying at the same time.

Trying to sound full of faith again, which was totally out of character for her, Emily said, "I guess you need to let God give you someone to fill the potholes."

"Well, J.P.'s not gonna be able to fill any potholes. He'll be simply trying to keep his own head above water," Caroline said, with skepticism.

"Stop bein' so pooh pooh! I heard you say that you love him, too, and I b'lieve it."

"I'm sorry, but I feel pooh pooh right now."

"Caroline, in the past few years, I've not seen one single thing that you didn't handle well."

"Why was I so dumb to think that having a difficult childhood somehow entitled me to an easy adult life?"

"Who told you that crap?"

"Emily, you just said God, so don't say crap!"

"Pardon me, Mrs. Post. Life's not gonna be a piece of cake, but you can choose how you want to color your own picture, how you want to view the events, and shape your own world. You can be creative or you can bellyache and never have a chance to make somethin' of your life, with the good times and the bad; you don't know what sweet is without tastin' bitter."

"Girl, you sounded so artsy. I know you're right, but I didn't want to taste bitter at this point of my life when I'm graduatin' from college, I'm lookin' for a job and a place to live, and I don't even have any transportation. And J.P. won't be able to attend my graduation ceremony." She looked like a little child who'd just lost her puppy. "I guess I'm bellyachin', and I need to get a grip and stop it."

"That's my best friend talkin'. You gotta climb this mountain, but look at it like it's a molehill."

"At least you agree that it's a mountain," said Caroline.

"It is one, girlfriend. Think you are ready to go back in there in case he wakes up?"

"Yeah, I do want to be the first person he sees when he opens his eyes this time. Thanks my friend for listin' to me; I guess I needed to vent." She hugged Emily, and Emily held her embrace and patted her on the back.

It was already six o'clock. One of the nurses came in to check J.P.'s blood pressure, temperature, pulse, respiration, urine output, the IV, and EKG at the scheduled interval. Caroline was standing on the other side of the bed. When J.P. did wake up, from hearing the nurse make comments as she poked and prodded, he gave Caroline a faint, "Hey!"

She put her hand on the side of his face and greeted him with, "Hey, honey. I'm glad you're wakin' up."

"Mr. Andersen," the nurse said, "you took a little tumble today."

He looked at Caroline, trying to smile, and said with rather slurred speech, "Yeah, I believe I busted my butt today."

Caroline was nodding, trying to look chipper. She felt a lump in her throat, like she was going to have to fight again to stop the tears from coming.

The nurse read and filled out paperwork. Once she was finished readjusting the IV, and exited the room, he appeared to relax quickly and fall asleep again.

Caroline, Emily, and Butch walked down to the waiting room, with Chris joining them. Emily said to Caroline, "I'm glad that I'm not off in New York."

"Oh my goodness, I completely forgot about that when I called you to come down here. Why aren't you in New York?"

"Jason's daddy talked us in to goin' after graduation. He said he'd sweeten the pot and let us stay in NYC for the whole month of June. He's just glad Jason wants to go somewhere with a girl."

"That's great! Y'all are gonna have loads of fun. I'm envious."

"Don't be, Caroline, you've found love, and I haven't. Sure, I'll have a great time with Jason, but it won't be anything like you had goin' at Christmastime with J.P., because y'all were already in love and sharin' somethin' special together. Jason and I are just great friends."

Caroline retorted, "Sometimes it's easier to have a friend than have a boyfriend."

Emily replied, "I know, darlin', cus I've had a few here and there, but they weren't worth a hill of beans."

Butch walked over toward the windows and stood there looking out, forlornly. Chris joined Butch for a minute while Caroline and Emily finished their conversation.

"You're right. I shouldn't be envious at all, and I need to be optimistic. Here I am in the beautiful city of Charleston, and somethin' tells me that I'm gonna get a job down here and be livin' downtown. And J.P.'s gonna get through all this mess, and we're gonna make it together."

"That a girl," cheered Emily!

Then the girls joined Butch and Chris to discuss J.P.

Butch spoke up, "I think it might be better that everythin's out in the open when the doctor gives the okay. When J.P. does become lucid, I don't want him to feel like we knew about his condition and he didn't. It ain't right, 'cus he's a grown man.

Chris, you should prob'bly be the one to talk to him if you're here. If you have to go back to work, which I assume you do, Caroline and I should be here with him for the next few days. Emily, maybe you could be here on Thursday when I take Caroline for her interview."

Chris and Emily nodded in agreement.

Butch continued, "Now we have to rally 'round him and give him the support and encouragement he needs. We all gotta stick by him. And help each other."

"Amen, brother," chimed in Emily.

Caroline curtailed her negative thoughts and heehawed because she'd never heard Emily say something like "amen, brother," as if she were in a revival meeting. Caroline didn't have a clue about what had gotten into Emily; plus, she needed to rid herself of some tension, remembering the comments Butch had made earlier about laughter.

Chris told Butch and Emily that he would go on home since the two of them were there to support Caroline. He needed to get in touch with his parents to tell them what had happened, and he dreaded it like the plague.

Butch mentioned to Emily that neither he nor Caroline had eaten since the morning, so they decided to go get some sub sandwiches and bring them back to the hospital.

Caroline had been absorbed in reading her novel, and hadn't realized how much time had passed while Butch and Emily were out getting subs. She didn't want to be eating a sub in the room if J.P. woke up, so Butch suggested that he stay with J.P. so that she and Emily could go eat in the lounge.

"How you holdin' out, friend," Emily asked?

"Okay. He's been sawin' logs the whole time y'all were gone. I been sittin' here readin' this crazy book. Lordy, I'm hongry now. Gimme that sam…wich, quick."

"I'm glad to see you're more like your insane self. I was gettin' worried 'bout you."

"You should worry. This is stressful. Emily, I have no idea how I'm gonna get my act together for that interview on Thursday."

"You're gonna go in there lookin' like a million bucks and put on that sweet charm, and you'll be fine and dandy, Mandy."

"I luv you. You're such a nut. I don't know what I'd have done if you were in the Big Apple right now."

"You'd probably be boo hooin' a lot more."

"Got 'at right," Caroline admitted. "Cryin' ain't gonna change a thing, is it? If I thought it would, I'd cry a bathtub full."

"I'm 'fraid not; but your optimism will go a long way. If he senses that you b'lieve in him, he can do this."

"I do b'lieve he can do it, but it's so scary. I keep thinkin' I'm havin' a bad dream, just like when Daddy had his accident. I try to deny reality as long as I can until the truth slaps me up side of the head."

Emily said with sincerity, "You're the strongest person I know, a pillar of strength. Try to keep tellin' yourself that this situation is totally separate from what happened with your daddy."

"I guess you're right, but it doesn't seem like I'm strong sometimes. I feel more like I'm a statue of salt in the middle of a sand storm, bein' chipped away one grain at a time."

After they ate, Butch and Emily left so things could settle down for Caroline and J.P. Hopefully, he would sleep most of the night, and she might be able to eventually get to sleep and possibly sleep through some of the frequent checks being made on J.P.

Caroline found herself alone again in J.P.'s hospital room. He was completely out, sleeping soundly. She viewed the room. It all seemed so cold and impersonal. The wall of outlets, monitoring equipment, stark white walls, colorless bed linens, and an abundance of fluorescent lighting made Caroline feel uncomfortable. She stood by his bed for a few minutes; there was no arousal from him. She was in for a long night, but she wasn't going to let him be alone.

She didn't last long standing next to his bed, her back was already aching and the sleeper chair was looking better with each passing moment. One of the attendants brought her a couple of sheets, a pillow, and a blanket. She opened the sleeper chair, put a sheet on it, and propped herself up with the pillow. At least she could stretch her legs rather than sit in a straight chair next to J.P.'s bed. She pulled up the white, thermal weave blanket. She always got cold in hospital rooms. Maybe there was some psychological reason for that kind of chill. She had to get her mind off of these things she was looking at and old deep-rooted horrors. She pulled out her novel and began to read.

Caroline eventually got used to the nurses entering the room frequently, and she drifted off to sleep. She had been emotionally exhausted for hours and the catnaps helped to ease her troubled mind.

About midnight she heard the door creak as it opened. She lifted her head to get a glimpse of the nurse entering the room. Instead of seeing a single figure enter the room, she saw a woman holding a bundle in her arms and she seemed to be levitating rather than walking in. Then she heard the piercing cry of a distressed baby. An eerie feeling came over her. She rubbed her eyes and blinked a few times. Then she sat up ramrod straight in the chair to see the nurse by J.P.'s bed checking the monitors. Caroline swung her legs over the side of the make-shift bed, slipped her feet into her clogs, and headed for the bathroom. Looking in the mirror, she was horrified to see awful dark circles surrounding her eyes, reminding her of a raccoon. Her mouth felt stale and dry. She retrieved a royal blue toothbrush and a travel sized tube of toothpaste from her small paisley toiletry bag and brushed her teeth and then used the bathroom.

As she slowly opened the bathroom door, she could definitely tell that the nurse was still there. The nurse was polite when Caroline traipsed past her and stood on the other side of the bed. She gently stroked his cheek and told him that she was going down to get some apple juice. If the truth be known, she was really downright spooked and had to get out of that room for a while.

She looked at the nurse one more time before she exited the room. She had to have been dreaming when she saw the figure of a woman holding a baby. *Why did she continue to have this dream over and over? Was it a dream or some kind of a message to her from some other realm?* All of the sudden, she remembered the night that J. P. had taken her to Grove Park Inn, the faint image she'd seen or imagined of a woman rocking a baby, at the entrance to the inn, and she shuddered to think that perhaps it was a message from beyond the veil of life and the hereafter.

CHAPTER 19

LOOKIN'

The routines continued for the next 48 hours with J.P. slipping in and out of consciousness. His parents were to arrive on Friday from New Jersey. Although Caroline did stay with J.P. quite a bit, Chris, Frank, Emily, and Butch came up with a rotation schedule so that one of them would be in the room with him during that critical 48 hour period.

The timing for such a dreadful thing to happen to J.P. was horrible for Caroline, going through a crucial time in her own life. She left the hospital on Wednesday night to get some rest the eve before her job interview. Chris stayed with his brother that night.

Emily's mother was very accommodating toward Caroline as she stayed in their home. Fortunately, she was genuinely concerned about J.P. and not just meddling in Caroline's business. She encouraged Caroline to use their home phone freely to stay in contact her family members about the accident, which she did.

On Thursday morning, Emily went down to MUSC to stay with J.P. while Caroline was at her parent's house getting ready for the interview. After she dressed, and did her hair in a fashionable coiffure secured by an attractive barrette, Caroline went out to the kitchen to get an objective point of view from Mrs. Price. She couldn't help but think of her as Debutante Deb although she knew it wasn't nice. To Caroline's surprise, Mrs. Price said she loved her outfit, hair style, makeup, and accessories and told her that she'd made an excellent choice for an interview with a school district. She looked in the mirror and actually felt like an adult and not an adolescent.

Caroline had another copy of her resume, printed on linen paper, tucked neatly into a professional looking black folder. She also had a gray, tweed, fabric-covered notebook of annotated photos of her student teaching experiences and projects, copies of her grades, copies of reference letters from professors and her student teaching supervisor, and evidence of her involvement in extracurricular activities.

She heard the doorbell ring about nine o'clock, knowing that it was Butch. Emily's mother greeted him cordially and invited him to come in.

When Caroline walked down the long, dimly lit hallway and into the foyer, she was surprised to see Butch standing there in a pair of nice slacks and a sports coat, looking very handsome, smiling at her. She realized how thoughtful he was to have dressed up to chauffeur her to an appointment, a gentleman of the Lowcountry.

She commented before he could say a word to her, "You look very nice today, what's up?"

"I turned on the radio this mornin' and heard that today was gonna be a scorcher, and I didn't want to take you to an interview and drop you off. That wouldn't look good for you to have to stand there in the swelterin' heat waitin' for a ride home. So I dressed appropriately to enter the buildin' with you and wait for you in the office. I wouldn't want your future boss to think you had a bunch of beach bums as your friends, so I'm tryin' to look as professional as you do, my dear."

"Well, that's mighty nice of you sir," she exclaimed!

He asked, brightly, Miss Carter, Are you 'bout ready to go?"

"I'm ready, but let me go back and get the things I'll need for the interview and get a change of clothes to wear in the hospital this afternoon. I won't be able to stand this outfit for long."

"Okay, I'll go cool the car for you. I've got J.P.'s car because the old Mustang needs a new alternator and the Volvo has a glitch with the air. Come on out when you're ready."

As they drove to Charleston from Summerville, Butch tried to strike up conversation about Winthrop and Caroline's student teaching experience. He didn't want her to focus on J.P's accident and get all flustered before the interview. He warned Caroline about the Gullah dialect that she might encounter and told her how difficult it is to understand folks on the islands sometimes.

After a 25 minute interview, Caroline came out of the Dr. DuBose's office smiling. Butch told her that he'd go out and cool the car again. The black interior of the Toyota was extremely uncomfortable if the car had been sitting in the sun for a while, even with a sun shield in place and tinted windows.

Butch drove the Toyota up to the circular drive area nearest the office, and Caroline came out when she saw him drive up, walking carefully in her heels. She got into the car and hugged Butch without saying a word. She looked like she was on cloud nine. He felt honored to be the person to have taken her to her first job interview.

He said, "I take it you had a good interview."

She commented, "Lord have mercy, it 'bout killed me to speak correctly for 25 minutes."

"I bet it did, I wouldn't wanna do it for more than 10 minutes, it ain't natural," agreed Butch.

"Actually, Dr. DuBose said that he thought I'd be perfect for a position in his school. I'm glad I took my portfolio, because he seemed impressed by it. He did say that, due to enrollment, grade level teachers may be switched around, and it's possible that I might teach first grade."

"So you think you'd like teachin' the little fellows?"

"Oh yeah, I'd love teachin' first graders, but I have to watch my grammar all the time. Dr. DuBose, seemed like he was tryin' to cover up his own accent as much as I was mine durin' the interview. We both spoke slowly, meticulously, and professionally, but like it was painin' us. I wondered if he was possibly native to James Island or some other sea island because he didn't sound like he was from the Upstate and definitely not from the North."

"Sure, 'nough," he paused, as if reflecting. "Well, I got my drawl and it's hard to let go of what you heard all your life just 'cus there's a bunch of Yankees in the house. They pick on me all the time and its heck to pay when they have their people come to visit. The whole doggone bunch of 'em coax me to say this and that, so they can have a good laugh. I give in and laugh with 'em."

She asked, "Hey, where're your people from, anyhoo?"

"My daddy's from South Georgia, real close to the Florida border if you're goin' Highway 301. Momma grew up in Greenwood."

"Oh, that's it. You sound different from folks 'round here. Sorry, I didn't mean that in a derogatory way."

"I know. That's the way things are. Some of the Charlestonians I've had to deal with through work sound like what I call movie star Southerners. But I get ticked-off when people treat you like you're an idiot, 'cus you drawl. Shoot, most of the students at Clemson have accents, unless they're transplants."

"Come to think of it, most of the students at Winthrop do, too, some a little more grammatically correct, but still distinctly Southern." She suddenly thought of Joost, his correctness in speech and how fake she felt trying to speak properly with him. She hadn't done that with J.P. because he'd purposely lost so much of his accent, and she felt that he wasn't going to judge her. "By the way, I didn't eat a bite of breakfast, how 'bout you?" She was starving.

"No...oo, I didn't eat either, but I don't want to eat lunch yet. Why don't we go down to East Bay, there's a great bakery. Do you feel like havin' all kinda stuff we shouldn't eat? Celebrate today, for havin' to tawk correctly all that time in your interview. It musta nearly wore you out."

When Butch and Caroline got back to MUSC, bloated and hyper from heaps of sweets, they ran into Emily, on her way to the snack machines. She said J.P. was definitely aware of the condition he was in. He cursed and yelled, trying to let go of his anger. He sort of wore himself out and slept a while after pitching a fit. When he woke up the second time, he was much more mellow and able to talk about things. She mentioned to Caroline and Butch that J.P. was being evaluated by the physical therapist.

Thank goodness, Dr. Nielsen came in, too, and explained to J.P. that he's hopeful that his spinal edema is causing temporary paralysis. He said that if J.P. works hard in physical therapy, he might be a candidate for full recovery. He gave him some hope, and J.P.'s attitude changed drastically.

Amanda, the PT, was in the room working with J.P. when Butch and Caroline went up to see him. Amanda was tall and slender. She was about J.P.'s age, twenty seven or twenty eight. She had long blond hair, pulled back with a clip to the back of her head. Her olive complexion looked tanned; perhaps she'd just vacationed in the tropics. Amanda wore tortoise shell glasses, but behind those glasses were incredible blue eyes, almost the color of turquoise. Her teeth were perfect and gleaming white; Amanda was strikingly beautiful.

While Amanda was doing stretching exercises with him, J.P. heard Butch and Caroline come in; he definitely heard Caroline's heels clacking on the waxed linoleum floor. When they walked further into the room, he noticed Caroline's expression, using his peripheral vision. With her chin tucked down and her eyes focused straight forward, she appeared to be looking Amanda over from head to toe. Knowing Caroline's unfounded insecurities, he felt that she was fighting hard not to be intimidated by Amanda.

J.P. called to Caroline to come to his bedside. He had no hesitation about introducing her to Amanda as his girlfriend.

After introductions, he said to Caroline, "You look fantastic today. I mean really good, very professional. I can't wait to hear about your interview."

Caroline nodded and then went to take a seat in the room. Butch also took a seat to give the PT time to finish J.P.'s therapy session.

Amanda continued to do the evaluative stretching exercises. J.P. spoke up and said, "I didn't introduce you to Butch. He's my good friend and housemate. To tell you the truth, I can't remember his real name. We've been calling him Butch for years and years."

Butch said, "My real name is Elmer, doofus. You don't remember 'cus most of the time you'd had a few beers when the other guys started pickin' on me. Doesn't Butch sound a lot better than Elmer? Unfortunately, my parents named me that after my grandpa. I guess that's tradition in my family to name the first-born son after the grandfather, if not after the father."

"What the heck is your father's name," Caroline asked?

"Horace."

"Ouch, that ain't much better than Elmer," she said. Sorry, but I'm glad you go by Butch."

Amanda finished the stretching exercises and told J.P. that they would continue to do those exercises at bedside daily until she'd be getting him up in a wheelchair, with the help of orderlies of course, and going down to the therapy room to work. As she left the room, she exuded Southern charm by drawling a fine, "Bye now. It was so nice to meet y'all."

Caroline secretly gagged because those would have been her exact words, in that exact tone, if she were in that position. Trying to conceal frustration, she used her most seductive walk in her heels as she went back to J.P.'s bedside.

He asked, "So, how did the interview go?"

"It was great. The principal, Dr. DuBose, said that I'd be perfect for almost any position in the school. In addition to my resume, I'd prepared a professional lookin' notebook containin' annotated photos of my student teachin', my grades and awards, reference letters, that kind of thing. Dr. DuBose perused the portfolio and seemed impressed."

"So if the principal likes you, the district hires you?"

"I think there's a good chance of it. The district did all of their necessary screenin', such as a SLED report and verification of grades and credentials. When I applied, I put Jasper Elementary School as a place I'd like to interview, since I knew there was goin' to be a vacancy there."

"That was good thinking. You're a smart cookie."

Caroline proclaimed, "I gotta get outta these heels or I'm gonna die. Lemme go change into my comfortable clothes."

J.P. beat Butch to the draw and started talking to him first. He asked Butch, "How do I thank you enough for taking care of her and doing the things I would've done?"

"Man, that's thanks enough. By the way, we drove your Toyota today. I didn't want Caroline to get all sticky and get her hair messed up b'fore her interview. The air in the Volvo is still not coolin' well and I didn't want her rollin' up in front of the school in a truck."

"That's fine, I'm glad you did."

"I guess your parents are comin' in tomorrow. Do I need to pick them up at the airport?"

"No, they'll rent a car so they'll have transportation over the weekend. They'll probably have to go back to Jersey next week. Usually, Friday and Monday are the only days they can take off. It's a different world up there. Most employers don't show much mercy, even when a person asks off to take care of family. It's all rush, rush, rush, to make money, money, money, to pay taxes, taxes, taxes."

"So you don't wanna go back up there to live, do you," asked Butch?

"Heck no! Who'd want to move back up there after living down here?"

"I suppose we're too hospitable if y'all Yanks don't wanna go back home." They were both laughing when Caroline came out of the bathroom. Butch went in there to change out of his dress pants and into a pair of long khaki shorts and a teal colored T-shirt.

J.P. said that Chris was getting off early and coming at three o'clock, and then Frank and Beth were coming after Chris. Caroline was planning to spend the night there but mentioned that she and Butch might go somewhere when Chris arrived. J.P. agreed that it would be good for them to go out for a while, assuming they'd probably hit the beach and find some good eats; after all, it was a special day for Caroline.

The Toyota was terribly hot sitting on the black asphalt for a while, the new parking lot feeling like the asphalt was melting and soft. Caroline and Butch sat wiping perspiration from their foreheads with napkins they'd snatched at the bakery.

After what seemed like an eternity to Caroline, the car began to cool off, and Butch asked, "Have you ever been to Fort Moultrie on Sullivan's Island? We could go bum 'round the fort, walk on the beach, and get dinner at one of the restaurants on Shem Creek on the way back. You don't want to go to the hospital cafeteria when you can eat seafood."

"I like seafood, and I'd like to go to Sullivan's Island," Caroline replied. "I haven't been to Fort Moultrie before."

They left MUSC and drove through downtown Charleston. They were approaching East Bay when it dawned on Caroline that she'd have to go over the killer bridge again. She asked, fearfully, "Am I gonna have to cross that bridge again?"

Butch answered, "Yes and you're gonna have to get used to it if you're gonna live in the Lowcountry. It's a part of our life."

She wanted to punch him in the ribs, but she dared not to. She got her eyes shut just in time.

When Caroline opened her eyes, they weren't quite over the bridge, but they'd passed the really high, scary part of it. She looked up to see the big signs for Sulliivan's Island.

It didn't take long to get to Fort Moultrie, and there was ample parking behind the Visitor's Center. Like tourists, they stayed in the cool brick building for about fifteen minutes looking at various artifacts, brochures, and video clips.

They walked across the street to the old fort, the wind blowing warm, sticky air and the sun beating down on them made them feel sweaty in seconds. The coolness of the underground bunkers felt somewhat better. For Caroline, it was interesting to a point, but looking at barracks, powder magazines, and cannons didn't hold her interest the way it might for a guy.

As they left the fort, she could see a pathway leading to the beach in the distance. When they got there and rid themselves of shoes, the deep sand on the pathway was hot, but not unbearably so. Sea oats were oscillating in the wind along the path, and she could hear mewling cries of the gulls and the soothing roar of the ocean. She inhaled deeply, taking in the smell of the salt filled air, and suddenly the sweaty stickiness of the air turned into healing sea breezes.

The beach looked nearly deserted, and she could see why when she looked at the signs warning of strong currents and rip tides. One lonely, leather faced fisherman was manning four fishing rods. He had driven pieces of PVC pipe into the sand and put the handles of his rods into the pipes. He was sitting in a beach chair, and watching intently to see if he'd gotten a bite on one of his lines.

When the old fellow realized that Butch and Caroline were walking toward him down the beach, he got up and lurched toward his large stained cooler to proudly show them his catch of a big pompano. Butch stood there a few minutes, speaking to the stranger.

Caroline walked further, standing at the edge of the water as the tide slowly flowed out, and looked out toward the horizon to marvel at the vastness of the ocean, feeling that she was viewing one of the most beautiful sights in the world. A brown pelican swooping down into the water to scoop up a fish, delighted her, and a semicircular view reminded her of how different everything was here in comparison to beauties of nature of her birthplace.

She looked down at her bare feet. As the waves surged up on the shore and then retreated, she watched the water and sand washing out beneath her feet. She took deep breaths, inhaling the wonderful salinous air and exhaling slowly, trying to relax. She thought, as she had many times before, that the ebb of the ocean symbolized a cleansing of one's spirit. She knew that to live, really live and enjoy life, one has to let go of the bad and focus on the good things that each of us experience. She hoped this was a place that she could learn to do that when the tough times came.

CHAPTER 20

TRYIN'

Caroline stayed with J.P. on Thursday night and most of Friday morning. She was exhausted, not having slept much the night before, being very anxious about the interview. J.P. didn't sleep well, and she didn't want to leave him lying in bed awake, with no one to talk to.

They'd talked quite frankly together for nearly two hours. She'd have to leave in a few days and might not be able to return until she graduated. J.P. told her that it was not her responsibility to be there cheering for him; he had to have the guts to tackle this thing straight on and regain his physical abilities. She felt confident that he would have the initiative to work hard in therapy. He told her that his greatest regret at the moment was the fact that he wouldn't be able to see her graduate from Winthrop, after she'd spent four years of her life working so hard to accomplish something that even he'd not chosen to do. She understood his feelings, but she didn't want him to beat himself up for something he had no control over; an accident was an accident and nothing could change that now.

Although they talked for a long time, J.P. didn't completely open up to her. He was trying to protect her from his own misery. Emily actually knew more about his real feelings than Caroline did because she was in the room with him when he became lucid enough to know what condition he was in, when he cursed and yelled at the top of his lungs. He'd always been the kind of guy that could hold things in, not let his true emotions show, so he wasn't going to let Caroline leave seeing him depressed and scared. He might need the pastoral counselor and psychiatrist after all.

As scheduled, Amanda came to do bedside therapy on Friday morning. Caroline didn't wake up until Amanda greeted J.P., in her disgustingly honey dripping drawl. Not having braided her hair and having tossed and turned half the night on the uncomfortable sleeper chair, she had a terrible case of bed head, a tangled mass of hair at the nape of her neck. Her mouth felt like cotton since she'd had a lot of soft drinks rather than water, what she thought was nasty tasting Charleston water. She was wearing a T-shirt and boxer shorts that she didn't want Amanda to see her in, or anyone else for that matter. She scampered into the bathroom and was aghast when she saw her reflection, feeling that she looked like a sloth, having failed to wash off the makeup she'd worn for her job interview.

Amanda was friendly toward Caroline when she started working with J.P., surprising Caroline that she remembered her name. She had to admit to herself that she was discriminating against Amanda because of her good looks - how different was that from discriminating against someone because of their race or ethnic origin?

When she came out of the bathroom, Amanda asked Caroline, "Would you like to step over and actually see us working?"

Caroline glided to J.P.'s bedside and Amanda said, "Okay, Mr. Andersen tells me that you're about to graduate from college and probably won't be back here for a few weeks. I thought it would be nice for you to see where he's starting from in terms of physical therapy so

when you come back you can definitely see the progress he's made."
Amanda was a believer in the power of positive confession.

"That's a great idea."

Amanda asked J.P., "Are you game for having an observer?"

"Of course I am if it's Caroline. She's my girl, and I'm going to get well for her."

Caroline gently ran her fingers through his hair although he was certainly due for a good shampoo. She wanted to kiss his forehead but refrained from doing so in front of Amanda.

After hearing J.P.'s comment, it dawned on Caroline that he really loved her and he wasn't going to change that fact simply because another pretty face came his way. This would be something she'd need to remember many times in their relationship in the future. She needed to lighten up with her attitude toward Amanda, because she and J.P. did need to develop a close patient/therapist relationship in order to get J.P. back to where he was before the accident. If there was any jealousy on her part toward the PT, she'd only be hurting J.P., and she didn't want to hinder him because of her own insecurities; they both had to toughen up.

Amanda was very thorough in explanation to both J.P., Mr. Andersen as she referred to him, and Caroline, keeping the session very personable but also very professional. Caroline wondered if Amanda would be different in that regard when she had to go back to Winthrop. Let it go. Let it go. It will be what it will be and there's no amount of fear that will change the issues.

Emily came down right before Mr. and Mrs. Andersen were due to arrive. She'd gotten a few leads on summer jobs that might be available in the area, because she needed a job, too, for a period of time after she and Jason planned to return from their New York trip. She was still hoping that her parents would break down and send her to school in Savannah, in the fall.

Chris came in at eleven o'clock, so Caroline and Emily left to go shopping and job hunting. Frank and Butch both needed to go to work for a while since they'd missed several days that week. Chris had worked most of the week except Monday, the day of the accident, and Friday because he wanted to be at the hospital when his parents arrived.

Caroline and Emily were taking the elevator down to the mezzanine. When the elevator doors opened, Caroline got a glimpse of her sister, Rhonda, about to get on the other elevator going up.

Caroline was so surprised to see her sister it was hard for her to come up with something goofy to say to her before she could step foot in that elevator. Off the top of her head she said, "Look who the milkman left on Momma's doorstep."

Rhonda whirled around and she and Caroline squealed simultaneously and said, "Hey, girl! Jinx, buy me an ice cream."

Rhonda said as usual, "No, you're buyin' me one."

"I'll do it this time. I'm so surprised and happy to see you. I had no idear you'd come this far to find me," Caroline said as she hugged Rhonda.

Rhonda was true to form, dressed in a very short, pink and gray, cotton skirt with pink platform sandals. She had on a pink, short sleeved, form fitting knit sweater, and loads of costume jewelry in shades of pink and gray mixed with shimmering silver. Her hair was in a French twist, and she actually looked good except she'd gone overboard with the accessories, as she usually did. Of course her makeup was so thick it looked like you could peel it off in one large piece, and she had so much mascara on her lashes that they looked like fakes. That was Rhonda. She earned a decent living transforming the appearance of women, and she had to project a certain image herself. She wouldn't be caught dead in public without all that makeup, being afraid a client or potential client would see her, as she would say, "lookin' homely".

Emily had not met Rhonda before so introductions were in order. "Emily, this is my older sister Rhonda," said Caroline, cautiously, wondering what Emily might say. Caroline always confided in Emily when Rhonda would treat her like a mindless child.

"Oh, Rhonda, nice to finally meet you. Caroline's told me so many things about you."

Rhonda shot a look at Caroline and said, "My ears are burnin', little sister."

"Rhonda, your ears are always burnin' and it's not always my fault."

Rhonda conceded, "True, but I'm still gonna get you back when you least expect it."

"Oh boy, caint wait."

Emily could tell that she was going to have to be attentive to keep up with the conversation between the sisters because they would yank her into the dialogue at any point in the conversation.

Caroline said to Rhonda, "Emily, lives in Summerville. I guess you saw the signs for Summerville on your way down."

"Yeah, I remember you tellin' me that she was the one who introduced you to J.P. when you visited Summerville for the first time. Speakin' of J.P., how's he doin' now?"

"He's definitely doin' better than he was. The first couple of days, he was out of it," Caroline said. "We were scared shitless for the first 48 hours, but now he's stable and has started some physical therapy. But don't let me get started telling you 'bout his therapist, Miss Amanda Johnson, 'cus you know there's nobody I hate werst than a gorgeous smart blond. And even werst than that, I caint stand a smart blond who acts like sorghum is oozin' from the corners of her grin. On the other hand, I guess it wouldn't be a good thing to have a dumb, grouchy blond physical therapist workin' with my boyfriend, would it?"

"Prob'ly not, darlin'. Maybe she has to bleach her hair to get it blond."

"Not likely, she looks like she's of Swedish descent," said Caroline.

"Maybe not. Try not to worry yerself sick 'bout something you caint change. By the way, Momma and Troy send their love and want you to know they've been prayin' for all y'all. Momma would've come but she's a little under the weather."

"Whut's wrong with Momma?"

"She thanks she's a comin' down with a bad strain of sprang flu."

"Oh gosh! That's just whut she needs on her spring break."

"For goodness sakes, you talkin' werst than you did afore you got yer education."

"It's Emily's fault. She influencing me with her Anderson County tawk."

They stood there laughing.

Rhonda asked, "So, you're from Anderson?"

"No, my daddy's from Anderson. He met Momma when he was a student at Clemson. They moved down here to be close to the beach. Both of 'em love to go down to Isle of Palms, have a few beers on the way, and bake in the sun for a while."

While she had speaking room, she invited Rhonda to go shopping with them. She said to her teasingly, "Listen Rhonda, if we get in trouble for anything, like the security guards thinkin' we shoplifted something, we're gonna depend of you to help us out."

Rhonda asked, with a look of seriousness, "What in creation are you talkin' about?"

"Well, Caroline always told me you could talk your way outta a croaker sack with a rope tied around it and tossed in the river." Then Emily roared with laughter and hoped Rhonda would, too.

"Car...o...line, I'm gonna git you back, just wait!"

Caroline explained that they both were going to be applying for a few jobs, and she updated Rhonda about the positive teaching interview she had. She expressed her thanks to Rhonda for driving four hours to be with her over the weekend.

Emily invited Rhonda to stay at her parent's house. She knew they wouldn't mind because they had an in-law suite, and there would be plenty of room since her grandma was down in Florida visiting friends.

Rhonda said, "I'd love to go shoppin' with y'all, but we need to stop at a burger joint first and get a cheeseburger and a choc...let milkshake, 'cus I'm 'bout to starve."

"I'm getting' some good old greasy fries," chimed Caroline."

Emily added, "I guess I'll get all three."

In the space of two hours, the three girls had lunch and did their shopping. Fortunately, the outfits they selected needed no ironing, and they slipped them on in the restroom at the mall. Caroline applied for a job at a department store for sales in fine jewelry, a specialty store for sales in doll houses and miniatures, and a receptionist in a dental office. Emily applied for a job in an art supply store, a toy store, and a courier for a law office.

Rhonda made a comment after the girls applied for the jobs, "If I was y'all, I'd try sellin' makeup. It's u easy job, sorta like paintin' all day."

"Rhonda, how could I sell makeup when I caint hardly stand wearin' it myself," asked Caroline? "I woke up this mornin' lookin' like a panda. I forgot to wash my face last night."

"I guess you got a point there."

Caroline added, "I think I could sell fine jewelry or doll houses. Remember how much I loved to play with Aunt Lou Ella's doll house when I was a little girl?"

"Yes, you were in there usin 'yer imagination while I was in the bathroom experimentin' with her lipstick and blush."

Emily joined in the conversation, "Y'all are as different as night and day, sorta like me and my prissy momma."

"Rhonda, Emily's momma is rather formal. Just tell her you're totally exhausted tonight from the long drive. That way she won't pepper you with questions," suggested Caroline. "Sorry 'bout that comment, Emily."

Looking perplexed, Rhonda was still standing there mouthing *pepper me with questions.* She shook her head from side to side and rolled her eyes.

Caroline took Rhonda by the arm and said, "Come on, time's a wastin', girl. It's a busy weekend.

Rhonda said, "I caint wait to see an apartment in one of these old houses."

She was already dreading taking Rhonda along with her to meet Clay and Anne. Caroline thought that Rhonda would need a muzzle on her mouth, so her sister wouldn't embarrass her.

Emily shifted the conversation to something that included her. "Can you believe we're graduatin' in three weeks?"

"No, I can't, but I'll be soooo glad. I don't wanna go to school anymore right now. I'll have to take a couple of classes in the next five years to update my certificate."

Emily said with yearning in her voice, "I hope I can go on to school in Savannah, if Momma and Daddy pay for it or I can get student loans."

"Why would you wanna go to Georgia rather than stay in South Carolina," asked Rhonda.

"Savannah's a hop, skip, and a jump from here. I could drive home every weekend if I wanted to. I wanna go on to school in art, and I can't really find what I want around here."

"Cosmetology classes at the vocational center just about did me in. I nevah liked school, and there's no way I could've made it like Caroline has. I wanna compliment both of y'all for doin' what it took to get a degree. Don't git me wrong, I'm thankful for my trainin' and I love whut I do, but Caroline followed Momma's example, and Troy and I didn't. We're all very proud of her."

When Rhonda finished her little spiel, Caroline had tears in her eyes. She hugged her older sister and said, "Thank ya Rhonda, for bein' here to support me."

Late in the afternoon, Caroline, Emily, and Rhonda picked up some subs and went back to the hospital. Chris was there with Mr. and Mrs. Andersen. Although they welcomed Caroline with open arms, she could tell their hearts had been broken by their son's tragedy. Introductions were made by J.P. having awakened in a confident mood. Rhonda over dramatized a bit, telling J.P. how sorry she was several times. J.P. thought: "God in heaven help me to withstand this girl, because she gets on my nerves. I know she's Caroline's sister, but..."

It was time for an evening meal, so Chris took his parents out to a nice restaurant in downtown Charleston to get a bite to eat. They mulled the situation carefully over dinner. Chris explained that J.P. would have 90 days to remain in the hospital setting or rehab. It would be hopeful that he would be rehabilitated and released to go home with continued support from various therapists. In particular, he'd be seen by the physical therapist two to three times per week and also an occupational therapist.

Caroline planned to stay the night again. She figured she needed to be with J.P. as much as possible, because Saturday was a big day to meet with Clay and Anne to see the apartment. Sunday, she and Emily would have to go back to school and tie up all loose ends.

Chris and his parents stayed a little longer when they got back from dinner. The nurse came in asked if she could elevate J.P.'s upper body, doing so very slowly and cautiously to see if it made him dizzy.

While he was able to see the T.V., he wanted Caroline to select a movie or program that they'd both be interested in. She felt so much love for him for the everyday selfless acts he demonstrated, always thinking about her rather than just himself. He was amazing.

Saturday morning, Butch called to ask Caroline if he should pick up Rhonda at Emily's house. Caroline warned him a little about Rhonda's straightforwardness, but Butch was perfectly capable of dealing with her, having dated girls like her while at Clemson.

Obviously, that's one reason he was still single at thirty years of age, ouch!

Butch had already called Clay to arrange a specific time for their visit. He and Rhonda arrived at about eleven o'clock that morning. Caroline was neat and clean, but unadorned in comparison to her sister, wearing some khaki shorts and a colorful peasant top of swirling tan, rust, turquoise, and chocolate colors. Her worn sandals were the color of her khaki shorts. However, Rhonda looked like a typical tourist going to lunch in a swanky Charleston restaurant. She had on a lavender and light green striped skort with a matching silk camisole and a light lavender jacket draped around her shoulders and tied in front. Her earrings were matching in color to her outfit but seemed much too oversized for such casual attire. She had been tanning before she came down because her short skort accentuated her skinny tanned legs. Her flat sandals were the exact green found in the skort, sporting large leather flowers on the top of the sandals. Her hair was nicely done in a free form updo and secured by Japanese chop sticks.

Caroline complimented Rhonda about her outfit and hair when she arrived with Butch. She wouldn't dare say but she really thought: *Yeah, that's cute but a little over the top for going to check out real estate. At least she's not gaudy looking today. I pray she'll be able to control her waggin' tongue while we see the place.* Caroline always described Rhonda's being a born blabber.

Before they left the hospital, J.P. cautioned Caroline a little about the Clay and Anne. He told her that Clay was a loyal friend, but Anne was very temperamental, a spoiled girl from a well-to-do family in Greenville. When J.P. mentioned that they were at his fall oyster roast, Caroline suddenly recalled a mental image of Clay and Anne and the impatience that she seemed to display that night. J.P. reminded Caroline that once the couple move out, she'd have very little contact with them. There was something else about them that she tried to call to her recognition, but she couldn't quite put her finger on it.

Rhonda kept Caroline laughing in route, reminding her of funny things they did and said as kids, and she relaxed and resolved not to get nervous. The apartment was a very short driving distance from MUSC, and they were there much faster than Caroline anticipated.

The house was in walking distance to the battery. Like all surrounding houses, it was beautiful because of the architecture and obvious high quality of maintenance of it. The house was three stories with upper and lower porticos. They opened the wrought iron gate and passed an immaculate garden courtyard that led to the apartment, part of which seemed below ground level, perhaps a cellar originally. It was obvious that a larger garden, separated by wrought iron fencing and huge camellias, was used for the occupants of the upper stories of the house. The thought crossed her mind that she might be looking at what once was housing for the servants who cared for the family living above, in the main house, so many years ago. For a fleeting moment, Caroline entertained the thought of ghosts or spirits, but she forced herself to dismiss it when she heard Rhonda's comments.

"Law, this place is somethin' else. You ain't gonna find a house like this anywhere in Greenville. Everything's so old, but well preserved. Honey chile, I'd do whatever I had to, to get this place, even if it meant flippin' burgers all summer."

Caroline turned around and whispered, "You gotta be kiddin'. I'd rather rent a room in a boarding house than flip burgers in the Charleston heat." She was grinning from ear to ear at Rhonda.

Caroline stopped fretting and got ready for the occupants to come to the door. Clay came to the door and invited them in. Of course the couple knew Butch quite well and made small talk with him avoiding proper introductions at first. Just as he was about to introduce Caroline and Rhonda, Anne said, "I remember you from the fall oyster roast."

Caroline commented genteelly, "Yes, I was there as J.P.'s guest. He and I have been dating ever since. To refresh your memory, I'm Caroline Bethany Carter, and this is my sister Rhonda Jean."

Rhonda could see Anne looking at her from the crown of her head to the soles of her feet.

With her snotty tone of voice she looked at Rhonda and drawled, "Is that Carter, like in Georgia peanut farmers?"

Rhonda, gracefully retorted, "Well, actually it would be more accurate to say like famous politicians, now wouldn't it?"

Caroline was thinking: *Go Rhonda, put that snob in her place. I don't wanna have to deal with her. On the other hand the Greenville thing might open a can of worms.*

Fortunately, Clay took over before a full-blown catfight started. He said, "My cousin should be here any minute. She's looking forward to meeting you, Caroline."

Caroline said, "I'm looking forward to meeting her, too."

Clay was gracious and showed the rest of the apartment to Caroline, Rhonda, and Butch. Anne went over to sit in the armchair and put her feet up on the ottoman. Caroline imagined that she used the woes of pregnancy to the hilt to be a lazy princess.

There were two small but separate bedrooms, one bath, and a galley kitchen with a tiny round bistro table with bar stools and the far end of the kitchen. One wall of the kitchen had exposed old brick which gave it a lot of charm. A piece of pegboard had been painted and surrounded by a beautiful old picture frame. Kitchen utensils had been suspended from hooks on the pegboard. An attractive pot rack, adorned with copper pots, hung from the ceiling just above the top of the frame.

The apartment was a little lacking in natural light, but a great deal of recessed lighting and track lighting had been added.

Rhonda was cautious about what she said, but a few oohs and aahs came out here and there.

They all heard a knock at the door. Clay opened the door, saying, "Hey cuz', how you doin'? Glad you could make it."

Introductions were made, and Caroline liked Clay's humble cousin, Tara, right off the bat. She seemed to be very sweet and intelligent, and not one bit uppity as her cousin's wife was.

Tara spoke directly to Caroline saying, "I've heard you're going to be teaching, and I'm going to be busy working in a salon. We probably can share this apartment just fine. Daddy's going to help us out in the beginning so we can get a good start. Clay has told me so many good things about you, Caroline. I think we could make this work. I'd be far too lonely to be living here by myself."

Anne was again on her feet, standing there with her hand over her belly, projecting that yeah, yeah, yeah, kind of attitude, wishing they'd get on with it so she could get on with her day, shopping for the bedding and accessories for her baby's nursery, with Daddy's credit card.

"Wow, it all sounds great to me! Tara, you seem to have such a sweet personality, I'm sure we'll get along just fine."

Anne, with a sour look on her face, seemed jealous of Caroline. Butch knew that Anne couldn't stand to keep her nose out of things for long. She said to Caroline, "I heah that you and your sistah are from Greenville. I grew up on McDaniel Avenue in Greenville. I graduated from Greenville High School, in the top ten percent of my class, of course. Daddy wouldn't stand for anything less from us. My sister and I both had our choice of universities to attend."

"You don't say, that's interestin'," Caroline said, hoping that her conversation with Anne would be short lived. She certainly offered no information about her high school alma mater.

Glaring at Caroline, and switching to her sarcastic tone of voice, "Caroline, I do hope you'll enjoy livin' here. Heaven knows you'll have so many unpleasant things to cope with dealin' with

J.P.'s taxin' recovery and teachin' those colored children on James Island. I couldn't stand it anothah year, even if we weren't expectin' our baby. I told Clay that he'd simply have to do somethin' to get me out of that dreadful situation. I'm so glad he was finally made a partnah in the firm. Of course, Daddy's bein' such a deah, too, helpin' us get into a larger home in Mt. Pleasant. The racial climate is so different there."

Butch was infuriated with Anne's display of rude behavior, and racial slurs, and he couldn't stand there and let her get away with it. He felt that, at that moment, he had to come to Caroline's aide. He looked at Clay, who already looked a bit flushed, and said, "Pardon me for what I'm about to say. Anne, you've nevah stopped to think that the colored children, as you say, the other teachers, and even the principal might not be able to tolerate you another day with your dreadful attitude." Again, he apologized to Clay saying, "Sorry, Clay. I know your're stuck in the middle of this. You're a saint."

Anne looked like she'd seen a ghost and said, "Well, I nevah..."

Caroline and Rhonda stood there staring at one another wishing they were telepathic.

Clay was certainly embarrassed by the whole exchange. To diffuse the situation, and save face, he spoke up and said, "Girls, most of the furniture was here when Anne and I moved in, so it's basically a furnished apartment, at a very affordable price for Charleston. With Uncle Jackson's help for the first few months, I think it would be perfect for the two of y'all. There might be a little getting used to the water here. It's different from that mountain water that you get from the watersheds in the Upstate. Our new place in Mt. Pleasant will be ready by May 30th, so this place would be available on June 1st. If y'all are interested, Uncle Jackson and I will take care of everything to get y'all in here."

Tara and Caroline looked at one another, said a silent prayer, and smiled. Caroline said, "Okay, let's go for it." With a smile, Tara nodded in agreement.

Anne stood there looking like a rich, but very pregnant, snob. She was beautiful, but her mannerisms were disgusting to Caroline, Rhonda, and Butch. Rhonda could no longer control her tongue and interjected, "Good thing y'all won't be neighbors; I don't think Caroline couldn't stand it if y'all were all livin' in the same vicinity."

Anne absolutely had to have the last word saying, "Y'all will enjoy this comfy old furniture. You won't even have to worry about if you get a pet. Daddy's furnishin' our new house, and it will take us a while to break in all that nice new furniture. Now take care girls, and Butch, it was so nice to see you again."

He said feigning conviviality, "Likewise, Anne."

Rhonda and Caroline exited first and waited for Butch in the garden.

Rhonda was still angry with Anne and whispered to Caroline, "I don't care if she is Mrs. Clayton McMahan, the eighth or the thirteenth, that bimbo is gonna git her comeuppance here direc'ly. That baby's prob'ly gonna be a little bitty fussy gut, too, and she's gonna have to work for a change."

"Hope you're right on that one, Rhonda. I hope you're very right," she responded, smiling at her elder sister like she did as a little girl. "I wouldn't want to deny anyone the opportunity to work. You done good on your come backs to her."

Then the two sisters simultaneously said, "Witch," and really cackled. Then Rhonda added,

"And I hope Daddy Deah refuses to pay for a nanny."

"Who's buyin' the pizza today?"

CHAPTER 21

LEAVIN'

Caroline and Emily visited J.P. early Sunday morning, as Rhonda was feeling a little under the weather when she awoke, possibly to be attributed to the five or six slices of pizza she'd eaten the night before, then washing it down with a half of a pitcher of sweet tea. Caroline couldn't fathom how the girl could eat so much junk and still be so skinny, like a Biafran; she figured Rhonda must have been adopted to have such a different metabolism as she did.

J.P. tried to be upbeat, but beneath the surface, Caroline could sense he was as scared and worried as she was about the road ahead of them. Reassuringly, she reminded him that she'd be back immediately after graduation, not letting him know how heartbroken she was that he wouldn't be able to attend. She'd begin to settle in, nearby in the apartment, acclimating herself to her new life. It was clear to him that she wanted to spend time with him daily when she returned and had every confidence in him that he'd work hard in physical and occupational therapy programs. She wanted so for him to believe in himself. Caroline could only imagine how she'd feel if she were the one being left alone in a hospital, although she felt that Chris and his many friends would be supportive as much as was possible. And she'd been told that he had a lot of friends, which was apparently evident from all of the encouraging cards, balloons, and plants he'd been receiving all week.

The parting was bittersweet, being painful but in some ways a relief for her. She was exhausted from the lack of sleep while staying in the hospital with J.P., and it was hard to concentrate. And the constant weight of worry had been bearing down upon her for a week, other than the times that Butch, Emily, and Rhonda had pleasantly distracted her, and she felt stressed to the maximum. Not to mention, the tenseness of preparing for a professional interview was also maddening, but she was grateful for a seemingly positive outcome, even though she knew nothing definite at this time. Dealing with her own insecurities around two blond knockouts such as Amanda and Anne had exacerbated her anxiety. Of course Anne was married to Clay, but being from Greenville and Caroline knowing that she grew up on the "good" side of the tracks, so to speak, made her uncomfortable around Anne. In addition, the condescending remarks Anne had made to her on Saturday, added to Caroline's dislike of her. Caroline said to herself, *"This has been one heck of a spring break for my senior year of college. One that won't be forgotten, I suppose. Who am I to be complaining; I'm the one walking outta here on my own two feet?"* How she wished she could get back to school and have a week to herself to cry and overdose on oatmeal cakes and orange soda, but that couldn't happen.

J.P. had made arrangements for Butch to go up to Rock Hill to see Caroline graduate and to help her move her belongings down to Charleston, but he hadn't told Caroline about it yet. He would have Frank order flowers midweek with a message card attached to let her know. If he couldn't be in Rock Hill himself, he could think of no one better suited than Butch to support her on a day of such importance. Chris was great in terms of dependability, but he didn't have the rapport with Caroline that Butch did. Both she and

Butch were Southerners to the core, and the ease with which they communicated, both verbally and nonverbally, had been apparent a number of times.

Clay and Anne also came to visit J.P. that week, and Clay had generously offered to J.P. to store Caroline's belongings in the guest bedroom of their Charleston apartment until they actually moved out at the end of the month. Anne didn't breathe a word about Caroline, trying to maintain favor with J.P. and cover her covetousness toward her in front of both her husband and J.P. She was painfully aware that her conniving ways, during their Clemson days, had alienated her from J.P. Although her basic nature was still the same, she seemed to control herself somewhat better and still achieve her wants; she was a snake in the grass, a bona fide manipulator, and a taker. She'd married Clay out of necessity, knowing that he'd eventually be able to lavish her in the lifestyle that she was accustomed to when she was growing up. But there was still that underlying attraction toward J.P., and she was deeply worried about his current condition and what his future would hold, always secretly wondering if she'd be a part of his future. For now, she had to appear to be a loyal friend as was her husband.

Clay couldn't help but notice how his wife seemed to find the good in J.P. but find all of the flaws in things he did. His relationship with his wife was already dysfunctional.

J.P. wouldn't be fooled again by Anne! He basically took her with a grain of salt; he tolerated his contact with her because of his friendship with her husband. To be honest, Anne made him sick to be around her with her rotten, selfish personality.

⬌ ⬌

At MUSC, J.P. was working very hard during physical therapy sessions. In the beginning of his sessions, he would be placed in a wheelchair by two hospital orderlies and taken down to the therapy room where Amanda was waiting for him to arrive. The orderlies would then place him upon a therapy mat. Fervently, Amanda would do stretching exercises and assessments to determine his muscle strength, both upper body strength as well as strength of his lower extremities. The fact that he'd worked in construction and worked out regularly put him in good physical shape before the accident which was certainly a plus for him in therapy. At the end of each PT session, J.P. would work with a female occupational therapist doing fine motor muscle strengthening exercises.

Both of the therapists took a shine to J.P. in a therapist/patient kind of relationship. His outgoing and positive nature pleased them, and he was already making great strides due to his own drive and initiative. He kept telling the therapists that he was in a serious relationship with Caroline, and he couldn't give up until he could do all of the things that he used to do for her, making him admirable for his dedication and devotion.

For Caroline, it was very different when she arrived back at Winthrop. She felt no contentment there for she longed to be back in the Lowcountry, even though the tensions were high, and waiting three weeks to graduate seemed like an eternity. She felt lonely back on campus despite seeing friends. There was absolutely some kind of force that drew her back to that beautiful lower part of the state. She tried to enjoy the freshness of spring there on campus at Winthrop, alive with vibrantly colored azaleas and yellow jonquils. It was nothing like the beauty of Summerville when J.P. took her to the park, but the flowers were still lovely beneath the towering oaks on the campus grounds and in the flower beds placed in the sunlight. Pink and white dogwoods were in bloom everywhere. She wanted to sit down beneath the centuries old oaks and write to J.P., but she didn't want to pour her heart out on the page only to have someone else read her love letters to him.

She nearly exhausted Emily, daily asking all sorts of questions about Summerville and Charleston. She would vacillate between tears of joy and sadness and would often seek a pep talk from Emily when she was feeling inadequate to help J.P.

Emily said encouragingly, "Just think, last month you didn't have a pot to pee in and now you're gonna be living in the beautiful city of Charleston, in a lovely restored home, somethin' that you couldn't afford to do on your own."

Caroline was elated to receive a letter from Dr. DuBose, the principal of Jasper Elementary School, stating that she'd been selected to fill the vacancy there. Several days later she received a large packet of information and forms from the school district for selection of her health and dental benefits, tax withholdings, and state retirement election. Both stores where she'd applied for summer jobs were interested in having her work for them. Realizing that she'd need two part time jobs to take care of her needs until the paychecks from the school district started coming in on a monthly basis, she was thrilled to hear about the summer jobs. Things were looking up for her.

⊷⟊ ⟊⊶

J.P. was doing great in therapy. Amanda and her male assistant, Evan, were able to get J.P. to a standing position much more quickly than Amanda had originally projected, still using a gait belt to help him stand and to protect him should he begin to fall. He was given a forearm walker, a tall walker that enabled him to rest some of his weight on his forearms as he tried to take small shuffling steps initially. Amanda was superb in cheering him on, and he was convinced that she'd been a cheerleader in high school; she was so full of enthusiasm that he absolutely couldn't get discouraged.

J.P. tried very hard to use humor to keep his spirits up. He spent a lot of his exercise time cutting up and telling jokes, and his will was indescribable. Those around him kept fighting and would win in the end.

As time went by, Amanda had him walking on an oval track around the therapy room using his forearm walker. The other physical therapists and assistants were astounded by the amount of progress J.P. was making in a relatively short period of time.

Caroline was surprised to find how many things she'd accumulated in the past four years. She had an affinity for thrift store shopping and antique hunting. Having a job on campus wasn't very lucrative, but it did give her a little cash to shop for things she loved. No, she couldn't collect antique furniture, but she'd been a scavenger for unusual pictures, beautiful old frames, porcelain figurines, toile patterned china, Mason jars full of buttons, and vintage hats.

As Caroline began the arduous task of packing, she feared that J.P. might think her to be a pack rat. On the other hand his house was quite cluttered. She found it difficult to part with items in her dorm room, her abode for the past years of her life, things reminding her of specific events during her college days. Her loot was supplemented by items her mother and aunts had passed on to her, and she surely couldn't part with those things, things like her great grandmother's quilt, vintage jewelry, her grandfather's hand stitched baby clothes, a collection of crocheted doilies made by her granny, and glassware in mint condition. School materials that she'd prepared for courses and student teaching had to be saved in case she needed them for her position on James Island. She got rid of a few things as she packed boxes, but she rationalized that if her belongings fit into one room in a dormitory, they should fit in her new bedroom in the apartment in Charleston.

The phone rang as Caroline was packing. It was Cheryl, the student on duty in the dorm office, a good friend of hers, saying that something had been delivered to her via the office. She raced down the stairwell to get to the office, feeling in great need of some kind of surprise. When she got there, the office worker pointed to the most beautiful bouquet of flowers Caroline had ever seen. She opened the card immediately to read that J.P. had gotten Frank to order the flowers because he wanted to let her know that he was thinking about her. He told her that he'd also asked Butch to attend her graduation ceremony on his behalf, and Butch would be helping her move her things to Charleston.

She was smiling at Cheryl with tears of happiness flowing down her flushed cheeks.

Cheryl commented, "Man, that guy must be crazy about you, girl. You better hang on to him."

"Oh, I plan to," replied Caroline. "B'lieve me, I have every intention of hangin' on to him."

"That thing's so big it might take both of us to get it to your room. Let me lock the office for a few minutes to help you take it up to your room. You can't hold those big heavy stairwell doors open while you try to hang onto that huge vase."

"I think I'm gonna have to take you up on that."

How badly J.P. wanted to make an impression on Caroline when she returned to Charleston. He wanted her to see tremendous progress that he'd already made and see that he had the drive and determination to get better. He loved her, and he couldn't allow himself to be disabled, less than what she needed him to be, less than how he'd been when she met him. He couldn't let her down! He presumed that she did truly love him or she'd be trying to get a job in a location other than Charleston. From all he'd seen of Caroline, she reminded him of the strong fearless women that he'd read about in historical documents, those women who had colonized and settled the state of South Carolina. The ones who'd cared for their families and managed estates when their husbands fought in wars and often died. The heroines he'd read about who'd buried their valuables to keep the enemy from confiscating them, hid themselves and their children from invaders, watched their homes occupied by soldiers, nursed the wounded, or saw their homes destroyed by fire and had the will to rebuild. Caroline was from good stock; she'd seen hard times in her life and overcome many obstacles with strength of character.

J.P. had a great deal of admiration for her and a tenderness of heart that he'd never felt before for anyone else. Now he had time, when alone in his hospital room, to reflect upon their courtship, consider the way that he felt about her, and evaluate her every response to him. She'd chosen him over the handsome European, Joost, one who'd probably never want for anything, one who'd be able to give Caroline the material things she might desire. She'd never said so, but he knew, instinctively. But she'd chosen him knowing that he had to work hard to get ahead and didn't have unlimited income to buy the finer things that many women feel they must have to be happy.

J.P. also felt compassion for Caroline that she'd worked hard to get through school with little financial resources. Teaching on James Island, or anywhere else for that matter, was not going to be an easy task. He wanted to be strong and capable, to be supportive and able to give her comfort at the end of a hard day of work. He wanted to take her back to New York often and show her sights that they'd been unable to see during their short stay in December. He longed to take long walks with her on the beautiful beaches near Charleston and stroll with her on the back streets and alleyways of The Holy City, listening to her tell him what enchanted her most. He wanted to ask her to spend the rest of her life with him and be able to love her completely, giving her children for both of them to love and cherish forever. All of this couldn't be over for them before it could begin. Tears were flowing over his cheeks and wetting his ears and the pillow beneath his head.

J.P. loved Caroline Carter without a doubt. His thoughts engrossed him. *Will she feel the same for me as time goes by or is she just feeling sorry for me? She has no way of knowing that this week is the week I'd planned to propose to her. Will there ever come a time when I can share all of this with her? Not now; everything is on hold. God, help me! I don't want to lose her; she's the love of my life.*

CHAPTER 22

LIVIN'

On the day of her graduation, Caroline got up at the crack of dawn. She stripped her bed and took the linens downstairs to wash and dry them and didn't know what to do while the laundry was getting done. With her mind excessively occupied with the major issues in her life, she couldn't read the book she'd brought with her, and she couldn't write on the paper she'd folded and placed in the book before she left her room. It seemed like the first time in the past four years that she didn't have something that had to be done, some assignment to be completed or some lesson plan to be written. She felt free but didn't know what to do with her freedom, yet.

As soon as the laundry was done, she was back in her room placing the light pink blanket, fresh floral sheets, and pillowcases in the last box to be packed. Everything else had been packed for a couple of days with the exception of a few articles of clothing, a couple of pairs of shoes, linens, toiletries, hair styling equipment, and some bathroom cleanser to satisfy her obsessive and compulsive need to clean the bathroom after her last use. Inspecting the dorm room, there seemed to be so many boxes stacked up, already making her feel somewhat self-conscious about the amount of things to be transported to Charleston.

For Caroline, a sweep of emotions was swirling inside. During those college years, she'd repeatedly told herself that her life would be easier if her daddy were alive to help her; she envied other girls who seemed to have things easier because their fathers took care of everything for them. She'd learned to toughen up, having grown up seeing her momma be independent, and she'd somehow been able to care for most of her needs for the past four years. Were the tables turning? Now, she had a man in her life wanting to help her, and even hospitalized, J.P. was still looking out for her in every way he possibly could. If he was physically unable to do it for her, he asked his friends to help him show kindnesses to her. This morning, she didn't quite know how to handle all of that. Would she be letting herself down if she started to depend on a man? What if something more tragic happened? Could she simply let her faith in God and in the goodness in others carry her through anything to come?

The commencement ceremony was scheduled for eleven o'clock. Momma Carter, Rhonda, Troy, and Caroline's grandparents were to arrive at eight thirty to take her out to a breakfast bar, which wouldn't tie them up too long in the restaurant. She wasn't sure exactly what time Butch would arrive in Rock Hill, having a longer drive than the others, but Caroline was sure conscientious and dependable Butch would be there.

It was seven thirty, and she planned to get her shower and style her hair. She put the navy blue mortarboard on her head and tried to decide what to do with her hair as she looked in the mirror. Opting to leave her hair parted on the right side, she'd use the large barreled curling iron to give her hair body rather than leave it straight as a stick. There was no use in trying to actually curl her hair because the humidity was too high, with afternoon showers in the forecast, and the curls wouldn't last through the ceremony must less afterwards for pictures.

By eight fifteen, Caroline felt a little queasy, probably a combination of hunger and excitement. In fact, she was as nervous as a long tailed cat in a room full of ol' timers in rocking chairs. She looked in the full-length mirror on the back of her door for the last time, feeling proud and accomplished. The navy blue dress she'd purchased to wear beneath her graduation gown was very flattering. The bodice of the sleeveless dress had small horizontal pin tucks in the front, and a form fitting skirt. When she'd found the dress at a department store in Charlotte, she had hopes that she'd wear it one day in the future when she and J.P. could go out for the very first time after his accident. That day would have to come. There'd be no giving up on him because she loved him, and she'd felt the love from him over and over again. Even on this special day, her day, she was already deep in thought about him, loving him, hoping for him, and dreaming for him.

After weeks of strengthening muscles in the upper and lower extremities, a new exercise was going to be incorporated into the schedule, the therapy parallel bars. J.P. would come down, from his room on the neuro floor, in a wheelchair. A gait belt would be put in place, around his waist. He would have to rise with assistance and walk forward supporting his weight with his arms as he gripped the parallel bars. The occupational therapist had been pushing him hard to improve his hand grip. Still, he was apprehensive at the first mention of the parallel bars, fearing that he'd be unable to bear his own weight and fall flat on his face, humiliating himself. But he thought Amanda was going to bubble over with enthusiasm, like boiling grits on a hot burner. She kept telling him how great he was doing and that he'd caught the attention of the entire therapy group and fellow patients. How could he turn her down? How could he impede his own physical progress? He had to do this for himself and for Caroline. She deserved that from him. It was no time to be a wimp, but he still felt like a heavy lifeless log as he tried to ambulate with the forearm walker.

⚔

The family arrived early as scheduled for the commencement exercises. Momma Carter had been the Pritchett's only child to have earned a college degree, and Caroline was the first Pritchett grandchild out of many to earn her degree. She hoped that some of her little wild cousins would settle down and do the same in the years to come. Unfortunately, Caroline's other grandparents couldn't be there due to the resent hospitalization of her Grandma Rena.

Rhonda and Troy weren't going to let Caroline get through this day without razzing her unmercifully. It started in the restaurant.

Troy started the ruckus by saying, "Gol...lee Caroline, I ain't nevah seen so many grits on a girl's plate 'fore. They gonna have to mop up the floor in here to git up all them grits that's gonna spill off your plate. You should'a got a bowl, or better yet, a bucket."

"Now Troy, you leave her alone," reprimanded Momma Carter. This is her special day, and if you graduate from anywhere, you have the right to eat all the grits you want."

Granny chimed in, "That's what I told Paw after his gall bladder surgery. I said that once he healed up, I'd cook him grits three times a day if he wanted 'em. Go on, baby, eat all the grits you want, just don't make yourself feel sick before you walk across that stage and make us the proudest Granny and Grandpaw in the whole world."

As they sat down at the table, Grandpaw couldn't resist getting into the conversation. He said, "Caroline, honey, people north of that Mason Dixon don't understand why we love grits so much down south. Well, I can't understand how they can eat them tough bagels ev'er mornin' with cream cheese and fish, what you're used to, I reckon. I been eating grits all my life, and that ain't what caused me to need gall bladder surgery. I can't hardly go a day without my grits, coffee, and some of your Granny's buttermilk biscuits smothered in mo...lasses." Grandpaw always drawled, with every word he spoke, so it seemed like forever, before he finished his little speech.

Then Rhonda started up, "Gracious heavens, what I wouldn't give to eat some of Granny's hot buttered biscuits with her churned butter meltin' in the biscuits and spillin' onto the plate. I got to smother mine in some of them sweet fig preserves she makes every year. I take a biscuit and sop up that melted butter and sugary sauce from the preserves. I keep a jar of fig preserves in my refrigerator, but they don't taste the same on toast, and I couldn't make a biscuit fit to eat if I was starvin'.

Caroline, eat all you want today, but one of these days you gonna have to watch it or you won't be able to wear yer good old faded jeans. My legs are still as skinny as ever, but I can't get my butt in my old jeans I wore when I finished the cosmetology program."

"You don't say," said Caroline. "I didn't think you ever gained weight, Rhonda. You still look like a beanpole to me."

"All, right, punk, if you wanna start that name callin', I'm gonna plan a counter attack and git you back. I won't do it today, cus you graduatin' and all." Then she stuck her tongue out at Caroline, before she started eating from her fruit plate.

Caroline had a mouth full of grits, and started laughing. She was trying to keep her mouth shut, but it was getting harder and harder. Troy was sitting next to her and grabbed his napkin. Just as he covered her mouth with the napkin, he said, "Sweet Jesus, she's gonna blow."

Then Caroline lost it. She could feel grits spewing out of her mouth. She leaned over her plate out of fear that she'd mess up her new dress. Everyone sitting at the table started handing Troy their napkins. Finally, Caroline managed to stop laughing and swallow what was left in her mouth. Other people were staring at the entire family, in total shock at the silliness being displayed in a public place.

Even conservative Mrs. Carter put up her hand to the left side of her face, as if she could shield herself from other patrons, and started to snigger. She'd always taught her family to have good manners in public, but this day was different. It was a family day, home away from home, and she really didn't care a rat's behind what other people thought about her grown children having fun together as they'd always done.

"Caroline, git a hold of yourself; I didn't mean to make you git your dress all messed up."

Caroline could see all of Rhonda's front teeth, grinning like a Cheshire cat, as Rhonda bit into a fresh strawberry. Caroline almost got tickled all over again, but Troy grabbed her by the shoulders and said, "You gonna start havin' spasms in a minute, if you don't eat your bacon."

Then Caroline had to get up from the table to go to the bathroom. She could not, for the life of her, get control of herself. As she walked to the bathroom, she tried to think good thoughts of J.P., not think of him in the hospital. She remembered Thanksgiving Day, at Granny and Grandpaw's house when Uncle Doyle Earle said such a long prayer, almost as long as a funeral eulogy and J.P. got tickled. She missed him something fierce today.

═╬═╬═

J.P. told Amanda that he was going to work on the parallel bars as soon as possible after Caroline's arrival. He felt that he should work harder using the forearm walker, so he asked if he could stay in the therapy room longer each day. Although Amanda didn't want him to get fatigued knowing that he would need strength to work with the OT at some point during the day, she agreed to let her assistant stay nearby to insure his safety walking on the dark green, oval track that surrounded numerous tables where other therapists worked with patients. Each day that he walked he seemed to get a fraction of greater sensation in his extremities.

━╪╍━

In Rock Hill, the clan tried to behave themselves in the restaurant for fear that they'd be asked to leave without having time to finish their last meal with Caroline before she graduated and left for Charleston. But in the parking lot, Rhonda and Troy had her hee-hawing before they went back to the campus. Caroline's big day would soon be over, and she'd have to come down from the clouds and deal with life. Momma Carter and Granny were both keenly aware of her need for their prayers, so they would continue to "exercise their knees", as they called it. Grandpaw would probably toast her with a bottle of whisky in his hand. Granny Pritchett couldn't straighten him out if she lived with him a hundred years. She always said that he was the best looking man in those hills, and she'd done hooked him for life, but sometimes he was too big of a fish for one woman to fry. He was a mess, but he loved Caroline and his other grandchildren.

On campus, her family went with her to her dorm room to wait to go to Byrnes Auditorium. Shortly after they got to her room, her phone rang. It was Butch calling her from the lobby of one of the high rise dorms. Apparently, he had no idea what dorm she was in. With her family sitting on the beds, stripped of linens, talking and having fun, she excused herself to walk over to Wofford dormitory to get Butch.

When she saw him, he already had his arms open wide to give her a brotherly hug.

She said, "Oh Butch, I'm so glad to see you. It means so much to me for you to be here for my graduation. And believe it or not, Miss Emily Price is going to be graduatin', too."

"Yeah that's amazin', isn't it, but don't you dare tell her I said so."

"I reckon, I feel like a princess bein' rescued from captivity in a foreign castle with you comin' all the way up here to help me move."

"Well, you've been locked up in a tower long enough, haven't you?

"Butch, I really loved my time here at Winthrop, and I'll leave havin' made friends with many sweet people and gathered many precious memories that I'll never forget. Four years was a long time though to be in some place other than your own home. Now, I'm ready to be moving on and goin' down to the Lowcounty today."

"You've got a great place to move into in Charleston. That apartment is wonderful down in that part of the city. I'm goin' to feel like I'm rubbin' shoulders with the rich when I come to see you."

"You will be rubbin' shoulders with the rich since Tara's daddy's loaded. In addition to being a surgeon, I understand he owns a great deal of real estate, doctor's offices all over the state."

"I'd heard that, too. Payin' for that apartment is nothin' for him. You were really lucky on that one."

"Not lucky, Butch; when it comes to luck mine is usually bad. I'll say I'm blessed on this one, especially when I talk about it to Momma and Granny. Now Grandpaw will say I was in the right place at the right time, and he'll drink to it."

Then Butch said, "Mercy me, I'm parched. Is there a drink machine in this buildin'?"

"What do you want? I'll go get it for you," she said.

"See if they have a lemonade, please."

He handed her some change. She walked toward the door that led to the vending machines. She turned around to smile at him. He felt happy for her and was glad she was feeling cheerful today.

She handed the drink to him and said, "Let's go have you meet my nutty family before it's time to go to the auditorium."

"So, I take it I can be myself and act down home cuntry with yer kin."

"You better b'lieve it. If you don't act cuntry and tell 'em where your momma's from, they prob'ly won't trust you to take me to Charleston."

"I guess I'll just act grits and gravy crazy," he said.

"Throw some ham bone in there and make 'em love you to pieces. Gracious! I'm glad you got here, Butch. Come on."

J.P. had been working laboriously for the past four days in the therapy room. Amanda was keeping a close eye on him both physically and emotionally, from a physical therapist's point of view. She'd seen cases in which accident victims had the drive to get better but not the patience and endurance it would take to complete the journey.

She asked, "What do I call you today, Mr. Andersen or J.P.?"

"I feel old when you call me Mr. Andersen. I think you're speaking to my dad."

"J.P., I know you want to be ready for the parallel bars by the time your girlfriend arrives, but I want you to remember that this is a goal. You'll reach that goal over time, and I'll be cheering for you all the way."

"I had you pegged as a former cheerleader from the first time I laid eyes on you. Were you a cheerleader?"

"As a matter of fact, I was a cheerleader in high school and in undergraduate school. How did you know?"

"Well, number one, you're pretty enough to be a cheerleader. Secondly, you are always about to "bust", as you folks say, with loads of enthusiasm."

"Oh, is that so? I thought I always maintained a professional façade around my patients."

"That's hogwash. You were prim and proper the first couple of days, but after that you've been like a helium balloon filled to maximum capacity."

"I hope you see that as a good thing," she said, needing some validation.

"Yeah, it's been a very good thing. I don't think I would've progressed as rapidly as I have if you hadn't been so bubbly."

"Just keep on doing what you have been doing with the same will to succeed, and you'll be there before you know it."

"Thanks, Amanda, you've been great. I don't think I could have had a better therapist."

"I don't know about that," she said humbly, "but I appreciate the complement."

＝┿ ┿＝

As Butch and Caroline walked over to her dorm, she tried to gently warn Butch about her family.

"Momma is pretty laid back and every now and then has a good ol' time, but only around family. Grandma and Grandpaw love me dearly, but some of their cuntry sayings crack me up, and no telling what they'll say 'round you. They can be very serious and be funny as heck at the same time; it's hard to know when to laugh or when to keep a poker face. On the other hand, my brother, Troy, and my sister, Rhonda, will do every outlandish thing they can do to razz me and embarrass me, to make me snigger and giggle like a juvenile."

Butch laughed and said, "Don't worry, Caroline, It'll all come out in the wash."

They walked into the room, and Rhonda didn't waste a minute. She said, drawling like one of the daughters of the confederacy, "I swanny, Caroline's managed to git a rock star to come to her graduation."

Caroline thought she was trying to come on to him, right away, but not doing a very good job, making idiotic comments.

He kindly responded to Rhonda, "Don't know what I'd do with 'at kind of fame, ma'am."

Troy rose from the dormitory bed and shook hands with Butch and introduced himself. He turned toward his momma and said, "This is our mother, Mrs. Carter, and this is our grandmother, Mrs. Pritchett, and our grandfather, Mr. Pritchett."

Caroline was about to gag, because she'd never heard her brother refer to their family members as mother, grandmother, and grandfather. It sort of freaked her out. He must have thought Butch was some rich Charlestonian.

Grandpaw also rose to shake his hand. Then he asked his standard question, "Where you from, or I guess I should ast you where your people from?"

"Mr. Pritchett, my daddy's folks, the Whites, are from South Georgia. Momma's people are from Greenwood; her maiden name was Turner. Momma and Daddy kinda made a compromise and brought us up in the South Carolina Lowcounty so each of them could visit their families without drivin' too awfully far."

"Well, lucky for y'all they didn't take you outta the state. I ain't nevah lived nowhere else but up in the 'em hills north of Greenville, and I'm mighty proud of it. Some people say it's the Dark Corner, on 'count of moonshiners a long time ago, but it ain't dark. It's God's country up there, and I'll live there til the dew don't fall on Dixie."

Troy saw that Butch was a genuine kind of guy and couldn't last long without starting in on Caroline. He said, "Now Butch, don't let nobody fool you. Grandpaw knows exactly who's a runnin 'em stills up there in the hills, to this day. My dear little sister can drink some 'shine when she tawks Grandpaw into gettin' her some."

"Oh Troy, you've always been known to tell tall tales," said Mrs. Carter. "Caroline nevah has had a taste of that stuff."

Caroline just smiled and rolled her eyes at Butch, having remembered that she'd already teased Butch that she knew all about drinking moonshine. He probably didn't believe any of it anyway, a girl drinking that strong stuff; that kick your butt and leave you to die stuff.

In her defense, Butch replied, "I can't see Caroline touching home brew. She knows that stuff will eat your liver up."

Troy came back with, "Caroline's not as prudish as you think. She's just tryin' to make a good impression on you today, graduatin' from college and all. She's street wise, you know, a city girl with mountain kin, knows a lot."

Caroline looked at Troy, with fire in her eyes, and exclaimed, "Stop! Stop right now before I air your dirty draws right here in front of Granny and Grandpaw."

"You would not," he said with a hint of questioning.

"Take your pick, big boy; you can stop pickin' on me or I'll tell everything I know. And don't think I won't just cus it's my graduation day. You best leave me alone, Troy."

Granny piped up, "Law, law, law. You'uns better hush or I'll knock the stuffin' outta your ears."

The group erupted into loud, uproarious laughter, with the exception of Granny and Momma Carter. This situation might have been one of those times when Granny had been hilarious and serious at the same time.

Caroline sat down next to her granny, put her arm around her neck and said, "Granny, I love you so much. You're always the peacemaker in the bunch. Thank you for comin' all this way to make this day so special for me."

Then she looked around at Butch and her other family members and said, "Thank all y'all for comin' today."

Momma Carter looked at her wrist watch and said, "It looks like it's nearly time to go to the auditorium. Caroline, put on your cap and gown, and I'll take a picture of you in this ol' room for the last time."

"Okay, Momma, that'll be fun. I'm so excited. Thank the Lord, last night was my last time to sleep in a dormitory on these rotten mattresses. Hallelujah!"

Butch laughed and said, "You might be sleepin' on a corn husk mattress in that ol' basement in Charleston."

⊶ ⊷

J.P. woke up that morning feeling down that Butch was up in Rock Hill and he couldn't be there. He appreciated Butch beyond measure, but he couldn't help but be saddened by the fact that he couldn't be with Caroline today.

Betty, a full-figured woman, with her graying hair greased smoothly to the back of her head, one of the hospital cafeteria assistants, came into his room after the grouchy morning nurse had done her rounds.

Mist' An'ersen, "How comes you looks like you los' yo' best friend in de world?" Not really expecting an answer from him, she set the tray of food on the beige Formica table at the end of his bed and came and patted him on the arm. "Let me get you cranked up so...z you can set up chea and eat yo' eggs and bacon. I gots you some good ol' hot grits wif butter dis mornin', too."

He said, trying to act cheerful, "Betty, thanks for asking. You met Caroline, my beautiful girlfriend. She's graduating from college today, and I'm having it rough wishing I could be there with her."

"Well, sir, I sho' do wish you could be dere wif her today, but you dere wif her in de heart, an' she know dat, too, 'eah? Sometime dat be better for a man an' woman to be together in de heart eben when dey is far apart. Some peoples lib right up under dey noses, but dey hearts be far apart. De heart of bof of dem gots to be close all de time, no matta where dey is."

"Betty, you're an angel. That's just what I needed to hear this morning to get me through the day. Thank you so much for having the courage to tell me that. I've been feeling sorry for myself this morning, I suppose."

"Yo' welcome, Mist' An'erson, and I thanks you fo' tellin' me you thinks I be de angel fo' you dis mornin'. You keep on b'liebin' in angels and de Gawd who sens dem angels, an' you gone be blessed. Now you set up chea and eat yo' food 'fo it git cold. I'll he'p you wif de feedin' all you needs me to. I know you has been gettin' better eber day, so maybe you can git dat bacon to yo' mout' if I puts it in yo' hand. Let's try dat, okay?

Betty was so kind to him and made sure that he was satisfied from his meal before telling him it was time for her to move on to other patients on the neuro floor, many of whom would have to be fed totally.

She put the lid back on his near empty plate, moved the table out of the way, and turned on the T.V. for him. She asked, "Does you wants to watch some sports dis mornin' o some news? Isaac, he be comin' in soon to gib you yo' baf."

He answered, "The sports channel would be good. If I get tired of that, I can sweet talk one of the nice little nurses' assistants into changing the channel for me.

"Oh, Mist' An'ersen, a good lookin' man like you is can git any-thin' done dat you wants in dis hospital; just smile lots an' show dem pearly whites and keep on soundin' like de nice man you is. And you gonna hab a nice day, sir. Maybe I see you again when I serb de lunches. Keep on keepin' on, sir! And ol' Big Betty be prayin' fo' you today, 'eah?"

He pursed his lips as if to kiss her and blew out a tiny puff of air, blowing her a kiss.

She smiled as she was leaving the room and responded, "Lawd, I hopes you is better soon, cuz I be waitin' fo dat, 'eah?"

"Waiting for what," he asked?

"I be waitin' fo de real t'ing." And a great gush of laughter erupted from her, her rotund belly jiggling as she laughed heartily.

Sunlight streamed through the branches of the oaks in front of Byrnes as Caroline's family and Butch exited the auditorium with the crowd of other families and friends of the graduates. Before long Caroline found her eager group.

Caroline's momma used up two instant cameras taking pictures after the graduation ceremony for what seemed like fifteen or twenty minutes. Caroline surveyed the grounds under the oaks until she spotted Emily with her parents, brother, and grandparents. She said to her own family, "All y'all gotta meet my best friend Emily. She kept me sane while I was here, and she introduced me to J.P. Butch and Rhonda are the only ones of y'all who have met her."

Excusing themselves from Caroline's clan, momentarily, she and Butch walked over to Emily. After a quick photo taken by her brother, Emily turned to see them approaching. She and Caroline ran to one another for a congratulating embrace. Butch followed suit to congratulate Emily.

Emily said almost out of breath from excitement, "Can you b'lieve, we finally made it to this day?"

Caroline countered, "Sometimes, I wondered if you would. Did you change your hair color for the graduation ceremony, you don't look so bleached blond?"

"Caroline, don't ever stop bantering me; if you do I won't feel your friendship in the same way."

"Well, darlin' you're my only friend that I can do it to. Nobody else would take the verbal abuse. I learned well from Rhonda, that's how she shows affection, and I feel as close to you as I would if you were my younger sister. I'm a few months older than you are, anyway."

Butch interjected, "Glory be, I can't believe both of y'all made it. I know the sacrifices that y'all both have made to get here. I couldn't be more proud of y'all."

Emily said to Butch, "Caroline doesn't think art majors have to do much to get a degree. But I'm here to tell you that I did plenty to get this dang piece of paper."

"Emily," said Caroline in a reprimanding tone of voice, "You know I pick on y'all the time 'cus I love you. I know art majors have their share of seemingly useless knowledge to acquire as any of us do to get a degree. But now we've gotten it, and we can do as we wish with all that information that was crammed into our brains."

Butch added, "You nevah know when some of that comes in handy when you have to impress someone to get what you need, like a job."

Both girls cocked their heads to the side and shrugged their shoulders, a questioning gesture, but then nodded in confirmation to his statement indicating that he might be right.

Emily asked Caroline, "Do gestures count as a jinx, you buy me an ice cream kind of thing?"

"Yes, and I'll buy you an ice cream next time I see you in Summerville or Charleston. Would your family mind if I steal you away for a couple of minutes to meet my folks and take a few pictures with me?"

Emily was able to take a few minutes to meet Caroline's family before leaving with her own family to go to lunch at some swanky restaurant in Charlotte. Her brother, Drew, would go on to Clemson to visit friends. Emily and her parents had plans to stay in a nice hotel in the city and tackle moving Emily's things back to Summerville the day after graduation.

Now, it was time to solicit help from Rhonda and Troy to help pack the truck. Caroline insisted that her momma and grandparents go to the library and sit in more comfortable seating while Rhonda and Troy helped them load her belongings. They agreed, so after changing into a pair of shorts and a Winthrop T-shirt, for old time's sake, Caroline drove them over to the library in her momma's big, gas guzzling Ford LTD, escorted them into the library, and showed them where the magazines were located.

Granny and Grandpaw seemed excited about getting to relax in comfy seating for a little while and looking at magazine pictures; it was something they'd never done before. Momma Carter would be busy trying to locate quilting and hunting magazines for her parents, if able to find them, then, she'd find some teaching magazines to get ideas for the ending weeks of school.

Caroline sprinted back across the street toward the main campus, leaving her momma's ugly, long olive green car in the library parking lot. She looked up to see countless small birds exploding from the crown of a well-shaped maple, like dandelion parachutes in a puff of wind. She felt as free as an eagle soaring, no restrictions, and no one to dominate her. Safely on the other side of the street, large oaks were alive to her, with each graceful dance of the leafy branches blowing in the gentle wind, saying goodbye to her today. Pigeons scattered, flying up and outward, making a passageway for her to run, to launch into her future. Despite all the hardships of her past, she was free today, and it had never felt so good to her.

When Caroline got back to the room, Butch, Troy, and Rhonda were all cutting up, telling jokes, and having a good ol' time. They were all basically from the same mold, having grown up in the South, and with Butch having gone to Clemson and remembering things his momma had told him, he knew almost as much as they did about the Upstate, the jokes and idioms.

Rhonda had changed into a skinny pair of jeans, ready to shred from age and wear, a purple T-shirt, and a pink baseball cap. Troy simply stripped off his tie and dress shirt and was down to his undershirt and khakis, looking tough with his large, muscular biceps on display. Caroline knew it was a miracle of God and her momma's constant admonishment that led to Troy's dress attire in the first place. Butch had worn a pair of brown corduroys, a plaid shirt, and a yellow knitted tie. He had removed his tie, folded it, and placed it on the desk along with his keys, and had rolled up the sleeves of his blue plaid shirt ready to get to work. Caroline looked at Butch and thought, *he's such a neat guy. I hope he finds his other half someday. That girl will be as lucky as I have been in finding J.P.* She liked Butch and was so grateful he was there to support and help her.

Troy shifted the conversation to Caroline, "Good...ness, young'un, what on earth you got in all these here boxes; you too young to be cartin' 'round this much stuff. You gonna be busier 'an a moth in a mitten tryin' to put all these things away. Hope your apartment is bigger than this cracker box, cause you gonna need some space to unload. Good Gussie, Butch, you better have brought a heck of a lot of bunji cords, or we gonna need to take a trip to the hardware store."

"We're good," Butch responded calmly, trying hard not to laugh at Troy's statements.

Rhonda had to stick her two cents in and, leaning against the side of the stacked boxes, she commented "I nevah seen the likes of so much stuff in all my born days. Hopefully, some of this mess is your teaching stuff you can take to your school over the summer." She looked at Troy directly and said, "I've seen her new apartment when I visited her in Charleston; her new room is gonna be like the Taj Mahal compared to this tiny depressin' dorm room. But this is a big load of stuff, and Caroline, you ain't gonna have much room for decoratin'."

Caroline was flabbergasted by Rhonda's statement, having no idea that her redneck acting sister was savvy enough to know about the Taj Mahal. And she knew her sister was tempted to say a crude toilet word to describe her possessions, but she was watching her tongue in front of Butch.

Nevertheless, she had to respond to her, "Rhonda, I won't have much money for decoratin' my new apartment. And I ain't gonna make a room divider outta danglin' crushed beer cans like you did in your apartment."

"Pshaw, Caroline, that wall of cans, suspended by fishin' line, is a work of art. All my friends always compliment me on that wall. They say it's kinda like a real life mobile."

"What friends you talkin' 'bout, Billy Joe Bryan and Travis Holbrook? Good land, Rhonda, they prob'ly guzzled all the beer outta those cans."

"So, it don't matter where the cans come from, it's still art."

"Well, suit yourself, but I have to admit it covers up all your big mess of junk boxes."

"Now, honey, don't get huffy on your graduation day," Rhonda said as she kissed her sister on the cheek.

Caroline put up her hands and curled her fingers like a hissing cat. With one more stab and in mock defensiveness, Caroline made it clear that her belongs were not to be considered "mess" and that many items were family heirlooms that no one in the family trusted Rhonda enough to give them to her, afraid they would end up in the flea market in Anderson, to be sold for practically nothing, or donated to the Salvation Army. Rhonda looked shocked that her little sister would say things like that about her.

Caroline stated, "My new apartment is considerably larger than this homey, but suffocatin' dorm room, and I'll have plenty of space to store everythin', even if some things have to stay in boxes," said Caroline."

"Honey, you have to watch out for roaches. They love to take up residence in these cardboard boxes, and I know you've seen some roaches in this dormitory. A whole crowd of 'em are gonna go on a trip to the Lowcountry today. Am I right?"

"I reckon you are, Rhonda. I'll just have to get some roach spray, or call an exterminator after I start earnin' some income. It'll be no big deal. I hope!"

"Baby, you'll prob'ly be a spendin' more on extermination than on your own groceries. I hear Charleston is the worse place in the state for bugs," she said still taunting her little sister.

"Rhonda, the boxes behind your wall of beer can art are filled with roaches, too.

Butch interjected, "Oh, you get used to bugs, sand, and humidity in the Lowcountry. It's a trade- off for the beautiful sunsets and the charm of antiquity. I been there a while now, and ain't no roaches run me off, yet." He was smiling and looking directly at Caroline, and said, "You just have to cross your floor, gingerly, in the middle of the night, ignore the crunches, and don't turn the light on to see what you'd rather not see."

Then Troy gave one more jab, "Caroline, I heard you really gotta look out for those fire ants in your fancy new garden; the one Rhonda is so jealous of." Rhonda elbowed him in the ribs. "I heard them fire ants, in the Lowcountry, will bite your butt and then sass ya when ya cuss at 'em."

They were nearly hysterical, including Caroline. She was going to Charleston, no matter what, and she wasn't going to be spooked by her brother and sister. It was apparent that they were going to miss her, giving her such a hard time as they always had done, wishing she'd abandon the whole plan to take off to Charleston and remain in the Upstate with them.

She went and hugged both of them, and exclaimed, "Your baby sister needs to grow up. Now, shut up and help us load the daggum truck, purddy please."

⊷⊶

Mist' An'ersen, "You ready fo' yo' baf dis mornin', asked Isaac, the good natured, talkative, mature orderly on the neuro floor of the hospital? His kinky hair was nearly all white, and J.P. suspected that his days serving as an orderly would soon come to an end.

"Isaac, you've been helping me now every day for the past three weeks. Don't you know by now that I don't want you to call me

"Mist" anything. My name is John Paul, but most people here in the South call me J.P. Now you can have your pick between John Paul or J.P., but please don't call me "Mist". It makes me feel old."

"How 'bout I calls you John Paul? Dat name gots a nice ring to it. I think I heard dat name befo'. Oh, yes, I heard dat name down on Shem Creek one day. I sho did. We sees dis man when we be eatin,' swimp and my wife say he be a pries, wid dat black suit and white colla'. She work fo his sister a long time ago on Sullivan's Island."

"Now Isaac, you have to get me looking and smelling great today."

"John Paul, is dis de day you tol' me dat yo girl gone be graduatin' from de college up yonder in Rock Hill?"

"Yes, but it's also the day that she'll be coming to see me. She'll be here in Charleston this afternoon. I haven't seen her for three long weeks, and I'm sure I was looking and smelling terrible when she left. To tell you the truth, I was feeling so rotten, I don't even remember everything we talked about before she left. I do know for sure she landed a teaching job on James Island, to start in August, and she'll be living here, downtown."

"Where she goin' to lib down here?'

"She'll be living in an apartment on the lower floor of one of those big houses down near the Battery."

"Lawd, how a teacher gone pay fo' some place like dat?"

"Her roommate's got old money, family money."

"Oh, yo' girl done be blessed from de Lawd. You bes keep a hol' dat girl."

"I plan to Isaac, and I am going to get better and better each day so I can take care of her in the future."

"Okay, John Paul, I needs some mo' towels, but I'm gone be gittin' yo hair clean right soon, and I gib you a shabe. You gone be smellin' so good, you can't hardly fight off all de womens in dis hospital. And when I git done heppin de other mens on dis flo', I'm gone come back in here and git you all fresh again 'fore she come."

"That'll be terrific! My brother brought me some cologne from home that I know she likes."

"What her name is again?"

"Her name is Caroline, and she's the sweetest, smartest, and prettiest girl in the world."

"O Mist', I mean John Paul, Miz Caroline, she gone luv that good smellin' stuff yo' brother brung you, womens luvs dat stuff, black womens and white womens."

"Isaac, it's okay for you to call her Caroline. Her name is Caroline Carter."

"O like dem peanut farmers down in Jawjah."

"That's right Isaac. I know you're busy today, so I'll see you later."

"You hab a good mornin', John Paul, and I sees you dis afternoon."

"Isaac, you're the best!"

"Thank yah, sir, do 'preciate dat."

⚊╬⚊

Within a half an hour the truck was packed.

Rhonda said, "I do declare, this truck looks like a hillbilly truck, fer sure, fer sure. You got not class at all, moving to Charleston like this."

Caroline retorted, "I don't think so Rhonda. Everythin' is packed neatly and secured by the bungy cords. I don't see any furniture stacked on top or pots and pans danglin' from ropes."

"Caroline, it looks like you're movin' everythin' out of that dorm room but the bathroom sink."

Caroline asked, teasing her sister back, "Oh heavens, did we forget that? Troy, be a sweetheart and run back up there to get that sink. Can't nevah tell when I might need a bathroom sink!"

Playing along with it to taunt Rhonda, Troy said, "That's right, can't nevah tell. Maybe I better pull out the toilet, too. Rhonda might need a toilet."

Rhonda was standing there with her hands on her skinny hips with a look of revenge on her face.

Caroline asked Butch, "Can you drive across the street to the library? It's right next to the student center; you can't miss it."

"Sure you trust me not to take off with your goods," he asked jokingly? "I might still be able to get to the flea market in time to peddle everythin'."

"Whose side are you on?"

"Yours, always, I'll see you in a few minutes," he said.

Caroline, Rhonda, and Troy walked down to the dorm office to return the room key. Then they walked across the campus to the student center, still acting silly and preparing themselves for the final farewell.

They went to the student center first so Caroline could check her mailbox one more time, and to her pleasure there was one letter postmarked from Charlotte, but it had no return address.

They got a few snacks for their trips back to Greenville and to Charleston and then walked over to the library to get Momma Carter, Granny, and Grandpaw.

The group met Butch in the parking lot. The men made conversation while the four women started their boo hooin'. After the release of some of those emotions, all were smiling with joy and wishing Caroline the best on her move. She made it short and sweet with her grandpaw and Troy, and then jumped into the cab of the truck. She blew kisses as she and Butch drove away with her family standing next to the car, all waving and with tears in their eyes like she was going off to war. Maybe she was and didn't even know it. Her momma had always told her that teaching was something like a battlefield with a lot of obstacles to dodge.

Frank came by to see J.P. during his lunch hour, bringing him a submarine sandwich for a change in his lunch routine. Big Betty popped her head in the doorway and saw Frank there helping J.P. with the sub. She put his food plate back on her cart and asked, "Y'all wants me to go git some dranks to go wif dem sam…wiches?"

"Sure Betty that would be great. How about some lemon-lime sodas?"

"Oh sure, I can get dat."

"Sound's perfect, Betty, thanks!"

When she closed the door, J.P. looked at Frank, both of them smiling, and said, "I guess I'll never remember that soda means baking soda dissolved in water, to people around here. Caroline told me all about that."

"Yeah, you got that right. That bakin' soda and water is all I ever had, as a kid, if I had heartburn. I got some fierce heartburn every time I ate real I…talian food."

J.P. was ready to roar when he heard Frank's pronunciation of Italian. He tried hard to hold back his snigger and said, "We were loaded up with the pink stuff if we were feeling sick to our stomachs."

"Mercy," exclaimed Frank! "I'm so thankful to see you able to eat this sub. I've been so worried 'bout you in all this mess." Frank kindly helped J.P. with the sandwich. After chewing and swallowing a bite of his favorite meatball sub J.P. said, "I know it must have been really hard on you seeing me fall and get carted off in an ambulance."

"That was crazy, not knowin' what kind of shape you were in," replied Frank, earnestly.

"You know, I was semi-conscious part of the time in that ambulance and wondered what had happened to me, but I guess I went back out so fast, I didn't have time to struggle over it."

"Do you remember much of being in the ER?"

"I know that every time I opened my eyes, another stranger in a scrub hat was hovering over me doing something. Other than that, it was just a blur for a few days."

"How's your meatball sub," asked Frank?

"It tastes great. I just hope I don't get indigestion. Don't know what the word would be for a phobia of soda water."

"You ain't gettin' that in this hospital. I'd have to smuggle it in here."

They howled with laughter for almost a minute. It felt so good to J.P. to laugh, really laugh.

The ride to Charleston was going to be worse in the truck than it was in Emily's VW. Butch had already commented that it would probably take them more than four hours to get there since they were so loaded down, and he had to keep an eye on things in the back, through the use of his mirrors, to be sure that everything was still secured adequately.

Caroline first asked about J.P. She wanted to know about every visit Butch had with him and every conversation they engaged in since she left, unless of course, it was something confidential. He indulged her to a degree because he knew how terribly hard it had been for her to leave J.P. in the hospital when she returned to school for three weeks. The conversation about him was long and intense, and Butch noticed that Caroline began to get anxious as they went on and on about J.P.s daily routines of nurses rounds, doctor's visits, and therapy sessions. In the course of the discussion, she started sounding very stressed and indicated that the real situation was not at all like what she expected to be happening for the two of them after she graduated and moved to the Lowcountry.

Butch wanted to redirect her attention to another topic to give her some respite from the constant thoughts of the difficulties ahead, but he suddenly couldn't think of anything to suggest they talk about. He very politely said, "I don't mean to be disrespectful in any way, but maybe we should talk 'bout somethin' different for a while, give you a little break from worry. You did just graduate and leave the place where you've worked hard for the past four years. We should be hootin' and hollerin' all the way to Charleston."

"I declare, we've been talkin' 'bout pretty heavy stuff. You don't have anythin' interestin' to tell me 'bout the Lowcountry?"

"Well, let me think 'bout it a second."

Caroline said, "Hey Butch, let's see if we can talk with correct grammar and pronunciation for ten minutes."

"Lord Caroline, you sound like a teacher for sure."

"Now Butch, I know you're all into design work and don't have to speak with a lot of people outside the office you work in, but it'll do you some good. Mostly, I want to see if I can start trainin' myself to speak correctly more often."

"If you do that, we won't even know who you are anymore," replied Butch.

"I reckon that's true, but I do need to practice. Give me ten minutes."

"Can't promise you much; it's been a long time since I tried," he admitted.

"Ten minutes hasn't started yet. Didn't you have teachers in school to model Standard English for you?"

"Yeah, I had one Scandinavian teacher named Miss Jensen, who came to the Lowcountry from Minnesota. She was very proper. We laughed about her at recess, but I liked her 'cus she was so pretty. I guess her parents had the money to send her to Furman, and for some reason she wanted to have the experience of teaching in rural South Carolina for a few years, maybe like some kinda religious mission. She indeed experienced the rural South in our community, poor thing. I actually had her for two years 'cus I was in a combination class, not enough students in our little school to have a teacher for every grade."

"That was pretty good for speaking properly, only a tad of dialect. Okay, the real ten minutes starts now, Elmer," she said with a slight lilt in her voice. "Try to eliminate the use of contractions, also, just to see if we can do it."

"Oh, please Miss Carter, do not call me Elmer," he pleaded. "I am much fonder of my nickname, Butch."

"As you wish, Butch, now let's get down to business. As you know, I am very excited about the teaching opportunity that I will have on James Island, beginning in August."

"Miss Carter, Caroline, if I may, I believe you will have your own educational experience while teaching there."

"Why do you say that I will have an educational experience there?"

"Well, Caroline, the culture on the islands is different from what you may be used to."

"I can understand that. The culture is different in various parts of Greenville County. The roots of the cultural differences are the same."

"I think it will take you some time to learn the different words and phrases that you may hear. That Gullah is hard to decipher at times."

"Believe me when I say that you would have a difficult time understanding the people who live in the heart of Greenville."

"I believe you. In my opinion, it does not matter how we speak in our own surroundings as long as we learn enough of the mainstream language to get by when we must use it."

Then Caroline said, "Lawsy me, that hasn't been ten minutes, and I'm wore slap out. I reckon the possum's on the stump!"

"I knew you couldn't last ten minutes, now, but you will when you absolutely have to. You told me you lasted twenty five minutes in your interview a few weeks ago. What's the possum's on the stump, ain't heard that one?"

"It means that's as good as it gits. Thanks for your vote of confidence. I bet I can last eight hours a day, when pigs fly. What you want to blab 'bout now for the next four or five hours?"

CHAPTER 23

MOVIN'

Upon arrival in Charleston, Caroline suddenly noticed the run down side of town, still the very old clapboard houses with long porches, but unkempt. When they came off the exit ramp and stopped at the first traffic light she asked Butch to turn right and drive through a few of the streets. What she saw were black people everywhere, on foot, adults and children on bicycles, men both young and old sitting mindlessly in front of neighborhood taverns, and discouraged souls sitting at city bus stops. In fact, she'd never seen so many black people in one area before. There were small local markets, A.M.E churches, a few housing projects, crumbling old houses, and children playing ball in the streets.

She asked, "There's a distinct difference in social class Charleston, isn't there?"

Butch admitted that there was such a difference but added, "Caroline, there are plenty of black folks who have become very successful and live in the Charleston area, doctors, lawyers, and businessmen. Like those of us from the middle to lower middle class, they have to be willing to work hard and take advantage of the help they're given along the way to attain success."

She replied very emotionally, "When we drove toward the North in December, I kept seeing billboards photos of somber lookin' black youth, advertising for the United Negro College Fund; but I don't think I ever saw one of those billboards in the South. Are we still crippling bright individuals in our public school system in South Carolina, perpetuatin' this misguided notion that whites are supreme, and we need not worry about the blacks that were oppressed for so long by our ancestors?"

"Girl, I know you're goin' to answer that question yourself when you start teachin'. If anyone can make some changes to a system needin' reform it would be Caroline Carter. You can use your knowledge, ingenuity, creativity, and compassion to help kids down here and make an impact on this community. I know you'll find a great many children who need a teacher like you're gonna be. Give it a little time; you haven't started yet."

"Okay, I know I get fired up on the inequality issue and discrimination problem. Had I been born up north in the 19th century, I'd have been a sure fire abolitionist."

"How 'bout avid abolitionist rather than a sure fire one?"

"You're as much of a smarty pants as Troy. So, what's on our agenda, now that we're finally here in Charleston," she asked?

He filled her in saying, "When I saw J.P. yesterday, he said that Clay and Anne McMahan had come down to see him on Thursday night and brought your new apartment keys to him. Their house in Mt. Pleasant has been finished early, so the downtown apartment is vacant and clean. They told J.P. that Tara's brothers would be there with her to move her things in, late this afternoon. I think it's important to J.P. to be able to give you the keys himself. So, I was wondering what you thought about swingin' by the apartment to see if Tara and her brothers are there, and then we can go on over to the hospital. Chris is plannin' to meet us at MUSC, and if you'd like, he and I can go unload the truck while you spend some time with J.P. alone. There'll be plenty of time for you to unload boxes to get settled in."

"It sounds like a plan to me. I'm sure that Tara will be expectin' me to be there to spend the first night in the new apartment with her, and I don't blame her, I wouldn't want to be there the first night alone."

"Looks like you were very organized in your packing, so it shouldn't be too hard to find what you're gonna need right away." He laughed heartily and then added, "Hope some of those organizational skills rub off on J.P. That boy's a procrastinator for sure and a hoarder. God bless him!"

"You don't mean it, do you," she asked?

"Of course I mean it. J.P. believes that overly organized men are either effeminate or anal retentive, neither of which he wishes to be called. Not that he would treat any such fellow badly, he's too nice of a guy for that, but he has no ambitions to become the most organized man in America, if you know what I mean."

"I got you! I'll try my best to be a positive influence on him without pushing him into somethin'."

"Believe me when I tell you that you've already been a very positive influence on him. In the past months, he's been like a different person. You gave him a reason to want to better himself."

"I hate for you to tell me he's disorganized because I was hoping that the mess in y'all's house was from you and Chris. I don't want an effeminate or an anal retentive kinda guy, but I don't want a slob either."

"Oh, he'll change to please you, but it may take some patience on your part."

"It seems like everything is requiring patience on my part these days. I could nevah have had a better teacher than my mother on that subject. She's the most patient saint I have ever known, besides Granny."

"They both seemed like sweet and considerate ladies. It's hard to believe that Rhonda is your mother's daughter, too. Pardon me, but she's full of herself. She don't hold back at all, does she," he asked dramatically?

"I guess she's had to be that way to make it to where she is now. She already owns her own salon, and she lives in a nice apartment even though it's cluttered, in my opinion.

Troy's done well for himself, also. He's about to be made the top construction engineer with the comp'ny he's workin' for, and he hasn't been there long. He has hopes of buying the comp'ny when the owner's ready to spend the rest of his days on a golf course in Hilton Head."

Butch said proudly, "I'm gonna be goin' to Hilton Head next week. I don't know if you know it or not but the comp'ny I work for designs golf courses. I just started a couple of years ago, but all of the civil engineerin' courses I took at Clemson have given me a great advantage. I've got my own dreams 'bout that line of work in the future. The ultimate experience would be to design a series of courses. The business can be quite lucrative."

"I didn't realize that, Butch. I'd heard that you did some kinda design work, but I didn't dream it was golf courses."

"It just so happens that I'm ah crackerjack golf player. Daddy made a mock drivin' range on our property, and I created my own miniature golf course. When I went to Clemson, Daddy bought me a membership at Boscobel in Pendleton, between Clemson and Anderson. I played every spare minute I had, at least when I was sober.

Look, Caroline, we're here!"

"I can already see some of the garden plants in bloom through the wrought iron fence and gate," she said, gaily. I know I'm gonna feel like I'm livin' in heaven here."

"You will once you get used to the heat and humidity. I don't know how people took it when there was no such thing as air

346

conditionin', but they did and they loved it and nevah returned to their homelands."

She said eagerly, "Let's go meet Tara's brothers and tell her that y'all will be comin' down later to unload my things. I know she's gonna be a blessin' to me, to help me stay on the straight and narrow path."

"You're already the straightest girl I've met so far. I feel I can trust you to be my true friend."

She closed her hand around his wrist and said, "You are a wonderful person, Butch. Thank you for everything you're doin' for me. You're one of my blessings, too."

"I have to confess something to you, Caroline.""What is it, Butch?"

"I'm a slob, too. My room is a royal mess just like J.P.'s room is. Chris ain't no better at keepin' house. You know from bein' a resident assistant at Winthrop that straight guys aren't neat. Maybe our mommas spoiled us too much by cleaning up our rooms. That's something we need to work on, but most of us secretly wish we could find some fantastic woman to help us with that problem."

"What you prob'ly want is a slave or in modern terms, a maid."

"Ooh, that hurts, cus we want our mates to be beautiful and interested in the things that interest us most."

"What, like football," she asked with a hint of sarcasm?

"Yeah, that would be ideal to have a lover, a maid, a companion, and a sports enthusiast."

"All y'all are absolutely hopeless," she said laughing, "but we don't seem to want to live without y'all."

"I hope you're honest about that one," he said.

"Let's get out b'fore they think we're full-fledged hillbillies, settin' in the truck all afternoon."

After checking in with Tara and her brothers, Butch and Caroline drove on to the hospital. J.P. chatted with Chris, sitting fairly upright in bed wearing a royal blue pocketed golf shirt, clean shaven; his hair had been washed and was slightly hanging over his left eyebrow, his fabulous blue eyes gleaming. The scent of his manly cologne wafted across the room, attracting Caroline, like a bee to honey. She cried at the sight of him. Butch saw the tears and quickly suggested that he and Chris go and unload the truck. Just as they were leaving, J.P. told Caroline to reach into the pocket of his shirt and take out the key to her very first apartment. Tears were dripping from her cheeks leaving little wet spots on his shirt. She handed the key to Butch without a word, unable to utter anything, with not one iota of instructions, just waiting for the two of them to leave the room.

She immediately dimmed the unwelcomed fluorescent lights, slipped off her brown leather clogs, lowered his bed rail on the left side, and crawled up into his bed to lie down beside him in a space barely wide enough to keep her there. She caressed him, running her fingers through his hair and stoking his face, and he took in the scent of her. And he smelled dangerously irresistible. Reprimands by nurses or doctors never crossed their minds. They said nothing but let their hearts speak to one another. Their tears of joy flowed together, none of them to be wiped away. To her astonishment at his improved strength, he raised his left arm to basically let it drop and rest it across his chest. She took his hand by her right and laced her fingers through his. Following a long silence, he whispered in a slightly dry raspy voice, "Thank God, you've come back to me, love."

She replied ever so sweetly, "I couldn't bear to be anywhere else." They both closed their eyes and listened to the breathing of one another and remained like that for tender moments in time. In his mind, he was saying, she doesn't know yet that I want it to be like this between us every single night for the rest of our lives, but one day she will, at the right time. Oh God, let me get better!

CHAPTER 24

FORGIN'

Caroline had a fitful night of sleep the first night in her new apartment. Tara was still up unpacking and organizing when she got in from the hospital, and they sat down for a short tête-à-tête. Both of them were frazzled from the move and the excitement of being on their own for the first time outside the parameters of their respective schools.

After making her bed and getting a quick shower, she thought to say prayers of thanksgiving for the good things happening in her life. As soon as her head hit the pillow, she was deep in sleep. About two o'clock in the morning, she sat bolt upright, on her overly firm mattress, awakening from the nightmarish recurring dream of the woman and infant. Beads of perspiration covered her forehead, and she was panting for breath. She would tell no one about it because it was becoming an embarrassment to mention it to her friends or family. All she could do was hope that soon the dreams would cease, once she was settled in this phenomenal city.

Caroline had one week before she'd start summer jobs, still hoping that she'd be able to use public transit to get to work. J.P.

knew that she'd have to walk a long way to catch a bus. A bus stop wasn't something that many people needed in the area where she was living.

Frank picked her up to go to the hospital. She found J.P. in a very good mood that day. During the visit he told Caroline that he wanted her to use his Toyota while he was rehabilitating. He said that it did him absolutely no good to be sitting in front of his house in Summerville, and he knew she needed a car to get to work and to visit him.

Needless to say she was hooting and hollering and then crying, hugging and kissing him. He'd just given her another set of wings. She was so excited that she vowed she'd learn to drive over the Cooper River Bridge without fear by the end of the summer, a monumental aspiration.

That next week was fantastic for the two of them. She accompanied him to physical therapy and occupational therapy every day and was thrilled to see the tremendous progress he'd made while she was away at school. In only three weeks, it was miraculous to see him up walking around the track in the therapy room using the forearm walker. It boosted his optimism as much as it did his self-esteem to see her so excited about his accomplishments.

One day, when Caroline was in the therapy room, she overheard Amanda discussing J.P. with the lead therapist, Chris Thompson, who incidentally was the kind of man the women in the room couldn't take their eyes off of; tall, dark haired, and unmercifully handsome. The color of his eyes was a cross somewhere between Tufts blue and warm gray, rimmed with hazel; extraordinary eyes. Amanda was explaining to Chris that she hoped there'd be no need for J.P. to be transferred to Shephard Rehabilitation Center in Atlanta because he was making such good progress, and she felt that he'd be able to go home soon, continuing therapy on an outpatient basis.

Caroline's heart was pounding, and she wondered if she should tell J.P. But maybe it was Amanda's place to do it, as his therapist, and Caroline didn't want him to know she'd been eavesdropping. Just as she was turning her head away from the direction of Amanda and Chris, Caroline got a first-hand glimpse of the most eligible physical therapist in the city; he looked straight toward her and smiled before she could turn away.

The day arrived for J.P. to try the parallel bars for the first time. Although it might have seemed juvenile, Amanda had purchased the kind of horns used at birthday parties, the type that looked like an insect proboscis rolling out to sip nectar from flower blossoms. On the count of three, everyone in the therapy room blew their party horns to signal their support of J.P. to tackle such a taxing exercise, a major physical milestone. With all the attention and encouragement, there was no way he could put it off with Amanda. And with Caroline there, he couldn't stall out of fear of failure.

He yelled out, "Okay, I got the message, I'll do it. Here goes!" Amanda attached his gait belt and hoisted him from the wheelchair, making sure to support his knee with her own to keep it from collapsing. Her male assistant was behind J.P. to help with the lifting and to move the chair out of the way. They made sure he had a firm grip around the bars. After his first few steps, the group blew their horns again and erupted into long, sincere applause, and he heard Amanda, with strong emotion in her voice, as she prompted him to keep going. Although he was using all of his strength, he glanced upward to see great streams of tears flowing from Caroline's eyes, dripping from her jawbone and dampening her shirt. He nearly had tears in his own eyes, but he fought the tears back and tried to keep up that tough guy façade.

Late that afternoon, Butch and one of his friends from Summerville brought the Toyota to Charleston and parked it in the MUSC parking area. Caroline left the hospital early that day due to total exhaustion from both the move and a poor night of sleep from her disturbing nightmare. As she was driving out of the visitor's parking lot, she had to slam on the breaks to avoid hitting a brand spanking new, red Nissan 300 ZX convertible, the driver cutting her off to speed out of the employee section of the lot. When he took a sharp left, she recognized that it was Chris, the dreamy lead physical therapist she'd seen Amanda talking to. A fleeting thought flashed before her sentience that made her wonder what it would be like to be fancied by a bachelor with more than adequate disposable income. She figured he probably had a charming beach house as well as the swanky new Nissan convertible.

Shame engulfed her! She immediately suppressed her thoughts. And after some time to clear her head and remind herself that most guys that drive new sports cars spend their time showing their butts and treating women like objects, with no regard for their feelings, she basked in the warmth of J.P.'s signs of affection toward her.

Several days later, Caroline was having lunch in the hospital cafeteria. It was her day off from her part-time jobs, so she'd planned to stay the bulk of the day with J.P. After a morning of watching physical and occupational therapists working with him, she needed a breather during lunch.

She went through the cafeteria line wanting to select greasy fried chicken, macaroni and cheese, sinful Mississippi Mud cake, and sweet tea. But she opted instead to get a healthy salad topped with broiled chicken strips, a large green Granny Smith apple, and boring spring water. She grabbed a big fat package of blue cheese dressing before she got to the register. Go, girl!

She paid for her lunch and then took a table near the window bathed in natural light. The cafeteria furniture looked very sleek and modern with wooden, Birdseye Maple, polyurethane coated tables adorned with glass vases and simple silk flowers, Gerber daisies. The chairs were constructed with brightly colored plastic and metal. Eggshell painted walls were covered with wonderful, floor to ceiling, textured wall hangings with brightly colored strips of cloth woven into frayed ropelike materials.

Caroline was sitting there gazing out the window, amused as she watched the tiny furry squirrels scamper up the tree trunks as if the street traffic was making them skittish. Could she blame them, the traffic made her skittish, too? Suddenly, she turned to see Chris, the lead physical therapist standing in front of her.

"Do you mind if I join you for lunch since you're all alone? I usually sit at this table to watch the squirrels."

Dumbfounded, she had no idea how to handle this other than to say, "Sure, have a seat and watch the little critters with me."

In close proximity, she could tell that he was a little older than she was.

He said curiously, "Tell me about Miss Bethany Caroline Carter. I've seen you in the therapy room a lot lately with J.P." Flaw number one, she thought, he has a social sequencing issue, messin' up my name, or maybe that's inattentiveness. I reckon he's 'bout thirty years old.

They made proper introductions to learn one another's names, officially. Trying to act cold fish, she said her name, from her repertoire, first-middle-last name.

His cheeky grin and searching eyes were telling her that he was trying to find out information about her relationship with J.P.

She said with a wan smile, "It's Caroline Bethany, but please call me Caroline", and then she explained her relationship with J.P. to be sure that he didn't misconstrue the situation and let him assume that she was just a good friend. She was very uncomfortable as she gave that brief synopsis of her status, so she tried to shift the inquiries back to him asking, "What about you?"

"Well, for starters, I'm from Albuquerque, New Mexico," he said crisply. I'm an avid mountain bike rider and a connoisseur of the best Mexican food in the United States."

The exchanges between them were sparse as Caroline concentrated on her salad, making sure she was chewing her mouthfuls for lengthy periods of time, until the lettuce became pulp between her molars, so that he did most of the talking. When there was a lull in the pleasantries, playful verbalizations on his part, she focused on the perky rodents climbing the impressive oaks out along the street. She was thinking, "This is another test, and I'm not fallin' for it. I'll eat quickly and stop this thing before it gets blown out of proportion. Law me, he's one fine lookin' man. Oh mercy Jean, I should slap myself silly."

She summoned the strength to nip it in the bud, then gracefully dismissed herself from the meeting with carefully chosen responses and left the cafeteria like a prima donna in a much too demanding role.

With Betty's constant insistence and encouragement, J.P. was feeding himself finger foods of lightly steamed carrots, apple slices, and pieces of boned chicken, and rolls. In the mornings, she'd place a strip of bacon or buttered toast in his hand, he'd feed himself, and she'd clean his hand thoroughly. She was more to him than just someone who was part of the cafeteria staff; she was his friend, as was Isaac, his orderly. They were much more personable with him than some of the nurses and nurses' assistants. They cared a great deal about him.

He continued to improve daily, his strong determination fueling his recovery. In his mind, there was no time to waste. He didn't want to go to rehab in Atlanta at Shepherd, and he knew he had limited time to stay at MUSC. He now had Caroline there, near him in Charleston, and he had to do everything he could to stay in the area to be able to see her often. She was becoming his life, but she didn't know the depth of his feelings toward her at this point in the relationship. Timing was everything to tell her how he really felt!

⇒⊱ ⊰⇐

Caroline busied herself with working two part-time jobs, visiting J.P., and helping Tara keep the small garden outside their apartment meticulously groomed. It was such a beautiful place to live and had to be respected with pride. She and Tara did everything in the garden with the exception of the lawn which was handled by the main gardener of the property. They wanted to do this to learn more about gardening. The main gardener was there to answer questions, silently observe their efforts, and make any final corrections to be sure the garden was as well manicured as the main garden.

June was gone and part of July had vanished, too. She was finally getting more acclimated to the sweltering heat and drenching humidity of Charleston, doing her gardening beginning at six in the morning, after coffee and light breakfast outside, and finishing no later than eight thirty, avoiding feeling overheated. If you allowed yourself to get burned out with the heat early in the morning, your strength seemed to be sapped for the remainder of the day.

Soon she'd have to start going to the school to arrange her classroom and prepare materials to teach first grade. She was excited and nervous at the same time.

Since the accident, J.P. had received short term disability insurance benefits. Butch and Chris had been managing fine with the rent on the old house in Summerville. Basically, all that needed to be paid was liability insurance on the Toyota, because the loan had been paid off a year ago. J.P. received one lump sum check of a little more than eight thousand dollars. The Toyota had a lot of miles on it, but it was still in good shape. However, with that car having bucket seats, it would be a difficult vehicle for J.P. to transfer himself in and out of it from a wheelchair, using a transfer board, even on the passenger's side of the car. He'd already been given a dismissal date from the hospital staff. He was glad that he'd made a decision to use the short term disability money to buy a used car for himself and let Caroline keep the Toyota. He'd handle the car insurance on both vehicles from the sizable nest egg he'd been contributing to for several years. All Caroline would need to do would be to take care of the gas for the Toyota.

With a couple more weeks of outpatient therapy, Amanda felt that a walker would be a sufficient mode of mobility, and they'd be working toward using Lofstrand canes. Being able to use the canes would enable him to go back to work doing research for ongoing restoration projects. He would work on a half day basis at first so that he could continue his physical therapy in the afternoons.

So he'd be going back to Summerville soon. Once he was able to get back to work he'd be able to see Caroline in Charleston, and sometimes she'd be able to drive to Summerville on the weekends.

J.P. had been dismissed from MUSC before the end of July. Within weeks he was managing well with the walker on an independent basis, and using the canes during outpatient therapy sessions.

Before he left the hospital, the occupational therapist had ordered assistive devices to help make dressing himself easier. Fortunately, the shower stall at home was easy to enter. Butch thoughtfully purchased a shower seat and a new electric razor for him as welcoming home gifts, and he and Chris constructed a temporary ramp over the front door steps.

There was no definite schedule for J.P. to go back to work, but with the tremendous progress that he'd already made, Amanda felt that he'd be ready to function independently within a few more months. Not another soul at work was interested in spending time in the archive rooms at the public library, and he thought that he'd be psychologically prepared to continue some of the research he'd started before he had the accident. Research was one of his passions, and the library was a great place for him to get back into the routine of work. Like his beautiful Caroline would do, he bowed his head and thanked God for his amazing recovery, his precious girlfriend, many loyal friends, a compassionate employer, his faithful family, and numerous competent medical professionals and caring hospital workers. He could never have made it this far without them, and he'd never forget what they'd done for him. The accident had changed him in so many ways, positive ways. He'd finally learned what gratitude, humility, and spirituality were all about.

CHAPTER 25
TEACHIN'

Caroline had been working at school on her days off and on days when she had to go in to work in the afternoons. She'd met a new teacher friend named Leona. Leona was a former friendly checkout clerk at a grocery store on Savannah Highway, who'd become sick of minimum wage jobs and gone back to school to get certified to teach. At forty five years old, she was now a veteran teacher of two years. She had a heart the size of a soccer ball and wanted to help Caroline get off to a good start teaching her first year at Jasper. She also wanted to shield her from some of the teachers in the school who were cutthroat ladder climbers who might sabotage her good efforts to make sure that they'd appear to excel above her in all things, using any means to destroy, downright grown up mean girls who are found in almost every school and at every level. In the classroom, Leona well knew how difficult the first few weeks were going to be for Caroline; trial and tribulation to the nth degree.

The first day of school was there before she knew it and Caroline started the day with a welcoming "Hello, boys and girls. My name is Miss Carter, and I'm going to be your first grade teacher. Now, how are my new boys and girls today?" She got nothing but blank stares from the children. Some looked as if they wanted to crack a smile, others looked completely expressionless, one little mulatto girl looked almost like she was going to be sick, and others looked scared or downright mad to be in school, almost as if they'd been captured and put in prison. Maybe she'd been imprisoned, too.

Caroline's next thought was, *Oh Lord in Heaven, what do I do next?* Then she had the children stand up and told them that they were going to learn the Pledge of Allegiance. She said, "Listen as I recite it for you. I will be looking at the red, white, and blue flag of the United States of America and placing my right hand over my heart; but don't be afraid that I am having a heart attack," she said, trying to coax some smiles from them but got no responses at all. "And don't worry that I am going to make you say all of the pledge today because I know it will sound long to you. We can learn it a little at a time."

She went to the back of the room to stand behind the children so that no monkey business would be going on while she said the entire pledge. Surprisingly, the children were as quiet as could be while she recited the pledge respectfully. Then Caroline asked the children to put their right arms in the air. Of course, some of them put their left arms up, so she walked behind them and gently helped them to correct the error, emphasizing the word right frequently. When everyone had the correct hand in the air, she told them to put their hands over their hearts. She heard little slaps across the room, like dominoes falling on a tabletop. She looked at them with delight. A thought suddenly came to her: *Momma had reminded her that the Confederate flag still flew above the dome of the South Carolina State House. Slavery had been abolished for over a hundred years, but the evil remnants of it were still fueling hatred in the twisted hearts of many white Southerners, including racist teachers.* Caroline knew she had to make some changes and she was starting now with her own attitude, giving respect to these little ones and believing in their ability to learn as well as any little children in South Carolina.

Trying hard to focus and maintain her composure before the young children grew weary of standing at attention, Caroline recited the pledge in its entirety making sure she articulated each word with a second's pause between the words so that the children could sharpen their auditory processing skills.

Caroline said, "After I say the first few words again, we are going to say those same words together. Keep your right hands over your hearts." She then proceeded to model the first three words of the pledge. What she heard as the children tried to mimic her was unusual to her. With somewhat staggered onset, she heard something like: "I's pled a gent, I's pleg a bence, and "I's plegga a ten." Then she thought, *Lordy, I'm gonna have to say those three distinctly all day long. I feel like I've just started my first day of teaching on a foreign mission field. Maybe I have.*

She went back to the front of the room and said, "I am going to write the first two words of the pledge on the board, and we are going to say only the first two words as we learn to read them." Even with her previous apprehension to do so, she found it possible to speak each word slowly, using Standard English, as she gave directions to the children knowing that many of them might never had heard some of the words she'd use throughout the day. She was trying hard to refrain from using contractions at this point to get them to enunciate every word. The contraction lessons would come later.

As she was writing the first two words of the pledge, she said the name of each letter she was writing on the dull green, worn chalk board and had the children repeat the letter name as she placed her unbroken stick of white chalk beneath the letter. She politely said, "Children, we are going to say I and not I's when we say the pledge. There will be many things I teach you this year that you may not say when you get home speaking, or tawkin', with your folks, your parents, but I am going to teach you anyway. I am not going to say that your way of speaking, or tawkin', at your house is wrong. There are lots of ways to say the same things. Suddenly, she saw a few half smiles from some of the girls. Most of little boys sat there and remained stone faced, with the exception of one little darling, whose face was as round as a moon pie, his expression telling her that he yearned to be taught many things. She knew many of the other boys felt the same way but weren't ready to show her.

When they finished their practice of the first two words in the pledge, Caroline announced that she would call the roll. She stood there looking at a name she'd never seen in print before, trying to mentally sound it out by syllable and getting somewhat flustered in attempting to do so in a timely manner. She suddenly realized that she should've reviewed the role before class started. Finally, Caroline spilled out Charlesena. A tiny little girl with her hair plaited in corn rows secured by rubber bands said, "Yez'um Miz Cotta, I be here."

Oh, Charlesena, I am so happy that you are here today. And I am so proud that you already remember my name, Miss Carter. Let's write the letters of your name on the board, and if anyone knows the name of the letter I write, please say it with me." Speaking to the entire class, she instructed, "After we write your names on the board, I will give each of you a name tag to wear today so that I can learn all of your names. Then we can play some games with our names so you can learn each other's names."

Charlesena, already having spoken to confirm her presence, spoke up and said, "We don't needs to lern dese other chill'uns names cus we plays together all de time at we house." The rest of the class nodded in agreement.

"I bet you do play together, but I sure have a lot of names to learn."

Caroline continued the activity with the names of the other little girls in the class: Belle, Pinky, Carolina, Ruby, Emma, Nellie,

Mary, Eva, Hannah, and Myra. Then she announced that she was going to call out the boys' names: Thompson, William, Samuel, Joe, Isaiah, Chester, John, Hercules, Peter, Dontrell, and James.

After the roll call and the name tags were prepared, the portly child with a cherubic looking face raised his chubby hand.

"Yes, William," she said after glancing at the name tag on his dingy white T-shirt.

"I thinks you be a good teacher cus you smiles a lot."

"Thank you, William, and I like you very much as well as all of my new friends in our class."

"What yo name is, again?"

"My name is Miss Carter."

"Oh yeah, Miz Cotta, you can calls me Will'um if you wants to. But my friends mights be callin' me Big'un out in the play yard. Dat be okay wid you?"

"Certainly, William if you don't mind that I call you by your given name."

"Them done give me bof names on dis island, Miz Cotta."

"Yes, I guess they have, William," she replied, brightly.

Then Myra, raised her delicate hand and stated, "Miz Cotta, We gwine he'p you lern all we chill'uns name. We know you is smaat 'cus you is a teacher. Momma tole me teachers is smaat."

Caroline smiled and told Myra that she appreciated her compliment. She continued with instructions, "Now children, this afternoon, I will be sending home some forms about payment for your lunches."

One little fellow, Isaiah, spoke up and said, "Momma, she don't be readin' so good and you not learnt me how to read yet so I cain't helps her wif dat. What is we gonna do 'bout dem papers, Miz Cotta?" His little face was filled with worry wondering if he'd be able to get his meals at school.

She looked out at the class as a whole fearing that many would have the same worry just expressed by Isaiah. "Well, you tell your mommas to come to the school in the afternoons, and I will help them fill out the papers. We have to do it to make sure you get breakfast and lunch. Tell your mommas that this is very important. It they can't find a ride to the school or it is too far to walk here, I can come to your house and help your mommas with the papers."

Then Samuel said, bobbing his little head up and down, "Miz Cotta, yo sho be a sweet teacher. You is like honeysuckle on dem vines. All we gots to do is pick you off the vines and smell that sweet smell."

She smiled sincerely and said, "Samuel, it sounds like you've just started your first poem."

"What you means, Miz Cotta; what be a po'm?"

"Samuel, tomorrow I'm going to read some poems to all of you. I have a very nice book with wonderful pictures and poems. Maybe then you'll have a better idea of what a poem is. I can write what you say on a large piece of paper, called chart paper, and we can all read it together."

Then Samuel said with a look of disbelief on his face, "Miz Cotta, you means you be gone writes what I say...s to you?"

"Yes, I will, if you would like me to. And if your friends would like to help you write more of the poem, and you say that's okay, I'll write down more lines in your poem."

"Miz Cotta, why is you goin' to make lines on dat paper, we needs to make tawk on that big ol' paper? We ain't nevah done dat 'fore."

Then the other children said, in unison, "Yez!"

Frail looking little Joe said, loudly, as if his voice could somehow increase his stature, "She gone be writin' a whole lots, cus we gots a lots to say...s"

Following a morning of activities designed to get to know the children and informally assess some of their abilities, a tour of the school, and the first day in the cafeteria, which was quite an experience for her, Caroline took the children out for recess. She was ready for a breather and vowed to herself that she would not look at her watch this first day outside. When the children reached the threshold of the steel double doors at the end of the hallway, they each let out a series of sounds of exhilaration, and began to run like free spirits in the wind. She proceeded to put down an old towel on the sandy soil under a large oak tree, with low branches festooned with silvery moss, to try to get some shade over her fair, Scots-Irish skin. Her red jersey dress hung well below her knees when she stood so it made it easy to sit in a ladylike position, on the ground. Several little girls headed straight for the basket used to tote the jump ropes, ready to jump and chant their intriguing mantras; and the boys dove for the rubber kick balls that Caroline had purchased herself for fear there might be none to use for her class.

Some of the little girls began to gather on the opposite of the huge old oak, using the stumps as stools to sit upon. Caroline could hear them as they conversed with one another.

Mary commented first, "Momma she be gone to Meggett when she be in skoo. She say...s all de chill'un, big'uns and little'uns be in Meggett. She say...s no white teachers comes to Meggett. All de chill'un and teachers be dark. She say...s she's big when she go to Meggett and she ain't lernt much 'cus she done quit when grand-momma gots so sick."

Nellie asked, "Who yo momma iz?"

"Momma be Lizzie, yo momma know Lizzie. Momma can makes dresses," answered Mary.

"Oh, yez, I done seen yo momma 'fore," said Nellie.

"Momma say...s we done got it good now-uh-days. She say...s when she gone to Meggett, dey ain't had no good books, and it be cold in de winner-time. She say...s we ought to be a so we be lernin'. She be sad she ain't lernt much in skool."

Emma, who seemed catatonic in the classroom, added, "Momma say...s we chill'un be luck to be gone to white skoo. We knows we gots a white teacher, Miz Cotta, but we ain't got no white chill'un with Miz Cotta. I likes Miz Cotta."

Nellie responded, "I seen some big white chill'un gets off dat shine bus dis mornin'. I was thinkin' where dem white chill'un be now. I reckon dey ain't in the fuss grade like we is."

Ruby said, "I likes it when Big'un say we teacher be a good teacher 'cus she be smiles a lot. She do smiles a lot, and dat be makin' me be feelin' good."

Emma again added to the conversation, "Dis mornin' I don't wants to get on dat bus wif that mean ol'white man a-drivin' dat bus; he be lookin' like de debil and makin' me feels scert. But momma say...s she be goin' to get she...s switch, so I gots on dat bus. I cries all the way to dis skoo. But I likes Miz Cotta 'cus she sweet to me. I likes skoo today."

Nellie got as quiet as a little mouse while the other girls chattered away. Caroline wondered if she was missing her momma, and she was nearly in tears hearing the children pour out their feelings.

By that time the little boys were hot and sweaty playing tag or kickball on the playground, and the girls jumping rope had beads of perspiration on their faces, she knew she needed to get them back inside to get water. The sun was unbearably hot as it had been every day for weeks. August, in Charleston, is always fiery, heavy, and humid, miserable as the air feels like steamy woolen blankets heaped upon you. The little girls under the oak had been smart to know that they'd burn up if they jumped rope in that brutal sun.

At the end of the first day, Caroline passed out the large white envelopes containing all of the important forms to be filled out by the parents or their designees. Again, she reminded the children not to worry about the forms being completed, that she would help if needed. When the students had packed their bags, if they had them, she explained, "I am going to play a tape now that has sounds you might hear in a tropical rain forest."

Thompson raised his hand and asked, "Miz Cotta, is we comin' ta skoo tomorrah?"

She answered, "Yes, y'all are coming to school tomorrow, and I will be very glad to see you. We will learn some more about a tropical rain forest." For the first time that day, she believed, she slipped a bit and talked like a true native in saying 'y'all', but she was glad she did because her babies probably never heard someone say you all. She smiled to herself.

Then jolly little William, Big'un, said, "Maybe I brung you a cootuh tomorrah. You does be likin' cootuhs, does you?"

She smiled sweetly, "To tell you the truth, William, I have nevah had a cootuh before, but you bring it and we'll find out what to do with it. I sure the other boys and girls will have some good ideas about the cootuh."

A rumble of little voices said, "Yez, Miz Cotta, we be knows all about cootuhs."

As they were loading the bus to go home, Caroline spoke loudly standing outside the bus, "I'm sure I'll be glad to learn about a cootuh if William finds one." Oops! There go the contractions.

Several of the boys popped up to make themselves visible through the bus windows and said, "We be heh'pin' Big'un find a cootuh fer you, Miz Cotta."

Most of the children left the school grounds smiling and waving. Caroline's heart swelled and streams of tears flowed, dropping from her cheeks onto her red dress, her forever contrary, red dress. Maybe she did have the guts it would take to be a teacher in this little spot in the world. But it would take a lot more than just guts; it would take prayers and dedication and a willingness to put her neck on the chopping block at times to deviate from the educational guidelines to give these little precious children what she felt they needed. As Granny would say, "It would take a river of love and a whole bushel basket of prayers."

With the yellow busses now dots in the midst of oaks and moss, Caroline, feeling wilted like a delicate daffodil on a hot day, turned and walked back into Jasper alongside Leona. Leona asked, "How was your first day, chile? They didn't give you no, excuse me, any trouble on your first day, did they?"

"Oh, no Leona, they were little angels," answered Caroline proudly. She was profoundly grateful that another teacher would care enough, at the end of a busy day with an equally hectic one to follow, to ask the little old new gal how things went.

"Well, give 'em a few days," said Leona laughing. "You might not describe 'em as angels all the time. Come on into my room. I've got two cold dranks in my new insulated lunch bag. I'm so proud of that bag 'cus my baby boy bought me that new bag. I saves me, excuse me-save, something special for the end of the day, and I thought 'bout you this mornin' as I packed my bag."

"Bless your heart," Caroline said, as any good girl would say. She realized that her new sweet friend was in the same boat she was in, trying to force herself to use correct English all day for the benefit of the children and to keep her job. But the school day was over and they could both relax and be themselves, slang, errors and all.

Sitting there in uncomfortable, old oak chairs turning up their small green glass bottles as fast as they could, needing refreshment, they began to chug. Caroline set her bottle down on the desk before she drank half of the cool liquid in one big swig. She looked down at the floor, unexpectedly burped, apologized, and said she was afraid she was about to have a nose spew. Then she screamed, as if she'd been slashed by a razor blade.

Leona screeched, "What is it, chile? Is you hurt?"

"No, I'm not hurt. I just saw the biggest roach I've ever seen in my life. There it is on the floor beneath your Social Studies bulletin board."

Leona started cackling, her dress gyrating as her shoulders bounced up and down. She said, "Lawd, you just saw your first Charleston Palmetto bug.'

"Mercy, it's like a roach on steroids; that thing's as big as a Goliath beetle. Thank heavens I haven't seen any of those in my apartment, or I would've been freaked out. I think the owners must have had the house sprayed around the perimeter, and maybe inside the apartment when my roommate and I were gone, because I haven't seen any kind of roaches or those hideous monsters. My sister Rhonda told me to get rid of my packin' boxes as soon as I moved in so I didn't bring in roaches from Rock Hill."

"Honey, these Palmetto bugs make Rock Hill roaches look like teeny weeny fire ants. You've been blessed if you haven't seen any Palmetto bugs, yet. They plaque people all over the Lowcountry." She was rubbing her thumb against her index and middle fingers to give a sign for making money. "Sometimes, I wonder if I should've gotten into pest control instead of teachin'. Walkin' around the schools sprayin' bugs instead of writin' lesson plans might make a lot more sense." She started her pleasant cackling again.

Both of them laughed a while and finished their refreshments. Caroline thanked Leona for the drink and then asked her, "Why do you have black and white children in your second grade class, and I have only black children? I thought integration was enforced."

"Caroline, "Do you know how many of us still live in the Charleston area? The racial make-up of your class is based on enrollment here on James Island. Social workers and medical personnel remind these mothers that they must get these babies in school. Some mommas had such a bad experience themselves, or not much of an experience at all, that they don't really care about their babies goin' to school on the busses mostly driven by white men, but they know they have to send 'em or they're gonna get their tails in the fryin' pan. A lot of white folks send their children to private school if they can afford it, especially for first grade. It sure has nothin' to do with you bein' a new white teacher."

"How can I help the people here," she asked earnestly?

"Chile, be yourself and love these chil'run. Show interest in their world, the things they love."

Caroline got up from her seat and enthusiastically told Leona that she needed to get back to her room to get ready for the next day. As she was leaving the room, she turned back and asked, smiling, "Leona, what on earth is a cootuh?'

Leona heehawed and said, "Baby, a cootuh is a turtle."

"Oh, thanks," Caroline left the room grinning. "I can handle a turtle. I need find a thrift shop ASAP to see if I can spot an old aquarium. And Leona, can you start teaching me Gullah?"

"Yez, now gwone girl!" Leona just about laughed herself silly to release the tensions of the day. "I'll check 'round, too, for a habitat for yo cootah. You gonna love it here chile, if you don't burn up." Her shoulders jiggled again as she added, "Charleston feels like the Lawd put us in a steam baf."

Wiping the sweat from her brow, Caroline agreed and then left to go to her own classroom. She spent the next few weeks teaching the Pledge of Allegiance, basic reading readiness, numerals and calculation, and science. She found the world of her students was filled with science, she just needed to give them the words to describe all that they were accustomed to. Not only did they study the animals of the rainforest, they learned about all kinds of cootuhs and such: Red Eared Slider Turtles, Eastern Painted Turtles, Eastern Box Turtles, Spotted Turtles, Snapping Turtles, and Loggerheads, and many more, and they learned about the geographical areas where these different "cootuhs" were found.

She got ideas from J.P., because he'd lived in the area so long, and she had to spend a lot of time each night preparing for the next day, even if he were visiting with her. How was she ever going to have a life with so much to do all of the time? Some days she, too, considered pest control.

CHAPTER 26

SEEIN'

Caroline heard a familiar knock at the door, one she'd heard a million times at Winthrop. After a holler to come in, Emily popped in the door and said, "Helloooo."

"Caroline hugged her and asked, "What brings you to this neck of the woods?"

"Since you don't come to Savannah to see me, I thought I'd step in on you and see how you're doin'."

"Emily, I can hardly bl'eve nine weeks of school have passed already. Next week report cards go out. I've been workin' my tail off," said Caroline breathlessly. "I wish I did have time to come to see you. Heck, I wish I had time to pee without looking at my watch!"

"Caroline, I haven't seen hide nor hair of you since our Labor Day picnic. Do you like this, workin' day 'n night like a mad-dog," asked Emily?

"Well, no, but it has to be done, especially durin' my first year of teachin'."

"I think what you're doin' for the pay you're gettin' is a crime, absolutely a crime."

"Get somebody you know to take that up with the South Carolina state government. We 'mad-dogs' would kiss your feet."

"How are things with J.P.," Emily asked?

"He's doin' great, Emily. His therapist thinks he'll be able to get rid of the canes in a couple of weeks. Miraculously, his strength is almost back to normal. His ace was the fact that he was in great shape before the accident."

"Is he still seein' the tall, willowy, bomb shell therapist?"

"Stop that right now!"

"Ouch, touched a nerve."

"You know that's why I felt so insecure with Joost Van Ness. He talked a lot about tall, thin Dutch girls."

"Caroline, you know that guy really liked you," Emily added trying to console her.

"He did as a friend," Caroline said, a tad sadly. "It was sorta bad for me 'cus I developed an inferiority complex."

"Good Lord, Caroline, there's no need for that," Emily said emphatically. "You know you attract guys like flies to hamburgers on a picnic table."

"What a choice analogy!"

"Well, what do you expect from me," Emily questioned?

"Not much by way of language."

Emily was grinnin' in silence.

"What," Caroline asked, abruptly?

"I heard through the kudzu line that you had lunch with some hunk in the cafeteria at MUSC."

"My granny has nightmares about the crazy stuff you come up with," Caroline stated, with her face all scrunched up and shaking her head from side to side.

Emily responded bewilderedly, "Your granny doesn't even know me. She's only seen me one time."

Caroline tossed her head back, laughing and said without detail, "Premonition!"

"So, was it true or rumor?"

"That was just the lead physical therapist. He wanted to see the squirrels."

"What is blazes are you talkin' 'bout?"

"I was havin' lunch, and lookin' outside to see the squirrels dancin' on the tree branches. The guy asked me if he could join me to look at the squirrels. That's all sister, and that was a long time ago."

"So, no need to worry 'bout you and J.P.?"

"You need to quit being goofy, Emily. There never was any reason to worry 'bout us. We've gone through too much and come so far together, no one should wonder."

"Okay, I'll give it a rest," said Emily, sheepishly.

Caroline changed the subject and told her that the only good thing about having to do report cards and holding parent conferences was that she had a teacher work day and was going out to lunch with her new friend at work, Leona. They'd planned to go to East Bay Trading because the food was great and prompt service could be guaranteed. Emily ended up staying a couple of hours, but Caroline was glad to see her. Her report cards were completed, and she felt that she needed some time to sit and gossip.

"J.P. today is your big day to rid yourself of these cumbersome Lofstrand canes," said Amanda encouragingly. "I'm going to refer you to a private physical therapist in Summerville or here in town if you wish, since I must dismiss you from our program. The new therapist will evaluate your strength, gait, flexibility, posture, and balance. Of course your treatment plan will be different than what you had here because your needs are different now."

"Everything about therapy will be different. Amanda, you've been a great therapist. I'll never forget you going out to buy party horns for my first attempt on the bars. I can't say that I'll miss coming to the hospital, but I'll miss the people I met here. I'll have to come back to visit you all."

"Darlin' that's: visit y'all served up with a side of grits," Amanda said with that hypnotic smile of hers. "Whatcha gonna do tomorrow, your first day downtown without the canes?"

"Oh, I'll definitely go out to eat with friends for lunch. I've hated trying to maneuver in tight fitting places with those bulky canes. It will be so nice to be seated in a restaurant like a normal person with no one staring at you as if you shouldn't be there."

"That sounds like a good plan to me. Go enjoy yourself. What about Caroline? I guess she's kinda stuck at her school all day."

"As a matter of fact, she has a teacher work day. Her friend from work invited her to go to lunch. I surely don't want to intrude on a hen party."

"No, it's not a good idea to do that. You'd be bored to tears with the school gossip, and you need a better day than that."

※

On Friday, Leona said excitedly, as she drove toward East Bay, "Caroline, I've been waitin' a long time to go to this restaurant for lunch. You know chile, I was always strapped for money when I worked at the grocery store, workin' just barely 'bove minimum wage. You can get benefits, but the pay is low, and you have to work there forever to get any kinda raise.

"Leona, I really admire you for goin' back to school to get your degree. Not many people do that or can do that."

"The good Lawd has a plan for your life, and you gotta go when you get the call," said Leona with conviction.

"I bl'eve that, too. My momma instilled that in me."

"She's a good momma then."

They found parking and started to enter the restaurant with Caroline leading the way. She opened the big heavy door and stopped suddenly. She thought she saw J.P. on the other side of the large room. His back was toward her. It looked as if someone was standing in front of him. As he was turning around, Caroline saw Anne McMahan standing there with her new baby in her arms, and his gaze met hers.

At that moment, Caroline felt like her heart had been yanked out of her chest, and she knew that her recurring dream of the young woman holding a baby was a portent of this horrible scene of J.P. and Anne. What was he doing here with her, just the two of them? Suddenly, she felt that she couldn't breathe, and the room was closing in on her, squeezing the life out of her. She turned around and Leona knew, instinctively, that Caroline was mortified and that it probably had something to do with her man. She took Caroline by the arm and got her out of the restaurant as fast as she could. Before they reached the car, Caroline wept. She got into the car and put her head down between her knees, feeling light headed.

She had a flashback of an image of the letter she'd received at Winthrop, the anonymous one. The image was burning in her mind, and she tried to block it out. She'd torn the letter up immediately after reading it and had never thought of the mentioned names again, Anne's name, Anne and Clay. Oh Jesus, how could she have failed to remember the names after all this time, after meeting them? She really loved J.P. when she received the letter and didn't want to reject him for his past mistakes. It was Anne who'd snubbed her at the oyster roast, on her first visit to Summerville, when she didn't even know the relationships between J.P., Clay, and Anne. That's why Anne was more than a b...otch the day that she and Rhonda went to see the apartment, and that's why Butch tried so desperately to expose Anne as the snake that she was; she's always been after J.P. She's a conniving, manipulator from a rich and powerful family. She hung on to Clay to have the promise of wealth and prestige, the wife of a lawyer; it was expected of her. How dare she show up here in public with my boyfriend, using her precious baby as a pawn? Caroline felt like going back in the restaurant and jerking the hair out of her head, but she wasn't a fighter, at least not physically.

Leona was patting Caroline's back, trying to get her to settle down. She said, "Baby, I don't know exactly what this situation is all about, but I know you're hurt real bad by your man. I'm gonna get you away from this parking spot 'fore any more drama gets stirred up out 'eah?"

As they drove away from the parking area, Leona, having gotten a glimpse of the J.P. with a woman and baby inside, saw him slowly come out of the door of the restaurant, alone, with a terrified expression. Caroline did not see him, and Leona said nothing about seeing him. It wasn't the time to tell her grieving friend. They drove further down East Bay and parked in a space at the Battery. She let Caroline cry for a while, but then she told her that she had to get it together because neither of them could afford to lose their jobs.

CHAPTER 27
SHOCKIN'

As he walked away from the restrooms, Clay saw Anne standing next to their table in the restaurant, holding the baby. But J.P. was gone.

"What happened, Anne," Clay asked, bewilderedly?

"I really don't know, but its par for the course for J.P. We were ready to leave the table and walk to the entrance to wait for you. All of the sudden, J.P. said he was sorry but he had to go. Something urgent had come up. He walked out the door as fast as he was able to, and left me standin' here all alone. His behavior was extremely odd, to say the least. I know how close you two were at Clemson, but sometimes I wanna say we should stay away from him. He doesn't seem all that enthused to see us anyway." She had to stop, because she was lying to Clay, when she wanted to see J.P. any way that she could, even platonically.

By the time they were coming out of the restaurant, J.P. was driving away. He drove toward White Points Garden, but turned on a side street before he got there, assuming that she and her friend might be there. He was getting more rational at this point and realized that running after after Caroline when she was upset would only add fuel to the fire. He was finished at work for the day and decided to do what he always wanted to do when he was down, go to the beach and maybe have a few beers. He wound his way back to East Bay, took a left, and headed toward the bridge. Isle of Palms would be the choice of beaches for today. The weather was a little breezy, but he had his windbreaker. His ancient canvas deck shoes were in the back of the car, so he got them out and put them on. He rolled his dress pants up a cuff, and headed toward the time worn boardwalk. As he started to walk on the beach, it seemed to be more difficult than he thought it would be on this first day without the canes, trying to walk across the dry sand. He felt fearful about his relationship with Caroline. How could such a misunderstanding happen just weeks before he planned to propose to her? He could see how badly she could be hurt, how it appeared to her, back at the restaurant. Something kept standing in the way of a proposal both times he'd planned to make it happen? What kind of force was stopping that?

He walked until he was feeling completely exhausted, and he collapsed at the base of the sand dune. Foam frothed waves rolled in toward the shore as he sat there and looked out across the ocean, and the cries of the sea birds soothed his spirit, and the boats in the distance kept inching along, sort of like his life, one tiny increment at a time.

After admonishing Caroline to try to calm down before they had to go back to work, Leona gave her a few more minutes before she said anything. She started up her car and said, "We're goin' to the drug store to get some eye drops for your red eyes. Then we're stoppin' by to get some cheeseburgers and fries to take back to school. I know you may not feel like eatin' anythin' now, but you may need to eat later. When we get back, you're comin' into my room to work on your permanent records, 'eah. I heard you say earlier that you didn't have many responses to confirm parent conferences this afternoon."

They rode in silence to the pharmacy, and Leona went in to get the eye drops. It always seemed like when a new hurt bombarded her, Caroline felt the old hurts so deeply again, missing her dear sweet daddy to comfort her. The hole in her heart felt like it was getting larger by the minute. She tried hard to start suppressing her emotions. She'd spent many years doing that, so not another soul knew how she'd grieved all of her life. There'd been no one who really knew how those feelings affected her but Joost Van Ness; he knew more of the details than anyone outside of her family. And Lord knows where he'd be after all these months of non-communication, in grad school working on his MBA, and by now planning to go back to Spain and marry some rich girl and live the big life. She knew how to contact him via his brother living in the states, at least she knew his brother's name and the city he lived in, but it would be ludicrous to do that. What was she doing even thinking about him right now? Why did she always think of him when the times got tough? Had she messed up the one real chance she had to be happy, maybe with him? She felt so confused, so hurt, so insane. She had to stop this and get it together to go back to work in a few minutes. She could do what was required of her, she always had. She could! She had to!

⚊⊹ ⊹⚊

J.P. looked at the rolling Atlantic for as long as he could. He felt numb, not physically numb although his back was beginning to ache, but he was emotionally drained. His heart ached for the pain that he'd unwittingly caused Caroline. He should have told her about the luncheon plans with Clay and Anne, to see their new baby. He felt like a butt for keeping something like that from her, but he rationalized that she was probably going to have to settle for burgers or chicken from some place near her school, and he didn't want her to feel sad that she couldn't have lunch in a nice restaurant with him.

J.P. left the beach but drove around for a while. He went down to Sullivan's Island and had a couple of beers and sat and thought some more. In his anguish, he wondered if Anne had anything to do with the fact that Caroline had chosen East Bay Trading for lunch. She certainly knew when Caroline would have a work day release for lunch, and she knew which other teacher might be willing to help. He began seething, angry at the thought of it.

Charleston was crawling with florists, so he went back downtown to a florist on King Street. He wasn't quite sure what to buy her and was oblivious as to what to write on the card. He walked down King Street until he began to feel tired and turned around toward the florist. It had to be two dozen coral colored roses, her favorite rose. But what would he write on the card? In retrospect, if he mentioned the luncheon appointment with Clay and Anne, this mess would never have occurred, and Caroline's feelings would have been spared. She would've known that he wanted her there with him even though she might not have been able to make it.

Maybe he needed to talk to Butch before he sent the flowers. Good ol' Butch was always level headed, and he was the closest of friends with Caroline.

⥤⥢

Caroline filled her reddened eyes with drops. She'd wiped her nose so many times using napkins and anything else she could find in Leona's car, she looked red and chapped beneath her nostrils. She had a powder compact in her back pack, so she powdered her face; it didn't help much. When she got back to school, she'd find a tissue, and then do a lot of fake sneezing when she had to see others in the hallways or meet with parents for conferences. She was hoping that the rest of the parents wouldn't show up since they'd never responded to her invitation, and she could do a home visit on another afternoon when she no longer looked like a crybaby. She was not going to continue to be a blubbering schoolgirl about this. She hoped that J.P. wouldn't even contact her for a while to give it a rest and let her calm down and cool off. She had an important job to do, her teaching was crucial for her little first graders. Furthermore, she wasn't married to J.P. nor engaged to him. So there was no need to pitch some kind of hissy fit or drown in a pit of despair. She was in Charleston now, and she could be as strong as Scarlett O'Hara, with indefatigable spirit, when Rhett left her standing on the steps of her mansion in Atlanta. Couldn't she?

Butch cringed when J.P. told him what had happened at East Bay Trading. He leaned his head back and sighed deeply. He said, "Caroline's been through so much lately, and you, too. I feel badly for both of y'all. As far as I'm concerned, Anne creates drama wherever she goes. I wouldn't put it past her to have stirred up this hornet's nest. What if she set y'all up, makin' such a mess of things?"

"She hasn't been very loyal in the past, but I don't know if she'd go that far. I thought about it, though. Clay's the one who called me and wanted us all to have lunch together so I could see their new baby. It's unfortunate that he was in the restroom when Caroline walked in."

"Well, I never mentioned this to you while you were in the hospital, and I didn't think it was the time nor place to tell you, 'till now."

"What is it, Butch?"

"When Caroline, Rhonda, and I went to see the apartment for the first time, Anne was true to form. She was as sarcastic and rude as she ever has been and right there before Clay and Tara."

"What did she say?"

"She used her familiar condescendin' tone with Caroline and Rhonda, like they were nothin' more than poor white trash. She rubbed it in that she grew up on the ritzy street in Greenville where old money is passed down from generation to generation, McDaniel Avenue. She also made it sound like she and Clay were doing charity work by turnin' over that great apartment, which she trivialized. She pumped herself up, rubbin' it in that her daddy was takin' care of everything to make life more comfortable for her before the baby arrived. She was unwittingly embarrassin' herself and humiliatin' her own husband."

"I know Clay had to maintain a certain social image, and he must have let his hormones take over his brains, when he married her. I can see it; she's beautiful and convincin' when she wants something," acknowledged J.P.

"She was so raw to them that day I couldn't handle it any more so I stepped right in the middle of it. I apologized to Clay before I gave her a little taste of what she'd dished out."

"I can imagine how that went down!"

"Man, if I were you I think I'd talk to Clay. Tell him what happened with Caroline; he prob'ly has no idea. He knows how Anne is, but there's no tellin' what she said to him 'bout you that day. It's all about her self-preoccupation, her arrogance."

"It may be hard for me to talk to Clay about this kind of stuff, you know, I was a little bit close to the situation back at Clemson when the whole attitude thing started."

"Are you kiddin'? She's had that terrible attitude her whole life. Remember, I met her 'fore you ever came down from Jersey. Her wonderful daddy spoiled her, still does, and her mother prob'ly kept reminding her that she was better than anyone else, except maybe her sister."

Tumultuous laughter filled the room.

"If you feel that uncomfortable," Butch said, supportively, "I'll give him a call to set up a little gathering with all three of us at one of the sports bars."

"That would make it easier for me. I don't want to lose my friendship with him; we go way back, back before Anne got in the way of things."

⬛⬛ ⬛⬛

After work, Leona invited Caroline to come home with her for dinner to offer more support. She said, "Honey chile, you wanna go to my house, I'm makin' some jollif rice, and it's gonna be some good eatin'?"

"Thank you, Leona, you're so sweet to me, but I think it might be best to go on home this afternoon." Caroline knew that if she went there'd be whining and crying because she already realized that Leona was a good listener.

"Are you sure," Leona asked again?

Trying to be strong and not be a crybaby at work, much too dangerous to do that, Caroline responded, "I'll go home and take a nice, hot bubble bath, read a book, or watch a movie. I've 'bout had my fill of men."

"I don't blame you there. I had my fill 'bout eight year ago. That's when I come to realize that grocery store chain wasn't gonna take care of me and neither was my lazy man. So I started back to school. But baby, you just might have a good un, after all, and some she devil is tryin' to screw it up fer y'all. I could smell a she devil when I walked into dat restaurant. Oh heck, it was probl'y full uh she devils." She threw up her hands as if she was releasing negative energy, and then she shook her head side to side vigorously and laughed heartily.

As miserable as she was, a fit of giggles flooded over Caroline, and she had to chuckle out loud to get rid of some of her anxiety.

Leona gave Caroline a little slap on the back and said, "Atta girl, let go of some of dat misry, honey. Ain't no good to hold all dat mess inside of you, 'eah?"

Leona took a little piece of paper from her scrap box. She wrote down her home phone number and handed it to Caroline.

Then she said to her, "You call me tonight if you wanna talk, and if you get up tomorrow feeling good and hongry, you call. I'll make you some ham and eggs with a side of my famous cheese grits. I can even top it off with some fresh hot biscuits, served up with homemade jam and butter oozing outta 'em and a cup of piping hot coffee." With emphasis, she added, "Glory to Jesus, I'll make you a brefast you ain't seen in all of Char...ston." She gave no thought to grammar and diction; she spoke to Caroline from her heart.

"Leona, you are too sweet to me. I'm feeling so bad because I feel like I ruined your day off, lunch away from the school," Caroline said.

"Baby, you don't think another thing 'bout dat. That weren't none of yo fault. We can try it again in only 45 days. You know that's how we survive in our business, counting the quarters of the school year," she said and chuckled again.

"Leona, I love what I'm doing with the children, but when other circumstances start to weigh on me, the stress of teaching becomes huge. Today, I wonder if I can handle it." She had tears in her eyes but managed not to start a major boo hooing session.

"Lawd Caroline, you made it this far. Have the most faith you can muster up, and things will be good again. Please call me. We black folks in Char...ston wanna love you and feed you till you feels like you is gonna pop. Sorry that ain't correct English 'but we is 'bout to leave this joint, 'eah? I'll catch you later sweet chile."

"Don't worry 'bout me, I'll be okay. Thank God it is Friday." Caroline doubted what she'd said to her friend, but it seemed to be an appropriate way to end the conversation.

CHAPTER 28

HEARIN'

Clay met Butch and J.P. after work on Friday in a bar in the city. Fortunately, Clay was the one to bring up the incident that occurred in the restaurant. He was as bewildered as Anne had seemed to be about J.P.'s sudden disappearance that day.

Clay asked J.P., "Man, did anything major happen last week when Anne and I were havin' lunch with you? You vanished, and we haven't heard a word from you."

Butch was sitting with a silent stare, looking intently at the other customers as he drank his dark beer, heartily.

J.P. responded, "Actually, it was a very awkward situation. Of course, you'd gone to the head, so Anne and I stood to free up the table and planned to wait for you near the entrance. As I turned around, I spotted Caroline at the door. She had this very disturbed look on her face; then, she said something to her teacher friend and they turned and walked out the door. I told Anne that I had to go, but I didn't say that I was going to try to catch up with Caroline in the parking lot before she left. Anne probably didn't even see Caroline, so I'm sure I confused her."

"Oh, livin' with Anne's insane jealousy, I can imagine how that might have been a problem with Caroline," said Clay kindly. "I don't think Anne saw Caroline either or she would have understood why you left so abruptly."

Butch interjected, "I think Caroline has had too many tough blows since she came to Charleston; it was somethin' she couldn't understand because she wasn't aware of the arrangements. She's still young."

"Have you been able to tell Caroline that all three of us were in the restaurant together," Clay asked J.P.?

"No, she hasn't answered my calls for the past week."

"Ooh, it did bother her, badly," Clay exclaimed! "Would you want me to try to give her a call to explain that we all had lunch together, or do you think that would embarrass her?"

J.P. said, "I know her answering machine is going to be on because she's been screening my calls, so if she doesn't answer your call you could at least leave a message. But buddy, do me a favor don't mention any of this to Anne. Even when we get it ironed out, it will be embarrassing for Caroline."

"No problem, I'll take care of it tomorrow, from the office," Clay said. "I'm terribly sorry that all this has happened. I hope y'all can get things straightened out. Anne has no idea we're having this little discussion. If she asks me 'bout you, I'll play dumb." He raised his mug to cheer and said, "Here's to letting sleepin' dawgs lie."

Their conversation switched to a more appropriate exchange with Butch. He seemed especially down and J.P. couldn't figure out what was eating at him. Butch was basically the opposite type personality from J.P., who was very outgoing and carefree. He was very personable, but Butch gave a lot of serious consideration to everything he did. J.P. figured he was in one of his deep thought type moods even though he was trying to converse with them. After a few more beers and some butt kicking, spicy Buffalo wings, they decided to call it an early evening so Clay could get home to help Anne with the baby before World War Three ensued.

J.P. decided to give it a rest with Caroline, no more messages from him for a while, to give her time to digest the word from Clay. He didn't want to suffocate her, to make her feel that he was trying to control or manipulate her in any way.

The next Friday, when J.P. and Butch got off work early and had a couple of beers, Butch suggested that they go down to Caroline's apartment together. They drove by the area where she parked her car. When they saw her car and knew that she was at home, they went back down to King Street to the florist to get a peace offering. Luckily, they had her favorite coral colored roses, and J.P. splurged for two dozen.

Within the hour they were back at Caroline's apartment, ringing the doorbell. Hearing the bell, she peeked out through the peephole and could see Butch. J.P. was standing to the far right of him, like a florist's delivery boy.

She opened the door just as she was, wearing a pair of droopy, gray jersey, lounging pants, a tattered Clemson T-shirt that J.P. had given her, and aged pink fuzzy slippers. Her hair was pulled up in the back with a giant clip, but part of her hair had fallen out of the clip. Her makeup had already been removed for the day, but she had a few smudges of mascara under her eyes. She didn't even seem self-conscious about her appearance, which was highly unusual for her.

She was a bit reserved but most hospitable and invited them in, looking at J.P. with an unmistakable longing. Of course, she was hoping that all of this mess with Anne was truly a dreadful misunderstanding. She'd believed Clay when he'd called and left a message. He certainly would've had no cause to be untruthful with her; for goodness sakes, Anne was his wife.

Caroline had been watching the news on WCSC when she heard the doorbell ring, so the TV was still on. She indicated that Butch and J.P. were welcomed to the sofa, while she graciously accepted the flowers and commented on how beautiful they were. She took the time to take in their delightful fragrance as she placed the vase of flowers on the small round table in the corner of the living room.

Not knowing exactly what to say next, she turned around and said, "Golly gee, what brings y'all down this way, other than to bring me such a lovely bouquet of my favorite roses?" She looked straight at J.P. and continued. "I'm so glad y'all came. I'm afraid I look very, very relaxed, but TGIF, thank God it's Friday." She spoke rapidly because she was nervous. Her smile had broken into laughter as she took a seat in the drab olive green, velvet chair, the upholstery nearly threadbare and the piping already frayed.

Caroline stopped laughing and turned her head toward the television when she heard the news anchorman, Jim Allen:

Don Harbin was on the scene within minutes of the impact somewhere near the end of the Cooper River Bridge/Mount Pleasant side. Here's Harold Simmons live with details:

Traffic has reopened here just off the Cooper River Bridge in Mount Pleasant. The right lane was closed for the past couple of hours. Investigators have cleared the scene about forty minutes ago. The nature of any injuries is not known at this time and police will not speculate. But we did talk to some witnesses who were here just seconds after they saw the dreadful impact. One person told us they believe that a female was actually ejected from a white Chevrolet Monte Carlo. Another witness said there was a baby involved. It appears that the vehicle veered right at high velocity and struck a cement barrier about fifty feet from the main thoroughfare to Mount Pleasant. We'll get back with you as soon as we have more details, Don.

Caroline got a cold chill running up her spine and felt like she was going to faint, slumping back into her chair. She was having a flashback of her recurring dream of the young woman holding a little baby in her arms.

J.P. was watching her intently as she turned toward him. Her face was as white as a sheet, as if she'd seen an apparition. Her lips were slightly parted, she was breathing deeply, and she broke out in a cold sweat. At that point Butch saw how she looked, too, and ran into the kitchen to find a glass to fill with water. He found a black coffee mug in the dish drainer and partially filled it, almost running back into the living room with the water, water sloshing out of the mug onto the worn planks of the aged floor. With J.P. giving her a drink, Butch then scooted off to the bathroom, having remembered that Caroline once told him that she liked to have a cool cloth on her forehead if she wasn't feeling well.

It was several minutes before she could say anything. Then she said in a terrified voice, "Don't y'all know that Anne drives a white Monte Carlo? I have a bad feelin' about this y'all." She didn't want to tell them about her flashback, her vision. "I'm not crazy, but I know something bad has happened. Y'all know I'm not fond of Anne, but I wouldn't want anything bad to happen to her and her baby. I do think a lot of Clay, and I know both of y'all feel the same way. If I get cleaned up, maybe we should all go down to MUSC just in case it was Anne who was involved in that terrible accident. There'll be no harm done if it wasn't her."

J.P. said, "Caroline, it does sound a little crazy, but I'm going to trust your instincts on this one. What do you think, Butch?"

"Well, since it did happen in Mount Pleasant and it was a white Monte Carlo like she drives, we better go."

"Okay, give me a minute and I'll look more presentable, don't want to embarrass y'all," said Caroline.

Caroline scrubbed her face again to remove the mascara from beneath her eyes, slathered on and smoothed some lotion on her face. Under the circumstances, she didn't bother to apply fresh mascara or blush. She changed into a pair of soft tan corduroy pants and a black v-necked sweater. Her hair was a mess and there was nothing more she could do but brush it well and pull it back up with the large hair clip. She pulled on comfortable black trouser socks and slipped her feet into her black leather clogs. She was ready to go.

The three of them found themselves in the ER waiting room with all types of people, both sick and well. Some were coughing, hacking, and wheezing like they nearly had pneumonia. Others were doubling over with abdominal pain. One old man had his right arm in a soiled makeshift sling, obviously broken, moaning as he moved his thin frail body in the uncomfortable chair. These people could've had their illnesses or injuries taken care of in a doctor's office, possibly, but probably didn't have the financial resources to do so. They end up in the ER because they're in pain and the hospital doesn't turn them away. It seemed to Caroline that the healthcare system was so screwed up. *Why didn't they have more 24 hour clinics set up to service these people, so only the serious emergency patients came to the overcrowded hospitals?*

Butch went to speak to one of the receptionists, to find out if Anne was in the ER. After what seemed like an eternity, he turned around toward Caroline and J.P. with a disheartened look on his face.

Caroline was first to ask, "What is it? Are Anne and the baby here?" She knew the answer before Butch confirmed it.

"They are, your insight was correct, unfortunately," reported Butch, wearily. "They're both here."

J.P. was stunned, holding Caroline's arm as her body dropped into the chair in the ER waiting room. She began to weep about the sheer terror of it all. An accident that had traffic backed up for two hours was no mere fender bender. Caroline was afraid for Anne and the baby, for she was the one who had dealt with the nightmares, visions, portends...the appalling recurrent images of a young woman holding a baby. *Were they deceased in those images, spirits from immortality?* For the past week, she'd thought the dreams were foreknowledge of seeing J.P. and Anne in the restaurant. Now, knowing that scene was a misapprehension, she feared that her perceptions were meant for this situation: she already knew the outcome of a horrible accident. She felt faint and asked J.P. if he would see if he could find her a cup of water.

Minutes later J.P. walked back up with a cone shaped paper cup of water. As Caroline drank, Butch pulled J.P., aside out of earshot.

Butch said with concern, "She sure is taking this hard."

"Think of her intuitiveness to get us down here without even a phone call from Clay," commented J.P. "I think she already knows what you and I suspect will happen. We need to get her out of here as soon as possible. There's nothing we can do here."

"I agree with you whole heartedly. Let's see if we can get her to leave, and we'll stay with her for as long as she wants us to. If something tragic has happened it may be quite some time before we hear anything since we're not part of the family."

"I hope she wants us to stay with her, but I won't push her in any way. You were so right when you said she'd been through enough since she came to Charleston."

Butch had driven to the hospital, and as they left the parking area he asked Caroline if she wanted to go somewhere to get coffee or dinner, if she felt like eating. They ended up having coffee with Kirshwasser, and chocolate cake, with Caroline taking only a few tiny bites of J.P.'s slice of cake. Having left Caroline's apartment around six P.M., they all had warm jackets in the car. The wet cold had not come to Charleston, yet, so it was still pleasant to walk outside after dark, wearing jackets. They drove down to White Points and took a little stroll on the Battery. All three of them were all talked out about the accident, Anne and the baby, the hospital, and poor Clay; it wasn't going to change a thing by talking about it over and over.

The harbor beyond them was illuminated with lights from incoming ships in the distance. Cool breezes blew the loose strands of Caroline's hair. Her hands felt chilled enough to fumble for the pockets of her tan corduroy jacket. She looked toward J.P. and saw that he was looking at her. The three of them were silently standing there, listening to the susurration of the gentle waves moving against the sea wall. Then she looked back out across the water, suddenly feeling very badly that she'd ever doubted J.P.

The funeral was to be held in Greenville at Mackey Mortuary, the interment in the burial plots belonging to Anne's family at Greenville Memorial Gardens, not far from the home on McDaniel Avenue, where Anne had grown up. Both the McMahan's and her family wanted only the immediate and extended family to attend. It seemed peculiar, but there were so many friends, things would have gotten out of hand with droves of sympathizers, draining all those who were grieving so terribly for the loss of two young lives.

The entire situation seemed surreal to Caroline. It was as if she'd awakened from the last horrible vision of the young woman holding a baby, with sweaty palms and a sick feeling in her stomach, a nightmare that had been recurring now for almost as long as she'd known J.P. She wondered if the nightmare was finally over, an end to the portentous repetitive dream. Lord, she hoped so as she stood there shivering and feeling very alone in her apartment.

CHAPTER 29

ANTICIPATIN'

Thanksgiving came and went, as fast as a snowstorm in the next day's sunlight. Caroline and J.P. had gone back to the Upstate for the holiday. Again, food was plentiful, and he wasn't shy about stuffing himself silly, just like he'd done on the first exposure a year before. After the gut busting meal, they stayed one night in Greenville before returning to the Lowcounty.

Only a few weeks of school were left between Thanksgiving and Christmas holidays for Caroline. She'd taught her little first graders the entire Pledge of Allegiance so that they approximated Standard English when reciting it. As well as the other required subjects, the children had developed a great love for writing poetry, group style on chart paper. Their poems, along with darling little illustrations, were attractively displayed in many areas of the school, and the emerging writers showed a great deal of pride in their work.

Plans were made for Caroline to go to Jersey with Chris and J.P. for Christmas holidays, but they'd be back in Charleston to celebrate New Year's Eve with Butch. Although she was tired from teaching and emotionally drained from the tragic death of Anne and the baby, she was excited that she would see things that she didn't have a chance to see on her first trip to NYC, and she needed a chance to get out of Charleston. She was not really a "home body" kind of girl, and the confines of her tiny city apartment were making her a tad claustrophobic.

This time around, Caroline was much better prepared to deal with Mrs. Andersen's questions. After all, she'd been with J.P. during most of his recovery from the fall and had remained loyal to him even in the most difficult of circumstances; that fact should have earned her a few points with his mom.

If she could steer the conversation in the direction of J.P.'s accident or her teaching career, she'd have plenty of answers to Mrs. Andersen's incessant questions; the rest of it would have to come from J.P., to fill in the gaps when a lull in the dialogue occurred, that awkward silence.

Even though there was eagerness to see Manhattan again, the trip seemed longer this time to Caroline. She felt she'd been much more intimate with J.P over the past months and found it harder for them to communicate in their usual fashion with Chris being in the car, too. And she didn't want to be rehashing all of the horrible events of the past year, which Chris tended to go on and on about like a mass of local news reports on the same subject. They were traveling on Interstate 95, and Caroline found it to be an insipidly boring route, with no familiar landmarks to discuss. She definitely didn't want to talk to J.P. about teaching because she wanted to feel as far away from that responsibility as possible, to give herself a mental recess from the daily stresses of dealing with her demanding career. It wasn't that she didn't love what she was doing, love her students dearly, but enough was enough! She needed to relax, take a real break, and recharge her batteries. She just wasn't sure how to go about it, cooped up in a pee-wee Japanese import for hours on end.

On this trip, they began very early, before the crack of dawn, and would arrive late in the evening, hoping to avoid the early morning traffic jams in Jersey, with truckers left and right. After the taxing twelve hour drive, with only three major stops, constantly wedged between eighteen wheelers like an infant warthog in the middle of a wildebeest stampede, they hit the Garden State Parkway. With nice music in the background, Caroline sat silently with her eyes closed trying to ignore the disturbing rush around her, reflecting on the year between her two visits up north. So much had transpired, and she'd grown from a college girl into a young adult. She felt she was now J.P.'s equal in terms of maturity, and she instinctively knew exactly where their serious relationship was headed, even though J.P. had not officially popped the question. Furthermore, she knew how she'd respond to him, once he finally got the nerve to ask. She was curious about what venue he'd select for such an important life event, how it would all come about, and wondered if he'd be cool and collected or nervous. She didn't think she'd be nervous or shy at all. She'd known for some time what she really wanted despite all of the drama that had taken place during their courtship.

The first day back in Jersey was similar to their arrival the Christmas before, with everything meticulously organized by Mrs. Andersen to receive and accommodate them. Again, sitting down over a lovely brunch, the queen bee began her lengthy update with the local happenings. Then, the barrage of questions gushed forth, largely directed at Caroline. Somehow, she reacted to the verbal onslaught of the overpowering female as if she, herself, were on autopilot, mechanically answering when inundated with questions, but feeling no emotional response, certainly no anxiety. She was sure that she was in love with this Yankee woman's son, and neither hell nor high water was going to come between the two of them, not even the irritation of nosy questions or Mrs. Andersen's air of superiority that seemed to continue to linger regardless of time or circumstance.

Thank God, within a couple of hours J.P. and Caroline were on their way to Manhattan. Chris was meeting a group of old friends at a pub in Hoboken, so Caroline and J.P. would have a day to themselves in the city. Secretly, she wondered if the arrangement had been set up at J.P.'s request. If not, she preferred to think of it as taking place this way and never know anything to the contrary.

As they passed the toll booths to enter the Lincoln tunnel, she felt no fear this time, yet when they exited the tunnel, she felt the same sense of awe at the magnitude of the skyscrapers at every turn. And it was far more than what she was visually soaking in; it was that overwhelming sense of disbelief, the question that she had turned over in her mind, time and time again when she asked herself, *"Is all of this real? Am I really here in NYC with a man who truly loves me?"* She couldn't imagine any more shock than she would experience if J.P. were a foreigner and she were revisiting his country. By comparison, NYC was a world away from all that she'd known living in South Carolina. It was dirty, busy, and massive, yet it was teeming with life and once again stirred loads of excitement within her. No, she could never live here, but it was vastly interesting to be a visitor to this fascinating city of millions of inhabitants on this small plot of land; she loved the amalgamation of cultures creating a constantly changing group called New Yorkers.

The air was extremely cold, but fortunately, the sun was shining high above the gargantuan edifices, and it was not a blustery, windy kind of day. Caroline's new down filled jacket proved to be much more comfortable for city walking than the heavy woolen overcoat she'd worn on her first visit. J.P. seemed to handle cold much better than she did; perhaps that was due to the fact that he'd spent most of his life facing bitterly cold winters.

Parking near Port Authority, they took the blue line train that runs up and down the western border of Central Park and then walked a little more than a mile to Rockefeller Center. The smell of hot pretzels wafted toward them and the sight of them tantalized Caroline. She resisted but was ready for hot chocolate to warm up a bit.

The wind began to blow slightly causing the colorful United Nation's flags to dance in the breeze. Standing there sipping hot chocolate, they looked toward the mammoth Christmas tree behind the bronze gilded statue of Prometheus, ice skaters floating around in a circle. It was a beautiful sight to her.

"I wanted you to get a look at this before the sun goes down, but we'll be coming back here in a few hours to see it all lighted. It'll be really awesome then," said J.P. with the enthusiasm of a young lad.

"Oh, great! I bet it's a stunning view to see at night," she contributed, with fervor.

"Now, I'm planning to take you to FAO Schwartz. Do you know anything about it?"

She responded proudly, "Yeah! It's one grandiose toy store, right?" He nodded to affirm. "That'll be neat! Doesn't it have some giant floor piano? Seems like I saw it on T.V., last Christmas."

"Yeah, that's it, and real-life toy soldiers. Did you know it's the oldest toy store in America," he asked, using his intellectual, historian tone of voice?

"No, I didn't know that. Thanks for enlightening me," she said with her honey colored eyes twinkling and sporting her cutie pie grin, knowing it made him melt when she looked at him that way.

"We could spend hours in that store looking at all kinds of fascinating toys."

"Yeah, yeah," she responded, while secretly thinking that she'd hoped for a more romantic day with him in the city than spending hours in a toy store. "You darn tootin', we'll have a good time," she finally managed to spew out, cheerily.

FAO Schwartz proved to be interesting to her, and they had a load of fun spotting classic toys that they'd played with as kids, some modified to accommodate the modern market. As they strolled past the doll section, he chuckled at her comment, "Barbie's butt shoulda been filled full of buckshot. Lord, that toy has destroyed the self-esteem of so many young girls...caused life-long inferiority complexes."

"So, how many guys do you really see built like G.I. Joe? We simply don't give a rip," he admitted.

"True, y'all don't. We shouldn't give a rip-roaring snot about Barbie, either." They both cackled at her comment.

As they neared the end of their time in the toy store, J.P. made a suggestion, "I'd like to take you to this cool Ukrainian restaurant called Veselka. It's famous for incredible borscht, and the pierogis are out of this world. I think you'd enjoy having lunch there today. Does that sound okay with you?"

"Sounds fine, but I don't have a clue what per...go...ies... are." She knew from the smile on his face, that she'd mispronounced pirogues, so she tried once again only to come up with per..roadies and finally a "whatever."

"Pirogues are kind of a soft pie, you could say, filled with meat, potatoes, onions and cheese; that kind of stuff. They're not sweet pies."

"Oh, okay. Never had borscht either, but I've heard of it. You know, we don't have that many ethnic restaurants in South Carolina. At least, not like y'all have up here."

"I know," he said, understandingly. He never made her feel embarrassed when he'd had exposure to something that she'd not experienced. He wanted to share with her the kind of things he'd been fortunate enough to learn about and liked her open-mindedness and curiosity.

They took the subway to the East Village and leisurely wandered in and out of art galleries before arriving at Veselka. Once seated, J.P. ordered a bottle of wine to warm them from the chill of the cool air on the city streets and to help Caroline relax after taking the subway filled with people from all walks of life who seemed stone-faced to her friendly, mannerisms. She'd made no comments about the people in the subway, but he'd felt some tension as she'd squeezed his hand while they rode.

As they were chatting at the table, J.P. looked toward the back of the restaurant and exclaimed, "I'll be gobsmacked, there's my old pal Russell sitting over there!"

"Gobsmacked," Caroline queried with an inquisitive look?

"Yeah, means astonished, think you guys say flabbergasted down south, or when your Granny says, 'Don't that just blow yer dress out,' she's gobsmacked. My grandma used to say gobsmacked all the time."

"So which one is Russell," she asked, craning to see beyond other patrons, but still giggling about his imitation of her granny?

"Oh, he's the cop sitting over there near the bar. He's been a New York cop for eight years or so. I'd love to introduce him; do you mind?"

"Of course not."

"Okay, hang on a second, sip some wine while I go speak to him, and I'll get him over here to our table in a couple of minutes." He seemed so proud of her and eager for his friend to see his beautiful gal from Carolina.

She sat there looking out the window at passersby, savoring the flavor of the wine, and munching on a slice of mouthwatering, hot bread. Unavoidably, she listened to the restaurant staff calling out to one another in their European dialect when suddenly an image of Joost danced across her consciousness. She felt flushed, guilt ridden and confused at the same time. So, as quickly as the thought of him had come to mind, she tried desperately to dismiss the musing and refocus upon J.P., to keep her head together. That kind of thing hadn't happened for a long, long time.

"Caroline, I'd like you to meet my old friend, Russell," J.P. said as he gently placed his hand upon her shoulder. She was thankful to feel his warmth to distract her from her thoughts of Joost, to snap her out of something of a trance like state.

Russell thrust out his hand to shake hers as she began her spill of politeness in her best drawl; knowing that J.P. would be proud of the novelty of it. "So nice to finally meet you. I've heard really good things 'bout cha for some time now."

"Hope there were a few of my best attributes that you've heard about. Paul and I have been friends most of our lives. We lost touch when he became a traitor and went south."

He looked at her smiling and said, "Well, good thing I did migrate south, you don't find girls like Caroline up here."

She felt a little embarrassed, but grinned at him and let out a hint of appreciation. "Thanks," she said and then turned to Russell. "This is a first for me, to meet a New York City police officer."

"Well, I guess you would say it is a first for me to meet a true Southern woman. Do you have any sisters," he asked, grinning from ear to ear?

"Russell, to tell you the truth, I do have one sister, but I don't think you want to tangle with her."

Then she and J.P. chuckled, and he backed her up saying, "Nope, better stay as far away from Rhonda as possible, unless you're a glutton for some verbal abuse."

Russell glanced at Caroline, wondering if his pal's comment would be misconstrued. Caroline nodded her head and confirmed, "We say her kind could start uh argument in uh empty house. Best leave rabid animals alone!" Russell and J.P. were both cracking up.

Time with Russell passed quickly as he had to be on his way for duty. Caroline and J.P. took their time enjoying the wine and meal. It was already late in the afternoon, and the sky had turned an ominous grey. He so hoped they would not get caught up in a storm before he had the chance to show her Rockefeller Center lighted for the evening, and he sure didn't want the winds to kick up and make it miserable to be walking around looking at the holiday decorations she loved to see.

He made sure to give her full attention in the subway as they laughed and talked about a gamut of topics. They weren't tipsy from too much wine, but were comfortably relaxed. Oh, it felt so good to him to share his life with her. He never thought he would need it so much, had never been to that point of wanting to settle down, until now. And suddenly, it seemed like the right time to move forward.

The weather remained conducive to being outdoors, but as they walked from the subway to Rockefeller, he knew it wouldn't be long before she would start to feel chilled. Looking down on league of ice skaters, she commented, "Wow, it really is pretty here at night, with the tree all lighted." She put her head on his shoulder and whispered, "It's special."

He took her hand, tightly clad in a soft, kid leather glove, and ran his fingers around her ring finger. She held her breath for a moment. She felt him reach inside his jacket, unzipping the pocket over his chest. Frosted breath seemed to be billowing in front of them both. She resisted the urge to shiver, somehow feeling like it would interfere with the moment. She looked down as he knelt before her with a small black velvet box in his shaking hand. He looked up at her with a tender look in his eyes, almost ready to weep, but with a look of joy and happiness. He swallowed hard, once, still smiling at her and calmly asked, "Will you marry me, Caroline Carter?"

All she could manage to squeak out was, "You bettcha I will, you Yankee boy!"

CHAPTER 30

HITCHIN'

"Good nest..........Momma, you and Granny are 'bout to drive me crazy 'bout this weddin'. You'd thank that the Queen of England was gonna be there, the way you two been carryin' on."

"Oh, Rhonda, stop it with that battery acid tongue of yours. Do you have to be so dad blastet hateful today," asked Mrs. Carter?

Then Granny chimed, "You ortta be 'shamed to talk to yer elders, the way you do. The good Lord will convict your soul."

"She's prob'ly too mean to listen," added Grandpaw Pritchett. "Ain't that right, Rhonda?" He was sniggering so much he had to pull out his white cotton handkerchief and blow his nose.

"Geeze Louise, all y'all just gangin' up on me now. It ain't fair."

Then Grandpaw said, "Oh lawt, you ain't seen nuttin' yet, till you see how they gonna lite into me after I enjoy myself at that reception. Talk 'bout gaingin' up on somebody."

"Daddy, you better not plan to get rowdy at that reception. Me and Momma are gonna ration your liquor."

"Like hell, y'all are," mumbled Grandpaw.

Then Granny said, "Now Paw, you best behave yerself today, don't be dippin' any of that nasty snuff while I got my back turnt and stay outta that whisky cab...net. I'm uh goin' shoppin' with the girls. We only got one week to get ready for this weddin'. I hope we have good luck findin' the right dresses. And you're goin' with me on Friday to look fer yer new suit."

"Durn, I was uh hopin' I could wear my overalls," said Grandpaw, squeezing his eyelids tight, making his face look shriveled, and shrugging his shoulders like he did when he thought Granny was going to smack him with the rolling pin.

"Granny started wringing her hands and said, laughing, "Lord Jesus, protect this man before I kill him. I ain't nevah seen the likes of nobody like him 'fore. Mercy, let's skedaddle gals. Where's my car keys?"

Rhonda and her mama followed Granny out the back door as the warped screen door slammed behind them. Granny gently kicked the old lazy cat out of her way as she bounced down the stone steps. Then the elder woman put her hand up to her mouth, like she was hiding her words, and said, "Sometimes, he's about as useless as a tit on a bull."

"Granny, you don't mean it," said Rhonda.

"Do, too," Granny exclaimed!

"Lawd, help this family get through this weddin'," her daughter chimed.

Three days before the wedding, as they entered Summerville on their way back from Columbia, Caroline once again marveled at the Spanish moss dangling from the oak trees, and the magnificent blue violet wisteria in bloom as twisted vines spiraled down tree trunks cushioned by the delicate blossoms of the azaleas below. It was indeed Flowertown. "Honey, let's walk in the garden,"

she suggested. They soon stopped, got out of the car, and walked hand in hand to the white gazebo in the middle of the azalea garden.

He rested his arms on her shoulders and clasped his hands at the back of her neck. "So here's where we're gonna tie the knot," said J.P., with a look of genuine happiness on his face.

She smiled back and commented, in a rather aloof fashion, "It'll be warm, but I know we'll have a beautiful wedding here. I've never seen a prettier place than this garden, in the spring; it is a paradise garden in full bloom."

He could tell something was bothering her, but tried to keep things lightened up. Then he laughed and said jokingly, "It's gonna be hot as hell, and you know it. We'll have to make it short and sweet so our guests won't melt like chocolate in a Carolina parking lot."

That comment did the trick to cheer her, and he had to stop and snort with her for a few seconds. "Seriously Caroline, I don't want you to worry about the wedding. You know we have so many friends here who are all pitching in to help us. Butch and Chris have put in the order to rent the chairs and will set them up early, the morning of the wedding. My buddies have their wives and girl-friends making bows out the wazoo to decorate the gazebo; love your idea of using white netting and dried flowers. And Ricky will be here to do the music. All of them are so good to help us out of the goodness of their hearts. It's gonna be great!" He then grabbed her at the waist and twirled her around the gazebo as she squealed with excitement.

"Oh Lord, what about the preacher? Have you heard from his secretary? Momma and Granny will both have ultimate hissy fits if we aren't hitched by a preacher."

"Yes, my dear, you'll have your minister. Calm down!"

"Grandpaw could care less as long as somebody pours bourbon at the reception," she said sniggering.

J.P. was about to crack up and said, "Maybe the preacher with slip him a mickey. You know those ministers have to slip a drink in, now and then.

"Ain't gonna happen with a Baptist preacher," she added to make him smile.

Some of J.P.'s friends had a large historic home in the center of Summerville, within a short walking distance to the azalea garden. They'd offered to have the reception at their home. Since they entertained quite frequently, they had linens, white china, and plenty of glassware. Another friend owned the local bakery and wanted to give the couple a wedding cake, as his gift to them. Caroline and J.P. had been making finger sandwiches for weeks and putting them in the freezer to be thawed and served at the reception; she vowed she'd never want to eat chicken salad again. A variety of nuts had already been purchased, and fresh fruit plates were ordered.

Invitation to the wedding had been done by word of mouth, so there'd not been the stress and expense of ordering, addressing, and mailing formal invitations. What could have been easier for Caroline than this lovely simple garden wedding they'd planned and financed together? That's exactly how she'd wanted it to be, because she liked to keep all things in her life simple and natural. Even her wedding gown was simple, made in layers of white cotton gauze fabric in a medieval style to be worn off her shoulders. She and her teacher friends had made her headpiece using ribbon covered wire, baby's breath, and other tiny delicate dried flowers secured to a single comb and wrapped at the back with strands of narrow ribbon to trail down Caroline's hair. She planned to wear her hair straight and wear just a touch of makeup. J.P. had given her a pair of silver looped earrings early in their courtship that she was going to wear, but she'd chosen not to wear a necklace because she felt it would detract from the simplistic beauty of the dress. She'd bought delicate white flat sandals and knew they'd look divine with her simple dress.

J.P. was going to wear a baby blue, linen suit and a pair of light colored, suede leather dress shoes. Neither of them wanted anything to do with a tuxedo. He was like minded with Caroline when it came to comfort, shoes or clothing, even on their wedding day. They both wanted to be comfortable, relaxed, and able to enjoy every moment of beauty that day; not wearing some miserable hot outfits to please everyone else, and they hoped their guests would do the same.

"Since so many things are being done by our friends, could we go to the beach tomorrow?" asked Caroline.

"Good idea, sugah," he said, trying to imitate her. "I think it'll be good for us to spend the day at the exact spot where we were when I first knew, without a doubt, that you were the kind of person I wanted to share my life with. Even though we'd known each other only three days, I knew you were the one."

Caroline smiled at J.P. but at the same time felt a single tear stream down her face, which she swiped away as fast as she could hoping he'd not noticed it. From that first day at the beach, when she told him of her father's death, he'd always wondered about the pain that she'd experienced most of her life, and he possessed the maturity to know that getting married, without her father to give her away, would be difficult for her. She had asked her grandfather to step in and do it.

J.P. had never dreamt that she might be holding something back, at least, not until now. He felt some uneasiness with the fact the she could seem so happy one minute as they talked about the wedding plans, yet be upset enough, below the surface, to shed tears. He'd never asked prying questions, and she'd never divulged much about her father's accident, but suddenly, the tears gushed forth, from his bride to be, and it made him feel unsettled. What should he say or do to make her feel better? He felt rather helpless in the situation. He just pulled her close to him so her head rested upon his shoulder and held her until she released a great heave of emotion.

⪤ ⪥

The tide was beginning to go out when Caroline and J.P. got to Isle of Palms. Native seabirds hovered over the water waiting for their lunch. The couple could see a container ship, far out in the distance, inching along to the next port. And the gentle breeze made a child's purple and orange windsock flutter as he ran, squealing with joy.

As they walked holding hands, damp sand feeling as if it were melting beneath their feet, Caroline was reserved; not much was said. They wandered the beach aimlessly, with Caroline occasionally bending down to pick up angel wings, small whelks, or scallop shells entangled in seaweed, hoping to discover a lettered olive. J.P. unearthed a shark's tooth, digging his big toe into the sand.

Suddenly, a stranger's golden retriever darted in front of J.P., with a fetching stick in his mouth, trying to solicit frolic. Behind them, sea oats on the dunes arched in the prevailing wind, as the grains of dry sand below were swept away.

In an attempt to get her in a more jovial mood, he poked her with his index finger, yelling, "Tag, you're it," as he darted toward the pier freckled with fishermen who were waiting for a bite. He ran so fast, he almost kicked sand up on a young mother slathering sunscreen on her petite children, with damp sand glued to their legs.

Caroline looked at him and laughed, thinking to herself that it was good to be young and in love, waiting for their wedding day to roll around. She didn't want to be down and depressed, to be dwelling on her haunting thoughts, those images that never seemed to leave her no matter how hard she tried to suppress them. Chilling thoughts of her daddy slumped over his blood covered table saw, dismembered.

She turned her head to gaze over the white capped waves and ran toward the sea until the water rushed over her bare feet. She could faintly hear J.P. yelling, "Remember, you're it. You gotta tag me," as the gulls overhead mewed, flapping their wings, with their webbed feet dangling from beneath their feathered abdomens. From her peripheral field of vision, she could see the fishermen casting their lines and someone at the end of the pier reeling in his prize, with all his strength and might.

She stood there, as she had done time and time again, wishing that the cleansing, receding water could wash away her pain, once and for all, *out with the tide.* Without warning, tears started to flow again; she tried to fight them but she had to vent, somehow. He realized that she was no longer attending to him, as he played like a teenager, so he ran back toward her and caught a glimpse of her tear filled eyes. She tried to hide them as he approached her by tucking her chin toward her chest; her long brown hair flying in the wind. Finally, he reached her, slipped his hand around her waist and pulled her close to him. Her body shook as she let out the overwhelming waves of emotion while he ran his fingers through her hair. He pulled up the bottom of his t-shirt to wipe the tears from her cheeks. His hand supported her, at the nape of her neck, as she lay her head on his shoulder. Finally, she told him how her father had died and that she was the one who had found him in his workshop. After moments of silence, still in his affectionate embrace, she felt some peace, some comfort; she felt his love and his understanding.

And he softly whispered to her, "It's all gonna be okay. We'll work through it. Fight for our happiness, darling. Don't let it be robbed by the sadness for the past. We've got what most people spend their whole lives looking for."

She managed to squeak out, "I know."

⭑⭑

"Rhonda Jean, get outta that bathroom! You been in that shower for 30 minutes," bellowed Mrs. Carter.

Rhonda turned off the water, dried herself with the stiff, economy towel, and wrapped another pygmy towel around her head. She slipped on a cotton nightgown and entered the motel room.

Mrs. Carter was still ranting and exclaimed, "This room is like a Navajo sweat house! I'm 'bout to burn up in here. Ain't no way I'm gonna be able to get into that chiffon dress, all sticking to my sweaty body."

Lawt, Momma, how do you know anything 'bout a Navajo sweat house; you ain't neveh been out west before?"

In an aggravated tone, Mrs. Carter responded, "Rhonda, sometimes, you act dumber'an a sack of hammers." At that comment, Rhonda was laughing until she was almost breathless. "I'll have you know that I teach social studies, and I know uh plenty 'bout a sweat house."

"Okay, Momma, keep yer tail feathers intact. I'm outta the shower now, and we'll crank up the air conditioner fer you in case you havin' one of yer menopausal attacks." Then she mumbled under her breath, "It's a hell of a lot more humid than a sweat house."

Mrs. Carter and Rhonda broke out in laughter, simultaneously.

Then Momma Carter said, "I'm just so blame nervous with it bein' Caroline's weddin' day, an all."

Rhonda sprayed her hair with detangler and began the difficult task of combing her boar's nest, as she called it. "I bet little sistah is uh sweatin' like a pig right now," commented Rhonda, with a chuckle.

"Don't confess it, girl" admonished Mrs. Carter. "The good Lord is gonna bless my baby today, and she won't sweat one drop."

408

"Get outta here, Momma! You know it's gonna be hot as hell in that azalea garden. We all gonna die in that heat. I do hope it ain't no long winded preacher, so we can get outta there before we melt."

"Well, you bettah not voice one single complaint," commanded Mrs. Carter, with her index finger pointed at Rhonda. "This is one day of your life when you're gonna act like you've been given some kind of decent upbringing."

Rhonda said sarcastically, "I won't have to say a thang, 'cus them damn Yankees will do all the bellyaching." Again, laughter filled the room from both women.

"I reckon you're right about that one," her momma added.

Granny was seated and whispered to her daughter, "Hope you got a handkerchief in your purse, 'cus I'm 'bout to sweat like a banshee in hades."

Mrs. Carter smiled and honored her mother's request. Then Granny Pritchett put her arm around her daughter's shoulders, put her other hand over her lips and said secretly, "You look ten times better than that prissy momma over thair."

Mrs. Carter put her hand on her mother's arm and squeezed. "You're the purddiest granny, too, but behave yourself, Momma. Don't' get me too tickled till after all this is over with."

Caroline's loyal friend, Ricky, a professional musician, played his acoustic guitar to accompany his tenor vocals of the medley of beautiful love songs. Handkerchiefs and tissues were being whipped out of pockets and handbags by all attending, perspiring in Summerville's heat and humidity. Bees gathered nectar from the purple wisteria winding up the tall tree trunks, and butterflies hovered over spreads of multi-colored, pink and yellow lantana. The wedding party came in sight on the winding path, lined with fuchsia azaleas, and then joined the smiling minister in the white gazebo.

Granny couldn't resist whispering, "Look at Paw uh lookin' so fine today. Ain't they somethin'? And look at our baby girl."

Mrs. Carter nodded as a tears escaped and coursed down her cheeks before she could wipe them away.

Within a few minutes time, J.P. and Caroline were pronounced to be husband and wife.

The crowd gathered at the far side of the shaded bridge over the koi pond. As they got to the other side of the bridge, the happy couple was showered with rice, some of it sticking to J.P.'s sweaty neck and some lodged in Caroline's long brown hair. They smiled with delight as they looked toward the cameras. It couldn't have been a more perfect simple wedding.

EPILOGUE

In an almost fetal position with her knees tucked toward her chest, Caroline sat on the beach next to Butch, watching little Jeremy Paul run toward them, giggling as he raced ahead of foamy line of the tiny incoming wave. Her memories were still crystal clear, both terrifying at times and consoling at others. In her meditative state, she thought of those first two glorious nights, filled with tender love making, that she and J.P. had spent together at one of Charleston's historic inns, after their May wedding.

As usual, Butch was patient with her in her silence as she mentally recalled the more than perfect weeks that followed their wedding ceremony, the precious short time that she and J.P. had lived together as newlyweds. For almost four years, she'd tried desperately to think of the good times, the sweet and lovely thoughts of her time with J.P. Yet, she still suffered from an overwhelming sense of guilt, of the type that can't be purged by any effort toward self-forgiveness, and the haunts still visited her to steal away her happy memories. On bad days she still blamed herself because she'd been the one to suggest a trip to the Outer Banks of North Carolina. They'd waited for her teaching year to officially end in June, making it possible to have a couple of weeks for a real honeymoon getaway.

For a few days before the trip north, she'd been trying to keep her secret, not to tell J.P. that she'd seen the OB/GYN and had been informed that she was already pregnant. She wanted to wait for some sublime sunset or for a quiet, romantic dinner by the water, the perfect venue and moment to tell him the blessed news.

They'd only been in Nag's Head long enough to take their bags to the motel room before he'd begged her to get to the ocean for a swim. Those hours of driving in the cramped Toyota had left him feeling restless, and the heat and the humidity of a June day made him want to seek relief in the coolness of the ocean water. She'd almost declined, feeling queasy and tired but not wanting to tell him why, but he refreshed her with a light snack of trail mix and a cold orange juice to drink. She'd finally agreed to head for the beach with him.

On a remote section of the beach near the old pier, the sand was scorching hot, causing them to run quickly to hit the damp sand near the water's edge, never even noticing the warning signs of dangerous riptide currents. They'd been diving into the waves for thirty minutes or more, laughing and having a good time with one another, and before they knew it, they must have been fifty yards out from the shore. The swells of water were becoming higher and more forceful, but they didn't pay much attention to it, acting more like irresponsible teenagers than responsible young adults. They were in love, and they were happy; and that's all that seemed to matter at the time.

The mood changed as she looked toward the next incoming wave, and screamed, "This is a big one, hold me," and with their hands clasped tightly together, they tried to take the huge wave, taking in deep breaths right before the wave covered them. She felt the swirling force of the water pulling them apart, and then, could no longer feel his hand. When she resurfaced, she felt disoriented, the forceful water turning her full circle; she searched for him. Horrified not to see him at first, she screamed his name until another wave rushed over her head, filling her mouth with water. When her head bobbed back up, and she spat out the mouthful of salty water and caught her breath, she looked toward the near empty beach, with stilted beach houses and motels in the distance. Instantly, she became aware that they'd drifted out much too far for anyone to hear her call for help. She turned and caught one glimpse of him, now some distance further away from the shore than she was. The sun's reflection was blinding and with every second passing and the strong current pulling her, the feelings of panic and terror set in; and for the second time in her life, she felt intense loneliness and helplessness.

She tried to head back toward the beach but soon found it impossible to swim against such an incredible force. She was already feeling fatigued. She kept turning around trying to see J.P., but the waves were continuously rising and obstructing her view from anything toward the horizon, but a wall of water. She felt numb, alone, and frightened. Within a short period of time, she stopped the futile attempt to swim back toward the shore and concentrated on treading water to keep her head above the surface. She called his name repeatedly, yelling at the top of her lungs, but she heard no response. She tried her best to relax, to attempt to float as the waves swelled, but it seemed like she was drifting out further from the shore, and the roars of the mighty sea, with her ears underwater, made her feel more and more terrified. She managed to float on her back and took three deep, cleansing breaths when some fleeting thought came to her, the remembrance of a nautical documentary she'd once seen on television, and she started to crawl parallel to the shore. At intervals, she stopped, craning her neck to try to get a glimpse of J.P., but she was fighting the powerful forces of the unrelenting water. Her legs were burning, and it felt difficult to breathe. For the first time in her life, she literally thought she was going to die, to be swept *out with the tide*.

Suddenly, instinct took over her conscious thoughts, and rushes of adrenalin strengthened her to swim toward the distant, partially dilapidated pier. When the waves rushed over her, thrusting her body downward, her feet never hit the bottom. She'd eventually spring back up to the surface, gasping for air at what seemed like the last moment. Swallowing the salty water made her miserably nauseated, and she ended up vomiting to get relief.

Her recollection of the haunting events was interrupted by an innocent wee voice saying,

"Mommy, I lub you."

Butch watched the little three year old put his short, stubby arms around his mother's neck and try to console her.

Now, she was fighting back tears, wiped her fingers underneath her eyes, and summoned a smile to her face for her toddler. She put her arms around him, and softly said, "Darlin' Mommy loves you, too. Mommy loves you more than chocolate cake, and that's a lot." She gave him an affectionate squeeze and buried her face into his neck, causing him to feel a tickle. She sat erect and asked, "Jeremy, honey, do you want Mommy and Daddy to help you build a sand castle today?"

He squealed with delight and stomped his little Flintstone feet in the damp sand. "Yeah, Mommy, a sam caskel." He turned toward Butch and took him by the hand asking, "You wanna play, too, Daddy?"

Butch had never been more proud of Caroline for her courage and determination to give this little boy as much of a normal life as she possibly could. He couldn't begin to imagine how hard it had been for her to lose her first love and still have to keep on going, to bring a baby into this world as a single mom, such a young widow. Caroline had gone to hell and back during the ordeal, but Butch, Leona, and Emily had been there with her every step of the way, to support and encourage her and to help her with Jeremy. He didn't know if he could have done it if the same scenario had been put on his plate. But there was something about Caroline that he'd never seen in another young woman before. She had a strength of character that is rare. He had the greatest of admiration for the woman he also loved.

Then, Caroline requested that Butch set up the umbrella, fearing that her fair skin would be burned and wanting to protect ginger haired Jeremy as they began creating the sand castle.

They sat that under the shade of the umbrella, with the salt breeze blowing and entertained the little boy as he tried with all his might to lift a heavy bucket of damp sand. Caroline looked out toward the vastness of the sea, and finally asked in a searching tone, "Butch, I'll always wonder, why?"

He put his hand over the wedding band he'd recently placed on her finger, as she patted a mound of sand, and said sympathetically, "I know Caroline, it doesn't make sense. We both loved him, and we'll never forget him. And this little J.P. will always remind us of his daddy."

In these early years of her adulthood, Caroline had learned that tragedy doesn't have to steal one's hope for a brighter future, and that the dark clouds of adversity spawn the most spectacular rainbows. She knew that her painful struggles had graced her with incredible strength to move on and enjoy each day with little Jeremy and her loving husband. Caroline had always loved Butch, as a confidant and supporter for the first few years after they met; but now she treasured him as her intimate lover, her understanding mate. She was so grateful for him, for without him, her life would be very difficult and bleak. He and Jeremy introduced happiness back into her life, and as she thought of J.P., she thought of these things, too, and felt contentment in her soul. Affectionately, she leaned toward Butch, rested her head on his shoulder, and said, "I love you, Butch."

Then, she looked out across the Atlantic and silently wondered where he was.

ABOUT THE AUTHOR

As a veteran educator, Lola Faye Arnold has written oodles of fictional works used by educators. *Out With the Tide*, was imagined while she was a graduate student in Charleston, South Carolina. Exposure to the supernatural, while in the romantic port city, spurred her to write her captivating tale.

Lola currently travels abroad in Europe and Oceania, stimulating her senses and gathering fodder for subsequent novels. When she is not reading, writing, or gallivanting abroad and hemisphere hopping, she finds great pleasure in spending time with her three children and six precious grandchildren.

Reviews, comments, and inquiries are welcomed at:
lolaarnold@hotmail.com

Made in the USA
Charleston, SC
14 January 2015